EVENFALL

In the Company of Shadows

Evenfall: Volume I
Director's Cut

Santino & Ais

.

For OG ICoS readers and new ICoS readers.

JUST A NOTE

Evenfall Volume I covers the first half of the original *Evenfall* but with a weight loss of nearly 100K words. The result is still a relatively long novel of 120K words, but one that is the first step in the ongoing process of refining the *In the Company of Shadows* series.

It is the first step because, someday, we do plan to self-publish the series. We just refuse to do that until we can have it edited and proofed by professionals. ICoS started as a free read and there will always be a free version, but that means the free version will have only been edited and revised by us.

Spoiler: This Director's Cut is still exclusively a Santino & Ais production.

So it ain't perfect, folks. But we tried hard to get it right with the expectation that there will be something (or several somethings) that we missed. Even so, we hope you enjoy the ride and understand why we made the changes that we did, and get on board to read (or re-read) the future Director's Cuts for the rest of the series.

PROLOGUE

To an outsider, the Fourth Floor Detainment Center would look innocuous. The thought revisited Chief of Staff General Zachary Carhart each time he descended from his office in the Tower to pay a grudging visit.

The Agency considered the Fourth to be a necessary evil, but unease snaked through Carhart whenever he strode through the shining white corridors. Each section of the Fourth was silent and sterile, giving nothing away of what happened behind the soundproof doors of each cell. That deception was no better than in the Maximum Security wing. There were rumors, but other than the guards and physicians who attended to the inmates, most of the Agency's staff was unaware of what truly happened behind those walls. But Carhart knew.

He knew the inmates ranged from enemy captives to Agency employees who had committed a serious enough infraction to warrant punishment, and he knew about the mental torment used to tame one of the Agency's most infamous assassins; a man considered so wild, the Agency kept him on the Fourth between his uses. The same man Carhart had been maneuvering to free for the past six months.

Two guards stood outside the cell and they both turned smartly, greeting Carhart upon noticing his approach.

"Sir!"

Carhart inclined his head and regarded the cell with hooded eyes. Unlike the other cells in Maximum Security, this one had an expanse of glass along the side to expose the interior. Inside, half a dozen guards in riot gear were inputting the codes to gain access to a reinforced metallic box. Feeding tubes funneled into holes at the side, but other than that, there was no way to see in or out until the door was unsecured.

The box was small, and seemed smaller every time Carhart saw it. That fact was emphasized when the door was breached, and the guards hauled out Hsin Liu Vega or Sin as he was called by the Agency's staff.

Sin was unconscious. Months of receiving nutrients through a tube had emaciated his sinewy body and his typically bronze complexion was chalky. Fine black hair fell over his face like a curtain.

The guards dropped him to the floor without ceremony. They stood around him in their armor, hands on their weapons. The contrast of their force and Sin's weakened condition was grotesque.

Carhart maintained his placid expression. "His status?"

When the question received no response, Carhart forced his eyes from the cell. The two guards, Officer Luke Gerant and Travis Randazzo, were young and newer than most. Luke was a fresh face on the Fourth and he could not seem to look away from Sin. The rumors about the assassin were so extreme that Luke had likely expected Sin to burst from the box snarling like an animal.

"Officer Gerant."

"I'm sorry, sir." Luke recovered. "The dosage of his sedatives was lessened this morning."

"When will he be functional?"

"In approximately—" Luke flinched when a loud laugh emanated from the open door of the cell.

This time, Carhart did not hide his sneer. Two of the guards were squatted down beside Sin and were pawing at him; their grasps left red marks and impressions on Sin's skin.

"In no more than an hour, General Carhart," Luke responded finally.

"I see." The guards inside noticed Carhart watching and moved away from Sin. "Have him cleaned up. The Inspector will want to see him immediately."

"The Inspector?" Travis exclaimed. "With all due respect, sir, The Monster—"

"Do not use that term with me."

Travis winced. "Sorry, sir. But as I was saying, Senior Agent Vega is dangerous. The Inspector isn't trained in combat, and Vega might be unstable when he wakes up."

"Then see to it that the collar is installed before then."

"Collar?"

Carhart turned. "The staff in the Med Wing will know to what I am referring. See that it's done. Now."

"Yes, sir..."

With nothing to muffle the words, Carhart heard Travis mutter to his colleague that they likely found a new way to control The Monster, and Carhart could not deny the truth of those words.

THE PROJECTED TIME frame of Sin's lucidness turned out to have been too optimistic, and he did not fully emerge from the sedation for hours. When Carhart returned to Sin's cell, Vivienne Beaulieu was at his side. Her pale blue eyes were unreadable; her face a mask of indifference even as they passed a battered inmate being dragged back to his quarters.

Carhart was not surprised. In the years he had known Vivienne, despite working for an organization that reeked of death, he had never seen her flinch.

He looked back at the inmate, putting a name to the face, and recognized him as a low-ranking member of an opposition group with ties to a larger terrorist organization. Carhart made a mental note to check the status of the man's interrogation later.

When they approached Sin's location, Luke and Travis were once again standing side-by-side near the cell along with two other guards—Harry Truman and Dennis McNichols. The same two men who had manhandled Sin earlier in the day. They were tall, muscular, and dark-haired; similar enough to be related, although Harry had a series of numbers tattooed to the side of his neck and other symbols inked across his knuckles.

Carhart scrutinized them with distaste before addressing Luke and Travis.

"General. Inspector." The guards nodded with respect, all but Harry staring at her with obvious intrigue. Despite Vivienne being a constant fixture in the Tower, it was possible they had never met her face-to-face. Even on the Fourth, the Inspector's reputation of coldness preceded her.

She barely acknowledged the guards, and focused on the interior of the cell and Sin's slumped form. He was clad only in black shorts and a sleeveless shirt, and a slim metal band encircled his neck. Although Sin appeared subdued, but Carhart did not miss the intensity in Sin's green eyes or the way his muscles coiled.

"What is his status?" Vivienne asked.

"He is completely lucid, Inspector," Luke said.

"The way the staff speaks of him, I expected to find him foaming at the mouth."

Carhart broke Sin's stare and addressed Vivienne. "The staff exaggerates. They have since Sin arrived at the Agency thirteen years ago. I realize that you haven't had any interaction with him in the past, but I know you're aware of his history and his father even though Emilio Vega died before you were brought in."

"I recall hearing that his father was a vulgar man who was quite skilled at assassination. The previous Inspector's files indicated that the man was completely incapable of remaining discreet in or out of the Agency."

"Despite his behavior, Emilio was the best assassin the Agency has ever had. Until his son."

One of Vivienne's blond eyebrows rose. "To my knowledge, even as a boy, Sin was determined to be certifiably insane. Despite that, and his previous psychiatrist now being in a vegetative state, Marshal Connors insists upon using him again."

"There were circumstances behind the attack on the psychiatrist. There are... triggers to Sin's outbursts. Common consensus was that he experienced severe abuse as a child."

Vivienne appeared unmoved. "I have read that he is wild, impulsive, and his 'triggers' often lead to him slaughtering anyone in his vicinity. In previous attempts to control him, he killed all of his partners, did he not?"

"Yes. But he is the best fighter we have, and can perform a mission solo that would typically require an entire team. His skill is unparalleled."

"So I have been told." Vivienne turned to the guards. "I will speak to him. Those chains will hold if I walk in, correct?"

Again, Travis' expression turned uneasy. Even if Vivienne was giving the order, the guards would be blamed if Sin managed to harm her. There was a reason why Vivienne had been kept out of previous dealings with Sin. She was the second-in-command of the Agency, their link to the outside world, and if a known security risk murdered her, they would all be crucified.

"They should hold," Travis said reluctantly. "If they don't, we have a remote to activate his collar."

"The prototype worked according to plan?" She directed the question at Carhart.

"Yes. It's capable of very high voltage and is an improvement from the stun belt."

"Have you tested it?"

"It was tested on other prisoners."

Vivienne nodded briskly. "Who has the remote?"

Harry stepped forward. "I do, Inspector."

"Test it. Now."

Carhart did not miss the ghost of a smirk that formed on Harry's mouth. The guard turned to the cell and pressed the button on the remote. Carhart's stomach churned.

A normal man would have crumbled to the floor as the collar sent volts of electricity into his body, but Sin merely tensed up, his teeth clenching. He held out a slightly shaking hand to support his weight against the wall.

Harry continued to press the button, upping the voltage. Beside him, Luke and Travis exchanged subtle glances.

"His pain tolerance is extraordinary," Carhart said, maintaining an even tone despite the slither of worry that crept down his spine.

Sin paled and sweat broke out on his skin. A stronger shudder went through him, but he managed to maintain a relatively unaffected disposition until Harry put the remote at maximum power. Sin fell to the floor, trembling, and his eyes shut. He still did not make a sound.

Vivienne's attention riveted between Sin and the power selection on the remote.

Once it was clear Sin was incapacitated, Carhart pinned Harry with a dark stare. The guard's glee was so obvious that Carhart had to rein in his disgust. "Stop. It was a test, not an attempt to disable him completely."

Harry obeyed, exchanging a smirk with Dennis.

"The collar should be re-calibrated before he is released." Vivienne took the remote. "He should be incapacitated long before the highest setting has been reached."

"The other subjects suffered severe convulsions and fell unconscious after the highest setting was activated."

"That is irrelevant for someone who, as you said, has a pain tolerance that far exceeds the norm. Now, open the door."

Travis input a series of codes into the keypad. A low beep and a flashing, green light indicated the door had unlocked. Despite the indication that Vivienne wanted to enter alone, Carhart moved into the cell behind her.

Sin looked up at them with his teeth bared in a grimace.

"Can you understand me?" Vivienne asked.

Sin pushed his back against the wall, breathing hard. His mouth twisted into a grim smile. "Hearing isn't the problem at the moment."

Vivienne surveyed Sin's restraints with a clinical air and stepped closer. "Do you understand why you are here?"

Sin lifted his chin at Carhart. "Why is this woman in here bothering me? I was enjoying my six-month stupor just fine."

"Sin—"

Vivienne interrupted with steel in her voice. "You will address me as Inspector and nothing else."

Sin's mocking half-smile was in place. "Okay, Inspector, what the fuck do you want from my life?"

Carhart tensed but Vivienne did not activate the collar.

"I assume you are aware that the Inspector's position is to maintain the covert nature of the Agency. I cannot guess what your dealings were with previous Inspectors, but I am here to make this much clear: I do not take kindly to covering preventable mistakes. Do not assume you are ever out of my view, regardless of if you are on compound. If you cause unnecessary problems, I will recommend you be returned to this box. I know about your claustrophobia. I am aware of the effect confinement has on you."

Sin sneered. "I wonder who told you that."

"Make no assumptions on the source," Vivienne said curtly. "What is important is that you do not disappoint me."

At that, Sin's gaze turned hawk-like. "Why would I disappoint you? What do you people want from me now?"

"You will learn soon enough."

Vivienne turned and walked out of the cell without another word.

Sin rolled his eyes. "You people really get off on the mysterious crap."

"Just behave yourself, Sin," Carhart said.

"If I don't, just use the collar to keep me in check."

Carhart frowned, but instead of engaging with Sin in front of an audience, he followed Vivienne into the corridor. When they were away from the cell he asked, "What did you conclude?"

"Despite his attitude, he gives the impression of possessing more self-control than he has been credited with. I will go through with my recommendation for his newest trial partner."

"I didn't realize you had a candidate in mind. Who is it?"

"My son."

Question after question sprang to mind, but Carhart swallowed them. "Why?"

"He would be unaffected by Sin's belligerence, and he is intelligent enough to avoid power struggles and mind games."

"I see."

"I will inform him tomorrow."

As they began their walk back to the exit, Carhart could only marvel at how Vivienne had given her son a possible death sentence.

ONE

THE JOHNSON'S PHARMACEUTICALS compound loomed before Boyd.
He had been born and raised in Lexington, and the compound was
not far from his neighborhood of Cedar Hills, but he had never been
to the compound before. Sprawled in the northern part of the city
behind a towering gate and surrounded by trees, it was one of the
few locations that had escaped the bombs. The third world war had
exploded not too long after Boyd's birth, but the effects lingered even
now. He had never seen the city any other way than it was; desolate,
crime-ridden and destroyed in places but rebuilt in others.

Johnson's Pharmaceuticals was a reminder of the inequity of
Lexington. Private businesses were almost nonexistent while large
corporate entities dominated. Drug manufacturers in particular had
profited from the war. Survivors suffering from trauma or lingering
sickness were charged exorbitant prices for the chemicals needed to
thrive. While most people could hardly afford a roof over their head,
companies such as Johnson's had enough money to spend on sprawling compounds and private security firms.

There had been a time when Boyd had strong opinions about those
facts, but the inclination to care had long since faded.

Boyd stopped at the gates to the compound and watched a woman
do a retina scan before the guards let her in. The taller guard's gray
and black uniform had a silver tag that read 'Veliz' while the shorter
guard's read 'Garrett.'

"What do you want?" Garrett's hand rose to his weapon while Veliz
continued to monitor the street behind Boyd.

"I have an appointment with my mother."

"What's her name?"

"Vivienne Beaulieu."

Garret's head jerked back and Veliz's attention switched to Boyd.
They looked surprised but somewhat skeptical. Especially Garret,
whose lip curled when he gave Boyd a thorough once-over. Boyd was
used to it. Thin and androgynous, he had long blond hair and skin
made even paler by the all-black clothing he wore. It did not help that
Boyd's face was typically frozen in blank indifference. People often

did not know what to make of him, and their conclusions were typically unflattering.

"Show me your identification."

Boyd held out his driver's license. Garrett examined it and entered the guard tower, returning with a metal detector wand. Boyd held up his arms, staring into the trees, and said nothing as Garret scanned him. The wand whined softly, showing no metal on Boyd's body, but Garret did a pat down regardless.

"You're cleared. An escort will be here shortly."

Garrett rejoined his partner in watching the surroundings while Boyd placed a visitor's pass on his trench coat. He waited without caring or thinking, having only the barest of interest in the men even as they continuously sneaked glances in his direction. When another guard named Amos appeared, he did not seem to have the same intrigue.

"You taking him to Entry?" Garrett asked.

"No. The Tower," Amos said. "She wants him in her office."

"Really," Garrett drawled. "There must not be a long shelf-life on this one, huh?"

"Who knows," Amos said dismissively. "I don't make the rules; I just follow them."

"Don't we all?" Garrett snorted and turned away. "Later."

Amos grabbed Boyd's arm and hauled him through the gates. After two years of minimal contact with the outside world, Boyd's skin crawled at the feel of hands on him. He wanted to pull away, but did not bother; it would simply draw more attention. Instead, he redirected his energy to the task of analyzing his surroundings.

The interior of the compound was more expansive than he had anticipated. Beyond nearest building bearing the maroon Johnson's Pharmaceuticals logo, there were several others of varying levels with roads snaking in between. The larger buildings had parking lots while others simply had paths leading up to the entrance. It was not unlike a university campus.

Boyd expected to enter the Johnson's Pharmaceuticals building, but Amos led him down the main street instead. Together, they headed toward a skyscraper that dominated the center of the compound. Although there were much taller buildings in Lexington, this one was massive in its girth. The windows were reflective and black, making the place look like a modern monolith. There were no signs designating the name of it or even an address yet the majority of the people on compound were heading in or out of the main entrance.

After entering the busy lobby, Boyd tracked the people around him and felt a distant scratch against his wall of apathy. Bits of conversation surrounded them. Briefings, missions, storms—Boyd had no idea what any of it meant. After years of being in stasis, he was thrown into a world on fast forward where everyone spoke a language he did not understand.

More unsettling was the reality of being surrounded by more people than he had been around in years. Boyd spent his days confined to his house, barely thinking or moving, and only left when he needed something that could not be delivered. He had never been claustrophobic, but the crowd of people milling around caused his throat to close up and his chest to tighten. There were too many eyes all around him, ready to watch him. Hands that could touch and potentially hurt him. People he could not trust.

Boyd moved closer to Amos, seeking protection as they waited for the elevator. Now, Amos' touch felt a little safer. Now, Amos was the only barrier. The rising anxiety receded.

When the elevator arrived, Boyd noticed small, nearly hidden cameras in the upper corners of the lift. He focused on them, trying to ignore how acutely aware he was of the press of bodies around him. When the crowd decompressed, Boyd's attention moved to the panel of buttons. It had a screen and card reader, and Boyd could not help but notice there was no button for the fourth floor. Curiosity niggled at him again. To his knowledge, the only superstitions designers often had was of the thirteenth floor, but the thought left Boyd's mind as indistinctly as smoke.

When were alone, Amos swiped his ID card and pressed the button for the top floor. Instead of opening up to a hallway or reception area like the others, they were met by a heavy door with yet another lock.

Again, Amos swiped his card again and the light flashed green, allowing them entrance. Glass walls partitioned sections of the floor, and a corridor led deeper inside, but Amos stopped at the reception area to their left.

A woman sat at the desk, her hazel eyes trained on Boyd. Her nameplate read Annabelle Connors.

"Is that the ten-thirty?"

Amos dropped Boyd's arm. "I don't know, Ann. I was just told to bring him up here."

She nodded and pushed a thin tablet toward the edge of the desk. After Boyd signed his name and stepped back, she looked from the tablet to Boyd with raised eyebrows before picking up the phone. "Inspector, Boyd Beaulieu is here for an appointment." There was a brief pause. "Of course, Inspector."

Ann stood and unlocked the door behind her with her own card. "You can go in."

A flicker of doubt nudged at Boyd, but he entered the room without delay. He had not seen his mother in years, but she had changed very little; pale blond hair pulled back, intense stare that would not miss the slightest change in a person's expression or body language, and lips that were perpetually drawn down at the edges as if she preemptively disapproved of anything he said or did.

To distract himself from Vivienne's scrutiny, Boyd examined the room.

There were no personal effects; no pictures of family, and no items of sentimentality. Floor-to-ceiling windows dominated the right wall, and afforded a phenomenal view of the compound and city below; the buildings were nothing more than scattered toys from this height.

"You walked through the entire compound in that state?"

His stomach sank. Already, he was failing. "Yes."

"What could possibly have deterred you from looking presentable when visiting my place of employment? You appear as though you have not combed your hair in days."

"I apologize, Mother. I have no excuse."

"I already invest a disproportionate amount of money in your existence for the usefulness you provide. When I contact you, I expect you to put effort into the meeting. Do not disappoint me again."

"I won't."

Even with cotton muffling his emotions, there was a sharp twinge at the knowledge that once again he had done something wrong. She was all he had left and he couldn't even please her.

"Sit down."

Boyd followed her order, sitting with his back straight in the chair and hands resting in his lap.

"What was your impression of the compound?"

It was a strange question, but he responded after short consideration. "The compound is large and well-guarded. There are more employees, buildings, and vehicles than I would expect for the sole purpose of manufacturing and transporting pharmaceuticals. I also received strange looks in relation to your name. "

Vivienne's regarded him with some disdain. "And it did not occur to you to question any irregularities?"

"I lack the necessary information to compare this pharmaceutical company with others, so I haven't formed an opinion."

"If you were to visit the other locations of Johnson's Pharmaceuticals, you would find that the compounds contain multiple laboratories as well as a central administrative building, and little else."

"That doesn't seem to fit with the security and size of this compound," Boyd replied. "There are a large number of buildings, many of which don't seem consistent with a typical laboratory design. Several of the staff members didn't appear to be administrative staff or lab technicians, and their terminology didn't reflect either job description. And there was heavy security across the entirety of the compound rather than grouped around key points. The implication is that the valuable assets here are something other than pharmaceuticals."

The coldness did not recede, but she nodded.

"That would be an accurate assessment. Johnson's Pharmaceuticals is a legitimate company with complexes located across the nation. However, this particular location is a cover for a government-sanctioned organization that is so highly classified even the majority of the elite government entities are unaware of its existence. The CIA itself does not even have a file, although the Director is aware of our existence."

Tepid interest stirred inside Boyd, but it faded. The existence of such an organization was as meaningless as anything else. The fact that his mother worked for such a place was not surprising. She had worked in the CIA for many years, although he had never been clear about her role there.

The stretched silence told him she expected him to respond.

"What would be the purpose of such an organization?"

"If you cannot even venture a guess with such information then you have allowed yourself to lose your only useful quality." Her face hardened. "Have you become entirely incompetent since your little drama?"

The question, asked in the callous tone Boyd had come to expect from his mother, brought unwelcome memories to the surface, and flashes of pain and utter desperation felt like they were closer to today than they really were. Still, Boyd did his best to ignore it all because he knew his mother would not approve of unnecessary emotions. He built a wall against those memories and told himself they did not exist. They could not hurt him if they had not happened.

Boyd gripped the arms of the chair, but then forced his fingers to relax. "Given what I know, I would assume this organization can't technically exist according to the government—perhaps due to constitutional violations or actions that the public or policymakers would find unacceptable. I would assume the secrecy and lack of documentation is necessary for the government's plausible deniability."

Again, Vivienne gave a single nod. "This organization does not have a name you will ever hear aside from 'the Agency.' The purpose of the Agency is to protect national security against the terrorist and opposition groups that have formed since the war, threatening the stability of the United States. The Agency fights in secrecy on an international and domestic front."

"If the existence of the Agency is so highly classified, why was I invited here?"

"You will go through a trial for an open position. An agent has recently been released from imprisonment, and he requires supervision."

"Imprisonment?"

"The agent in question is an exceptionally skilled assassin. However, he has shown extreme levels of aggression in the past. Until recently, he has been in solitary confinement."

Boyd could not guess why she would recommend him for such a position. "I see. What does the position entail?"

Vivienne scrutinized him, likely looking for signs of hesitation or fear. "The agent is unpredictable, unstable, and has gone on rampages in the past. The position is to be his partner, and to control him. Additional details will be disclosed at a later date."

"I have no qualifications for such a position. I don't understand why I would be chosen."

"You have been nominated, not chosen." Vivienne's tone cooled.

Her lips tightened at the sides. "You and a number of other candidates will go through a rigorous process to determine if you have the qualifications necessary for the position. Should you be hired, you will receive further information."

"This decision isn't yours to make?"

"No."

Boyd wondered if not being the highest authority, despite her aspirations and need for control, was a sore point for her. Given how she had always put her professional life before her personal, he assumed it was.

"I am here to ensure the Agency remains a secret," she continued. "I ensure that Agency activities do not find their way into the public realm by way of the media. My jurisdiction primarily falls along those lines as well as anything to do with the public or external interactions. My position as the Inspector leaves me second-in-command to the Marshal and it is he who will make the ultimate decision."

"Would I return to this compound for the tests?"

"The process begins tomorrow morning at seven-thirty. You will remain on the compound in temporary quarters overnight."

Boyd's anxiety resurfaced, sweeping over him like a wave. "I'm not allowed to leave?"

"That is not a problem." Vivienne spoke with the strong confidence a person typically reserved only for their own lives, not presuming to speak for others. "You have no reason to leave the compound. I am well aware that your life is meaningless."

Boyd couldn't argue with the assessment.

"Do you have any questions? You do not even wish to know the name of the agent?"

Boyd shrugged. "That information is useless unless I'm hired."

There was the briefest flash of what may have been satisfaction in her face, but it was there and gone in an instant.

"Very well. Guards will escort you to your next destination. You will stay there until you are contacted in the morning." She looked away, making it clear that he was dismissed, and did not say goodbye.

Boyd took care to quietly close the heavy door behind him.

It did not occur to him to refuse the offer. There was no reason for him to do so. Whether he joined a covert government agency or whether he had continued his life having never known of its existence were equally unimportant. Boyd had nothing and no one to exist for. He had given up his desire to live years ago, and with it had gone all sense of hope or belief in a future that was anything but numb and pointless. All Boyd had was silence, and memories that stalked his dreams and transformed into vivid ghosts that loomed in every corner of his house.

If there was a hell beyond what he knew, Boyd would welcome it.

After all, a life without living was simply a death without dying. What more was there to fear or hate but life, endless life, with no respite?

TWO

Sin had long ago learned that the general populace of the Agency expected him to act psychotic. That fact was evident enough by the looks he received when Luke came to escort him from the Fourth to the upper levels of the Tower.

Luke unwisely chose to take the elevator. To say the Agency staff that had occupied it reacted strongly would have been an understatement. Some gawked at Sin, some attempted to stay out of his line of sight, and others stared with outright animosity.

He ignored them. With the vast majority of the Agency staff believing he was everything from a murderer to a cannibal, it wasn't shocking that many were displeased with his reinstatement as a field agent.

The elevator emptied quickly, but whether people were getting off at their designated floors or were simply trying to get away from him was unknown. He assumed the latter.

Within two stops, the elevator was empty except for Sin and Luke. The guard kept staring at him, and Sin debated doing something alarming just to test how quickly he could break Luke's hand before he used the remote. The test on the Fourth weeks ago would have given Sin a full minute to confiscate the device, but they had likely re-calibrated the voltage.

Sin ran his fingers along the collar. The metallic coldness resting against his skin felt unnatural, but he was getting used to it. He was also becoming accustomed to the idea of the collar doubling as a tracking device as well as a control mechanism.

Sin shot the younger man another deliberating look, but the sight of those big doe eyes reminded Sin of something else.

"I know you."

"What?" Luke frowned. "How? What do you mean?"

"When I was taken out of the box, you were there."

"Um..."

"With Harry." Sin leaned down. "Friend of yours?"

Luke shook his head rapidly, sandy hair brushing his forehead. "No."

"Are you sure? I could have sworn you were one of the ones

encouraging him to shove his hand down my shorts and see how hard he could squeeze before my scrotum burst."

"What? I didn't—I would never—" Luke took a step back. "Me and Travis defended you when Dennis and Harry did those things. I wasn't up there until recently so I don't know what happened before, but—even if you're a psycho I wouldn't abuse a defenseless person."

By the time Luke stopped speaking, he was practically pinned against the side of the elevator, and had failed to grab the remote even when Sin took a step closer.

"I'm not defenseless. I'm a cannibal."

"No, you're not."

"How would you know?"

"Travis said most of those rumors are bullshit."

"That's because he wasn't there the time I bit into a guard captain's neck."

Luke paled. Sin snapped his teeth.

The elevator dinged and the doors slid open. Sin turned away and exited without giving Luke a backwards glance. He heard hurried footsteps behind him and assumed the guard was trying to regain his composure.

Luke followed closely behind as Sin walked past offices and hallways, ultimately arriving in the lobby area of General Carhart's office. Two field agents, a Research and Development agent, and Carhart's receptionist were in the immediate area. Every one of them stopped to stare. When Luke bypassed them to open the general's door, Sin stepped inside, glad to be away from ogling agents even if it meant dealing with Carhart.

"You can go, Officer Gerant."

Carhart was the same as always. Fit, blue-eyed and blond-haired, and almost too fresh-faced for his role at the Agency. In the thirteen years Sin had known Carhart, the man had aged very little physically.

"But, Sir—"

"I said, you can go."

Luke nodded uncertainly and held out one hand. "The remote, sir?"

"I don't need it. Take it and go."

Sin smirked. "Pretty confident, aren't you?"

"Goodbye, Officer Gerant," Carhart said pointedly.

The guard shot him another worried look, clearly concerned about leaving the third-in-command of the Agency alone with a self-proclaimed cannibal, but left the office and shut the door behind him.

Sin sat in the armchair opposite Carhart's desk and made himself comfortable on the plush cushion.

"Have I bored you already?" Carhart sounded almost amused.

"No. But after sleeping on the floor for the past six months, I may just doze off from the sheer opulence of your chair. Or maybe it's the horse tranquilizers you pumped me full of for those six months that are still slowing me down."

The amusement faded. "Holding a grudge, Sin?"

"Fuck you." Sin closed his eyes. He heard a low sigh and the squeak of Carhart shifting in his chair.

"Are you hungry?"

"No. After six months on a liquid diet, I'm watching my figure."

This time the sigh was one of exasperation. "How many more 'after six months' retorts do you have left in you? You weren't nearly this witty after spending four years on the Fourth during your previous incarceration."

"Well, that was before the box and before I was left in a stupor for the entire period," Sin replied. "And speaking of the box, I still have to mention the abusive guards, my emaciated condition, and my dog collar. I heard the medics talking. Apparently this little gem was all your idea."

"Because it was the only way I could convince Marshal Connors and the Inspector to let you out of that damn cell," Carhart snapped. "An opportunity arose, a way to get you off the Fourth, but they didn't want to. They wanted to keep you in that box. The only way I could get around it was by suggesting a way to control you, for insurance."

"Interesting choice of words."

Carhart's broad shoulders tensed. "After what you pulled with your last four partners, what the hell do you expect? They paint you in the role of the murdering psychopath and you play the part while I try to be devil's advocate every time you get into trouble."

"It's not my fault you designated complete morons for my babysitters." Sin sat up in the chair and leaned forward. "Maybe you shouldn't have chosen people who thought the word 'partner' meant 'handler' and that I was their fucking pet."

"That was unfortunate," Carhart agreed. "After much debate, the

SANTINO & AIS

Marshal and the Inspector both agreed on that note. They went over the files, the reports, and debriefings, and agreed that perhaps we hadn't made the most suitable choices."

"And I see you didn't feel it necessary to share this news flash with the staff."

Not that it would have mattered. Sin's reputation and existence on the compound had been tarnished and despised for years.

Carhart asked again, "Would you like coffee? Something to eat?"

"Will you shut up about the eating?"

"You're skin and bones." Carhart indicated the threadbare clothes hanging from Sin's lean limbs. "If you're going to be reinstated you have to get your weight up and start rebuilding muscle. We're working with a specific timetable."

"Fine. Get me a chocolate milk and a donut."

Carhart stared at him.

Sin shrugged.

Sighing, Carhart pressed the button on the intercom. "Amy, can you bring in a coffee, some donuts and... a chocolate milk?"

There was a pause and a very uncertain sounding, "Right away, sir," in response.

Satisfied, Sin crossed his arms over his chest.

"You have to develop better eating habits, Sin. You're about twenty pounds underweight. That sweet tooth isn't going to help you in any way. I don't even know where you get that. Certainly not your father."

Sin went very still in the chair. "Don't."

"I was just sayi—"

"I said to shut up about my father."

The tension in the room was palpable and only broken by the appearance of Amy with a tray full of donuts, a mug of coffee and a large cup presumably filled with chocolate milk. She seemed mildly alarmed by Sin's icy glare and Carhart's stiff posture but instead of commenting, offered Sin a flexible straw before hurrying out of the room.

Sin looked down at the neon pink straw in bemusement and the moment was broken.

"So," Carhart said, grabbing his coffee from the tray. "The opportunity I spoke of—any clue as to what it is?"

"Mm." Sin took a bite of a chocolate donut and nearly moaned at the delicious taste of sugary icing. "Either you're in desperate need of my wonderful assassination abilities or your super elite unit is still short a high-ranking fieldie due to your relative lack of high-ranking fieldies?"

"Precisely. My options are limited to you and Senior Agent Trovosky."

"So go with Trovosky. I'm sure he'd come in his pants at the opportunity to be on your extra special team."

"Ha ha. Funny. Agent Trovosky has been on an extensive undercover assignment for the past two years, so you're the only option we have."

"It's so nice to be needed."

"Janus activity has been rearing up again and they're getting stronger with each passing day," Carhart said.

Sin licked the tips of his fingers, wondering if this would lead to another lecture about the importance of the Janus unit, and his own cooperation. The last time Carhart had attempted to press the issue, it had been six months ago when Marshal Connors had launched the unit.

"We need to act now before they induct every oppositionist into their fold. They've swallowed insurgent groups here and overseas, and their influence is spreading."

"Sounds dire."

Carhart glared. "Can you take this seriously?"

"No."

"This is your job, Sin. Your job—"

"My job?" Sin scoffed. "If you think I'm still here because of loyalty to the cause, you're more delusional than I thought. I'm here because it's too much trouble to bother trying to escape Connors' tentacles."

Carhart exhaled slowly. "In any case, the conditions of your release are to retrain, to become a full-fledged member of the Janus unit as well as taking on your previous duties. And once again we will be inducting a second field agent to the unit, a rank 9 who will be—"

"Fuck that."

"—trained specifically to be your partner."

"No way in hell." Sin was already standing up, his back stiff. "I'd rather go back to the Fourth."

"But you won't just go back to the Fourth, Sin. You'll go back to the box and this time, you won't be getting out. They're not using it as a temporary punishment anymore. That's your fate if this doesn't work out. Is that what you want?"

Sin directed his gaze to the windows. Below them, Lexington's skyline was broken, and the destroyed suburbs sprawled out beyond the city limits in a shadow. From the Tower, the area known as the Wasteland looked like charred rubble and fading decay. Once, the Wasteland had been tidy subdivisions, but the nearby military base had turned it into a target during the war.

"Sin, are you paying attention?"

"Yes."

"Then please—"

"Please, what? Please be a good pet now that I've been let out of my cage? Please behave while one of your thick-necked field agents treats me like an animal?"

"I'm telling you it won't be that way this time!" Carhart slammed his hands on the desk. Coffee slopped over of the side of his mug. "We're going through a very extensive process to find a suitable match for you, Sin. Psych profiles, background, personality assessments—and this time your input will be included. It won't be like it was before."

Sin frowned. "My input? Why bother? You know what they all think of me."

"It isn't about what they think of you. It's about what you think of them. Maybe if you have a say, you'll be less likely to kill them when they push too far."

"Maybe."

"Why are you so resistant?"

"Because it's a waste of time," Sin snapped. "Even if you managed to find a ready-made saint of a field agent full of white guilt and social justice instincts, just wanting to do the right thing and treat me like a real person, I will fuck it up without a doubt. I'm damaged goods. You know what happens with me. I'll always end up back up on the Fourth."

"Well, I'm not prepared to give up on you just yet." Carhart wiped the table in obvious aggravation. "You're the best we have and even if they hate you, everyone knows that. Now shut the hell up, drink your chocolate milk, and stop being a pain in my ass. For God's sake."

Sin watched the smoke-colored clouds drift across the oppressive sky. "I'll agree to it. For now." Carhart opened his mouth but didn't speak when Sin speared him with a dark look. "But if you pick the wrong person, it's his fucking funeral."

"Believe me, Sin. I know."

SIN'S BATTERED COMBAT boots left dusky smudges against the wall of the darkened conference room, but he didn't shift his position. He peered through the two-way mirror from beneath his lashes.

"This is boring," he drawled. "And unless you're completely moronic, it should be clear that the last two agents would be a disaster. Who exactly narrowed down your short list?"

Carhart sat on the edge of the table and touched the computer panel, bringing up a holographic image of the information. "Connors did," he replied, voice gruff. "He insisted on throwing in as many rank 9 candidates as possible to save the time spent putting a lower level field op through the rank 9 training."

"Since he likely doubts they'll last the initial trial missions, I can't say that I blame him."

Carhart typed something into the touch screen keyboard and Agents Eddy Baxter and Jenny White were marked as unacceptable. He sent their files to the virtual trash bin with a swipe of his fingers. The former was a flame-haired rank 9 agent from the Counter-Terrorism division who perpetuated the characteristics that had gotten Sin's previous partners killed. Agent White was a rank 9 valentine agent in Intelligence; she was a promising candidate as far as temperament, but Carhart had worried that she'd try to use her skills at seduction on Sin—the tactic of choice for valentine agents.

"And Agent Alvarado backed out at the last minute," Carhart scoffed, not hiding the irritation in his face as he marked off Michael Alvarado's name. "General Stephen said he's too frightened of you to be a realistic choice. I recommended Harriet Stevens, but she respectfully declined. It's too bad. She's an excellent agent."

"Does she think I'd eat her?"

"No, but she identified that she isn't the best at negotiation herself, which is a requirement for the other member of the team."

Sin was unsurprised this was proving to be a failure.

"So we're left with two level 8 agents and a civilian prospect with no training whatsoever who would be starting off as a level 1 trainee," Carhart said sourly. "Connors won't be pleased."

"How unfortunate. Let's get on with this."

The staff member conducting the interviews returned to the room with the next candidate.

"That one looks familiar."

"His name is Adam Blake."

He'd heard the name before, but Sin didn't remember ever speaking to Adam in the past. As he studied the agent's pale skin, black hair, and even darker eyes, Sin wondered whether Adam had ever been involved in one of the incidents that had led to him being dragged to the Fourth; Sin never recalled the specifics of those incidents after the fact. Just vague impressions, sounds, and feelings that returned as if it had happened in a dream. Or a nightmare.

Frowning, Sin reached backward across the table to bring up Adam's file. The man was an undesignated valentine operative, which was not surprising. The most attractive field agents usually were. Seduction was one of the oldest and most effective ways of getting information and flipping enemies to informants.

"He doesn't look very enthused," Sin observed.

Carhart gave Sin a wry look. "Let me guess—you're thinking how fun it would be to find out what makes him tick?"

"I said no such thing."

"Right."

The interviewer, a man named James who looked more like an insurgent than a staff member from Human Resources, explained the position to Adam. The opening was for a tactician in an elite and very confidential unit in the Insurgency division, one that required the agent to work with Hsin Liu Vega.

If Adam had any pre-existing opinions on Sin, it didn't show. Even when James referenced the infamous city center massacre of 2012, Adam's unaffected disposition did not shift.

"After the incident, news stories circulated about Agent Vega being behind many other murders in the city. Inspector Beaulieu stamped out the spread of that information, but the Agency staff still remembers. Many of them believe it."

James stopped speaking and waited. Knowing he was being observed, Adam glanced at the mirror.

"At that time there were also reports of widespread corruption in the police department. I think it's more likely they needed a scape-goat, and Vega was convenient."

Sin raised an eyebrow. "He's not too bad."

"I agree but I'm surprised to hear you say it."

Sin shrugged. "At least he's not a total fucking idiot."

The next interview wasn't as successful. Agent Carson spent twenty minutes feeding James rehearsed lines and clearly saying what he thought the Agency would want to hear, but even then, he began to falter when Sin's past crimes came up.

Carhart marked the man off the short list, and scowled at the only remaining name.

Boyd Beaulieu.

"I suppose you're going to have no choice but to do the trial with Blake," Carhart said as he flicked through Boyd's file.

"No faith in the Inspector's kid?"

"I'm not in the business of wasting time vetting civilians with nothing in their backgrounds but a few college credits in psychology," Carhart said. "And like you said—he's just a boy."

"I was fourteen when I was inducted as an agent. He's four years older."

Carhart watched as James brought Boyd into the interview room. "You were fourteen going on thirty-seven and trained by one of the best assassins the Agency ever had. It's hardly comparable."

Sin said nothing. Instead, he focused on the newest option.

The kid was average height but thin beneath a long black trench coat that concealed his form. It was difficult to tell if he was like Sin— wiry and well-muscled despite his leanness—or slender and waifish. He had fine blond hair that fell past his shoulders and partially hid his face. It would have been easy for an outsider to wonder whether Boyd was a man or a woman. Androgyny removed the sharp angles sometimes found in a man, and turned his features softer, more ambiguous.

Boyd turned to the two-way mirror, and Sin noticed the boy's eyes were amber. The shades of gold captured Sin's attention, and he missed James' first two questions. The kid was nothing like the typical field agents who were vetted by the Agency, and if chosen, Sin had no doubts they would prey on Boyd's differences.

The resemblance to Vivienne was strong in looks and even body language. Like her, Boyd gave nothing away in his expression. His face remained blank throughout the interview, his eyes dead, and mouth moving only long enough to respond to James in a toneless voice.

After a point, Sin wondered if it was an act. Many young people attempted to personify the bleakness that had encompassed the world after the war, and Boyd could be following the trend. However, his lack of reaction persisted even when the killings were mentioned.

James brought up holograms of crime scenes and still images from autopsies, but there was no recoil of horror or gleam of fear. Boyd was completely unaware of the incident in the city center; he had no recollection of hearing stories about a suspected serial killer on the news.

None of it seemed to mean anything to Boyd. Images, descriptions, witness accounts of the crimes—nothing sparked fear or even interest.

"Him."

Carhart approached the mirror. "It seems Vivienne had a point after all."

Sin willed the boy to react to James' words, but there was nothing there. Just an empty husk where a person should have been. "Getting him to break will be fun."

THREE

Boyd walked through the mostly empty hallways of the training complex. His steps echoed around him as he headed to his latest session with David Nakamura, Boyd's trainer for the past few months.

Given the brief job description he had been given by his mother, Boyd had not known what to expect. He had assumed training would primarily consist of self-defense techniques, but the sessions were far more intense than that. He was being trained in offensive combat, weapons, tactical planning, and strategy.

He had been confined to the training complex for the duration; a large building with multiple levels that contained everything from a cafeteria and training rooms to dormitories. The rooms were small, minimally furnished, and lacked even a single window. With only the artificial light to illuminate the building, it felt like time had ceased to move.

Over time, Boyd realized there were other people in the complex training to be rank 9, but he was separated from them. His training was more intensive so he could meet the qualifications within the allotted time frame, especially since he was starting as a blank slate while the others had likely been active field agents for years.

The classes he took were all one-on-one, and not all geared toward fighting. He also learned the Agency's goals and directives. They repeatedly stressed the importance of secrecy and success, and the consequences for the greater good if the Agency failed. Or, more accurately, if the agents failed. Boyd had deportment training as well. Those sessions focused on his behavior and appearance; the Agency took great stock in physical perfection. Boyd wondered if that was why his mother always noted when he did not adequately meet her standards.

His main concern with deportment was that he hadn't interacted with anyone on any sort of consistent basis for years, and he'd always been a quiet person who preferred to be left alone if given the choice. Still, Boyd realized he had developed some relevant skills over the years. He was often able to read even the least expressive of individuals. People would say a lot within hearing range of the boy who rarely spoke, so Boyd had learned to compare the body language they showed each other with the truth that came out in low whispers between friends.

The most time-consuming and labor-intensive of Boyd's training sessions were physical fitness and combat. He was expected to attain a specific physique in order to adequately function as a field agent, and the amount of time he spent weight training rivaled the hours spent sparring with David. After years of living a sedentary lifestyle, his new routine was exhausting.

Despite disengaging himself from the world for so long, a long-buried drive to excel began to surface as the sessions grew more and more trying. Even so, it was difficult to stay disconnected from everything and everyone else when he was constantly being thrown into situations where it was impossible to do anything but interact.

As he approached the designated training room, Boyd saw a man and a woman standing outside, leaning against the wall. They both wore training gear, but the man was laughing and tugging on her braid as she swatted him away. When Boyd approached, they both noticed.

"I wouldn't bother going in there yet," the woman said. "Nakamura is on the phone with Doug and that always takes forever. You know how Doug is."

Boyd assumed the Doug they were talking about was Instructor Douglas Ferguson, the man who was typically involved in all high-rank training sessions. When Boyd had first begun training, he'd been informed that the infamous instructor was out of the country, which was why David was filling in.

"Thank you."

When Boyd stood by the door with his arms crossed, the girl studied him and seemed puzzled.

"What training are you here for, anyway? I haven't seen you around."

"It seems to be specialized training so I've largely been separated from everyone else."

The two agents exchanged looks.

"Huh. That's odd. I've never even seen you on compound, and you look so young."

"I'll be nineteen in a week." Boyd paused, looking at the two of them thoughtfully. "Why? How old are people typically recruited?"

"It depends," the guy said. "If you're a military or government recruit it's usually older but no later than mid-twenties. They like to get them young. But if you're a jail recruit or something else civilian-oriented, it can be basically any age. If you have the qualities they want, they'll take you whenever."

"A lot of R&Ds and analysts get recruited pretty early, I hear," the girl added. "Mostly because a lot of them are geniuses. Once they go through IQ testing or enter Mensa, all kinds of Agency flags probably go off telling them to run and recruit new nerds."

Boyd nodded. That seemed to fall in line with his understanding of the Agency. Still, he didn't know how early 'pretty early' was, and wondered how the Marshal managed to gain custody of minors. Somehow, he doubted it was done legally.

"I'm Cecilia, by the way. And this is Dover. What's your name and rank?"

"Boyd. I'm not positive what my rank is."

Dover frowned. "That is beyond strange, dude. Are you a probie?"

Probie was the term for probationary agent and one that Boyd had learned quickly. Higher ranked agents seemed to enjoy using it.

"I've been training for three months. I think at the end I'll be assigned a rank."

The explanation didn't satisfy Dover's curiosity, and he pressed on. "Well where'd you come from? Why did they recruit you? Sometimes rank changes based on your background."

"I didn't come from anywhere in particular," Boyd admitted. "I'm one of several people being tested as a potential partner for Agent Hsin Liu Vega. I assume they're waiting to assign an official rank until they see whether I will succeed with the training."

Dover's eyes narrowed. "Why the fuck would a new kid with no background be training to be Vega's partner? That's beyond most people's rank and classification."

"Yeah," Cecilia chimed in, not looking too happy with this development herself. "Did someone recommend you for some reason? I mean, are you sure it's the Monster you're getting trained to be with?"

"I'm positive. My mother summoned me and explained the position. During the interview, they specifically stated his name."

"Your mother?" Dover asked, confused. "Who in the hell is your mother?"

"Vivienne Beaulieu."

Twin looks of contempt spread on the agents' faces.

"Ah," Dover said. "Now it makes sense."

"How so?" Boyd asked warily.

"You're off the street with no background in anything and they're giving you that position?" Cecilia demanded. "Do you know how hard we had to work to even become eligible for rank 9 training, and you're just being handed it?"

Dover shook his head. "Forget it, Cecilia. It's not even worth it. She'll do whatever she wants."

"But it's not fair," Cecilia insisted, her voice rising.

"I don't know what to tell you," Boyd said. "I've just been following orders. Perhaps you should talk to one of your superiors about it."

"Yeah," Cecilia sniped. "I'll get right on that, but oh wait—your mom is second-in-command of the Agency, and obviously she doesn't give a fuck about protocol. Obviously she doesn't give a damn that I've been here for six years and am just now in rank 9 training and even then, I'm not guaranteed promotion. But I wouldn't expect some PR bimbo who's never trained or worked in the field to understand. All she is, is a talking head."

Dover shifted uncomfortably, peering around as if he was afraid of her being overheard. "Alright, alright—let's just forget it for now."

"Six years," Cecilia repeated, getting in Boyd's face. "Always having to work twice as hard as the men, always having to prove myself three times over, and you get to skip all that and get the second highest field rank in the Agency. It's mind-fucking-boggling that this is even allowed."

Dover grabbed Cecilia's arm and guided her away from Boyd. "Don't be stupid. Just forget it. He can go whining to his mother if you keep running your damn mouth."

Irritation flashed through Boyd. "I won't tell her anything. We may be related but that is where the connection ends."

"Right. That's why she made sure her boy outranks 90% of the field ops in the Agency," Cecilia snarled. "Must be nice to get top pay and clearance right off the bat. Do you have any siblings that she's going to stick in here? Maybe she'll make the next one a captain."

This time Dover started to tug her down the corridor. "He probably won't live out the next few months, anyway. He'll be gone before you know it. I can't believe you're getting all riled up over some faggy little..."

Dover's voice trailed off as they disappeared around the corner.

Frustration settled in the pit of Boyd's stomach like a stone. He wanted nothing more than to retreat to his quarters for the remainder of the day, and to become invisible to the rest of the world. For weeks, he had interacted only with the training staff. It seemed that was for the best. Boyd had not known his mother was so despised, and there was nothing he could do to change that or the way people treated him due to it. Apparently, his connection to a woman who barely tolerated him would make him detestable to others.

Setting his jaw, Boyd forced the thoughts away and walked into the room. David had apparently finished his phone call, and turned to survey Boyd. He was Japanese, possibly in his forties, and shorter than Boyd despite possessing a more muscular build. Although David took his role as an instructor seriously, it was not uncommon for him to smile while they trained.

"I didn't think it was possible for you to look that angry," David noted as Boyd approached the weapon rack and selected a pair of expandable tonfa.

Boyd flipped the tonfa up to protect his arms and eased into a fighting stance.

David gave him a brief once-over. "I've got news for you, kid. You don't get to ignore your trainer just because you don't feel like talking." His jerked his chin at the tonfa. "And put those down. We're doing hand-to-hand today."

Still refusing to speak, Boyd flipped the tonfa up and caught them by the ends before transferring them to one hand. He bent to set them down, and David struck.

Off-balanced, Boyd fell to the mat on his back, his breath whooshing out of him. David moved to pin him but Boyd recovered, twisting out of the way and rolling into a stand. He danced away, eyes returning to the fallen tonfa. Before he could grab them, David hooked the tonfa on his foot and kicked them across the room.

They continued to spar, with David striking hard, fast, and throwing Boyd down to the mat more than once. Although David continuously had the upper hand, Boyd was becoming aware of his own improvements. He was fast and had developed a talent for slipping out of holds. Boyd tried to focus on that, on utilizing his speed and thinner build as an advantage, but David began to talk even as they sparred.

"What made you angry?"

"I'm not angry." Boyd blocked a kick to his sternum and whirled out of the way.

"Could've fooled me." Silence except the sound of their feet across the mats and their harsh breathing. "Did it have something to do with those trainees out there?"

Boyd put more force behind a punch than he normally would, and David blocked neatly.

"No."

David didn't respond for a minute as they traded blows and dodges.

"Let me give you a piece of advice."

David dropped down and swept Boyd's legs from beneath him. Boyd slammed back onto the mat and was pinned within seconds. David's eyes were alight with adrenaline.

"Probie mistake number one: letting emotions control you in a fight. It makes you easier to compromise." David's body was heavy against Boyd's. "You think your enemy doesn't notice when you're distracted? You think just because you pretend to be an expressionless corpse, it makes you one? A fighter can read you. A fighter can exploit your every weakness, and you could have gotten yourself killed just now, worrying about whatever petty issue you're having. When it comes to life and death, that's all those issues ever are: petty and not worth dying over."

Boyd tried to shove him away, but David accounted for the movement and held Boyd down.

"What's the matter? You want me to let you up?"

Boyd's heart thundered. "Get off me."

David didn't relent on his hold. If anything, his hands only tightened. His body seemed to grow heavier and more oppressive. With no way to escape, Boyd felt the distant claw of panic, growing closer and stronger and making his heart beat so hard he could feel it resounding in his chest.

"You're biggest strength is evasion," David said. "But I think it's for a reason. I think it scares you to be like this."

Boyd grit his teeth and did not make a sound. He squeezed his eyes shut and tilted his head back, willing himself to calm down. To think rationally, to relax, and breathe. But it wasn't working. It was never going to work. David was too heavy on him. He couldn't move—he wouldn't be able to get away—

"Why is that?" David's voice sounded very far away.

Boyd didn't hear the strained noise he made or realize when he switched to mindless, panicked struggling. He jerked fiercely; clawing and shouting until the fear swarmed and blanked everything else out. The next thing Boyd knew, he was a few feet away from David and crouched on the floor, panting.

David did not seem surprised. "Probie mistake number two; letting those same emotions show. Creating a weakness."

Boyd didn't answer. He trembled from the adrenaline, and his pulse raced.

Displeasure was clear in the instructor's face, but he declined to criticize the display further. "Take five. After that, we're going to weapons. You have an appointment at 1400. Since we'll have to stop early today, I expect you to work harder than usual."

Boyd tried to nod, but he could barely move. He waited until David crossed the room and only then uncoiled from his crouch to sit on the floor. Shaking, Boyd pulled his legs in close and rested his elbows on his knees. He dug his fingers into hair and focused on the rise and fall of his breath.

"Damn it."

He focused on the rise and fall of his breath. It took time, but he was able to return to the comforting darkness that allowed everything to pass him unheeded. Once the blanket of neutrality returned, Boyd was calm. The memories and panic vanished.

Boyd approached David again. This time when they engaged in their sparring, Boyd wiped every other emotion away. He attacked David with a single-minded focus, not relenting until David held his hand up, signaling Boyd to stop. It was only then that Boyd realized they'd been going for nearly an hour, and that someone else had entered the room.

"Oh, Luke," David called. He wasn't even out of breath. "I didn't see you there. He's ready unless you want to give him a chance to change."

A man with sandy hair had entered the room. He wore a guard uniform, but had a kinder face than most people Boyd had encountered so far.

Luke glanced at his watch. "If he's fast, I don't care."

Boyd went into the locker room to change and pack his things into a small sport bag. When he rejoined Luke in the sparring area, they left the training facility and went into the outer courtyard of the compound. It was the first time Boyd had left the training facility in so long that he was surprised by the cold November wind. For months, he had only felt the climate controlled air of the training complex.

There weren't many people around, but those he saw were going to or from the Tower. The place was the hub of activity on the property with the exception of the group of buildings he'd later learned were residential.

"Where are we going?"

"To the Fourth," Luke said. "I'm not sure what they have planned for you, but I figure it has something to do with Agent Vega."

"What's the Fourth?" Boyd had a vague notion of it being the sort of place one did not want to end up, but knew nothing else.

"It's officially called the Fourth Floor Detainment Center. Very high security, can't really get there on your own."

"Is that where Sin Vega is kept?"

"Yeah. He used to be kept in Maximum Security, but now he's just kept in a holding cell until they decide what's going to happen with him."

The precautions seemed excessive to Boyd. But then again, based on the impression he'd gotten from others, Sin was apparently a volatile individual.

"If he is as dangerous as I have been led to believe, why are they releasing him?"

"I don't know, really." Luke sounded so genuinely thoughtful that Boyd glanced at him again. "He's a scary guy. I guess he must be an amazing agent for them to release him. That, or not everything people say about him is true."

Luke was the first person who hadn't immediately dismissed Sin. David had refused to discuss the rumors, but he had also said nothing in Sin's defense. Others only referred to Sin as 'The Monster.'

"You have seen something that leads you to believe the rumors aren't all true?" Boyd asked.

"Somewhat. I'm not saying he isn't unstable, because he is. Undoubtedly. He's killed guards during his psycho fits, but I've also had a relatively normal conversation with him recently that made me think he isn't always out of control. People set him off and that's when things get hairy. But that's also why he probably shouldn't be back on active duty." Luke paused. "I shouldn't be talking about this with you."

"Is there an unspoken rule against giving that sort of information?" Boyd asked, perplexed. "I have noticed that it's difficult to get straight answers. I don't know how much of it is due to the inherent secrecy of this place and how much is because of the position."

"I think it's due to the position. Most people are biased against Vega because of all the rumors. Maybe the administration likes you being a blank slate."

Boyd didn't think the plan made much sense, and hoped the appointment on the Fourth would satisfy his questions once and for all. The lack of information about the position was becoming a source of aggravation, although he had to admit that he would rather receive the details from a reliable source rather than gossip.

They lapsed into silence and entered the Tower. They bypassed the main elevator bank and followed a short corridor to a steel-colored door. There were no markings around it, and Boyd did not even see a way to access it until Luke activated a hidden panel and swiped his key card. A door slid open, and Boyd realized it was yet another elevator.

"The floor is heavily restricted," Boyd observed.

"The main elevators don't even have an option for the Fourth. Even the main stairwells don't have access. The entrances have been completely blocked off and the only one that wasn't requires specifically coded access on your card."

After stepping inside, Luke scanned his card again in order to press the button for the Fourth. The door shut with a whoosh, and the lift glided upwards.

"If the clientele is so dangerous, why is it in the main building instead of a separate one? And why that floor?"

Luke shrugged. "No clue. I know that when this compound was actually owned by Johnson's Pharmaceuticals, there were a lot of secure labs in the Tower. The fourth floor may have been the location of one of them and already had a good setup. But to be honest, this whole compound isn't well-designed from a security standpoint. I heard they're eventually going to relocate to somewhere more updated, but who knows when that will happen."

The elevator made a clean stop, barely rocking. The door opened. "Who has access to the floor?"

Boyd followed Luke as he walked out onto a stark, white corridor. The fluorescent lights glaring down across the white floors and walls made the place feel sterile, like a hospital. Boyd crossed his arms over his stomach.

Two other guards entered just as they left and Luke grimaced, not bothering to greet them. He didn't respond until the door slid shut, and the other guards disappeared.

"Officers, doctors, special ops staff who work up here, and the guards assigned to this floor." Luke tapped his own key card. "There aren't a lot of us. Those two guys, Harry Truman and Dennis McNichols, have been here the longest. We don't rotate much."

Boyd though that made sense given the security.

"Keep up," Luke said. "It's easy to get turned around up here. Everything looks the same from the outside in every wing."

Despite the warning, it didn't take them long to reach their destination. The door was unremarkable, as was the tiny room Boyd entered after Luke unlocked it. A man was waiting inside whom Boyd had never seen before. He was younger than David, and had wheat-colored hair and cerulean eyes. There was a boyish look about him, but he was well built and handsome. At first, Boyd wondered if the man was another candidate, but then Luke stood straighter and nodded with respect. Something unspoken must have passed between them because Luke flashed a reassuring smile at Boyd and left.

Boyd hesitated, unsure of what to do.

"Hello Boyd," the man said.

Boyd remained standing. "Hello."

"I'm General Carhart. You could say that I am the one overseeing this endeavor. I would have introduced myself to you sooner but your training is more vigorous than most, and I didn't think it wise to interrupt your regime."

"Oh," Boyd said, then thought to add a polite, "It's a pleasure to meet you."

"Agent Blake will be here shortly. It's between the two of you now."

Boyd was surprised; he hadn't expected to make it this far.

"Did many people apply?"

"It wasn't a matter of applying so much as a matter of being selected for the trial," Carhart replied. "Since it has come down to you and Agent Blake, whoever successfully completes the trial will serve as Sin's partner and the other will serve as back-up in case the original choice dies."

Boyd thought the likeliness of death must be high but didn't care enough to ask. Instead, he said, "What are the requirements of successful completion? Will there be a test?"

"No." Carhart indicated a two-way mirror that spanned the wall. What resembled an interrogation room was on the other side. "The purpose of this endeavor is to find someone whose personality can adapt to Sin's. He is valuable material to the Agency but his behavior can be extreme. We need someone who he cannot mentally eviscerate, to say the least. Someone intelligent enough to handle him and the tasks that he refuses to perform."

"Are those tasks related to mediation?"

"Yes, but you will find that in our line of work, there is very little mediating with insurgents and terrorists. You would more often be dealing with contacts, double agents, and tasks that require going undercover. These are things Sin does not excel at. He excels at being a living weapon. For my unit, I need both."

"I see."

The conversation felt one step removed to Boyd. He may as well have been reading a spy novel about a character getting inducted to a secret agency for all that he felt personally invested in the situation.

"So you would be my supervisor," Boyd said.

"Your commanding officer," Carhart corrected. "Your role in the Agency exists within the confines of my unit. The purpose of that unit will be disclosed to you if you are chosen as Sin's partner or upon Blake's death if he is instead."

"Then whose unit would I be assigned if Blake is chosen? I assume the Agency would retain me in some function until the point I may be needed."

Carhart nodded. "Even though your training is intensive, it is still not proportional to the training a real field agent requires in order to achieve rank 9. In my unit it is acceptable because you would have a specific role. Outside of my unit, it's a handicap. If Blake is chosen, you would function in a menial administrative role on the compound until you are needed, unless you consign yourself to the years of proper training to make it as a genuine agent of rank."

Boyd nodded, unsurprised. "I was told I would be receiving a glimpse of Sin."

"Perhaps a bit more than a glimpse."

The door opened and Rank 9 Field Agent Adam Blake entered the room. He glanced between Boyd and Carhart. There was surprise evident in what Boyd had come to recognize as his typically somber face.

"Am I late, sir?"

"No." Carhart nodded at the seats. "Both of you can sit down. You will be observing a psychiatric session between Sin and an Agency doctor. It's an evaluation. You're not the only ones being tested during the next several months."

Boyd hadn't expected to be privy to Sin's psychiatric sessions, yet it made sense since the assignment relied on the ability to adapt to Sin's personality. Even so, Boyd wondered what would happen if Sin failed the tests.

They spent several minutes waiting, some of which was occupied by Carhart speaking to someone on his comm unit. Boyd didn't speak and Adam, as usual, acted as though Boyd were not in the room. The man never seemed very thrilled to be doing whatever task was assigned to him, although from what Boyd had seen, Adam completed them with neat efficiency.

After ten minutes, Carhart flicked off the lights and the door on the other side of the mirror opened.

The figure that appeared was not what Boyd expected. After hearing ominous rumors for months regarding the monstrous qualities of Agent Vega, the image Boyd had unconsciously formed was of someone older and more severe. He'd thought Sin would look wild, unkempt, or hardened like a convict. Instead, Sin was tall, well over six feet and thin for his height. The worn cargo pants Sin had on were practically hanging off his narrow hips, but a sleeveless t-shirt displayed sculpted arms. Apparently, the weight Sin did have on him was crafted entirely from muscle.

There was a slim metallic collar clamped taut around Sin's neck, and Boyd could not guess at its purpose. Sin moved in a manner that showed the extraordinary control he had over his body. Every movement was precise and simultaneously predatory, exactly what Boyd would expect from a man known to be a living weapon.

Sin sat down and stared at the mirror. It was obvious that he knew he was being watched. Perhaps he even knew who was watching him.

Now that his eyes were unwittingly locked with theirs, Boyd noticed that Sin's features were unique and contradictory. His cheekbones were high, and a straight nose sat above well-sculpted and full lips. It was his eyes, however, that made his appearance truly exceptional. They were almond-shaped, heavy-lidded, and shone like bits of jade. The hue was a dramatic contrast to his bronze complexion.

It was not immediately clear what Sin's ethnic background was, although the name Vega implied a Latin American or Spanish origin.

Boyd had not expected to become intrigued by his possible partner's appearance, but he found himself unable to look away. There had been a time when Boyd had enjoyed drawing, and Sin's was the sort of face even a former artist could not help but appreciate. The contradictions created questions in the back of Boyd's mind; what was Sin's background; how could he supposedly be so strong with a body like that; how had someone so young and attractive developed a reputation for being a monster?

Sin's mouth turned down as if he heard Boyd's thoughts. His stare became menacing. "Get on with it."

In the darkness, General Carhart chuckled.

Sin continued to look through the mirror. Even when the psychiatrist entered the room, Sin did not avert his gaze.

The psychiatrist introduced himself as Dr. Osland. For the most part, Agency staff was a step emotionally removed from typical civilians, and notably blasé about their jobs. At first glance, Dr. Osland seemed to fit that mold perfectly, but a closer examination showed otherwise. A glimmer of distaste crossed his face as he settled into the chair opposite Sin.

The evaluation began with formalities. Boyd learned Sin had a history of incarceration on the Fourth dating back nearly fourteen years when he had been inducted into the Agency as a teenager. He had an equally long history of psychological examinations. Osland claimed Sin's lack of cooperation made it unlikely he would ever receive a diagnosis for his issues.

Sin agreed and did not seem concerned. He mostly just looked impatient. "Can we get to the point?"

The doctor's lips pursed. "Suits me fine."

"So get to it."

Osland flicked his thumb over his tablet. "You have spent a significant portion of your career locked on the Fourth. One incident spanning four years that began in 2012 and the latest that kept you there nearly a year."

"Your skills of detection are quite unparalleled, Doctor."

"The incident in 2012 which led to your first major incarceration in the Fourth Floor Detainment Center—"

Sin glanced up at the mirror with a scowl.

"—also led to you being kept in isolation for two years. Upon completion of that term you were put into intensive psychiatric care with Dr. Lydia Connors in the hopes that you would be deemed stable enough to return to active duty so that your talents could once again be employed." The last part of the sentence sounded droll. "You then proceeded to once again act out violently—"

"Perhaps you aren't bright enough to have reviewed that entire case file."

The doctor went on as if Sin had not spoken. "—and found yourself incarcerated for another two years. Once again, your talents were needed and you were evaluated, and returned to active duty. But not even two years later you found yourself on the Fourth and in isolation for the deaths of four agents who had each been assigned to be your partner."

This time Sin gave a mocking smile although his eyes promised murder.

Osland stopped speaking. His hand slid into the pocket of his sports coat, and he pulled out a small remote. "Why should now be any different? You have made it clear that you won't cooperate with doctors and that you will continue to behave antisocially and compulsively."

"I never said it would be different. This wasn't my brilliant plan, in case you missed that."

"But you don't want to return to the Fourth, correct?" When Sin didn't say anything, the doctor went on. "So you do have something invested. And I assume, to avoid the aforementioned conditions of your failure, you will put more effort into this evaluation."

They eyed each other, the doctor with an almost condescending kind of patience and Sin with ill-concealed dislike, before Osland began circling the issue again.

"Your previous partners. I'd like to discuss what happened with them."

Sin's lip curled, enhancing the scathing expression permanently etched into his features. "Don't you have a file somewhere with this information, doctor? Complete with snapshots of their corpses? Well—the ones that were recovered."

"Yes," Osland replied without missing a beat. "But I'd like you to tell me what happened. Something other than, in all of their cases, it was 'self-defense.'"

"Not all were killed in self-defense. Some died out of sheer stupidity alone."

"Do you find it amusing?"

"Would it matter if I did? Stop pretending like any of this even matters."

"Meaning?"

"Meaning this whole thing is a joke. Even if I said I'd hacked them all to pieces with a dull knife before pissing on their bodies, it wouldn't change a thing. If Connors wants to use me for something, he will."

Osland set his tablet on the table. He smiled. "Take some things into consideration, Agent Vega. In your current state, you are a waste of resources. A being that must be fed and tended to despite not providing a use to the Agency. If I say that you will cause the failure of missions, Marshal Connors will listen to what I say."

Silence blanketed the room with only Sin's increasing tension to fill the void. He sat with his shoulders pushed back, hands flat on the table, and lips pressed together. His hawk-like stare roamed the doctor slowly, and again Boyd was reminded of a predator examining his prey. But despite Carhart shifting towards the door and muttering a low command for a guard to standby, Sin merely looked through the mirror again.

"Evan and Michelin thought being my partner meant I was their pet. Laurel, on the other hand, was too stupid to be saved. She tried to negotiate by pointing her gun. I wouldn't have attempted to involve

SANTINO & AIS

myself in that colossal failure even if I had planned to. She was killed on a mission, not by me. I simply didn't save her. Coral wasn't any better. For all of his rank 9 training, he was a complete failure in a storm. He put together a ridiculous plan and, unsurprisingly, it failed."

"You didn't attempt to rectify his mistakes."

Sin scoffed. "Why should I?"

"Because you were supposed to work as a team."

"If the team is doomed to fail, why bother? I'll die eventually but it won't be by someone else's stupidity. If they aren't capable of respecting me or my experience as a senior agent, then obviously the partnership would fail. I don't give enough of a shit to try to salvage it."

The comment was the end of Sin's cooperation, but the final exchange was the most telling. Cold and callous, maybe. Antisocial, definitely. But Sin nearly always had a reason for his actions. Boyd wondered what had happened to cause Sin's previous incarcerations, and what had triggered his "psychotic" behavior.

The evaluation ended and Carhart switched on the lights. "Comments?"

"Is he actually mentally disturbed?" Adam's voice held a hint of doubt. "He appears normal to me. Cruel and quick-tempered, but not as out of control as everyone says."

Carhart nodded. "For the most part he is. However there are times when he snaps and does behave psychotically and violently."

"Are there commonalities in what causes his psychotic breaks?" Boyd asked.

"It differs from occasion to occasion. In one case it was a threat that wasn't even directed at him, and in another he reacted in response to verbal abuse from a guard."

Adam stood. "It's interesting that missions would be assigned to such an unstable individual. If his triggers aren't even known, how can he be trusted at all?"

"He can't," Carhart said. "That's why the two of you are here—to ensure he does not act rashly and, if he does, that the situation is controlled and rectified. His skills as a fighter are too valuable to be lost completely. You two are expected to make up for where he fails."

"How are we to control or rectify his behavior when we clearly would be outmatched physically?"

Adam gave Boyd a dull look. The man likely did not appreciate being associated with the extent of Boyd's lack of physical prowess, but as far as Boyd knew, there was no one on the compound who matched Sin in skill.

Carhart stood beside the door, examining them. "Implements have been put into place to ensure the two of you have a mote of self-defense. First, there is the collar which is surgically installed in his neck. It serves as both an electroshock weapon and a tracking device. If activated by the remote control, it has the ability to completely incapacitate Sin. Whether or not you are able to use it before he takes it from you is entirely up to you. No method is one hundred percent."

The notion of controlling a man with electric shocks was appalling, and in a former life, Boyd would have protested the notion. Now, he said nothing. His words did not have the power to change the situation.

"Why did the doctor say he has more invested this time?" Adam said.

"The circumstances of future incarceration have been made considerably harsher for Sin."

"How so?" Boyd asked.

Carhart's face was the epitome of carefully constructed detachment. It wouldn't have seemed out of place if he hadn't been so impassive until torture devices had entered the conversation. "Sin has a weakness, and they have now decided to exploit that weakness when he is incarcerated. Now, he has reason to fear the Fourth. It's in his best interest to not return there."

"If I may ask a question, General?" Adam asked.

"That's why I'm here."

"You know him fairly well. What do you anticipate being the most challenging aspect of this aside from possibly being killed during one of his... fits?"

"I do know him well," Carhart said. "And my best advice is to not react to him the way he wants you to."

The general's eyes grazed over the empty room again as if he could still see Sin beyond the mirror. "Sin will bait you and he won't do it in the same way every time. He will try sarcasm, cruelty, intimidation— whatever he thinks will get a rise out of you. He expects the worst from people and he trusts no one. If you don't show overt hostility towards him, he will only expect it to come later. He is used to both physical and verbal abuse from the people here. He is used to being condescended to and treated as though he has lesser intelligence. He is used to not having an ounce of respect from anyone. He will be waiting for you to prove yourselves to be like everyone else and if he sees that, he will react to you exactly as he reacted to the others. It is your job to not let that happen."

Adam did not react to the words, but a niggle of curiosity reared up in Boyd's mind again. How could such a powerful, and talented, agent be demoralized to such an extreme degree? Was his treatment a tactic used by the Marshal to keep him dehumanized and isolated? It would be an ideal way to keep Sin as a tool to be used for especially difficult jobs rather than view and treat him like a person. Boyd knew, better than anyone, what a weakness humanity could be.

"Even if you think you're fully capable of not letting him get under your skin," the general continued. "You may be in for a surprise. What happens after you reach that point will determine everything."

AFTER VIEWING SIN'S evaluation, training consumed Boyd's life for the next several months. It left little room for speculation about the man who may or may not become his partner. Boyd returned to his grueling routine, his exhausted nights, and careful avoidance of other trainees. He immersed himself in the process, and lost track of days, weeks, and even months.

For that reason, Boyd was surprised to be notified, nearly three months later, for a meeting with General Carhart in the Tower. Still worn-out and aching from hours of sparring, Boyd barely took in his surroundings while he was led to Carhart's office.

"Boyd," Carhart greeted him.

"General Carhart."

"It seems that you're going to be our man."

The words did not fully register, and Boyd could only think to ask, "Did something happen to Adam Blake?"

Carhart did not look particularly surprised by the question but there was some scorn in his voice when he said, "Agent Blake lost interest in finishing the trial. He decided that dealing with Sin would be too much effort for very little gain."

"Oh." When Carhart waited for a reaction, Boyd asked, "When do I start?"

"Sin's reintegration is nearly complete and your training com-
mences in March. Around that time, the two of you will meet and
you will be fully inducted into the unit."

"Okay."

There was no camouflaging the disappointment on the older man's
face. Boyd knew, had always known, that Carhart did not want some
skinny, unskilled teenager to be in his elite unit. He'd wanted the man
who'd already put in years as an agent; the man who knew what he
was doing, and hadn't had years' worth of training crammed into
months.

But Carhart seemed kinder than most people at the Agency, and
he did not say the words aloud.

FOUR

THEY HAD BEEN waiting in Carhart's office for fifteen minutes when Sin arrived.

Six guards wearing full body armor escorted him into the room. They looked prepared to go on a full storm and siege rather than simply escorting a single man to another area of the building. In addition to their own safety measures, Sin's hands and ankles bound.

"This is fucking stupid." Sin jerked his arms away from his escorts, causing the flexible cuffs to dig tighter into his skin.

Carhart's brow furrowed, and he looked to the guard who had separated himself from the rest of the group. "Lt. Taylor, is this necessary?"

Taylor shrugged. "Marshal Connors stated that all precautions will remain until the Beaulieu boy's training has completed and the final psych evaluation is put through on Vega. It's a lot of red tape but he hasn't been able to roam free for years, and Connors isn't taking any chances until everything is in the system. If Vega causes another mess in the middle of the compound, the Inspector will flip her shit. She still has to conjure cover stories for dead staff with civilian ties."

"I see."

One glimpse in Sin's direction showed that his mood was escalating from irritated to homicidal. Boyd didn't know if it was his expression, his posture, or the gleam in his eyes, but the aura coming off Sin created a sense of imminent danger in the room. All but two of the guards were on edge and had their hands on their weapons.

Boyd recognized the two unaffected men as guards he'd briefly seen on the Fourth with Luke: Dennis McNichols and Harry Truman. Sin's glare burned into them more often than the others.

"I have authorization to use the collar at will, so your presence and the presence of the shackles won't be necessary any longer," Carhart said. "Considering the fact that his evaluation should be processed within the hour, I don't think they were necessary in the first place unless it was a mere desire to create a spectacle of him in the last possible moment."

"The situation remains the same. I can't change my orders." Taylor nodded at the rest of the guards. "Turn him loose."

Harry moved to stand in front of Sin, closer than necessary, in order to cut the flexible cuffs. The guard wore a grin that was nearly lurid and it grew as he jostled Sin around and jerked at his wrists. Sin didn't respond, but he resembled a coiled spring that was ready to snap. When the restraints were removed, the guards stepped back.

"Good day, gentlemen," Carhart said when they lingered.

Taylor hesitated, but eventually left with the rest of his men filing out behind him. Harry leered at Sin one last time before shutting the door.

"You can sit, you know," Carhart said when Sin continued to glower into space.

"I prefer to stand," Sin said through gnashed teeth.

"If you play nice, you will be able to avoid scenes like that in the future. Your cooperation in this project will ensure that your situation will change for the better. Indefinitely."

Sin snarled, and Boyd wondered why he was so enraged. From what Boyd had gathered, Sin was always restrained when escorted around the compound. Boyd wondered if Harry was the cause of Sin's agitation.

Carhart leaned back in his chair. "The arrangements have already been made for you to have your own quarters contingent on the success of this trial."

That comment drew Sin's interest. For the first time, he took in Boyd. One dark brow rose doubtfully.

"He looks more frail and pathetic up close. When he dies, they'll blame me anyway."

"So you should see that he doesn't die."

Boyd didn't respond. He knew his lifespan would be very short.

"The purpose of this is for the two of you to meet before being thrown into a mission together," Carhart said. "Introductions aren't necessary—you know all about one another by now. Boyd, you will meet the rest of the team in a more formal unit meeting tomorrow morning."

"Will I receive more information about the unit?"

"Yes." Carhart accessed the touch pad that was embedded into the table beside him. "Information about the unit has been withheld until now because, although every aspect of the Agency is highly confidential, what we do in my unit is even more so. The sensitive nature of our operations can be sabotaged if the wrong word gets out and there is always a chance of betrayal. Even within our own ranks."

"What is the nature of the unit?" Boyd asked.

"Are you familiar with the domestic terrorist organization called Janus?"

Boyd searched his memory but could not recall anything about Janus. "No."

"Considering your psych profile states that you have been isolated from the world for quite some time, I cannot say that I'm surprised."

From the corner of Boyd's eye, he saw Sin's head turn in his direction.

Carhart typed a command on the touch keyboard at his desk and a hologram appeared above the table. It was as detailed as the interactive holograms Boyd had practiced shooting in training. The images that rotated above the desk arranged themselves in a slideshow, depicting carnage and scenes from the war.

"After the Three Treaties were signed, a lot of people were angry. Peace," the word left Carhart's mouth with an acerbic edge, "was established between the three different sides, but millions of people all over the world protested." He stopped and glanced at Boyd through the hologram. "Are you aware of the cause of the war?"

Boyd nodded. "The United States and Russia were engaged in a conflict, and members of the European Union were drawn in after both nations refused to acknowledge UN directives."

"And after they were caught in the crossfire of a few battles. That is a very succinct version of events, but it will suffice for now." Carhart seemed satisfied that Boyd had an understanding of at least that much. "The general consensus was that after a decade of slaughter, the involved nations were brushing their squabble under the table because nobody was winning. The citizens of the world were expected to go back to business as usual as if none of it had ever occurred despite the damning evidence of mass graves, a destroyed environment, and a shattered economy worldwide."

Carhart flicked the touch screen again and images of rallies and protests appeared. One of them was a scene of chaos at the memorial park in Washington DC. There were dead or unconscious people strewn around a rectangular area with the remains of a monument in the middle of it all.

"Hundreds of groups formed internationally with the like-minded goal of revolution. They wanted every politician involved in the war removed from office and 'real democracy'. Some groups wanted anarchy. Janus is one of them. They started as a small group and eventually grew into one of the largest insurgent organizations we have seen so far in history. Their power has spread beyond the United States, and they now work side-by-side with groups in Europe and Asia to form an army that is dedicated to crushing the existing political systems."

"Tell him the part about how they're all nothing but terrorists." Sin pointed at the hologram and then at Boyd. "Let's not forget all of that Agency propaganda. Otherwise he will just start sympathizing with the bad guys and your indoctrination could fail."

It looked like Carhart may reprimand his senior agent, but instead, he opened a drawer and extracted a paper bag.

"Do you want this or not?"

"Depends on what's in it." Sin's tone was bland, but he took a step closer, attention piqued.

Carhart dangled the bag between his fingers, mouth easing into a grin that was almost fond. When Sin held out an expectant hand, Carhart tossed him the bag.

"Now sit down and stop interrupting."

Sin pulled out a package of chocolate-covered potato chips. He didn't smile, but he didn't look enraged anymore either. Sprawling in the chair next to Boyd, Sin opened the package and popped a chip into his mouth. Carhart turned back to the hologram, once again all business, but Boyd could not concede to the idea of the third-in-command of the Agency acting almost paternal to the alleged psychopath.

"Despite Janus' self-proclaimed desire to want change for the good of the people," Carhart continued. "Both their methods and their intent have become corrupt. Now, Janus' goal is power. They use guerilla and cyber warfare to attack the United States and other countries they wish to control."

Carhart indicated the image floating between them. "In 2009, on the one-year anniversary of The Three Treaties, they bombed a WWIII memorial. It turned into a massacre of government officials, military personnel, and civilians alike. Since then, the situation has deteriorated."

At one time, Boyd might have understood Janus' viewpoint; his father had died because of the war and his death had defined Boyd's life. Now, there was a void where Boyd had once felt passion. There was no point in forming an opinion or developing sympathies for either side. He was at the Agency until he died, so he would follow their lead.

"Your unit exists to deal specifically with the threat of Janus?" Boyd asked.

Carhart nodded. "We focus on Janus and the organizations that orbit them, which is why it is so classified."

"How many other field agents are in the unit?"

"None. You and Sin are the only field agents. There are two Research and Development agents and an analyst."

Boyd knew Sin was supposed to be a one-man killing machine, but the expectation of two people taking down an international organization was unrealistic. The demands on Sin, and the dependency on his skills, only gave more value to Sin's existence at the Agency despite his treatment. Each tidbit Boyd discovered about the senior agent only strengthened Boyd's belief that the alienation of Sin on the compound was a deliberate tactic by the Marshal.

"Why so few?" he asked after digesting the information.

"Because the Agency lacks people with high enough classification to perform in this unit. We only have two living rank 10 field agents. One is abroad on an extended undercover assignment, and the other is Sin. Despite Sin's difficulties—"

"I'm still sitting here, you know," Sin said around a mouthful of chips.

"—he can do what in normal cases would require an entire team."

Sin licked chocolate off a finger. "It feels so good to be needed."

If Boyd had not seen recordings of some of Sin's missions, he would not have believed Carhart's claim.

"And as I said before," Carhart continued, unperturbed. "It is necessary to keep the confidentially limited. People talk. Things leak."

"I see."

Carhart seemed satisfied that Boyd had grasped the necessity for discretion, but Sin looked increasingly uninterested in the proceedings of the meeting now that he had finished his snack. He brushed his hands against his pants and said, "You're acting like you actually think he will survive the first assignment. I've never seen a more helpless looking agent."

"I should think you of all people understand that looks can be deceiving," Boyd commented.

"So there's a fierce fighter lurking beneath that effeminate exterior?"

"Whether I am or not is irrelevant. Considering how little you know about me it's foolish to make assumptions based on my looks alone."

"Why assume I know nothing? They have a whole file on you. On every minuscule detail of your unimpressive existence. If I really thought you were going to last more than a day, I could very easily go look at it and then I would know things that you don't want anybody to know."

"The existence of the information is meaningless unless you looked at it prior to commenting," Boyd said. "Which you've as well as admitted you didn't."

Sin snorted. "Why don't we just see him fight without the training wheels and then I'll know?"

Carhart tilted his head and considered the two of them. His eyes settled on Boyd. "Do you oppose the suggestion?"

"It's fine," Boyd said impassively. Whether Sin broke his neck now or later mattered very little.

"Good."

THEIR TREK TO the training room drew more attention than Boyd would have liked. It wasn't too surprising given their trio was made up of Chief of Staff General Carhart, an infamously despised senior agent, and Boyd—whose relation to Vivienne and androgyny put him at odds with mostly everyone else on the compound. He ignored the additional attention and followed Carhart. Sin walked next to him without speaking, but Boyd knew the older man was watching.

A staff member in the training area of the Tower led them to a private sparring room with a padded floor, weights, and a rack of weapons.

"So, how seriously do you want me to take this?" Sin asked.

Carhart moved away from the middle of the room. "You wanted to see how well he can defend himself, so this is your chance. I'm assuming you have common sense enough to know you should not harm him seriously."

"I can harm him only slightly?"

Carhart glared at Sin, and Sin flashed a sardonic smile. He watched

SANTINO & AIS

as Boyd removed his trench coat and exposed his customary outfit of a long-sleeved black shirt, pants, and combat boots.

"What are the parameters for this?" Boyd indicated the wall. "Are weapons involved?"

"If you want to use one, by all means."

Sin didn't even give the weapons wall a glance. He was fiddling absently with a loose string at the edge of his frayed shirt.

With his still-amateur eye, Boyd studied the way Sin held himself and searched for signs of weakness, but found none. Given the fact that Sin did not make a move toward the weapon rack, he was clearly opting for hand-to-hand combat, but Boyd was not foolish or prideful enough to follow suit. If he was to fight someone stronger and more skilled, he would do so with whatever weapon he had available.

Boyd naturally shied away from knives, bypassed anything requiring skills he had not yet perfected, and gravitated to the blunt weaponry. He removed a pair of tonfa from the rack, holding the knobs on the sides, and returned to the center of the mat to face Sin.

Sin dropped into a fighting stance, watching Boyd with those luminous green eyes that didn't seem to miss even the barest of movements. For his part, Boyd scrutinized Sin's stance before moving in for an attack.

The fight began with quick, darting movements on Boyd's part. He struck at critical points such as key joints and Sin's throat and face, but Sin had an uncanny ability to read Boyd's intent before he even reacted.

When Boyd went for Sin's knee, Sin jumped to the side. When Boyd aimed for the kidneys, Sin spun away. He danced around Boyd maddeningly, a leaf just out of reach that tumbled on the wind. He let Boyd strike but deflected with no more effort than it took to swat a fly. Boyd put more strength into his strikes, but Sin stopped them, and Boyd could feel the powerful strength of the other man as it rebounded up the tonfa and into his arms.

Sin had the steadiness and strength of a mountain combined with the speed of a predator. David and Carhart had warned Boyd of this for months, but it was now undeniable; this was a man who could kill him. Easily.

Despite that, and Sin's reputation as a bloodthirsty psychopath, he did not try to harm Boyd during most of the spar. It would have been easy for Sin to hurt him and make it seem like an accident, so why wasn't he being more ruthless? Was he truly so scared of whatever lay in wait if he failed? Boyd didn't know the answer to the questions and for now he largely ignored them.

He doubled his strikes; both tonfa extended, swiping at Sin one after another, in an attempt to catch him off guard. Although Boyd's stamina had increased due to his training, the fight wore on his body.

A river of exhaustion and futility ate away at the granite of Boyd's mind. Sweat crept along his skin and strands of hair caught on the sides of his face and lips. It was a nuisance, and Boyd wished he had tied it back. His long-sleeved shirt was stifling and it too clung to his thin frame. Boyd's boots seemed heavy and he regretted not having removed the extra weight prior to the fight. Then again, he hadn't expected to last this long.

He wondered how long Sin would allow this to go on, and as the thought crossed his mind, Sin broke the pattern.

Fast as a snake unfurling itself and striking, one instant Sin was a few feet away and the next, Boyd felt a violent twist at his right arm. Sin wrenched the tonfa away, causing it to clatter and nearly hit Carhart's feet. Boyd pulled the other tonfa up but it too was thrown to the side.

In a last attempt at defense, Boyd jabbed at Sin's throat, but Sin responded too quickly for Boyd to track. It was an impossible speed for a man who had impossible strength packed into his lean frame. Boyd's arms were jarred to the side and a large hand snapped around his throat. He felt himself leave the floor, feet hanging and entire body dragging down on the one point. Boyd's head pounded and his throat closed even more from the pressure of gravity. When Sin squeezed, Boyd's windpipe was almost entirely cut off. Breath left him in a painful, clawing rush that his body automatically fought against. His chest strained for air, his lungs dragging out against a near vacuum.

But through it all, Boyd did not panic. His mouth could have fallen open; he could have kicked and struggled like a worm trying to dislodge a fish hook. He could have clawed at the hands around his throat, and he could have stared into Sin's eyes with desperation and fear. But Boyd felt nothing. He couldn't stop the automatic reactions of his body, the straining chest and pounding heart, the little nibble of uncertainty that ran in the back of his mind and asked: Is this it? Will I die here? But Boyd felt no fear, and he knew Sin sensed it.

As if to test him, Sin squeezed and completely cut off Boyd's air. His lungs screamed for air, but Boyd remained motionless even when his vision blackened at the edges. He understood the idea of dying should be frightening, but the feeling wasn't there. If anything, there was an overwhelming sense of relief.

For just a moment, Sin looked intrigued. He tilted his head to the side. Then, Carhart's voice cracked like a whip.

"Sin. Enough."

Sin's hand opened, and he allowed Boyd to fall to the floor like a discarded rag doll. Boyd caught himself and coughed, dragging in deep breaths. He wondered whether Sin would have killed him had Carhart not been in the room. He doubted it, since it would have sent the man back to the Fourth, but Boyd couldn't be certain. There was nothing in those green eyes to tell him what Sin had been thinking.

"He isn't entirely without skill," Sin said. "He's possibly better than the average new field agent."

Boyd concentrated on steadying his breath. When he could draw in a breath without much effort, he straightened.

"Good work." Carhart smiled in approval. "There was no expectation that you would actually defeat him. On the contrary, you exceeded my expectations as far as your skill with the weapon. David was correct in saying that you learned quickly. I think you would have been a good match for the average agent."

The compliment surprised Boyd, but he didn't react.

"If you play your role well I guarantee that you could become more than what this position allows you to be. I see potential in you. But keep in mind, your success or failure depends entirely on your partnership with Sin. That is your starting point. That is why you are here. Don't forget that—his previous partners did and they paid for it."

Sin scoffed. "Understatement."

"The only way a partnership can be successful," Carhart added, "is by trusting one another, which is—"

"A big fucking stretch at this junction in my career," Sin said.

"—not going to be something that comes quickly," Carhart spoke over Sin. "But the relationship that develops between the two of you will determine how this plays out. If you don't get along, you will both fail. And I am sure neither of you desires failure for your own very different reasons."

FIVE

ON THE DAY of his first assignment, Boyd learned that the typical procedure for a mission included a briefing followed by a visit to Artillery to obtain necessary equipment. The building was innocuous from the outside, but he soon discovered each room was filled with the kind of advanced tech, gadgets, and weapons that made Boyd feel as though he had been transported to a future world where holographic camouflage suits and HUD contacts were the norm.

Boyd found it fascinating that whatever government entity funneled money to the Agency could afford an arsenal that could supply an army, but could not tend to areas still in disarray over a decade after the war. Even as disconnected from reality as Boyd was, the sheer scope of technology and weaponry the Agency had available was surreal. In room after room, he found rows of weapons gleaming under the light; impersonal and well-maintained tools needed to carry out the business of murder.

Boyd did not know where to start, so he stuck to the basics. He had already been given the remote for Sin's collar although he did not intend to use it. Boyd had also received a miniature microphone and ear bud set that the Agency called a comm unit. The ear bud was little more than a thin, flat disc that was nearly invisible in his ear, especially when hidden beneath the fall of his hair. The wireless microphone came in a variety of types, but the default was a small pin. He could turn the transmitter on and off at his convenience but they were typically left on unless an agent was on a solo mission.

It was standard equipment for all agents, but the Artillery staff said he could find other models inside the building. Boyd didn't think it was necessary. Additional learning was not something he was interested in pursuing. The information he had to memorize regarding the Janus unit was more than enough to keep him occupied.

The insurgent groups orbiting Janus numbered in the hundreds, and Boyd was expected to learn the key players in each. During his first meeting with the Janus unit, Boyd had been given a palm-sized tablet by the Research & Development agents that held hundreds of pages of intel. There was so much to learn that the Agency assigned numbered codenames to each group, especially since they all seemed to have similar names relating to justice, democracy, or freedom.

The current mission's target was Faction 53, also known as True Democracy Movement, or TDM. The faction operated in and around Carson City, which was not too far from Lexington. Their objective was to infiltrate a location that several of 53's members were using as a safehouse and gather intel regarding their main base of operations.

After locating the area which housed blunt weaponry, Boyd equipped himself with a pair of expandable tonfa. It was a lighter weight version than he was used to, but still had the strength.

He toured the rest of the facility to determine whether he needed more , and he entered a massive room full of guns. The walls were lined with sophisticated displays for more pistols, rifles and shotguns than he'd even known existed. While taking in the scope of the room, Boyd spotted Sin's unmistakable figure clad in a black shirt and his usual frayed, black cargo pants.

Boyd approached his new partner. Sin had not shown up at the briefing, and Boyd did not know when they would discuss the details.

Sin examined a .45 ACP and cocked it, at first seeming to ignore Boyd. But then he said without looking over, "That's it?"

"What else is needed?"

"If there's a gunfight, I suppose you could always throw it like a spear and hope it takes out multiple shooters," Sin replied. He walked away without waiting for an answer and surveyed the rest of the guns although he continued to hold the .45.

It was a fair point, but Boyd wasn't particularly comfortable with guns, and he was still perfecting his aim. As the mission depended primarily on stealth, Boyd did not think he would need it.

When Boyd didn't respond, Sin's mouth crooked up minutely. He went back to collecting ammunition for what Boyd now saw was a .45 Ruger. Another agent entered the room, a tall Asian man with bleached blond hair, and came to a halt when he noticed Sin. He turned and left the room without much delay.

Sin's reputation certainly preceded him in every case on the compound. He was leaner than most of the field agents Boyd had encountered, usually had disheveled hair, and wore clothing that was time-worn, yet other men seemed to fear Sin even without making direct eye contact. It was an interesting phenomenon.

Sin finished gathering his equipment and strapped the weapons to his body. It was obvious that he was not wearing body armor. Even Boyd had thought to wear one of the Agency's suits. It was compact and sleek, molding to his body seamlessly beneath his clothing and trench coat. He wondered if Sin was that confident in his own abilities, or whether he knew something Boyd did not. If he did, he didn't offer the information, and Boyd did not ask. He merely stood by until Sin faced him.

"I'm fully at your disposal."

Boyd nodded and left the room. Together, they walked to the underground receiving area where agents departed and returned from missions. Boyd took the driver's seat of an Agency vehicle and did not speak until they were away from the compound and on the main road.

"We are to infiltrate a building with people from Faction 53 and retrieve information about the main headquarters."

"Exhilarating."

Boyd slowed to a stop at a red light and watched Sin out of the corner of his eye. When not making sarcastic comments, he didn't talk much, and Boyd wondered what he was thinking. Did he expect that Boyd would be dead by the end of the day? No one seemed to have much hope for any of Sin's partners lasting indefinitely, and Boyd had to wonder how transitory this seemed to Sin.

The light turned green and Boyd returned his attention to driving but, without warning, Sin leaned well into his personal space. The motion was abrupt, but Sin only turned the heat down low enough to be useless.

"What are you doing? It's cold."

Boyd turned the heat back to its original setting.

Sin smacked his hand. "I thought you weren't as delicate as you look."

Boyd was incredulous, but he immediately turned the heat up again.

"Turn the vents away from you, then. Not all of us are apparently frost-bitten across our entire bodies."

"What would you do if we became stranded and had to camp out?" Sin wondered, resting his head against the window and regarding Boyd. "I'm not sharing my body heat."

"Who said I would want you to? And for the record, having normal reactions to the cold does not make me inferior or weak as you seem to be implying. Perhaps it is you who would need help were we stranded. You could be at risk for hypothermia."

"I've survived a winter in Siberia when I was ten."

"What were you doing there at ten years old?"

"Searching for Santa Claus."

Boyd shook his head. Sin flicked the slats to his vents down with a decisive click and went back to looking out the window. Feeling a tiny sense of victory at that, Boyd sat up straighter. It was silly, yet showed Sin wouldn't necessarily win everything. Even if it was a disagreement over something so insignificant.

"Regarding the mission, we don't have blueprints of the building so the layout will have to be determined upon arrival."

"Number of hostiles expected?"

"Twenty."

Boyd slowed at another red light and noticed Sin breathing on the passenger window so fog curled against the glass. He raised one long finger and began to draw on it. It was such a child-like thing to do that Boyd again found himself distracted from the drive and guiding the car on autopilot. He steered his mind back to the mission even as he kept one eye on whatever Sin was drawing.

"It's expected that the hostiles will be—"

Through the lines in the fogged glass, Boyd caught sight of a familiar sign. First Bank.

His breath caught and the words died in his throat. Boyd hit the brakes harder than he'd intended, rocking the car as they came to an abrupt halt.

The street sign on the corner proclaiming Dauphin Street and the dilapidated buildings. The alleyway and the relative obscurity of the place—

In Boyd's mind there was a flash of cement and a puddle of water. Confusing clips of voices, laughter both cruel and happy, and the twist of a scream sounding far away and at the same time too close. Buildings reaching to the sky and a street growing too small. Red curling into the puddle, inch-by-inch changing it forever from clear water. And through it all, Boyd was being pressed down, harder and harder, lungs stilling with the feeling of suffocation—

A voice whispering in his ear... I want you to remember this forever.

Boyd turned away from the bank, from that terrible day caught in time. It was so much more vivid than usual. He could almost feel the stickiness of dripping blood.

For one damning minute, Boyd forgot where he was and who he was with. How had he gotten here? How could he have driven this way—

"And suddenly you look quite taken aback."

"What?" Boyd's voice was strained.

"The light is green."

Boyd grasped at the sense of normalcy and eased off the brake, resuming the drive. This time, he stared straight ahead. When they were further from Dauphin Street, Boyd's heartbeat slowed. As soon as First Bank was no longer there as a monolithic reminder, and his scattered thoughts were given the chance to realign.

Next to him, Sin made a tsk-tsk sound. "Bringing attention to our fancy Agency-issued car in the middle of one of the most rundown parts of the city? What would your mother say? Of course if a police officer did stop us, they'd turn back around as soon as they saw the plates which take us so far out of their jurisdiction that they wouldn't know who to contact."

Boyd barely heard the criticism. His mind sidelined by the off-handed: what would your mother say?

"Maybe you're having a panic attack," Sin said. "We can always turn back, you know. They'll understand."

"No," Boyd said sharply.

"It may be for the best. I just can't be certain of your mental or physical state with sudden attacks occurring at random."

Boyd's breath hissed out. "It won't happen again."

"Maybe. How could I be sure unless you tell me what the problem is?"

"The reason is unimportant and does not concern you. They did a full evaluation of me during training. They would not have sent me off as your trial partner if I could conceivably pose any type of threat to you."

"Believe me, sweetheart, I feel anything but threatened. But how could such a seemingly innocuous area produce such a strong reaction in a guy who appears to pride himself on showing nothing?

There wasn't a soul in the street except for the usual beggars. Maybe I should mimic the extent of your reaction."

"That won't be necessary."

"Are you sure? It was pretty visceral. If any other agent were here, they would likely be concerned about taking a probationary agent with an emotional issue into a red zone."

"Leave it alone," Boyd snapped. "There is no emotional issue. If you would stop focusing on unimportant minutiae, we could prepare ourselves better for the mission. At this rate, you're more distracted by any of this than I am."

"Actually, having a half-trained newbie freak out before a mission and refuse to explain why warrants me calling in an early abort. Connors would prefer that to a mission failed."

Boyd's jaw set. "Do what you must but if the mission is aborted, it should not be on my account. I am perfectly capable of doing my part. Whether or not you feel entitled to information that is none of your business is not my concern. I assure you that none of this will affect the mission. That should be all that matters."

"Oh, but it would be held on your account. Even if you won't deign to fill your partner in on your random attacks of fear, I'm positive that Connors and your dear mother would demand an explanation." Sin leaned against his seat. "If I were someone who actually gave a shit about this mission, or any mission, you'd have trouble."

Boyd's heart thumped at the thought of explaining to his mother. It threatened to reignite the trembling, the fear, but he viciously shut down any tangential thoughts.

None of that mattered. The past was the past. It couldn't hurt him anymore. He just had to focus. Everything else would fall away like it had for years, and he would be safe again. He just had to be stone instead of human; unfeeling and unanimated, and everything would be okay. Boyd repeated that to himself, and shut everything else out.

He ignored Sin and reoriented himself to their position and his purpose. He did not speak again until they were approaching their target.

"It would behoove us to have a plan prior to entering, and we're nearly at our destination."

Sin didn't respond. He seemed to have already lost interest in Boyd.

"We don't know exactly where the information and the hostiles are

SANTINO & AIS

within the building," Boyd continued. "However, if the building is like many of the others in the area it is likely to have two main exits: one in front and one off the alley. Given that many of the buildings in this area used to be for commercial use, there are probably a number of rooms in back which once functioned as offices with a larger show-room or lobby in front."

Boyd pulled over on an abandoned street a few blocks away from their target.

"Obviously this information will not be known until we enter. However, to speed the completion of the mission I suggest we split up, one entering in each entrance. If you have a preference for alley or street side entrance, you're welcome to it. We'll keep our comm units active and whoever is able to obtain the information first will alert the other. We meet at the car upon egress."

Sin slid his hands into his pockets and inclined his head submissively.

Satisfied there didn't have to be a prolonged discussion about this, Boyd opened the door. "Is your comm on?"

"Sure."

Boyd hesitated. There was something off about Sin's mild manner, but Sin failed to say anything further so Boyd got out of the car. He made his way to the targeted building, staying in the shadows and slinking low. He did not stop moving until he was across the street from the building. From what he could see, it was not equipped with a security system and there was one lookout on the second floor.

Boyd crouched at the mouth of the alley, watching. There were so many security breaches in the building that Boyd did not think they could all be manned by a guard. After a while, the lookout disap-peared from the window, and Boyd searched for other telltale signs of movement. He found nothing. Moving swiftly, he crossed the street and darted to the side entrance. After picking the lock on the rusted door, and after hearing no one, Boyd pushed it open.

The interior of the building was wrought with decay. It stank of rot-ting wood, the floor was uneven, and the walls discolored from water damage. There were a few doors within view; two on each side of the corridor, and one at the end that likely opened up to a larger space in the front of the building.

Boyd crept further inside. Each room he explored was either empty or void of anything pertinent to the assignment, and his comm remained silent. Either Sin had efficiently killed the man at the front of the warehouse, or he hadn't run into any problems so far.

Boyd assumed the latter until three hostiles appeared in the outer hallway.

He ducked into a nearby room but wasn't fast enough to avoid detection. Within seconds, the staccato burst of gunfire ripped into the open doorway. A disturbing trill rushed through him; adrenaline, alarm, and indifference all combined. There was a second in which his civilian brain froze, having no idea what to do with people shooting at him, but almost instantly the training took over. Boyd kicked over the dilapidated desk and crouched behind it. Gunfire sprayed around him, ripping into the walls and sending sheetrock crumbling onto him.

Boyd ran through Agency protocol in his mind, in part to calm his shattered nerves and pounding heart, and in part to focus past the chaos surrounding him. Never lose contact with your partner, the trainers had said. In the event of a problem, check in.

"South hallway," Boyd said into the comm unit. "I need backup."

Sin did not respond.

The impact of the bullets shook the desk; Boyd knew it was only a matter of time before they weakened the structure enough to shoot through it. Voices called out in the hallway, saying they had the intruder cornered. Boyd now felt fairly certain that Sin had never entered the warehouse.

Still, he hissed into his comm, "Where are you? I'm surrounded."

There was no answer, and Boyd knew there would not be one. Sin had probably never left the car. Boyd couldn't even be sure the man had bothered to turn on his comm given his lackadaisical 'sure' earlier.

Disgusted, Boyd dropped his hand to his utility belt. He removed a flash-bang grenade and threw it into the outer room, temporarily blinding the hostiles. He sprang out from behind the desk and dove out the fractured window, feeling the glass catch on his clothing but not penetrate his body armor. He was out of the warehouse before the hostiles had recovered.

Boyd sprinted back the way he'd come, knowing there was little time before the hostiles pursued. The Agency car was where he had left it, and so was Sin. The senior agent was casually leaning against the side of the car. The sight of him lounging around made Boyd's aggravation swell. He skidded to a stop and grabbed Sin's shoulder.

"What the hell were—"

Before he could finish the sentence, Boyd found himself pinned against the car. For a breath, he and Sin were nearly nose to nose.

"Don't touch me," Sin growled.

Boyd caught himself when Sin released his coat. He could hear the sounds of pursuit closing in on them, echoing in the alley and growing louder. With a tightened jaw, Boyd stalked around the car and jerked open the driver's side door. He hardly waited for Sin to get in before speeding down the street, the tires squealing in protest. The high-pitched whip of bullets ricocheted off the pavement around them, and he heard the dull thud of one of the shots catching the back of the car. They turned the corner and Boyd twisted the steering wheel to catch the next turn. In the rear view mirror, he saw the hostiles swarming around the corner.

Frustration continued to stain Boyd's thoughts even after they had made it another two blocks and all signs of the hostiles faded.

"Do not put your hands on me, either," Boyd said in a hard tone.

Sin once again appeared completely disinterested in his existence.

"What the hell were you doing back there? Didn't you have your comm unit on?"

"What do you think?"

"Why didn't you even try? The mission failed, and we'll both be held accountable. Doesn't that bother you?"

"The mission didn't need two people. Maybe you should have brought a gun."

Boyd didn't acknowledge that Sin was right and instead said, "What difference would that have made against so many armed hostiles? It may have helped but it wouldn't have fixed everything."

Sin half-turned in the passenger's seat. "Who exactly was it that trained you, out of curiosity? They should put termination down on their day calendar if you are their final rank 9 product."

"Not all of us were born superhuman," Boyd said coldly. "It's my first mission and I expected my partner to be where he said he would be. Apparently that was a mistake."

"Relying on anyone is a mistake. If you weren't taught that, you are more misinformed and ridiculous than I thought. This mission was a joke. If you aren't even capable of performing adequately on it, you won't last much longer whether it's me who snaps your neck or not."

"Is that what you want? Another failed attempt at a partner on your record?"

Sin released a short laugh. "Don't speak as though you know anything about me. And this partnership will fail regardless, judging from what I've seen today. You have the amazing ability to be both arrogant and completely stupid simultaneously."

"How am I stupid?" Boyd demanded. "My plan would have worked."

"Maybe but then again, maybe not. You didn't ask my opinion on the matter. Like I said, if I was anyone else, they would have aborted this mission at the first sign of you not listening to reason. Not to mention your weird-ass panic attack. They would also write up a detailed report of your ineptitude."

Boyd clenched his teeth. He wanted to argue the point that he didn't ask for Sin's opinion because clearly Sin was uninterested in ever sharing his, and nothing had stopped Sin from chiming in any time he'd wanted. But he couldn't discount Sin's other points and that annoyed him even more, along with the reminder of what had happened on Dauphin Street.

"And you plan not to?" Boyd challenged. "So far you've spent your time mocking me, ignoring me, or threatening to kill me. If you have such a problem with me I'd think you'd love the chance to tell your superiors."

"You'll die regardless. What's the point?"

At least they were in agreement on that point.

The rest of the ride felt at once too long and too short. When they returned, Sin walked away without a word and Boyd wrote the mission report alone. There wasn't a good way to word that he'd failed on his first mission so he was unsurprised when he was summoned by his mother within an hour of the report being submitted.

Ann led him into Vivienne's office and shut the door behind him.

"Sit down." Vivienne's words were clipped.

Boyd obeyed.

"I had low expectations of you yet even I did not anticipate such a resounding failure."

"Mother, I—"

"Inspector," she corrected.

"Inspector," he said. "The situation was such that it required two people. I did request backup, but I didn't receive it."

"A convenient explanation," Vivienne said. "You did not bring a gun on the mission."

Boyd hesitated. "No."

"Were you not advised to bring one prior to the mission?"

"I was."

"Was the reason for the recommendation not in case of a gunfight?"

"It was." Boyd had no idea how she knew all this. She'd probably found out through checking the artillery records and, if they had it, surveillance.

"And was a gunfight not what caused this catastrophic failure?"

"It was." Boyd forged ahead before she could say anything else. "However, it should be noted that even if I'd been armed with a gun I still would have been forced to retreat without backup. I was vastly outnumbered."

"Ineptitude is not an acceptable excuse. What was the nature of your incident prior to the mission?"

Boyd's heart jolted. "I don't—"

"All Agency vehicles are equipped with surveillance. There is always a thorough investigation following a failed mission, in part because agents have been known to lie to obscure their own mistakes."

No doubt if they had surveillance they also had GPS. There was no point in trying to pretend the incident had happened anywhere other than by First Bank. As if sensing his thoughts, Vivienne continued with the same dispassionate tone.

"I was under the impression that you were past that. Must you continuously be so weak as to cause embarrassments?"

"I apologize, Inspector." Boyd's stomach clenched with dread. "It will not happen again."

"Are you so certain?" She leaned forward. "I have my doubts that you are trustworthy in that regard. You have already proven yourself to be weak and susceptible in the past. I nominated you for this position based on the impression that you were suitably emotionless, yet you have already proven that you are incapable of success. It lends the question of what I should do with you."

A spike of distress shot up Boyd's spine; a guttural reaction that he couldn't quite keep from his expression.

"There are options available. We have facilities that would be ideal to give you an opportunity to recover from your lapse. Time need not be a factor. Is that what you wish?"

Boyd's breath caught and, again, the memories returned like creeping shadows. Expanding darkness and eyes glinting in the corner; the wounded ghosts hovering over him and watching as he struggled against the chafing of his wrists. Screaming until the metallic taste of blood was familiar in this throat; endless terror and an ever-consuming, pleading wish to die.

He blinked, pushing the images away. "No."

"Then I suggest you put more effort into this or I will enact a solution that you will find to be very undesirable. Is that understood?"

"Yes, Inspector."

"My reputation will be affected by your performance. I have worked too hard in this organization to have a child bring me disgrace simply because he is unwilling to function as expected. Do not make me regret the nomination."

"I won't, Inspector," Boyd said, voice dropping low. He wanted to look down, but her stare sucked him in. Or maybe it was simply that she had paid attention to him so infrequently in his life that he was unwilling to turn away now that she did.

Vivienne scrutinized every inch of him as if she were assessing him for a test for which he didn't know the criteria for passing. It was disconcerting.

At length, she focused on her tablet again.

"Dismissed."

Boyd left with a non-expression on his face even as anxiety gnawed him to the bone. He ran through the mission, every word and mistake he'd made, and vowed to make it the last time he gave them ammunition.

As he left the Tower, the cool slide of determination washed over him and replaced the fear.

SIX

BOYD SPRINTED THROUGH the woods, trees rushing by his peripheral vision like shadowy sentinels in the night. He ignored the throb of his knees and the sharp twinge in his shoulder, souvenirs from a mission that had gone awry.

After nearly a month of close calls, his number had almost come up in a rush of grabbing hands and shackles as he was forced into a dark, windowless room in the basement of an abandoned building. Once again, he had been outnumbered, but after several missions, Boyd had nearly mastered the art of escape.

He had learned to walk as silently as Sin when needed, his senses keener, and movements quick and sure. Now, Boyd could incapacitate a guard with two, sometimes one, motion if he came upon the person unaware. However, that could not always keep him out of trouble.

This time, Boyd had made it to the egress point with the intel in hand. He had no illusions that he'd have been thrown on the Fourth if he'd screwed up another mission involving 53. The goals of this mission had been the same as the first, but this time he had succeeded. Even though he was still operating alone.

Six assignments in, and Sin was no closer to helping Boyd than he'd been on the first, but the hostility between them had faded. Sin no longer went out of his way to mock or antagonize Boyd, although Boyd had no idea what was responsible for the shift.

Even running, it took Boyd several minutes to navigate the woods, a task made more difficult by the darkness. It was an issue that only plagued him in wooded areas. Boyd could review blueprints before he went into a building and instantly understand the layout, building a 3D image in his mind that he could mentally rotate to find a new route. But when every direction seemed to be filled with the same view of tree trunks and leaves that blocked out any reference points, Boyd got confused.

At last he reached an area with thinner canopies, affording him a much-needed glimpse of the vacant buildings rising beyond the park. Boyd reoriented himself based on the angle of the buildings and kept going. It wasn't long before he burst out of the park and back into the more familiar urban streets.

The mission had taken he and Sin to Carson, a city that lay just beyond the Wastelands. This specific neighborhood was largely abandoned and removed from the general populace; the kind of area where gunfire went unreported.

Once he was back on the street, Boyd found his way to the meeting point. He was breathing so hard that he couldn't even hear his thundering heartbeat, and his limbs tingled. Boyd was as quiet as possible until he determined that no hostiles were around. Satisfied, he approached the vehicle.

As per their new routine, Sin was sitting in the driver's seat, waiting. On a larger mission with a bigger team, it would be customary for the team leader to wait in the vehicle to run the mission and make sure everyone was on point. It didn't apply for their partnership since there were only two of them; Sin was needed in the field not the van.

Vivid green eyes analyzed Boyd's disheveled form when he climbed into the van.

"Surprisingly impressive," Sin commented, starting the engine.

Boyd shut the door. He looked askance at Sin, trying to determine if that had been a veiled slight. Judging by Sin's expression and tone, it had been a simple statement with no negative undertones. It was the first time Sin had said anything positive to him.

"Were you watching?"

Sin glanced in the rear view mirror. He went still as if he sensed something.

Although he did not accompany Boyd on the assignments, Sin was always diligent about ensuring they were not followed. As cynical as he was about the trial partnership and his own future as an agent, Sin still protected the integrity of their covert nature. He shifted the car into drive and guided them off the street, still focused on the darkness that pressed in on them from the outside. Streetlights in this forgotten neighborhood had long since died out.

Once they returned to the highway with no signs of a tail, Boyd assumed his question had been ignored and stopped expecting an answer. He went about ensuring the safety was on his rifle before he twisted to stow it behind his seat. Boyd ignored the protests of his bruised torso, and was fastening his seatbelt when Sin spoke.

"I was observing."

Boyd tightened the belt across his lap. "Why?"

"To observe you."

"Obviously. You didn't initially observe me, though. What changed?"

"I figured you'd be dead by now. It's surprising and I'm very rarely surprised."

Boyd tried to get a read on Sin and, as always, came up with so many conflicting signals that he may as well have drawn a blank. He didn't think he would ever get used to the enigma that Sin represented. The only thing he had figured out so far was that everything in the first mission, from Sin telling him to get a gun to the incident on Dauphin Street, had been a test. One that he had failed.

"What do you think, then?"

"I think that you're less likely to die as easily as I first thought." That seemed to be the end of Sin's analysis until a tiny smirk curved up his mouth. "Until we're assigned a mission that requires a lot of combat, anyway. The likelihood of you surviving a storm on your own is slim to none."

"It's possible I would surprise you on storms as well. Although, the difficulty of such missions is why we're supposed to be partners..."

Sin returned his attention to the road and did not reply.

"Why are you still so resistant?" Boyd asked when Sin remained silent. "The issues that arose on the first mission haven't been repeated. I understand that we didn't have a good first impression and you haven't had the best track record with previous partners, but I'm not them. I don't understand what I've personally done to warrant you being so unwilling to cooperate."

This time when Sin glanced over, there was definite surprise in his features. "Oh, I don't have a reason. I'm just making this up as I go because I'm insane and all of that."

"We both know that isn't true. If you don't want to answer the question, say so. There's no need to lie."

"For someone who allegedly was content to stare blankly at people and not talk for the better part of their training, you are certainly chatty these days."

"I don't see the point in talking for the sake of talking, and prior to today I had little to say to you." Boyd didn't turn away, wondering whether so much direct eye contact surprised Sin since most people avoided looking at him. "You seemed content to ignore or belittle me and I had nothing to contribute to that."

"Well, I still don't particularly like you, if that helps you in shutting up."

"That's fine. I don't particularly like you, either," Boyd said, unfazed. "However, for someone with a reputation of being unafraid of confrontation, it's interesting that you keep evading simple questions."

Sin accelerated as they moved into a higher speed limit zone. "I don't need to answer to you or explain my reasoning to you. I don't have any desire to even have a conversation with you. It's not my problem how curious you are."

"Why are you so defensive?"

"I'm not defensive. I just don't understand you. Why the fuck do you care about what I think? Doesn't it bother you that this is all getting you nowhere?"

"In what way?"

Sin pushed the vehicle faster and the trees along the highway rushed by. "How do you think this is going to end?"

"My partnership with you? Or my time at the Agency?"

That earned Boyd a humorless smile. "Isn't it the same thing? You're here because of me."

Boyd acknowledged that with a nod. "Then, to answer your question it will likely end when I die on a mission. Chances are that will happen sooner rather than later."

A flash of something crossed Sin's face, but Boyd could not discern if it was irritation, disgust, or something entirely different.

"Don't you have anything better to fucking do other than babysit and eventually get killed by some psycho?" Sin demanded.

"No," Boyd said without hesitation. "I don't."

They spent the rest of the ride in silence.

WITHOUT SIN, THERE were only five people present at the debriefing.

As usual, General Carhart sat at the head of the glass conference table. He was speaking to Jeffrey Styles, an analyst in his late twenties whose black hair was always perfectly in place much like his pressed suits. Out of the three support agents present, he was the only one who fit the mold Boyd had come to attribute to Agency staff. The two Research & Development agents, despite being tasked with the formidable job of accruing hundreds of Janus-related sources world-wide, were both idiosyncratic and offbeat in their own ways.

Ryan Freedman was easily the nerdiest person Boyd had ever met. During a briefing, Ryan was not above making chitchat about the newest MMO he was playing, hacker forums he frequented, or an anime series he liked. He was shorter than average, thin, and his black hair stuck out in a mess of cowlicks and curls. He was more like a geeky teenager than a twenty-five year old genius who'd been born and raised on the compound.

At the moment, Ryan was peering through thick-framed glasses at an outdated laptop while sliding his thumb across a tablet, and diverting his attention between the two.

The other R&D agent, Owen O'Connell, was several years older than Ryan. Despite being a much-coveted linguist at the Agency, Owen always looked like he'd jerked out of sleep without properly putting on his clothes. Pale and covered in freckles, his curly red hair was usually messy, and his shirts were perpetually wrinkled or untucked. As they finished debriefing Boyd's most recent mission, Owen worked his way through an enormous container of coffee.

"I'll have the analysis ready in a few days," Jeffrey was saying as he set his tablet down. "It will take some time to sift through all the data to find usable intel."

"Is it possible there isn't anything of use at all?"

"That's always possible; especially when the enemy gets forewarning that they're being spied on by an unknown group." Jeffrey didn't look in his direction, but Boyd knew the analyst was referring to his first disastrous mission. "But I won't know until I look through everything. They may have felt safe outside the city."

Carhart inclined his head and pushed his chair back. "Report to me immediately when you're done. We'll reconvene when we have more information unless something else comes up." He was gone before anyone could reply.

"Geez, he's always in a rush these days," Ryan commented.

"He could be outrunning a curse," Owen offered, frowning. "Do you think that's what's going on?"

Jeffrey's hand stilled as he logged out on the tablet. "That's easily the stupidest thing you've said this week."

"Just this week?" Owen's eyebrows rose. "What'd I say last week? Was it something awesome and enlightening?"

"Stop being such an imbecile." Jeffrey opened his briefcase with sharp movements. "I'll never know how someone like you made it into a unit like this. Some of us had to actually work for it." He speared Boyd with a pointed look.

Boyd was unsurprised. He had realized from the start that Jeffrey was another person on compound who seemed to hate him simply for existing.

"No really," Owen said, peering at Jeffrey with interest. He seemed to have woken up a bit with this topic. "Maybe I was sleepwalking at the time? I don't remember any cool conversations. Oh! Unless I was telling you the story about my dream, but if you actually believed I sprouted wings made of spatulas and could fly..."

The answer only irritated Jeffrey further. The two men bickered during most meetings, with Owen's obliviousness only fueling Jeffrey's annoyance. Boyd suspected that Owen enjoyed baiting Jeffrey since the analyst always responded.

"I don't know, guys," Ryan piped up seemingly randomly. He was chewing on the end of a stylus and peering down at his computer with a frown. It almost seemed like he was continuing a conversation although he hadn't been talking out loud to anyone else in the past few seconds. But that seemed to be how Ryan's mind worked. Always going, even when he was talking about something entirely different.

"I mean, do you really think Warren Andrews is in league with Janus? I know they've been swallowing up all of these teeny groups and whatnot, but his profile doesn't seem to be what they usually scoop up. Know what I mean?"

Boyd paused and, since this was work-related, settled back into his chair. Jeffrey and Owen stopped talking.

"Janus does seem to go for the assholes," Owen agreed. "And Warren's not really their style unless he held up an old folks' blood bank for the poor when I wasn't looking."

"Faction 53 isn't as aggressive as they used to be but they still have power," Jeffrey said. "Janus could simply be expanding their selection pool. It wouldn't be the first time they shifted their targets."

"Yeah, but something dreadful this way comes." Owen waved a hand. "Right? 53 has the right hand slapping the left from what your source said. And once they break up, they're gonna lose any power they held which makes them prime meat for the vultures. Or I guess rotting meat?"

"I dunno. It's just a personality thing is all I'm saying." Ryan put down the tablet, looking at the others. "He doesn't seem the type to want to be controlled by some giant puppet master, or at least that's what my sources have been saying. I hope we end up negotiating rather than just wiping them out. Even though 53 is extreme, they're dealing with a shitty situation over in Carson."

"The only indication so far is that he's thinking about it, correct?" Boyd asked.

Ryan nodded, his hair bouncing with the motion. "Yeah, from what I've found, he seems hesitant about it. But then again he's super paranoid about everything ever since the split with Aarons."

Before Boyd had joined Carhart's unit, Faction 53's two main leaders, Jason Aarons and Warren Andrews, had had a falling out. The group initially formed because of rampant corruption in Carson's governing body. 53 thought there was a lack of equity in the way resources had been allocated during reconstruction as well as the over-policing of poverty-stricken neighborhoods. Eventually, 53 had taken to terroristic acts to prove their point, but Jason Aarons was more aggressive which caused friction between him and Andrews. Jason left and formed his own group, leaving both factions in a vulnerable position.

Allegedly, some of the people in 53 wanted Warren to accept Janus' proposition, and his hesitance made them doubt his leadership.

"He should be paranoid," Jeffrey said, completely unsympathetic. "He can't keep his group together and he's letting enemy agents with inadequate training infiltrate his bases. He's lucky there hasn't been a mutiny."

Owen pointed at Jeffrey. "Being kind of harsh on the dude, aren't you? Warren doesn't seem like too much of a douche. Also, for our little blond nougat, I'm pretty sure half a year of hardcore boot camp isn't 'inadequate training.'"

Jeffrey stood. "I forgot; it's love the enemy day."

"Well, mark a calendar then. I won't always be here to remind you."

Jeffrey scowled and left.

Owen yawned. "It's way past my bedtime," he mumbled, even

though it was barely 10 am. "Night and bedbugs and all that." He ambled out of the room with another huge yawn that Boyd heard even as the door swung shut. Boyd stood to leave as well.

"Boyd, do you have a sec?" Ryan half-stood.

"Yes."

"Do you mind if I pick your brain a bit about your partner?"

"Why? Surely you know him better than I do."

"Ha! Not even close." Ryan reclined in his chair and raised his arms, threading thin fingers behind his head. The black jacket he wore over a faded anime t-shirt shifted with the motion. "I haven't had a conversation with Hsin since I was, like, I dunno... ten."

"Were you close prior to that?"

"No... That was like when he first got here. He stayed with the Connors for a little bit because he was so young, but it didn't work out and I never had direct contact with him again."

"Then why do you refer to him as Hsin? I haven't heard anyone else call him that unless they were saying his full name."

"People just call him Sin because it was originally mispronounced so everyone started doing it." Ryan gave one of his huge shrugs, his shoulders nearly going up to his ears. "Plus, I like his real name better."

Even if it was Sin's real name, Ryan was the only one who seemed to care. It was a familiar way to address a man who was not exactly approachable, and Boyd wondered if Sin had a preference either way.

"What did you want to discuss?"

"I'd just wondered what he was like one-on-one. He never showed up for briefings even back when he had the other trial partners." Ryan's words were coming out casually, but he'd begun avoiding Boyd's eyes.

"Why does it matter?"

"Because I want to know what he's like and you're the only person he's in contact with." Ryan started putting his belongings in a large backpack. "If you don't want to talk about it, it's fine."

"I don't mind." Boyd considered the question. "I don't have much of an answer. This latest mission was the first time we spoke on anything close to even terms. We don't converse much or, when we do, it's regarding the mission parameters or he's being sarcastic."

For some reason, the last part caused Ryan to grin. "The times I have seen him in the past few years, he's always such a smart ass. It's pretty funny, I think. He just doesn't give a crap about anything here the way everyone else does."

"I find it to be irritating at times, to be honest. Especially since he enjoys calling me sarcastic pet names such as sweetheart."

"Why does he call you that?"

"To be obnoxious or patronizing, it seems."

"Or..." The mischievous grin returned, making Ryan look far more youthful than he already did. He appeared to be on the verge of saying something but stopped himself and hid his grin behind the case of his laptop as he put it away. Boyd found Ryan to be exceedingly odd at times.

"Well, anyway," Ryan said. "He could just be trying to get a reaction out of you."

"I suppose. Did you speak to his previous partners? I assumed he did the same with anyone he was around for any length of time."

"The pet name thing? Nah, not as far as I can tell. None of the partners lasted very long. I mean, Laurel made it probably a month before she got killed and she was the longest. We actually had hope for her." Ryan said the last part dryly. "But they never made it sound as though he really... joked around or anything. To any extent."

That was interesting, and dredged up Boyd's continued ignorance about how exactly his predecessors had failed.

"What happened with them? I only have a succinct version of the events."

Ryan stopped putting equipment in the huge backpack he carried. He studied Boyd, gave a little nod to himself, and began digging around in the bag. There was an assortment of discs, flash drives, and memory cards in a large plastic bag, but he had no trouble finding the one he wanted.

"Give me a sec and I'll set up a whole demo."

Ryan moved to Carhart's position at the table and popped a drive in before fiddling with the computer. He made various 'hrm' and 'aha!' sounds before the hum of the holograph machine echoed in the room, and an image popped up between them.

The man in question had fiery red hair and a scarred face.

"That's Evan McCoy. He was bachelor number one and the mistake they should have learned from. At first they were hiring these big guys from Counter-Terror. Macho men with hero complexes."

Another image popped up, this one of a younger man with deep chestnut-colored skin and surprisingly light hair. "Michelin was the same way. He was bachelor number two."

Ryan's fingers flew over the keyboard and two images popped up side by side. It was a man and woman, both of whom were in their twenties. Boyd wondered what happened to an agent who passed his or her prime; he had yet to see a field agent much older than late thirties.

"Laurel and Coral. I wonder if anyone else noticed that they rhyme." Ryan grinned at his own joke.

Boyd studied the pictures. "How did they die? I know he let two of them perish on a mission after he deemed them too stupid to save, but I don't know any details. It would be helpful to know what sparked each incident."

"No one really knows," Ryan admitted. "Evan and Michelin had a definite power trip when it came to Hsin. A lot of people on the compound, them included, get off on feeling like they can put someone so strong in his place. And when they realize he isn't a complete lunatic... they underestimate him. Especially because of how he looks."

Boyd rubbed his jaw and examined the rotating images. He could imagine how agents like Evan and Michelin, brawny men who could double as bodybuilders would have underestimated Sin. For all that Sin had unparalleled skills, without having seen him in action, it was probably easy to assume he was not as strong as the rumors claimed.

"If they were abusive to him, why wouldn't he say so?"

"I don't know. Hsin doesn't provide any information even if it's in his own best interest. So there's, like, no way to tell if it was legit self-defense or if he just got annoyed and snapped their necks. I know for a fact that he allowed Laurel and Coral to die. They weren't as bad as the other two, but you could still tell they thought he was some kind of inferior creature." Ryan frowned and turned off the machine, causing the images to shimmer and disappear. "The problem is the administration. They treat him like something subhuman and everyone else follows."

Ryan's voice rose with each word until the explanation turned into a rant. The R&D agent put his things away again, his hands moving in quick agitated motions.

"If you've hardly spoken to him and rarely see him, why does it upset you so much?"

Ryan stopped packing and threw his hands up. "Why is everyone so dumbfounded by that?"

"Because no one else here cares."

"They don't," Ryan agreed. "And like I said, it's because of the administration. When he came here, they turned him into this little killing machine, isolated him and took everything—even his name. They turned him into a thing that belongs to them. He isn't a person, he's just property, and that gives everyone else permission to treat him the same way. As for me?"

Ryan finished putting his things away and hefted his backpack on one shoulder. "I respect him because he doesn't let anyone break him. They try so hard and he just weaponizes his dehumanization."

Boyd picked up his own messenger bag and could not help but look at Ryan with new eyes. "Do you tell everyone these things?"

"Oh, yeah! I'm not alone, though. The R&D crowd is way different than the fieldies, Boyd. One day I'll show you and you'll see. We're way more critical of things and we get away with it because we're the eccentric nerds." Ryan smirked, wiggling his brows. "I don't even hide that I have a monster crush on Hsin. The guy is gorgeous!"

Boyd had to agree that Sin's unique features were attractive. "You tell everyone that part as well?"

"Yup." Ryan looked proud of himself as he explained. "It's not like it's any big secret that I'm gay. I never date girls and I've been here since I was a fetus. Also, if anyone starts ragging on Hsin in my earshot, I let them know a thing or two."

"I see." Something about Ryan's proud smile and conviction reminded Boyd of someone from the past. Someone long gone. "It's a commendable attitude to stand up for what you believe in regardless of whether it's widely accepted."

"Thanks." Ryan's expression brightened. "You're pretty cool, Boyd. I'm glad you're not another asshole. A lot of that tends to go around here. It's in the air."

"I've noticed."

Ryan started for the door, walking backwards. "Well I have to jam but let me know if you want to talk or if, like, you want any additional info on Hsin. I may not be close to him as a person but I'm kind of a Vega lexicon. I've studied him like a creeper for a while. It's a little gross. This obsession should really stop sometime before they think I'm a stalker."

"I'll keep it in mind."

As Ryan walked away, Boyd could not help but think that although the invitation was one he would have almost discarded in the past, now the notion of finding out more about Sin had merit.

SEVEN

THE LIBRARY ON the fourteenth floor of the Tower was Boyd's favorite place on the compound. It was the original reference library from an era when printed books and desktop computers were common. A more advanced technology center had been added on the lower levels, but Boyd quickly ceased going there because it was so crowded with field agents all vying to submit their reports.

And, during his scant number of visits, Boyd had been subjected to glances and comments filled with vitriol not dissimilar to the level Dover and Cecilia had displayed upon learning about his connection to the Inspector.

Boyd tried not to draw attention to himself, but his status as Vivienne Beaulieu's son, Sin Vega's partner, and a civilian who was promoted to rank 9 and assigned to General Carhart's elite Janus unit, had spread throughout the general populace, and his looks made it impossible to blend in or escape notice.

So, Boyd avoided the tech center just as he avoided the compound's café. The library, in comparison, was usually empty and quiet. He could flip through books and write reports in peace without feeling judged for his very existence. He had even discovered a favorite table in a back corner that was always deserted.

He was on downtime for a couple of days, and Boyd was seeking the next novel in a series he had recently begun to read. After months of continued activity of the mind and body, it was difficult to return to the habit of drifting into a trance when alone at home. Now, he grew restless, and that restlessness prompted him to return to old habits such as reading.

Boyd perused the aisles, found his book and a large tome on architecture, before going to a lone table at the very back of the library. It was out of view and behind the stacks; a good location to sit quietly and avoid others. However, when Boyd approached the table, he froze.

Sin was slouched at the table with an elbow propped up and his cheek resting against his palm. A book was open in front of him and a couple scattered nearby, but Sin was not reading. At the sight of Boyd, his face took on a suspicious cast. "What?" he demanded.

"You're sitting at the table where I intended to sit."

Sin stared him down as if seeking a sign of deceit. "You're just randomly here?"

"Yes." Boyd set the books down so Sin could see. "I prefer this library. It's quiet, which is also why I prefer this corner. Fewer people come back here so I can spend time without being bothered."

"No shit." Sin slammed his book shut and Boyd saw that it was a collection of post-war poems. "I find it odd that you're here. I don't believe in coincidences."

"Well, that's unfortunate because that's what this is. If I'd wanted to track you down, why would I do something so obvious?"

Sin grabbed the other books and put them in a stack. One appeared to be a novel and the other was thick and wide like a textbook. "I was thinking more along the lines of someone sending you here, but thanks for the speech."

"No one sent me." Boyd hesitated, not wanting to chase Sin away. "Are you leaving?"

"Didn't you say you wanted the table?"

"You don't have to leave for that. I was only hoping to take one side of the table but if you don't want me to, I'll leave instead. You were here first."

Sin's hand curled around the spine of the book he had been reading, but he was still tensed to leave. When Boyd hovered by the table without moving, Sin inched backwards on his seat. "Whatever."

Boyd sat down and opened the architecture book. He flipped through the pages and soon felt eyes on him, but when he glanced across the table, Sin dropped his gaze.

Not for the first time, Boyd was perplexed by his partner. He could not decide if his presence was unwanted or if it made Sin uncomfortable in some way. Whatever the case was, Sin was not attempting to chase him away which was more surprising the more Boyd thought about it. He observed Sin, watching as he chewed on his lower lip and scanned each poem.

"How is that?"

"What?"

"The book. I haven't read anything by that poet. I was curious if it's good."

Sin shot Boyd an incredulous look. It seemed like he might say something scathing, but then he appeared to stop himself and said instead, "Dull."

"Do you read a lot of poetry?"

"I don't really read a lot of anything. Until recently, I haven't had access to books since I was a child." The response was spoken curtly but after a beat Sin added, "Even then, I only had a few classics. After having read Milton, this is amateur hour."

"You had advanced taste for a child. I used to read well above my grade level as well."

"And look where we both ended up in the world," was the dry response. "How far our good taste has gotten us."

Boyd's amusement showed in a nearly imperceptible twitch of his lips. "Intelligence doesn't always equate to common sense. Or, for that matter, the ability to choose one's path in life."

Sin gave Boyd another semi-confused look and resumed reading. Or appeared to resume reading. There was a distinct lack of page turning, and Boyd did not attempt to hide his curious observation. The apathy Boyd had felt in their earlier days as partners was replaced by intrigue the more he considered Sin's behavior towards him versus his previous partners; that sense of intrigue had heightened several degrees after a recent mission in Spain.

Days of reconnaissance in a hotel afforded Boyd the opportunity to pick up on several tiny aspects to Sin's personality. He worked out constantly, ate whatever he wanted, and relished long missions that allowed him to come and go as he pleased since the Agency was not watching. Also, Boyd realized his partner had zero modesty. He'd seen Sin fresh out of the shower, and the sight stayed with Boyd days later. Sin was made up of bronze skin, lean muscle, and puckered scars. He had a spectacular body that matches his face, and more intriguingly, a tattoo scrawled in cursive on Sin's back shoulder had read, *"So many and so various laws are giv'n; So many laws argue so many sins."*

The delicate script of the tattoo was at odds with the hardness of Sin's body and, after forcing himself to focus on something other than exposed flesh, Boyd had recognized it as a quote from Milton's epic poem Paradise Lost. He wondered when Sin had gotten the tattoo, and what artist had dared to press a needle to Sin's skin.

"Is your love for Milton why you got that tattoo? Initially I thought you simply enjoyed the irony of the quote."

Sin ran his finger along the spine of the book again. "I don't know about love, but it was both. Where I grew up, there were only about six real books to read and Paradise Lost was one of them. I didn't understand much of it because my English wasn't that great, but I kept the book. I appreciated it when I was older and knew what the fuck it was talking about."

"What language did you speak if not English?" Boyd asked.

Sin eased back into his slouch and said after some deliberation, "Mandarin."

"Really? Where did you live at the time?"

The hesitation was longer this time. Sin fiddled with the hem of his sleeve, slipping his thumb into a hole that had worn there over time. "Hong Kong, but my mother was from the mainland."

"I didn't know you lived in China," Boyd said, surprised. Sin's features were difficult to place, but Boyd had not guessed him to be Chinese. "For how long?"

"An amount of time."

The information only heightened Boyd's curiosity about what else Sin was, so he asked, "What about your father?"

The edge that had sharpened in Sin's voice eased. He shrugged and tapped his fingers against the table. "A conglomerate of Latin American things."

Boyd nodded, latching on to the topic. "Do you speak any language from that conglomerate or just Mandarin?"

"Spanish. He never taught me Portuguese." Sin closed the book and shoved it to the center of the table. "Here. Enjoy that awful book. It's depressing in all the phoniest ways."

"Thanks." Boyd touched the cover, sweeping his finger over the glossy texture of the title. "My mother is French. Did you know that?"

"No. I just know she's a blonde white woman."

Boyd briefly smiled. "When I was young, she spoke French at home a lot. My earliest memories are of her teaching me French. It was the only time she didn't…"

He hesitated to voice the hopes he'd had back then; that maybe she'd been proud or even briefly liked him on those special occasions. All other memories were of her belittling him, or looking past him like she wished he had never been born.

Boyd fiddled with the edge of the pages. "Anyway. That's the only other language I know. French."

"Oh." Sin stopped tapping his fingers against the table. "Well, you should learn Spanish."

"Maybe I will someday."

"Maybe," Sin replied. He seemed to struggle with what to say before flipping open his textbook. "Anyway, whatever. I'm surprised you recognized the quote."

"His wording is memorable."

"Indeed."

The conversation piqued Boyd's desire to fill in more gaps about his partner. "What else do you like to do when you aren't reading?"

"Why do you want to know?"

"No reason. I'm just curious."

Sin shook his head as if he found the prospect to be absurd. "I do nothing. I get junk food from vending machines and work out two or three times a day."

"That doesn't seem contradictory to you?"

"What's contradictory about it?"

"You're eating something unhealthy and then exercising. Why don't you eat healthily as well?"

"It's not like I'm trying to watch my figure. Besides, candy bars and chips are better than the shit they send to my quarters."

"What do you mean? Can't you choose what you eat?"

"No."

"Why not?"

Sin sighed and snapped his book shut. "Because I don't get to choose anything. The only time I can buy my own food is when we go on a mission. That's the only time I can go anywhere in general. I'm a fucking serf."

"You're stuck on compound between missions?" The information was new to Boyd. "Why?"

"Because I'm an out of control killer. Obviously."

"But you aren't. Surely the administration at least realizes that."

"Why are you so sure? You don't know what I've done to earn that reputation, now do you?"

"Then what have you done?"

"Enough."

Boyd wondered about the extremes Sin managed to present in only a handful of minutes. At times, it was almost as if Sin didn't mind talking about inane things, but he almost always lapsed back into the bristling behavior of trying to keep Boyd at arm's length. Did Sin want it that way or did he feel obligated to keep it that way? Boyd could not decide which it was, and always wound up with the frustrated feeling that Sin was an unsolvable equation.

A disjointed conversation floated to where they were sitting. Although the context meant nothing to Boyd, Sin went ramrod straight. There was no immediate indication as to what made him so tense until Harry Truman appeared next to their table.

"Study date?" He gave them a wide, leering smile. "Mind if I join?"

"I do, actually," Sin said. "I only give reading lessons on Sundays."

Harry's eyes did a slow circuit of Sin. "You're a real smart ass when they let you out of your cage, aren't you?"

Sin's expression went from withering to murderous.

"Is there a reason for your interruption?" Boyd asked.

"We're meant to check on Vega here from time to time and I volunteer for the job. He's like a pet of mine." Harry smiled, slow and vicious. "Aren't you Vega?"

"Go fuck yourself, Truman."

"Only if you watch, baby." Still smirking and leering at Sin, Harry gestured to Boyd. "Why don't you get lost, blondie? Me and Vega have some things to work out."

Boyd went rigid. He opened his mouth to say something sharp, but Sin cut him off.

"I hear there's a sixteen-year-old in the training complex, Truman." Sin put his remaining books in a stack and pressed his palms flat against the table. "Why don't you run along and go see if he's your type? A bit old but you seem open to variety lately."

Face flooding with color, Harry snarled and lurched forward. He cocked a fist back and swung it down at Sin, but the senior agent did not flinch or move from his spot.

Harry's fist came to a halt only centimeters from Sin's cheekbone but he didn't retract it right away. Instead, they stared at each other with an increasing aura of mutual rage, both tolerating the other's, and neither backing down. It was only when Sin leaned forward so Harry's hand brushed his face did the guard get a grip on his temper and take a slow step away.

"Are we finished?"

Sin's voice was soft, and Boyd's trepidation heightened.

Hissing out a low breath, Harry did not look anything close to finished, but he didn't stop Sin from leaving. Once Sin was gone, Harry's attention settled on Boyd.

"What the hell are you looking at?"

Boyd sized the guard up. "Nothing."

Harry's expression fluctuated between anger and indignation, as if Boyd's impassive tone made it difficult to discern whether or not he'd just been insulted. He must have decided he had, because he slammed his palm down on the table and leaned into Boyd's personal space. "Then move the fuck along."

"But this is a library, and I'm looking at library books."

"I don't give a fuck what you're doing. Get the hell out."

Boyd debated whether it was worth it to stay, and ultimately decided it wasn't. It would only lead to Harry harassing him until he felt in control again, which would defeat the purpose of going to the library in the first place.

Besides, now Boyd wanted to do research of a different sort.

He gathered his things and left the library without another word, digging out his phone once he was out of the Tower.

"Boyd?" Ryan sounded surprised when he answered.

"Are you still willing to share information on Sin?"

There was a pause before Ryan replied. "Yeah. Can you come to my apartment, though? It's easier that way."

"Yes."

After receiving the location and directions, Boyd realized Ryan lived in one of the residential buildings on compound which was common for Agency personnel. When Boyd arrived, the door swung open before he could knock. Either Ryan had a way of seeing who was at the door, or he had somehow heard Boyd approach.

"Hey! Come in. Sorry about the mess."

Ryan's apartment was full of mismatched furniture and eclectic knickknacks. Books, posters, action figures, and computer tech filled the space.

Ryan dropped into a chair and grabbed his laptop. "What made you want to find out more about him, anyway? I got the feeling you weren't really gonna take me up on that offer."

Boyd sat down on the only empty chair. "I find myself growing curious about him."

"Damn!" Ryan suddenly exclaimed, staring at his computer screen. "I forgot to send in my supply card! Anyway, why? What changed?"

"Nothing dramatic, but I'm consistently confused by him. I keep wondering which parts of his personality are real or an act, and the same regarding the rumors."

Ryan reclined in his chair and reached up to adjust his thick black glasses. "If I tell you stuff, you're not gonna somehow use it against him, are you?"

"No." Boyd frowned. "Why would I? It would serve me no purpose. I have no ill will against him; I'm just trying to understand him."

"Good. I didn't think so, but I got to worrying maybe I'd jumped the gun by offering up so much information. Sometimes I get too excited when I think someone is on the same page as me..."

"Like I said, it serves me no purpose to be malicious."

"Right-o." Ryan steadied himself. "So—do you want to know a lot or a little? I may make lunch while we talk if it's a lot. I need to take my meds like, yesterday, and I'll puke if I don't eat first."

Boyd wondered why Ryan needed medication, but did not want to be intrusive. "I'd prefer more information rather than less. If you want to make food, that's fine with me."

"Cool." Ryan got up from his chair and moved to a long counter that partitioned the living room from the kitchen. "Do you want anything? I forgot to send in my supply card so all I have is, like, sandwich fixings and junk."

Boyd considered asking for tea, but that wasn't a staple in everyone's kitchen. He didn't want to be more of an inconvenience. "I'm fine, thank you."

Ryan removed a large bag of pretzels from a cabinet. He put it on the counter and opened his refrigerator, digging around until he leaned back with his arms full of pre-sliced cold cuts. "Mike's has the best cold cuts, FYI. Anyway, what did you wanna know first?"

"Which stories are true?"

"Well, what all have you heard or been told?"

"I know about his partners and that he has injured people on compound in the past. I've also been told that he killed several people in the city, but I was not given a cause of the event." Boyd thought of the different rumors he'd overheard. "I suppose in general a clarification of what he's actually done would be of use. I want to know if he is as insane as they say, or if there is more to him as I have begun to expect."

"Well, when you put it like that, it makes total sense. They probably should have cleared that all up for you, anyway. I don't know what they think they gain by keeping you in the dark." Ryan slathered his bread with mustard and slapped a few pieces of lunch meat on it. He glanced at the clock and opened an overhead cabinet which was filled with different prescription bottles. Ryan took out two and set them on the counter next to his plate.

"So... let's see. Well, I guess people were always freaked out by him but the first big thing was the incident down in Vickland like ten years ago."

"That came up during my interview, but the full story wasn't explained."

Ryan's head bobbed up and down while he chewed a large bite of sandwich. "The Vickland thing is why they started thinking he was going completely insane and tried sticking him with partners." Ryan swallowed and wiped his mouth with the back of his hand. "He was coming back from some mission and walking through Vickland during that time when the neighborhood was still a complete shit hole, you know? Back when the scavengers would be out in droves."

Boyd nodded, remembering quite well the way Vickland had been.

Ryan jumped off the stool and went to the refrigerator again, removing a container of milk. He couldn't seem to sit still. "He came across this girl being raped in an alleyway and he killed her attackers. But the girl got so frightened of him that she started screaming and drew the attention of the scavengers nearby. They thought it was Hsin who started it all. They attacked him and he went nutso and took a lot of them out. It was pretty bad."

Boyd's eyebrows rose. When they'd say Sin got distracted by civilians, it had not occurred to him that Sin would want to protect them. "Why would he care what happened to her? Did he know her?"

"No, not at all."

"Then why did he interfere?"

Ryan talked around a mouthful of food. "It was a young girl getting gang raped. Any decent person would have interfered."

"That may be, but I'm trying to understand why someone who seems content with letting his own partners die would care about preventing a stranger from being hurt. What causes him to help one person and not another? Is it based on the type of crime committed or the age of the victim? Has he ever helped other people aside from that girl or did something about her specifically speak to him?"

Ryan shrugged. He swallowed some milk with a lip-smacking sound.

"No one knows what makes him tick. All I did was compile data and do a bunch of guesswork after he was assigned to the unit. But I do know that he considers just about everyone at the Agency his enemy so that doesn't help any would-be victims 'round these parts, know what I mean?" He wiped his mouth and opened the pill bottles. "There's been conjecture by his doctors over that incident—that he helped that girl because she was just a kid and was helpless, and it brought up stuff from his own childhood. In the end, though, they think he went berserk because he was so outnumbered and felt super threatened."

"His own childhood?"

"Yep. All sorts of issues there." Ryan began opening the pill bottles.

Boyd waited for Ryan to continue and, when he didn't, he pressed, "What happened?"

Ryan doled out pills of various colors and sizes and swallowed them with large gulps of milk. "There's not a full story. His earlier doctors thought his mother abused him as a small kid. Then his father, Emilio, took him on and trained him to be a killer from like age eight, so I don't think whatever method he used was child protective services friendly."

Boyd did not think so either.

"You said he went berserk and that he was in automatic kill mode. What does that mean exactly?"

"Didn't they tell you anything?"

"General Carhart said something similar but didn't explain what triggers him."

Ryan made a thoughtful sound and nodded. "Well, that kind of makes sense. They don't know for sure because Hsin never cooperates with psychiatrists so Zachary probably didn't want to give you wrong info and make you start jumping to conclusions. All of Sin's episodes have happened under different circumstances, so a person is liable to get freaked out and start thinking any random occurrence could make him wig out."

"Most likely," Boyd agreed. "But I want to at least try to understand what I'm dealing with. I don't want to only be given the convenient information."

Ryan leaned against the counter and crossed his skinny arms over his thin chest. "As far as I know there are five documented occurrences of him having those scary episodes. I'm sure it's happened other times, but those are the ones the Agency knows about and has evidence of. Two were before the Vickland thing and two were after. There's a difference between him getting sick of someone and beating their ass and going into automatic kill mode."

"What's the difference?"

Ryan held up a finger. "One is the normal reaction of someone who has been trained to be a lethal weapon since, like, before puberty but the other..." Ryan held up another finger and drew it across his throat. "The other is, like, Hsin becoming someone else. It seems like he completely shuts down mentally and only sees everyone around him as a threat and he starts just—well, killing. Usually it takes someone sedating him to get him to stop and when he comes to, he's fine."

Boyd could not help but think back to the library and the way Harry had antagonized Sin. If that wasn't a trigger, what was?

"You mentioned he targets those he sees as a threat," Boyd said. "Does that mean he only attacks aggressors once he's having an episode or does he attack everyone in the vicinity?"

"I'm not sure. I'd think you'd be okay if you just stayed away, but there's no way to be sure."

"And the other times? What happened?"

This time the hesitation was longer. Ryan began pacing the living room. "The first two happened when he first got here. The first one was because some of the older—well, you have to understand, Boyd. Even here, some people have a real stupid ass bully mentality."

Boyd nodded. He knew full well.

"Some of the guards and lower-ranked field agents are especially bad. They didn't like that this little kid was an automatic rank 9, right? So they decided to mess with Hsin one day after he'd been in the training room. They pushed him around, surrounded him, I guess to see what he's made of. Meanwhile it's all on camera. It triggered a bad episode. He put three in the infirmary and cracked two of their necks. Hsin was fourteen and almost a hundred pounds skinnier than any of those dudes, but they stood no chance."

It was a good reason to fear him, but Boyd still thought it sounded like the aggressors had had it coming.

"Was anyone punished for the incident?"

"The guards were. That was the first time something bad happened and since they provoked him outright, it wasn't really his fault. But then everyone knew something wasn't right with him so that's when a lot of rumors started."

Ryan sat down again, this time on a little ottoman near the couch. "I remember when I heard about that, I was scared of him. Connors didn't know what to do with Hsin because he was so young, so he attempted to treat him as a ward and have him live with us, but after that incident Connors put him in this secure room on the Fourth. Not a real cell, but a crappy room that was monitored all the time."

It seemed like Sin had spent the majority of his life at the Agency locked up. No wonder he had trust issues.

"You lived with Marshal Connors?"

"Yeah. My parents were a part of the Agency. My dad was a lab tech and my mother was an analyst. They both died from the lung sickness when I was young, and Connors took me in. I'd grown up on the compound so he knew I'd always be a part of it in some way. It helped that by the time I was six, I'd already tested beyond high school level. I was useful to him."

"Impressive."

"Not really. It's not like I worked for it. I was basically born this way. I could read before most babies learned how to speak."

"The fact that it's a natural talent doesn't make it less impressive. It just means that you'll be ahead of others and have the ability to go farther than anyone else."

There was no response to that. Ryan didn't seem to want to talk too much about the fact that he was a genius or anything to do with his IQ. "The next incident," Ryan said, switching back to the previous topic, "was during his rank 10 training. It isn't as well-documented because the training is top secret. I couldn't find video or specifics anywhere. Just that one of the people involved with the training got mangled."

"You never found out what started it?"

"Nope. Not one trace. It's referenced as a date in one of his doctor's files, and I traced it to the time he was in his rank 10 training towards the end, but that's it."

"And the other two times you mentioned?"

This time Ryan visibly squirmed. "I dunno if I should talk about it…"

"What are you worried about?"

"Nothing, really. I dunno. It's just a sore topic."

Boyd wondered what was so much worse than Sin mangling people or killing a number of civilians. "Without knowing what it is I can't say for certain, but I doubt it will drastically change my opinion. If you have the information in some form you can simply give to me rather than having to tell me; that would work too."

Ryan shook his head. "No, it's better if I tell you. There's back story involved. A real drama fit for TV. But, now that you mention it, I did compile all my data on a flash drive. When he was put in the Janus unit, I started studying him. Anyway, the incident started with Lydia Connors. She and her twin sister Ann are the Marshal's daughters."

Boyd recognized the name. Annabelle Connors was his mother's secretary. Somehow, he had never made the connection between her last name and the Marshal.

"They grew up here like me and both studied to be shrinks. Ann abandoned it but Lydia didn't. After the Vickland thing, Hsin was put in isolation on the Fourth for two years. When talk started about evaluating him to be let out, she pushed to be his doctor. Problem was, she had been infatuated with his dad back in the day and her infatuation shifted to poor Hsin because he is the spitting image of Emilio." Ryan scratched the back of his head. "Well, it didn't end well for her. She tried to take advantage of the situation when he was really unstable one day and now she lives up in the Willowbrook Home."

Boyd's eyes narrowed. The very idea of someone, especially a psychiatrist, taking advantage of their patient was disgusting. "Did she ever treat him like his previous partners?"

"Nope. She was gaga over him. Had a real Vega obsession." Ryan made a face. "When it happened, she was asking him questions about his childhood according to some of the notes."

"You said earlier that he was abused as a child. Was it sexual abuse?"

"Not sure. His mom was a prostitute so anything is possible. Apparently, when he first got here, he implied enough to make it sound like most of the abuse had happened while he'd been with her."

Ryan started to say more but before he could, his phone trilled. He fished it from the pocket of his skinny jeans and peered down at the screen.

"Ahh, I have to get back to the Tower."

Disappointed, Boyd stood. "Thank you for the information. And if you wouldn't mind, I'd be interested in borrowing your files. I feel like you have a lot more insight than others."

"Probably because I have too much time on my hands."

Ryan went over to his desk. The drawers were full of assorted implements just like the plastic bag he carried in his backpack. And just like with that bag, despite the disorderliness of the drawer, he found what he needed without a problem.

"If you ever want to talk or hang out without Hsin being the topic, that'd be cool too."

There was a lull as Boyd tried to figure out what to say. Ryan was so unlike the other people on the compound that it put him at a loss. "Oh," he said. "All right."

The response brought a loud laugh from Ryan. "I'll get you to loosen up. We can watch anime and eat nachos. But I have to jam so I'll talk about that more later."

Ryan dashed out of the apartment with Boyd following close behind. With the flash drive securely in his messenger bag, Boyd went home to research.

BOYD HADN'T TOUCHED his father's old office in years. He always felt uncomfortable entering the room.

As a child, he had learned early on to stay quiet and entertain himself. He remembered hours of sitting silently in the living room, carefully coloring between the lines, and watching the light glow beneath the office door. His father spent hours at a time inside, and Boyd would look up when he thought he heard movement.

Boyd still remembered the way his father would emerge from the office with tired lines etched in his face, and would pick Boyd up and hug him in a way that had felt inviting and safe. He remembered affectionate fingers ruffling his hair, Cedrick's warm voice announcing he was work with work, and the obvious excitement about spending time with Boyd. His father was the only person, other than Lou, who had shown true pleasure in having Boyd in their lives.

Now, Boyd was alone.

He shut those thoughts down as hard as he could, and focused intently on the topic of Sin. Once the flash drive was inserted and a window popped up on screen, he saw that Ryan had collected quite a bit of information. There were many folders and files, and judging by the extensions, Ryan had compiled videos, images, and documents as well.

Boyd clicked through a few of the images first. They were pictures of Sin over the years, and most were still-frames from security or surveillance cameras. The progression in age was interesting, not because of Sin's physical appearance, but because of the subtle change in demeanor as he'd grown older.

The image of Sin at the age of fourteen showed a thin, sinewy boy with delicate features. Long black eyelashes framed vivid green eyes that were intelligent and calculating. However, teenage Sin's face was void of any expression or emotion. In a way, it was disturbing. He looked soulless.

Several pictures of Sin over the subsequent years followed that trend. It was hard to imagine that scrawny, striking child going on assignments and taking lives, but Boyd knew Sin had.

After a point, Sin's mannerisms changed. He was more expressive and his stare became challenging, hostile, and accompanied the mocking smirk Boyd was familiar with now. More curious than ever, Boyd returned to the main folder and watched the videos.

The first one was of the incident in Vickland.

Grainy footage from a surveillance camera filled the screen. The date at the bottom of the video was seven years old, which explained why the area had not been cleaned up yet. This hadn't been long after the second major wave of bombs had scattered across the country, including Lexington.

There was no audio, but there didn't need to be. A young girl of thirteen or fourteen ran across the screen while three men pursued. They caught her and tore off her clothing before forcing her down to the ground; the attack happened just out of sight of a group of people scavenging through the rubble nearby.

Minutes later, Sin appeared in the frame. It did not take long for him to pass the scene, notice, and stop walking. The men halted their activity and words that Boyd could not hear were exchanged.

At first glance, Sin appeared to be unaffected, but when Boyd paused the video and examined Sin's body language, it told a different story. His posture was stiff, his hands balled at his sides, and his expression was almost too vacant. It was almost as if Sin wasn't really there. Then, without transition, his expression morphed to one of pure fury.

What happened next was a blur. One second Sin was facing three larger men, and in the next, he was slaughtering them. With quick, decisive moments, Sin snapped necks and bashed heads into the sides of buildings. The carnage was over within seconds.

Afterward, Sin was covered in blood. He stared, wide-eyed and snarling. The girl screamed in terror. This time it caught the attention of the scavengers, and the entire scene erupted in chaos. They swooped in on Sin with pipes, bats, bricks—whatever was in the debris that lay in piles in the area, and he responded with lethal force. Everyone who came near him fell to the ground. It wasn't long before police arrived in droves. It took several minutes for them to take him down.

The video ended.

Boyd moved to the next file.

The next video was the same night but several hours later. The picture was sharper and showed Sin sitting at a table in a small room. Dried blood clung to his flesh and clothing, but the wild look was gone and instead, Sin looked dazed and dismayed. He kept looking at his hands and scrubbing them against his pants, head bowed more often than not. After a while, Sin got up to pace the room, scratching at the blood and raking his hands through his hair.

Boyd could hear the brush of fabric and realized this video had sound.

It went on that way for a while until two men walked into the room. One stayed by the door and one approached Sin, ordering him to be still. He introduced himself as Detective Lyons and his partner as Detective Valdez. The next several minutes passed with them attempting to question Sin about the incident. Sin answered vaguely and then ceased to respond at all when Lyons became increasingly aggressive. Over an hour passed and at one point, Lyons shoved Sin onto the floor and pinned him there. The detective's gun was drawn and he pressed it against Sin's mouth.

"You're going to start talking or I'm going to make you blow my gun, you sick fuck."

In the space of a second, Lyons went from straddling Sin to flying across the room. He slammed against the wall, and then Sin was on him again. The gun flashed in Sin's hand just as Valdez shouted and drew his own weapon. A shot was fired, and Valdez crumpled to the floor, blood pooling beneath him.

Sin's expression was tight, his body taut with tension, but there was no trace of madness in him. At that point, Lyons climbed to his feet and threw himself at Sin.

"Fuck it," the younger version of Sin said flatly, and raised the gun. He unloaded it into Lyons head until nothing but pulp remained. He tossed the gun down and walked out of the room.

The video ended shortly after, leaving Boyd to stare at the screen.

He considered the events with objectivity.

In the first video, Sin had clearly been having some kind of psychotic break. Even then, he hadn't attacked the scavengers until they swarmed him. The trigger had been the girl. However, in the second video, he'd allowed the detective to abuse him for almost an hour before lashing out. Had he finally lost his patience after being pinned down? Was it the comment about the gun? Boyd didn't have an immediate answer so he continued to sift through the files until he found information about Lydia Connors.

There was a scant amount of documents and memos from Lydia's practice. None of it was very helpful or conclusive due to the randomness at which they were included because Ryan had probably been unable to recover the majority of her files. The main items of note were a scanned piece of scrap paper that read "basement on Shantung Street in HK?", and the surveillance recording from the session when Sin had attacked her.

The video had no audio, but Sin was visibly distraught as he sat hunched in on himself across the table from Lydia. He was pale, tense, and his head was bowed. Long stretches of time passed with Lydia talking to Sin and him barely responding so Boyd set the video to play faster until he saw Lydia reach across the table to administer Sin some kind of injection.

Within minutes, Sin's eyelids drooped. Lydia got up and moved to stand beside him before leaning down to whisper in his ear. To Boyd's disgust, she also began to rub Sin's shoulders, not noticing when he cringed.

Boyd wished he knew what she was saying to Sin because whatever it was only made his turmoil worse. He shook his head and put his fists on the table, curling them up and releasing them with repetitive motions. Again, Lydia missed the actions or chose to ignore them. She kissed Sin's neck and her hand snaked around to reach into his lap.

Boyd could not see what she was doing, but the motions of her arm made it clear enough. What happened next was quick and brutal.

Sin's eyes opened, and he had the same wild-eyed expression from the incident in Vickland, and he reacted with the same violence. He flipped the table, causing it to break. Shards flew everywhere and Lydia threw herself back, her enraptured look turning to one of terror. She held her hands up to ward Sin away, but it was clear that Sin had entered automatic kill mode. He slashed her with broken glass until the guards charged in and the video ended.

Instead of looking into her condition, Boyd coldly closed the video and moved to the next.

This one was only a year old and had taken place on the Fourth as Sin was escorted upstairs after the death of his last partner. For the most part Sin did not speak, but his body appeared to be brimming with impotent rage as Harry Truman hauled him down the corridor. They were accompanied by Dennis McNichols and two guards whom Boyd had never seen before. One of them had a badge that marked him as a lieutenant of the guards. Again, there was no audio, but the interactions were clear.

Harry and Dennis were taunting Sin, getting well within his personal space and touching him in a familiar manner which made it obvious this treatment was the norm. The lieutenant, if anything, looked amused by the entire exchange as he offered his own unheard comments. He grinned at Sin smugly, even when Harry pinned Sin to the wall outside of his cell and got very close to his face. He whispered something in Sin's ear.

After consecutive videos, Boyd could now pinpoint the signs of Sin's episode approaching.

Again, Sin's face slipped into a mask of indifference that ultimately shattered with blind rage. Harry threw himself back just in time, but the lieutenant wasn't lucky enough to escape. Sin yanked him back into the cell right before Dennis slammed the door shut. He locked the door with the keypad, his fingers shaking visibly.

There was a brief argument between the guards, but none of them opened the door. From what Boyd read afterward, by the time reinforcements came, the lieutenant had died of his wounds. Apparently, Sin had ripped open the man's jugular with his teeth.

There was an interesting mix of punishment and forgiveness when it came to Sin's episodes. He had received no repercussions for episodes triggered by abusive guards, yet he'd been detained for the high profile incident in Vickland, and the attack on Lydia. Boyd wondered if, despite the rumors and general hatred of Sin, the Marshal himself dealt with the senior agent with cold objectivity.

One would assume Connors would have had his daughter's attacker terminated, but instead, Sin had received a relatively light sentence. Boyd wondered if, deep down, Marshal Connors knew his daughter had brought the attack on herself by playing such a dangerous game.

If so, why didn't the administration attempt to dispel the rumors that Sin killed for enjoyment? Why did they imply he was a sociopath instead of an unstable man who was triggered by abuse; his reactions made more extreme by his childhood and training? The entire situation was baffling, but it also fell in line with Boyd's previous musings about Sin's alienation being a purposeful tactic used by the Agency to keep him as their isolated living weapon. There was no proof for that theory, though.

The only thing Boyd concluded with any certainty was that Sin had been systematically dehumanized by the Agency, and others, and he made no effort to do anything but live up to their poor expectations of his behavior.

EIGHT

THE LOCATION OF 53's headquarters was about sixty miles outside Lexington in an area between Carson and Cunningham Terrace. The gray ruins of Carson slowly transformed into open spaces and rich forests that would eventually lead to the affluent town known as West Cunningham. The area was deserted, and perfect for a base of operations.

53 had claimed an abandoned lumber mill for their purposes, and at first Boyd had assumed that would make the mission simple. The mill was large and constructed of steel with towering smokestacks, but there were a number of ways to slip inside. However, after one night of recon, Boyd realized that Warren Andrews was not utilizing the upper levels of the mill. Instead, they were working out of the sublevel. At some point in the recent past, someone had turned the sublevel into a bunker. It was reinforced and deep underground, making it impossible for Boyd to use his phone. He was completely cut off while exploring the maze of hallways and rooms below the mill.

Boyd spent nearly an hour inside the base, slipping from one shadow to the next, a task made easy by the unstable generators 53 utilized. But even without the cover of darkness, Boyd was prepared. Unit 16, the Agency group who outfitted employees for undercover missions, had provided him with clothing that allowed him to blend in with the hostiles. They had also replicated 53's signature red armband.

Heavy footsteps treaded toward him, the scuffing of soles against concrete. He reached into his back pocket and pulled out a radio he'd acquired from a supply room. Two men turned a corner and walked toward Boyd. He fumbled with the radio as if he did not know how it worked. As they came up beside him, Boyd adopted a frazzled expression but stood to attention. He gripped the radio in one hand and pressed the button. The radio blared static, and he dropped it on the floor with a resounding clatter.

"Sorry!"

One of the men scowled and continued on without incident

although they muttered about Andrews recruiting too young these days.

Boyd fumbled and cursed softly at the radio until their footsteps faded. He flipped off the radio and slipped out of the base. He moved through the forest to wait near a small grove by a bend in the river. Leaning against one of the trees, Boyd waited for Sin to arrive. When he did, he was as undetectable as always.

"There are two exits other than the one you used," Sin said. "One to the north and another to the east. They are guarded by two hostiles. Beginning at approximately 0900 hours they switch shifts every eight hours. It is done efficiently with no lapses, however at half past the hour, five hours into each shift there is a thirty-minute meal break for each man. When one leaves, the entrance is secured by a single guard and there are brief three minute lapses while he paces back and forth to observe either side of the forest." Sin met Boyd's eyes. "When you sneak in tomorrow, that would be the best opportunity."

Boyd nodded. He noted the term 'you' and was unsurprised to realize Sin had no intention of accompanying him on the mission the next day. Pushing himself away from the tree, Boyd replaced the radio in his back pocket and headed to their safehouse—a small cabin that had likely been owned years ago by an employee of the mill.

"I think I found where Andrews' quarters are. They utilize an underground facility that seems to have been constructed after the original mill. Unfortunately, it's so far underground that I can't get a signal. If they are unwilling to negotiate, that may make things more difficult."

Sin walked alongside him. "If you are able to speak with Andrews, they will most likely immediately disarm you."

Boyd slipped his hands into the pockets of his jacket. "Do you really not plan to come?"

After months of mocking Boyd about what would happen on his first storm, the occasion was finally here. Boyd would be heading into a base full of hostiles, and if negotiation failed, he would be expected to kill Andrews and take out the base. He would have to do it while trapped deep underground without a working comm. It was a suicide mission without his partner. But despite the previous sarcastic comments, Sin didn't seem to be in the mood for jokes. His body was tense, and his mouth set in a grim slash.

"Let's just get back," Sin said and strode ahead.

Boyd watched him go. As the gravity of the situation grew clearer, he wondered what his mother would say when she found out about his death.

THE SOUND RIPPED Boyd out of an already restless sleep.

At first, he could not identify it, but when he listened closer, Boyd realized the sound was coming from Sin's bed—a distressed mutter, a soft groan, and the sound of bed sheets rustling.

Boyd rolled over and peered across the room at his partner.

Sin was curled in a ball on the thin bed but as Boyd watched, he unwound himself with a muffled whimper, one of his arms dangling off the side of the bed. He said something in his sleep, voice low and strained, and sounding distinctly like Mandarin.

"Sin?"

Another distressed groan filled the air, louder. Sin's head turned toward Boyd, his face awash in moonlight and frightening in its vulnerability. Boyd stared in awe, but shook himself and padded across the room.

"Sin, wake up." After a brief hesitation, he touched Sin's hand. Boyd immediately regretted it.

Sin's eyes snapped open, but he did not seem to register his surroundings or recognize Boyd. Without warning, he lurched up and threw Boyd off the bed and across the room.

Boyd smashed into the table, and it flew a few inches off the floor, hit the wall, and fell over. Everything clattered around Boyd in a spray that peppered his shocked body. His bag fell down next to him, spilling its contents.

An iron grip flipped Boyd onto his back, and his head cracked against the hardwood floor. The pain was stunning, and Boyd could only blink as spots danced around him. When his vision cleared, Sin's face was inches from his own. He froze in the face of wild green eyes and bared teeth.

The words 'automatic kill mode' tumbled through Boyd's mind.

Hands wrapped around his neck, squeezing, and Boyd reached up to claw at the powerful fingers. He gagged, and a desire to live swarmed up from a place he had buried long ago. Apathy about survival gave way to a resounding desperation to stop Sin from committing this act while out of control and isolated in the middle of a forest.

But the grip was too tight, too unyielding, and Boyd could only gag and wheeze. He could feel himself fading, his vision dimming, but he still reached up to press his hand against the side of Sin's face. "Sin—Hsin... please."

The fingers around Boyd's neck loosened just slightly, and Boyd grasped at the thread of hope.

"Please stop," he rasped. His hand skewed up and threaded through Sin's hair. "It's... me."

Time stilled and silence draped the cabin but was broken intermittently by the distant howl of an animal, and the scrape of branches against the roof; sounds that were usually ignored but now served as indicators of Boyd's last moments. His vision dimmed further, but then awareness swept over Sin's face, and he scrambled backwards.

Coughs erupted from Boyd's throat and he clutched at his throat while shifting to an upright position. Everything went unsteady, but Boyd sucked in great gasps of air. "Sin," he wheezed. "You were dreaming. It wasn't me—I didn't hurt you."

Sin's only answer was the ragged pull of his breath, and the trembling in his hands when he held them up. He backed away from Boyd, eyes skewing between him and something on the floor. Boyd followed that frantic gaze and saw the remote for the collar. In the commotion, it had fallen out of his bag.

Boyd pitched it at Sin, and he caught it in midair.

"Take it. I'm not—I'm not a threat."

For the first time since they'd met, Sin's expression was completely open. Boyd could see shock and fear in Sin before the senior agent bolted from the cabin. He was there and gone so fast that it seemed like he'd disappeared within the blink of an eye.

Darkness stretched out beyond the door and the sounds of the forest grew louder, but Boyd did not hear or sense Sin in the vicinity anymore.

Shock held Boyd in place for several minutes before he managed to pull himself to a stand, limping over to shut the door. With his thoughts scrambled, Boyd moved on autopilot. He fixed the table and put his things away, ignoring the way his body protested in response as new bruises likely blossomed where he had been thrown across the room.

When there was nothing else to do and no way to expend his left-over adrenaline, Boyd sat on the edge of the bed. His mind inevitably replayed the attack. The Sin he had come to know had vanished. Replaced by someone violent, terrifying, and insane. But... he had stopped when Boyd touched his face and said his name.

He did not know why Sin had snapped out of the episode, and Boyd understood even less his own sudden desire to live. The lack of interest in survival had faded in the past few months, but it was still there like an old friend that visited whenever Boyd thought about his life and the never ending flow of missions. But for some reason, Boyd had wanted to stop Sin. Not so he could live, but because he had not wanted Sin to emerge from his episode and find his partner lifeless on the floor. Boyd didn't want his last moments to be the reason Sin was sent to the Fourth.

Boyd shut the thoughts down and realized he'd been rubbing his wrist. He jerked his fingers away as if they burned and stood.

It didn't matter anymore. None of it did. In a scant number of hours, he would be moving to infiltrate 53's base, and all of this would finally stop.

THE NEXT MORNING, Boyd prepared for the mission with grim acceptance. Every action he took would be the last time it occurred. The last time he tied his hair back to stay out of the way in a fight. The last time he straightened the clothing he'd been given by Unit 16. The last time he walked out of a safehouse. The last time he went on a mission.

His resignation did not slow him, and the infiltration went as planned. Boyd evaded the guards, moved through the old mill like a phantom, and used the same abandoned chute to access the sub-level of the building. Prowling through the maze of corridors the day before had imprinted an internal map in Boyd's mind, and he used it to make his way to the southwest corner of the bunker. It was the most secure location and the most inhabitable, which was why Boyd suspected it was where Andrews had made his base.

Voices emanated from a shut door further down the hallway, and Boyd crouched around the corner as he weighed his options. His best bet was to catch Andrews alone, but he could only lurk around the base for so long before someone realized he didn't belong. His luck would inevitably run out. The timing had to be right, and he needed the upper-hand.

The words on the other side of the door were nothing more than a jumble of syllables and fluctuating tones no matter how much closer Boyd moved. He peered around with caution before darting forward in a way that made every sore muscle in his body scream with agony. Ignoring the pain, Boyd swiped his finger at the narrow space under the door and pressed the adhesive on a small audio transmitter against the metal. He hurried back to the darker corner, and the sole of his shoe squeaking against the floor. Boyd scowled and hunkered down, pinning himself against the side of the wall. His heart sped with adrenaline, but no one came.

His comm unit was useless as far as contacting anyone on the outside, but he switched the channel so he could pick up on the transmitter that was now glued to the door. The sound was fainter than he'd hoped. On his next mission, he would have to invest in learning how to use a higher grade of technology. If there was a next mission.

Despite the volume, the voices came across clear.

"There's nothing I can do about it now," a man was saying.

"You can tell them yes!" a woman barked. Her voice came across sharply in Boyd's ear. "It's better for *all* of us, even if you don't agree with them about politics. Do you really think they're going to involve you in their plans?"

"Yes."

"Don't be a fool," the woman continued. "They just want to make sure that we won't turn into enemies."

"If I'm a fool, you're naive. Their goals are *not* ours. That was never what we were about. Not since the first sit-ins, not since me and Aarons started this group, and not now!"

"So what are we about?" she challenged. "Hiding in the woods while we run out of supplies? Raiding the mansions in West Cunningham? Petty attacks on civil buildings in Carson? How is that getting us—"

"We are the resistance whether you believe it or not. Everyone else has just rolled over and accepted the fact that the administration controlling Carson has become a dictatorship. The government sees everything as dissent, and more and more people who dare to speak out disappear. Things are getting worse. Especially since the Feds aren't paying attention to broken cities they could not even be bothered to rebuild."

Boyd digested the information. He had no doubts the man speaking was Warren Andrews, but he had no idea who the woman was. Andrews was married, but Boyd did not think his wife was actively involved with 53. If anything—

An explosion of gunshots ruptured the silence and fractured Boyd's thoughts. He threw himself to the side, scrambling for a nearby doorway as another spray of bullets hurtled in his direction. Boyd rolled into the room and kicked the door shut. The bullets ripped through it and shrapnel slammed into his thigh. Boyd bit back a cry of pain and dragged himself behind the open door.

"What the hell is going on out here?"

Boyd peered through the slit in the door and quickly identified Andrews. He was standing beside a woman with short, dark hair. She strode away from the door and looked up and down the other corridor, a gun in her hand. Their voices lowered so it was difficult to hear over the roar of pain in Boyd's ears, but he caught the gist of it fine. They were going to fan out and find him.

Swearing softly, Boyd ripped a smoke pellet from his utility belt and flung it into the hall. It hissed, and he ran out just as the air filled with smog. Boyd narrowly avoided another burst of gunfire. The bullets tearing into the wall behind him before the sound of coughing rang out in the hallway. He sprinted around the corner, hair whipping behind him as he headed for the egress route he'd planned, but each footstep caused pain to rage through his leg and thigh.

Boyd grit his teeth and kept running. Fleeing the mission was futile, but giving up to the hostiles was also not an option he relished, and that was what kept him sprinting through the corridors as his eyes teared and his body threatened to slow. He did not stop until the sounds of pursuit surrounded him; he was trapped.

Andrews appeared with the woman and another 53 operative. They rounded on Boyd and when Andrews raised a gun, Boyd leapt at him with his tonfa extended. He disarmed the man with three consecutive strikes to the arm, breaking it with the blunt weapon before spinning towards the woman. Her eyes were still squinting from the smoke, but Boyd went at her without mercy, aiming the end of the tonfa at her temple. It nearly connected when someone grabbed Boyd's ankle, jerking him back and causing the tonfa to glance off the woman's head with less impact. He fell to one knee, the impact so jarring that Boyd lost his grip on the weapon.

Additional hostiles flooded the corridor, and Andrews pressed his pistol to the center of Boyd's head.

"What are you doing here?"

Boyd turned his face up through a curtain of now-loosened hair. "I'm here to talk."

"Talk?" Andrews cradled his injured arm. "I don't think so. A man of your description has been stalking us for weeks."

"Yes, to feel you out." Boyd tried not to focus on the feel of the muzzle pressing to his skin, and the reality of being helpless and surrounded by enemies. "It's in your best interest to hear what I have to say."

"I don't think so. I'll get answers a different way."

Andrews nodded at the woman. She moved forward; her gait halting but fast with purpose, and she paused only long enough to retrieve a small gun from a man beside her. It was a tranq-gun.

Boyd surged to his feet but wooziness and the shrieking pain of his wound sent him wobbling, and she injected him. It was only a pinprick, but the drug overwhelmed his senses with near immediacy. Boyd listed forward and everything flickered and faded away like a candle being snuffed.

But it didn't last.

His eyes opened, but the scene playing out around him made little sense. There were running feet, and a flurry of motion he could not follow through his hazy hold on reality. A loud thump on the floor jolted Boyd, and a young man with bright blond hair collapsed nearby. He stared straight ahead with his face frozen in shock.

Sounds echoed in the maze of hallways. Peopled shouted and guns fired. Stray bullets ricocheted while Boyd struggled to remain conscious and move away. But unconsciousness beckoned him again. It was only the increasingly intense screams that drew him back to the real world.

"Shoot him!"

"Jesus Christ, kill him!"

"What the fuck—"

Boyd's eyelids lifted, and he saw a flash of green and black. Sin appeared in a moment suspended in time; his back was to Boyd as he stood calmly amid the chaos.

The lure of darkness deployed, but Boyd tried to claw away from it. His eyes opened sluggishly, once to an empty corridor, and again to the sight of a man aiming a gun at him. The flashes were confusing, but no one attacked him, and Boyd's foggy brain told him that he'd imagined Sin. His partner was long gone. Boyd was alone again and would soon die.

When the remnants of consciousness faded, this time, Boyd did not fight.

BOYD BECAME AWARE of reality in parts.

Everything was swathed in shadows. Boyd drifted with that for a while, the darkness and he coexisting together; symbiotic, calm. Soon, he realized he heard nothing and that was strange. When he remembered that he could hear, he also realized he could feel. Something light and soft covered him. There a soft object had been wedged beneath his head and back. At length, the words filtered into his brain. Pillow. Bed and sheets. The image of a cabin came to mind. The safehouse.

Belatedly, Boyd realized he felt pain, and that he was breathing. That shouldn't have been something noteworthy, but it was. His chest rose and fell, and the soft sheet rearranged itself. His fingers twitched and the pain grew more intense.

All of it joined together to prevent Boyd from returning to the serenity that had sheltered him just seconds before. His sense of time was warped, so it could have been seconds or centuries before he remembered why any of these innocuous details were noteworthy.

Images moved behind his eyelids; disjointed scenes as if someone took film, cut it apart, and put it back together haphazardly. He remembered Sin standing in the center of a bloodbath, and the more distant memory of being surrounded. The cocoon of sleep threatened to return, but the image of Sin would not fade. With it, understanding dawned and was followed by delayed disbelief.

He was alive.

Boyd struggled to sit up and looked around the cabin.

SANTINO & AIS

Warren Andrews was tied up and gagged in the corner, and considerably more bruised than he had been earlier. Nearby, Sin leaned against the wall with his arms crossed over his chest. He too appeared to have sustained some injures but was as unflappable as always.

Boyd focused on the sheet pooled in his lap. Beneath it, he wore a loose pair of drawstring pants that he didn't remember putting on. When he touched his left thigh, he felt bandages beneath the fabric.

Somehow, Sin had secured Andrews, saved Boyd, and bandaged his wounds.

It did not make any sense.

"Sin..."

"Boyd." Sin's nodded at Andrews. "I took the liberty of bringing him here for further negotiation."

Boyd gathered his focus and swung his legs over the edge of the bed to approach the bound man. His confusion could wait until after the mission was complete.

"I'm going to take the gag out, but if you start screaming or still refuse to cooperate, we may run into a problem. I suggest you work with us and make it easier on everyone."

Andrews' glare turned baleful, but he did not make a sound when Boyd removed the gag. He glowered at Sin with loathing.

"We've been following your progress," Boyd said. "And we've noticed that recently you've been in a bit of a bind. We're offering a solution."

Andrews jutted his chin at Sin. "If you want to talk, he goes."

"Why should he leave?"

"He slaughtered half my men. If you know anything about me, you would understand why I don't want to be in his presence any more than I have to."

Boyd considered that before turning to Sin. "Do you mind stepping out for a minute?"

Sin scrutinized the man's restraints. Only then did he give a short nod and leave the cabin, pulling the door shut behind him. Andrews jumped at the sound. The man was pale, sweating, but visibly relieved to have Sin out of the room. Instead of continuing to stand over the 53 leader, Boyd pulled over a nearby chair so they were eye-level.

"We've noted the pressure you've been under between Janus' recruitment and the expectations of your men. As of now, it's put you in a precarious position. Unfortunately, Janus will swallow up your group and give you little in return. As I said, we have a solution to your dilemma."

"'We'?" Andrews bloodstained teeth flashed in a sour smile. "I don't know who sent you or who you're with but obviously it's someone just like Janus if not worse."

"Better or worse are subjective terms that I can't help you with," Boyd said. "But although our strength rivals Janus, we don't indiscriminately attack innocents and targets alike. The innocent casualties of Janus attacks have been high in the past and are likely to only grow as further strengthen their army. As a man who started down this path by trying to protect the civilians of Carson, I'm sure you can see how this is a worrisome trend, and why we would want to stop it."

Andrews huffed out a breath, the sound raspy and wet. "You people are all the same. You think you can use us to get at your goals. We didn't form the True Democracy Movement to be pulled into your political wars. Our concern is the people of Carson who have been abused by the state, abandoned by the Feds, and forgotten by aid and relief organizations for decades. The only reason Janus, and you, give a damn about any of it is because you've all noticed that TDM is a real force. We can make a difference and the people support us. Unfortunately, we don't want your help or help from Janus."

"Well, unfortunately for you, you've already attracted Janus' attention. They aren't simply going to go away because you want them to." Boyd started leaned forward and hid a wince. "What we're prepared to offer you is this: You join Janus as our spy and hide it from your people."

Andrews' expression became incredulous, but he did not speak so Boyd continued.

"You give us information on Janus from the inside and when your mission is complete, we will provide protection and supplies for you and your operatives. We have no interest in interfering with your fight with Carson's government so you would be free to continue with your agenda. In addition, the individuals in your group who wish to join Janus will be appeased, and you will no longer need to fear defection to Aarons' side."

A harsh laugh filled the empty space that followed Boyd's words. "You forgot to add on that it will also ensure we're under another organization's thumb. We aren't mercenaries. We don't work for other people, no matter how powerful they are."

Boyd weighed his options. If Agency propaganda did not work, he would have to sink lower.

"I see. Then I will inform you that today a vehicle will be waiting outside your son Kaysen's school. It will be driven by a very friendly woman who will tell him she's a friend of his mother's, and that she's there to bring him home. It's possible he never makes it home."

With little inflection, Boyd listed what could happen to Andrews' two kids and wife. "It's equally possible that Lily drowns when she is sent away to that expensive camp in Georgia. The counselor with her group will be frantic when he realizes they lost her along the way. When they find her body, it will be deemed an accident. And as for Jaime, everyone knows your wife smokes, especially when stressed. Sometimes she smokes in bed. Following the family tragedies, no one would blame her for it. Unfortunately, that habit would be fatal if she fell asleep with a cigarette still burning and caused a fire." Boyd spread his hands, unflinching. "It's equally possible that instead of any of this, they could be brought in for rigorous questioning until you agree to work with us." Boyd paused. "Personally, I think the accidents would be more humane."

If Andrews had been pale before, he was now a ghost. "I'm not surprised you would do this," he whispered. "Any organization that would employ a... man like that—" he jerked his head to the door. "—does not truly care about human life."

Boyd did not bother to deny the claim. "It doesn't have to be that way. If I can assure my employers that you'll work with us, none of that will happen. Of course, we'll have to keep your family under surveillance in the event that you attempt to deceive us."

"So it's all up to me," Andrews said with a humorless smile. "I can save everyone by working for you."

"Yes," Boyd agreed. "Your cooperation can begin immediately by you answering some questions."

"What questions? It seems you know everything."

"To your knowledge, is Jason Aarons and his new group also being pursued by Janus?"

"No. My Janus contact works only with me. Jason wouldn't know how to get in touch with them."

"Who is your Janus contact?"

"What does it matter?"

"We have interest in Janus and the people who associate with them," Boyd said. "Especially since you said the contact only works with you. It would seem there's a reason for that."

Andrews seemed to roll this around in his head. He was silent for so long that Boyd readied himself to make the call to the Agency with the unfortunate directive, but then Andrews spoke up.

"Thierry Beauvais is my contact. I have a cousin who lives in England and keeps company with very wealthy people."

"Why?"

"She's a call girl and has made clients of the kind of people Thierry associates with. They met at a party and became friends and business partners of a sort. He started paying her to spy on certain clients who talked a lot when they were in bed. When she found out that I was looking for someone to buy arms from, she pointed me in his direction."

Boyd nodded. "How long ago was your first contact with Thierry?"

"About a year."

"And Janus learned of you through him?"

Andrews shrugged. "I'd never had contact with them beforehand. He said they were looking into expanding and liked our style. They liked the fact that we were not afraid to fight the government and take a stand."

Boyd said nothing. There was no need. Even with that small amount of intel, the deal would was invalid without Andrews' cooperation. They needed a mole, not just a single name, so Boyd let the unspoken question hang in the air.

"I'll do what you want. I can only pray that your people keep their word."

"They will."

Boyd made the arrangements. He found his Agency phone in the bag he'd stowed beneath the bed and sent a coded message to Ryan with Andrews' response: he would work for them so the Agency could surveil instead of abduct.

When it was all said and done, Boyd found Sin standing just outside the door. Boyd informed him of Andrews' cooperation, and nearly stopped in his tracks at Sin's exhale of relief. Boyd knew enough about

110   SANTINO & AIS

his partner to know the relief was not for Andrews; Sin would have killed the man in a second. No. The relief was for the man's family.

The mystery of Sin was ever-growing, and Boyd did not know if he would ever understand a man who could slaughter dozens, allow his own partners to die, but then show genuine concern for faceless civilians.

However, as they hauled Andrews out of the cabin and returned him to the base, there were times when Sin ensured he was in front of Boyd or demanded to scout ahead. There were also times when he checked Boyd's leg and the bruises on his neck before casting his eyes to the ground.

It would have been impossible months ago, but now Boyd wondered if Sin's fleeting concern for others had extended to him as well.

NINE

THE DRIVE BACK to Lexington felt shorter.

Boyd navigated the Agency vehicle through a road that appeared to have been retaken by nature. It was cracked from lack of care and the bowed branches of trees extended above, blocking out the ash-colored sky. With nothing but the unspoken questions in his head and Sin's stalwart silence beside him, Boyd could do nothing but stare at the rush of trees and remember how, many missions ago, the forest had so confused him.

"Why did you save me?"

"Does it matter? You're alive."

"It matters to me."

The setting sun cast muted rays across Sin's face. His skin was peaked and circles lined his eyes.

"It's pointless for you to die. That is basically what I decided."

"Why? I'm easily replaceable. Agent Blake could take over for me and it's unlikely anyone would have been surprised to find I hadn't made it back."

"Well, maybe I don't want Blake to be my partner."

"His temperament was relatively similar to my own," Boyd said. "I imagine after a day or two you'd hardly notice the difference."

To that, Sin did not bother to respond, but Boyd did not want the ride to pass without him saying the words that had been at the forefront of his mind since waking in the cabin.

"Thank you."

Sin yanked at a loose string in a tear at the knee of his pants. The rip widened. "Did I answer your questions the way you wanted me to?"

"What do you mean?"

"If I answered adequately, I'll expect adequate responses to my questions in return."

"Oh." There were so many questions that Boyd jumped at the chance to gain additional information. "I have additional questions."

Sin sighed. "What now?"

"In the past, you were unconcerned about whether the mission was a success. So why did you make the effort to bring in Andrews?"

"There would have been no point in saving you if I'd let the mission fail. They would just terminate you and lock me back up when we returned to the compound. I'm not unaware that this mission is important."

It made sense, but Boyd wanted more. The unknown had been out of reach for the past several months and he was hungry for answers.

"I still don't understand why you saved me. I've been trying to determine the reason. Judging by how you bandaged my wound and checked on me, along with what you said about Blake, it implies concern for both the mission but also my survival." Boyd stole a glance at Sin. "If that's true, I don't understand what changed in the past months."

"I don't either." Sin's eyes slit against the sun streaming through the window. "I didn't think... I didn't think you would make a good partner. I didn't think this would work."

"And at some point something made you believe it would?"

"Obviously," Sin said, starting to look impatient.

The admittance was pleasing even though Boyd had never expected the words to leave Sin's mouth. Or to occur to him at all.

"What did you want to ask me?"

"Why didn't you just use the remote and activate my collar?"

"Because I didn't feel it was necessary."

"Oh."

Boyd surveyed his partner. "And I truly have no interest in harming you."

"I didn't—" Sin cut himself off, frowning. "You should never touch me when I'm sleeping."

"I'll keep that in mind, but you were clearly having a nightmare. When I called out, you didn't respond. In the future, how do you prefer I wake you?"

Sin looked at him sharply. "What are you talking about?"

"You were clearly having a nightmare and murmuring in your sleep. If it happens again, I'd like to know of any alternatives for waking you."

Sin's breath gusted out in a disgusted sigh. "Well, that's just beautiful. But whatever. Just leave me be if it happens again. It's safer."

They lapsed into silence again. The trees began to thin as they left the woods of Cunningham Terrace and drove through the desolation of Carson and the Wastelands. The skeletons of abandoned buildings and neighborhoods jutted out of shattered subdivisions, unforgiving reminders of what the abandoned suburb had been like in the past. Once the skyline of Lexington loomed in the distance, Boyd's mind returned to the mission, and the report he would soon have to write.

"In case you don't read the write-up, I thought you should know that Andrews named his contact with Janus. His name is Thierry Beauvais."

"I hate that little French fuck."

Boyd raised his eyebrows. "You know him?"

"I've had to meet with him twice before. He tantalizes the Agency with information and makes us jump through hoops to get it. I utterly fail at dealing with him. It would be best if I didn't see him ever again."

"I see. Did something happen when you saw him before?"

"You could say that."

With only a mysterious smirk from Sin to go on, Boyd could only wonder what future meetings with Thierry would bring about.

SIN'S FILES WERE a lure Boyd found difficult to ignore.

With so much about the senior agent still uncovered, Boyd was drawn to them late that night after submitting the mission report. He stripped off the clothes he'd worn on the mission, changed the bandages on his thigh, and walked into the office with a cup of tea. The house was quiet around him, the lights off, and his father's memorabilia masked by shadows. There was nothing to distract Boyd from the seemingly unending wealth of information on Sin—the mission reports, mission recordings, still images, and transcripts of psychiatric evaluations. Despite all that, there was barely anything on Sin's early childhood.

By the time Boyd had investigated most of the folder's contents, he stumbled upon file extensions with curious names. One was called "cam01", and when Boyd clicked on it, it quickly became apparent why.

An image of an empty apartment filled the screen. The walls were white and the furniture was plain. There were no decorations. Nothing to imply that anyone lived there. Even so, Boyd heard a rustle of movement through the speakers and shadows shifted on the screen. Boyd closed the file and opened the others, flipping through a bedroom, and a kitchen until Sin's face appeared. He was looking directly into the camera.

Startled, Boyd leaned away from the monitor. These were not videos taken of some past event; they were live feeds of Sin's apartment, including a camera installed in the mirror of Sin's bathroom. Boyd's stomach curdled, but he could not look away.

Sin's bronze complexion was ashen. His full lips were parted and his breath was labored. He raised trembling hands to wrap a bandage around his upper arm. It was already stained crimson. He stepped back to reach for something out of view of the camera, and Boyd took in his partner's body with shock. Numerous lacerations and bruises covered his torso, one of them so dark it was nearly black. Of them all, the most serious injury was Sin's arm. Blood ran down the length of it, leaving small puddles in the sink. Boyd then saw the pliers, peroxide, and the unmistakable sheen of a bullet coated in blood.

Sin stepped back into view of the camera with a small bottle clutched in one hand. He swallowed a few dry before looking into the mirror again.

He was so pale, so worn and vulnerable, that Boyd wanted to turn the video off. It was too intimate, and Sin's expression was too raw, but Boyd couldn't make himself stop. He stared into Sin's hooded eyes, analyzed every aspect of his unforgettable face, and wondered how Sin had masked his injuries and pain for so many hours.

Sin took a long, deep breath. He stood up straight, teeth flashing when he flinched, and slowly turned away from the camera. He stepped into the bathtub and sat down, nearly disappearing from view of the camera. When Sin laid down in the tub, the screen showed nothing but a tiled wall and a shut door.

The spiky edges of guilt cut through Boyd. It was undeniable that Sin had been hurt saving him, but why hide it? Was the need to mask weakness ingrained in Sin, or did he not trust Boyd? The worst part was that even if Sin believed he could let down his guard in his apartment, it was only an illusion. He didn't have privacy anywhere. There was a camera of every angle in his home.

Was any of this with Sin's consent? Did Sin know about the cameras? Maybe he did, but Boyd doubted he'd known about the one in the bathroom. A man who had ridden in silence with a gunshot wound wouldn't have let pain show so easily if he'd known anyone would see it.

Who all had access to these feeds? Boyd wondered. Who else was watching and taking note of Sin's vulnerabilities?

THE NEXT MORNING Boyd was sluggish while he dressed, and distracted on his way to the Agency. His thoughts continuously returned to the live feed just as they had throughout the night, preventing him from falling asleep. Boyd tried to put the thoughts aside so he could focus on the coming briefing, but they flooded back when he entered the conference room and found Sin sitting at the table alone.

"Late."

Boyd could only stare. If he hadn't watched the live feed, he would have never suspected Sin was injured. He looked the same as always.

Clearing his throat, Boyd sat down next to Sin.

"What are you doing here?"

"If I'm going to start being your partner, I supposed it meant I had to show up here." Sin slouched in his chair. "Why? Do you want me to go?"

"Of course not. I was simply surprised to see you."

"I see."

It was difficult not to peer at Sin closely and look for signs of the vulnerable man who had shuddered before the cameras the night before.

"Incidentally, how are you?" Boyd asked. "I didn't think to ask yesterday."

"It went as expected," Sin said.

Boyd supposed that could be a true enough answer. Most people would expect Sin to be injured on a mission involving such heavy gunfire, but Boyd did not know if the vagueness was to avoid outright lying or whether Sin just did not want to discuss it at all.

"I appreciate your willingness to help and interact."

Sin made a face. "Don't start thanking me. I almost killed you five hours before the mission."

"It doesn't matter. It would have been an accident."

Sin shot him an incredulous glare. "Well, it matters to me. If I'd have killed your dumb ass, the odds of me finding as good a partner

SANTINO & AIS

are slim to none. So just ensure that you don't pass on too quickly. I'm starting to get used to you."

Boyd's eyes opened wider with surprise, but he smiled slightly as warmth filled him.

Then the door opened and his smile vanished. Sin scowled.

"Hola!" Ryan's voice sang out before the door had fully opened. "How—" Ryan froze in mid-step, gawking. "Hsin!"

Sin's scowl deepened.

"Uh..." Ryan trailed off, jerked at the straps to his backpack, and tripped his way to a chair. "Wow, I didn't expect to uh, see you... ever."

Sin didn't reply and his attention drifted to the wall.

Ryan laughed nervously. He unhooked his backpack and opened it but kept sneaking glances at Sin, who ignored him.

"Hello, Ryan," Boyd said. "Are the others on their way?"

"Owen's probably stopping to get coffee." Ryan's face was still flushed with embarrassment. He fiddled with his laptop. "So, how are you guys?"

"Grand," Sin said blandly.

"Fine. And you?"

"Oh, you know. Busy, not being able to sleep because of all of my projects—although... Oh! That reminds me," Ryan blurted. "I was going to ask if you wanted to come over when you have downtime. I just downloaded a series I've been searching for forever. It's super old."

Sin's gaze switched to Boyd but he said nothing.

"Is it the one you have on the walls with the robots?" Boyd asked.

"No, but if you're interested in mecha, I have a ton of shows like that. The series I found takes place in the 19th century and is about this awesome samurai guy in Japan."

"Where else would a samurai be?" Sin commented, eyes still on Boyd.

Ryan squirmed in his chair. "I dunno. I was just explaining..."

"I don't know what I'm interested in." Boyd didn't know what mecha meant but apparently it had something to do with young men and robots with wings. "The series you mentioned is fine. Is it historically accurate?"

"I'm not sure so far, it just finished today. I didn't want to start until

I had it all. There's a movie too." Ryan gestured at Sin. "Hey, you know, you could—"

"No."

"Okay..." Ryan didn't seem surprised.

The door opened and Owen shuffled in looking tired as usual. He stopped just inside the door and blinked. Owen looked down into his coffee cup and turned around.

"Where are you going?" Ryan demanded. "Owen!"

"Something's wrong with my coffee, Ry-Meist," Owen mumbled. "I think they gave me a shot of L-espresso-D. I'm seeing things now. I'm going to go away and come back and see if anything changes."

"Come sit down before Jeffrey gets here and starts badgering you."

Owen peered at Sin, who exuded every sign of being unimpressed, then switched his attention to Boyd, and finally sat down next to Ryan. He carefully set the coffee cup on the table. "Okay, but just so we're clear, Sin Vega is sitting there and I'm not imagining it, right? I've been having some weird dreams lately so I don't know what's going on right now. I might look down and realize I'm naked."

Sin slouched down further in his chair and rapped his knuckles impatiently against the table. Now that other people were in the room with them it seemed like he couldn't wait to leave.

"It's good that he's here." Ryan grinned in encouragement, apparently deciding to pay no attention to Sin's behavior. "I'm glad. We can all be one big happy unit now and everything."

"Oh yeah, it's all good." Owen lazily saluted Sin. "I just didn't wanna be hallucinating in the middle of meetings again. I got a lot of dirty looks the time it happened. I don't know why it's such a big deal, anyway. It would've been way more exciting if there really were tap-dancing penguins in there, even if it made it kind of hard to concentrate."

Sin looked so visibly annoyed to be around other people that Boyd wondered why he had come. It almost seemed like he was trying to be nice..

The door opened again and Carhart and Jeffrey stepped in. Carhart arched an eyebrow at Sin and took his spot at the head of the table.

"Nice of you to finally join us."

"No problem," Sin drawled. "Nice group of misfits you have here."

Owen rested his chin against his palm. He raised one hand with a look that clearly said "guilty as charged."

Jeffrey, on the other hand, displayed clear distaste from his thinned lips to his stiff posture.

There was a pleased tilt to Carhart's mouth but he evened it out quickly. They went over the mission with Boyd doing most of the talking. Even when he told the others how Sin had saved the mission, Sin refused to speak. He spent the entirety of the debriefing staring at Boyd and toying with the zipper on his hoodie. It wasn't until Boyd mentioned Thierry's name that the routine was broken.

"Oh no," Ryan groaned. "Not that guy again. Ugh. And also, my sources all dried up with him. They lost touch or don't have access to him anymore. We'd have to go through the civilian route to get in touch with him."

Owen took a long drink of coffee. "We're talking Mr. Suave in the tux? I know someone with the direct connect."

"Good," Carhart said. "We'll get a feel on how agreeable he's feeling lately and decide how to approach him from there. If he is having recent contact with Janus shot-callers, that goes directly against his previous claims that he'd fallen out of contact with them."

"Who is he exactly?" Boyd asked.

Looks were exchanged around the table, and Sin rolled his eyes. "A pointless asshole with a lot of connections."

"Basically," Ryan agreed with a snort of amusement.

"Yeah, I don't think anyone wants to claim him as their BFF." Owen finished off the rest of the coffee in one gulp.

"Thierry Beauvais is a wealthy entrepreneur who uses his vast wealth to either help or hinder different political groups in Western Europe. His father was one of the first benefactors of Janus when they were nothing more than a fledgling group. When he died, Thierry didn't show that same exclusivity and instead began playing various groups against each other seemingly for his own amusement." Carhart glanced at Sin. "We've had previous dealings with Thierry. In the past, he's shown interest in helping us, but he's very temperamental. Our most recent meeting with him ended in disaster when Sin took the liberty of insulting him to the extent of the man getting on a flight out of the country."

"He's a condescending fuck," Sin said, unconcerned.

Boyd could not imagine Sin dealing with a man like Thierry. The mission must have ended disastrously.

"Are there worries that he may be uninterested in negotiating with us again?"

"It's possible. But we won't know for certain until we contact him. At that time, we'll have a follow-up." Carhart indicated Owen. "Get your source on this as soon as possible. I want a contact number immediately."

"I'll be all over that after the meeting, like a mongoose on a snake." Owen frowned. "The trained ones, anyway."

Carhart pinned him with a flat stare. "If no one has anything further to add we'll wrap up for now. Owen, I expect you to be in touch within the hour."

Owen eyed Carhart warily but ultimately nodded again. Carhart left the room without ceremony. Jeffrey wasn't far behind, pointedly taking Owen's cup and throwing it in the garbage on the way out. Owen snorted but followed, no doubt to work on his assignment.

"Don't mind Jeffrey, by the way. He has a permanent case of stick-in-ass," Ryan confided, glancing at Sin with a brief, hopeful grin. When he got a non-response in return, Ryan sighed quietly and looked at Boyd. "Well, if you're interested in the anime let me know."

"I will. Thank you, Ryan."

Ryan flashed a smile and left. Once he was gone, Sin spoke. "Interesting."

"That does seem to be the best word to describe the unit."

Sin shoved his chair back, dropping his hands on the arms as if to push himself up. "Well, I'm off to the training room to likely be hassled by complete morons."

"Is that the one in the Tower?"

"Yes. It's an unfortunate place to go because it's used by every single idiot on the compound, but it offers a wide variety of equipment to work out and spar if you want to do that sort of thing." Sin stood. "My newfound freedom to roam the compound leads me there more often than not."

The questions surrounded Sin continued to mount. Why had he come to the briefing and why was he offering so much information? His behavior was at complete odds with everything Boyd had come to learn about the other man. Instead of pointing that out, he said,

"That's good to know. I'm primarily used to the training complex but I don't have access to it anymore. Are there places where a person can be left alone or does it get too crowded in the training room?"

"There are private rooms." Sin slid his hands into his pockets. "You should consider going sometime. To further your training. Because you're still too skinny."

"I will." Boyd gave a hint of a smile. "Thank you. I've needed a place to train. David said the same thing."

Sin nodded. "I'll see you around."

His gaze lingered on Boyd as he backed out of the room, and Boyd could not help but wonder if the offering of information had been an invitation.

TEN

WHEN SIN WOKE up, it was with a flash of panic. The last vestiges of the nightmare haunted his peripheral vision, but when he jerked his gaze to the darkened corner, he found nothing unusual there.

Slumping back against the bed, Sin took a deep breath. There was a distinct tremor in his limbs and his breath was still coming fast. Phantom aches echoed through his body as though he'd really experienced whatever had happened in his dream. Trying to remember the entirety of it was always pointless. He'd had the same nightmare countless times. Recently, it had started coming more often, but no matter how worn out he felt after waking up, no matter how dismayed he was, only fragments of the dream remained.

Green grass and rocks stained with blood, the moon hovering in a smoke-and-onyx sky. Flashes of a body being dragged across rough terrain, a slack mouth, and fingers trailing limply through dirt.

"Fuck."

Sin opened his eyes again and pulled himself into a sitting position. His head was pounding but the ghostly pain in his torso. It was always the same when he woke up—strange aches as though he'd just been in a fight and a clawing horror that made his heart catch in his throat.

Sin combed his fingers through his hair and stood. Disgruntled and irritated, he rolled his stiff shoulders in an attempt to relieve the tension. He didn't understand the dream or why it had such an effect on him. The fact that he woke up in a cold sweat was bad enough, but the idea that he thrashed and yelled in his sleep was even worse. It still annoyed the hell out of him that Boyd had witnessed it firsthand.

He headed to the bathroom, shoving off the loose gray pants he'd worn to sleep. Even with the sun muted behind thick, gray clouds, the daylight streaming into the apartment windows was too bright compared to the darkness of his bedroom. It made his head pound further, but he felt simultaneous relief as it chased the dream further away. The muddled feelings did not fully disperse until he stepped under the welcome pressure in the shower, and the water cooled his uncomfortably heated flesh. Sin smoothed wet hair away and kept his face tilted up against the cold water. It was stupid to continuously revel in the feel of a normal shower but he couldn't help it.

In all of Sin's life, he'd never had his own space. Although it was a standard Agency apartment and Spartan by default, it was still his own.

He was still confined to the compound unless he had supervision, and guards stood in front of his apartment door at all times, but it was better than living in a cell on the Fourth. Sin had no idea how Carhart had managed to convince Connors to finally let him have his own quarters, but Sin suspected they thought this tactic would prompt him to cooperate. If that was the case, he couldn't deny that it had been a motivating factor.

Well, that and the fact that Boyd had turned out to be a marginally acceptable human.

The thought of Boyd unsettled Sin in a way that he did not understand. He'd had mixed thoughts about the younger man from the moment he'd seen Boyd during the interview and now, months later, Sin was still unable to come to a clear determination on his partner. He didn't trust Boyd, not really, but somehow Boyd had morphed into not only a decent partner but a companion of sorts.

A random conversation should not have been so disarming, but days later, Sin realized why it had thrown him so far off his guard. During his entire time at the Agency, Boyd was the first person to really speak to him. Carhart consistently tried and failed, but Sin could never look at the general without thinking he had a motive. Boyd, however, didn't seem to have any. And that made no sense. If anything, Boyd should be either plotting against him or running away after their nearly disastrous mission outside of Cunningham Terrace two weeks ago.

The worst part of that incident was that Sin didn't remember anything until the point where he'd already been crushing Boyd against the floor. It was just like the other times, "episodes" as the Agency called them, when he'd blacked out completely. Even though Boyd had been able to bring him out of it, Sin didn't have too much optimism about that happening a second time.

After scrubbing himself and allowing the powerful jets of water to rinse him, Sin shut the faucet off. Stepping out of the shower, he wrapped a towel around his waist and gave himself a cursory once-over in the mirror. The bruises were slowly fading from his torso but the gunshot wound was still painful and raw-looking. After the first couple of days of caring for it on his own, Sin had been forced to go to the medical wing to make sure it hadn't gotten infected. As little as he liked having Agency staff attend to him, an infection wasn't something he could fix on his own.

After drying off and dressing for a morning of working out Sin left the apartment. He didn't look at his guards, Daniels and Kemp, and stalked down the hallway. Sin could feel their eyes on his back but didn't acknowledge them.

As usual, the compound was relatively quiet around his residential building. It was set apart from the others and was considerably smaller due to the fact that it was meant for special cases. There were the usual guards posted by the main doors who eyed him as he went by, but other than that, Sin was left alone on the walk across the courtyard. It wasn't until he got closer to the Tower that crowds of people began to appear.

The tension that had built in Sin's shoulders upon stepping out of the building only worsened as he walked up the steps to the Tower. He didn't have social anxiety, but he did have idiot agent anxiety. Especially when he was locked in a torture chamber for putting them in their place. Most people avoided Sin, but there was always someone who inevitably pissed him off.

It started out well enough; he'd managed to get the only remaining private room off the side of the main training space so that he wouldn't have to deal with gawkers. He spent over an hour doing various exercises and stretching in relative peace and quiet. Sin lost himself in the repetition of what he was doing. His mind cleared and the anger melted away. It lasted until he left the room to get a bottle of water and noticed Harry Truman and Dennis McNichols in the main area.

Harry focused on Sin right away.

The tension returned, and Sin drained his bottle of water before returning to the private room to wait.

A blanket of quiet rage swept over Sin, but he kept it in check. Harry was the only person on the compound who wasn't afraid to touch him. Harry knew better than anyone what Sin was capable of but that didn't deter him at all. In fact, Harry did everything in his power to get Sin to lash out. No one seemed to understand it, even dimwitted Dennis didn't seem to know Harry's motivation, but Sin had figured it out long ago.

Harry wanted him on the Fourth. Their interactions went back a long way but, after the introduction of the box, Harry had taken his harassment to the next level. While Sin was kept drugged, Harry was able to do whatever he wanted. Sin had enough muddled memories of large hands groping him and a hot wet mouth pressing against lips and neck to realize Harry had a sexual fixation with him.

After looking at the guard's file, Sin hadn't been surprised to see that in Harry's civilian years he'd been a registered sex offender with a long history of stalking. The Agency vetted Harry due to his military background and sociopathic tendencies, but even they had shied away from a field agent path once they realized the man couldn't rein in his sexual impulses. Instead, they'd stuck him on the Fourth to harass people who were already receiving far worse treatment.

"We just keep running into each other, Vega," Harry drawled as he entered the room with Dennis close behind.

"Imagine that, considering we both live on the compound."

"Oh, is that all it is?" Harry stopped less than a hand-span away from Sin. His eyes roved over Sin's sweaty form, focusing on the crotch of his sweatpants before sweeping back up to Sin's damp neck and pursed lips. "I thought maybe you were doing it on purpose."

Sin smirked, revulsion twisting with the hatred he felt for the man. "You wish."

"Why don't you give us a minute?" Harry said to Dennis.

Dennis frowned. "I don't think that's a good idea, Har—"

"I said get the fuck out," was the snarled response. The look Harry shot his friend was full of venom. Judging by the way Dennis quickly departed, it would seem that Harry's abusive personality came into play in his friendships too.

Sin uncrossed his arms and curled his fingers into loose fists. He cast a quick look around the room and noted that there was indeed a small camera mounted in the ceiling. It was nearly disguised by the light fixture.

"You just keep playing hard to get now that you're free, don't you?" Harry moved closer and forced Sin to back up unless he wanted the guard pressed against him.

"Groping someone who is in a drugged stupor doesn't count as compliance." Sin didn't flinch when Harry pushed him against the wall. "I know that must be hard for a pedophile—"

"I'm not a fucking pedophile," Harry snapped, cuffing Sin in the head.

It took all of Sin's willpower not to respond. He took a deep breath, but his fingers were now balled into white-knuckled fists. "Is fourteen the age of consent in your fantasy world? That was the age of the boy you attacked before the Agency recruited you, wasn't it?"

Harry grabbed the front of Sin's shirt, bunching the fabric. "That's a lot of talk from someone who kills civilians and rapes his shrink."

Sin didn't know how the rumor about him having raped Lydia had come about, but he wasn't going to respond to it. That was what Harry wanted—to get a reaction out of him.

Harry leaned forward again, raising a hand to slide down the side of Sin's face. "Now, when are you going to start playing nice?" He rubbed his thumb against Sin's mouth and parted Sin's lips. Harry's breath hitched. "I have to admit, Vega. I miss your fine ass. I miss having you up there with me."

"Do you?" Sin turned his face away, body going so tense that his headache returned.

"Yeah, I do." This time Harry nuzzled his face against Sin's neck and inhaled. "C'mon, don't act like you forgot, Vega. All of our quality time..."

"Is that what you're calling it?"

"Fuck yeah it is. But you know I like it better when you can fight. Thinking about that look on your face when you get angry... Mmm, it makes me come so much harder."

The rough, flat slide of Harry's tongue against his neck pulled Sin out of the forced calm he'd tried to adopt. He wrapped his hand around Harry's wrist and twisted it backward until the other man grunted in pain.

"Touch me, and I'll kill you. We aren't on the Fourth anymore."

Harry flexed his wrist, leering at Sin with obvious desire. "Attack me again and you will be, bitch. I'll activate that collar and zap you so hard your eyes will be rolling for a week. When you wake up you'll be back on the Fourth—" Harry stepped closer again and Sin tensed.

"—drugged, helpless, and fully at my disposal. And next time, you're mine. All of you."

The words caused a rush of memories to crowd Sin's mind. The feel of a heavy body crushing him, an erection digging into his thigh—unable to move, unable to defend himself. The power Harry held over him now was just as bad as what had happened then. The inability to react without even worse consequences made Sin freeze in place. He was just as helpless as he'd been in the box.

Everything Harry said was true, and Sin was damned either way.

His lip curled, nostrils flaring as his breath came faster.

"That's the face," Harry hissed, thick lips lifting in a filthy smile. "Right there. That's how I want you to look at me when I finally fuck you."

The image of Harry in front of him began to flicker. Everything around them dimmed. Sin's peripheral vision was nonexistent; he focused solely on the threat before him. Harry.

"Touch me and you will be sorry."

The threat only excited Harry. He chuckled deep in his throat. Just as his hand wrapped around Sin's arm, the door behind them opened. He turned from Harry. Sin's heartbeat sped and his hands trembled. He forced them to stay down, but he was losing the tenuous control he had over the violence that wanted to wreak havoc.

"Am I interrupting anything?" Boyd's disaffected voice filtered through the tension.

"Mind your fucking business," Harry growled.

"This *is* my business." Boyd stood behind the guard. "I suggest you take your hands off my partner."

Dennis rushed into the room. "Sorry, Harry, I walked away for one minute—"

"Shut the fuck up," Harry snarled.

Sin wrenched his arm away, but Harry grabbed the front of his shirt, ripping the collar. He yanked Sin against him until their faces were only inches apart. Boyd grabbed Harry's arm, but Dennis rushed in and slammed Boyd against the wall. He reared back his fist to strike Boyd just as Sin awoke from his hate-filled daze and wrapped his hand around Dennis' neck.

Luke Gerant entered the room before anything more could happen.

"What the hell is going on?" Luke demanded.

Harry pulled away with a scoff. "Nothing. Piss off."

Sin released Dennis. His fingers had already made red marks on the man's throat.

"Officer Truman was harassing Sin," Boyd spoke up, moving around Dennis. "He was using Officer McNichols to watch the door so no one would enter and obviously planned to escalate the situation. I attempted to intervene and you see the result."

Sin blinked at Boyd. Adrenaline was still pumping through his veins but the desire to eviscerate both men was fading. "Boyd—"

"Shut your mouth and mind your business," Harry interrupted, glaring at Boyd. "It's between me and Vega."

The hateful look Harry aimed at Boyd sent a sliver of unease down Sin's spine and shattered Sin's anger. When Harry set his sights on someone it was more of a promise than a threat, and that did not bode well for the future.

Shaking off the remnants of the episode that hadn't actually come, Sin waited for Harry to make a move. He wouldn't put it past the man to try to attack Boyd now—Harry had no control of his temper when he didn't get his way, although he usually didn't lash out with an audience.

"It isn't between you two." Boyd did not flinch away from the promise in the big man's face. "You're clearly a deranged man taking advantage of the situation. Sin may feel unable to properly respond, but I don't. I'll file a formal report on you if that's what it takes."

Sin's unease jacked up. "Let's go."

Luke glanced between Dennis and Harry, failing at hiding his dislike. "It may be a good idea for you to report this."

Dennis was incredulous. "You're taking their side over ours?"

Harry sneered, not appearing surprised in the least.

"It's an incident that clearly needs to be put on the record. You were on camera the whole time. It may be best if everyone has their side of the story documented," Luke replied. "Besides, others in the training facility were aware that something was going on. A maintenance worker grabbed me while I was passing to inform me that there was trouble."

Sin had no interest in filing reports or documenting anything. "I'm out of here."

Boyd didn't move. "How do we file official reports? Do I report what I've witnessed to you or should I write a report and send it in?"

Harry made another ugly sound at the back of his throat and stormed out of the room with Dennis on his heels.

Ignoring them, Luke nodded. "Go to the third floor—that's where the guard command center is. All incidents that occur on the compound are reported there before being distributed to the proper chain of command for the individuals involved. Since it involved Truman and McNichols, I'll make sure my captain gets it."

"I'll do that. Thank you."

Luke started to say something to Sin, but Sin walked out of the room. He almost kept going until he was clear of the training area but forced himself to stop. When Luke and Boyd left the private room, the guard stopped in front of Sin.

"I appreciate you not hurting Harry."

Sin raised an eyebrow.

"I knew you could have. And I know he would have deserved it."

"How are you so sure? I'm an out of control cannibal, remember?"

"No, you're not. You're not as crazy as you want me to think. Like I said, you could have killed him."

"Yes," Sin agreed. "And next time, I probably will."

They stared at each other, and then Luke raised a hand in farewell. He said to Boyd, "Let me know if you have any issues filing the report. You can find my number in the directory. Take care."

When the guard was gone, Sin addressed his partner. "Why did you get involved?"

Boyd was unruffled as ever. "It seemed like you were about to hurt him and I wanted to intervene before you could get in trouble for defending yourself. I also wanted him to know that not everyone will ignore such blatant harassment. By reporting it, maybe he'll see some consequences for his behavior."

Several things about Boyd's response were unexpected, but there were too many people focused on Sin, and he still felt the burning desire to bash someone's face in.

"Let's get out of here."

Boyd followed him out of the training room. Most people avoided looking directly at Sin when he came close, but as soon as his back was to the rest of the room, he felt the weight of their stares. A few mutters echoed around the room and Sin thought they undoubtedly believed he'd caused some issue. He couldn't help wondering what people would think if they knew the truth.

He and Boyd continued walking until they were outside, well out of earshot of anyone who would be brave enough to eavesdrop. Sin led Boyd around the side of the building and to a cluster of trees that provided them shelter from the steady stream of people on the path.

"You unnecessarily brought yourself to the attention of someone you would have been smarter to avoid," Sin said. "You should have stayed out of it."

"It doesn't matter. I wouldn't have stood by silently regardless."

"You're either being cocky or stupid. Truman is the pack leader of a lot of guards who run this place. And not the ones like doe-eyed Luke back there. It would be wise to not get on their bad side because of me."

Boyd's lips pressed together, and a hint of heat entered his voice. "So I should allow a terrible person to hurt others in front of me simply because it could be inconvenient for me to interfere? You're my partner and I'm going to help you. Even if it wasn't part of my job, I would not let that go. Besides, I'm already disliked because of my mother and my position. This changes nothing."

"You defended me. That was enough. And I..." Sin lifted his shoulders. "I appreciate it. No one ever has before. But taking it further isn't necessary. I don't want you to get hurt again because you were trying to help me."

Anger was still evident by the tightness in Boyd's shoulders and the flash of his amber eyes. After so many months, it was the first flash of intensity Sin saw in his partner.

"That doesn't concern me," Boyd said. "What concerns me is you have such low expectations that even someone speaking up on your behalf is enough for you. Harry seems too arrogant to stop until he's challenged. I'm not going to go halfway on this. If something happens to me on a mission, I want the incident on record first."

"Will you shut up about dying?" Sin said, exasperated. "I decide to go along with this shit, and you're still ready to drop dead at the first opportunity."

"I'm being realistic. I'm more likely to die before you. It has nothing to do with you being a good partner. I'm simply thinking ahead."

"You're an idiot."

"What are you worried about? Is there something I should know about Harry?"

It would have been smarter to end the conversation before he gave Boyd further ammunition for filing a report, but for some reason he kept talking.

"He's a predator and he views me as an ideal victim. The fact that I'm generally hated suits him because no one is likely to believe me if I tell anyone, but he doesn't care about what I've done. When he's denied what he wants, he gets worse and he will lash out. It doesn't help that his buddies tend to man the surveillance station."

Again, a flash of anger lit Boyd's face. Even as subtle as it was, it was more emotion than Sin was accustomed to seeing from his partner. "I see. As a predator, does that mean he's attacked or harassed others in the past? Or has it mostly been you due to your circumstances?"

"I know he had a record of it before he was recruited here."

"How long has he been here?"

"At least five years, maybe more. He first appeared on the Fourth two years into my first incarceration."

"Does everyone know what he's like? Officer Gerant didn't seem surprised by the situation."

Two women entered the small grove and stopped at the sight of Sin and Boyd. They looked from one man to the other and did an about face. Sin continued as if the conversation had never been disrupted.

"All guards in the Maximum Security wing of the Fourth know what he's like. Luke just seems more squeamish and moral than the others."

"And General Carhart?" Boyd demanded.

Sin combed his fingers through his unruly hair and exhaled loudly. "I don't think he realizes the extent of it."

"Why would you not want me to file a report, then?" Boyd crossed his arms over his chest; lean muscle was evident in his biceps beneath the long-sleeved black shirt he'd worn to the training facility. "Obviously he never plans to stop, and everyone knows and looks the other way. The ignorance and discrimination in that alone is astounding. Doesn't it bother you at all?"

Sin shrugged, tired of the topic. He wasn't interested in being seen as the victim in some unfortunate circumstance. Harry Truman was a nuisance and a danger only because he couldn't defend himself without making the situation worse. It was just something he'd have to deal with in order to avoid the box.

"I'm used to it. It doesn't make a difference to me anymore. People will do what they want because they think they can. After all, I'm barely human. The scary monster of the compound."

Boyd scoffed. "Well, I don't accept your status quo. He already dislikes me so not filing the report wouldn't help. I won't stand by and do nothing when it's within my power to at least put down in words what everyone else would conveniently ignore."

There was no point in arguing the topic. Boyd seemed determined to go through with his plan, and Sin wasn't going to keep fighting him on it. Besides, Sin couldn't deny that there was something intriguing about his partner's stubbornness. It was a change from Boyd's usual apathy and disinterest in the world.

"Why were you there, anyway? I'd never seen you there before."

"You told me it was a good place to train."

At the time, Sin had only said it to distract himself from his own curiosity as to why reclusive Boyd spent time at Ryan's house, and his own sudden desire to see Boyd's fleeting smile reappear.

When he said nothing, Boyd drew his own conclusions.

"Is it so strange that I went there?"

"No. I just—" Sin stopped. As usual, he didn't know how to explain precisely what he was trying to say. Expressing himself to others had never been necessary before. "I didn't think you would actually go. I took you for a loner."

"Oh." A warm breeze pushed pale strands of hair into Boyd's face, and for a brief, absurd moment, Sin had an urge to brush it away. He didn't, and Boyd kept talking. "There are times I don't mind being around others. But since you recommended it, I went."

Not knowing what to say to that, Sin looked down at his torn shirt for inspiration and realized it was worse than he'd thought. The entire collar was destroyed, and the shirt was ripped haphazardly to the left. Boyd noticed the destruction too.

"If you need to leave to change..."

"It's not like I have much to change into, anyway."

"Why not?"

"Because the clothes I have are the clothes I've had for over a decade. I don't get out much."

"Are you still not allowed to leave on your own?"

Sin shook his head, looking in the general area of the gates. "Not without an escort. I am not to be trusted in the city on my own, so says the good Marshal."

"Hmm." Boyd slid his hands into the pockets of his black pants. "Would you like to go now?"

Sin's head swiveled in Boyd's direction. "With you?"

"Yes."

Again, Sin was stunned to silence. Eventually, he released a low huff of laughter. "You're really not afraid of me, are you?"

"No. I'm not."

The irony of Boyd not fearing him despite nearly being killed by Sin a few weeks ago was so extreme, Sin nearly laughed. Maybe it made sense they got along; they were both apparently crazy.

"Do you drive?"

"Usually. My car's in the main lot."

Boyd headed toward the compound's gates and Sin reluctantly followed. He stole discreet looks at the younger man as they walked, trying to determine why Boyd was being so nice. Yes, they'd had more frequent conversations lately, but this was totally different. Being around Boyd for reasons unrelated to a briefing or a mission was not something Sin had ever considered. Now that it was occurring, he had no idea what to do.

Most of Sin's interactions with people in the Agency were either one way or the other; they ignored him or went out of their way to ostracize him. Not even Carhart had offered to escort him off the compound before. And there was always the possibility Boyd was playing a game; being nice just to keep the partnership running smoothly.

Frowning down at Boyd again, Sin hoped that was not the case. No one had been friendly to him before, and it would be unfortunate if it turned out that all of this was a lie. The willingness to plan missions together, the displays of curiosity about Sin, the random questions, and that smile... Sin was almost positive he would quit bothering to interact with people in even the remote ways he did now if it turned out that Boyd had managed to trick him. Just the notion nearly drove Sin to return to his apartment and stop pretending he was capable of being social.

Boyd's car was black and sophisticated-looking, more expensive than Sin expected. They got in and stopped at the gates while Boyd showed his identification and cleared their trip with the guards. It was easier than Sin had expected, and he could only assume that Boyd was already on the list of people he was allowed to leave with. Connors had probably never expected such a thing to happen, though.

When the car glided away from the compound, Boyd asked, "Do you have any preferences for price range?"

"Somewhere cheap. I'm kept on an allowance. I don't have access to my account."

"That's strange. Why not?"

"Because they control every aspect of my life." Sin watched as they drove through All Saints, the neighborhood that the Agency was in. Outside of the compound, the area was full of large houses and green spaces, especially with Silver Lake Park nearby dominating so much of the land. When they got further south, larger buildings cropped into view.

"I know of some affordable places. If you have no objections, I'd planned to bring you to a thrift store anyway."

"I don't care how I look. Wherever is fine."

Boyd nodded and led them southwest toward Vickland. Sin didn't pay much attention to where they were headed, although he did note Boyd was taking a few of the lesser-used residential side streets. They backtracked north, looped around to return south, and hooked up with Dauphin Street on the west side of Vickland just before the area transitioned into the Financial District.

It wasn't until Boyd parked the car that Sin realized the quickest route from the Agency would have been to drive all the way down Dauphin Street. Boyd had gone out of the way to avoid it. The information clicked in Sin's mind and combined with memories of Boyd's behavior on their first mission together. They had been on Dauphin Street that day too.

Sin glanced at his partner, more intrigued than ever. Maybe one day he'd find out what had happened to Boyd in the past.

"I thought you hated people as much as I do," Sin said as Boyd removed the keys from the ignition. "So why are you going out of your way for me?"

"Because I want to." Boyd's hand closed around the door handle, but he didn't push it open. "It bothers me that you have no one to rely on especially because most of your alienation is due to the Agency. I'm not in the habit of acting before I think, and I've taken the time to consider everything I know about the Agency and their treatment of you."

Sin's dark brows rose. "Is that a fact?"

"Yes. It is. And I've yet to find a reason why I shouldn't help you."

Wondering just how much Boyd knew about his history at the Agency, Sin pushed his own door open. "You really don't seem like the charitable type. You seem like the mind-your-own-business and try-not-to-give-a-fuck-or-get-involved type."

"Normally I am. It seems to be different with you."

Sin got out of the car without a response. Again, he wondered if the genuine-sounding words were nothing more than carefully crafted lines. Boyd redirected the conversation as he joined Sin on the sidewalk.

"There are a lot of second hand stores in the city but I think Aspen's Closet is best as far as the price and quality," Boyd said. "How much money do you have?"

"A couple hundred. They don't give me very much."

"That should be more than enough here, but what if you were to use it all on clothes? Do you get more this week?"

"No. It doesn't matter. I don't buy anything anyway except shit from the vending machine."

"It seems insulting to have your own money withheld."

A couple of people in front of the store gave Sin's torn shirt dubious looks. He sneered at them. "It's pretty tame compared to locking me in a box."

They entered the store as a woman and a teenage girl left. The interior was bigger than Sin had expected but was filled with racks of clothes and people. It was disorderly and cluttered, which made Sin want to return to the open space of the sidewalk. Instead, he swallowed the niggle of anxiety and forced himself to act like a normal person. As normal as he could get.

"Yes, but limiting your freedom in even small ways adds to the insult. Why does it matter if you have access to the money you've earned? It isn't as though you could buy your freedom."

The truth was, Sin hadn't given much thought to his allowance when it'd been implemented. In the past, he hadn't been given any of his money at all. He'd been told that it was sent to his bank account where it would remain for safe keeping until he was deemed capable of handling it on his own. Now, Sin wondered if it was a lie; if the Agency had never actually paid him. Whatever the case was, he couldn't change any of it now.

Boyd led him to a small alcove hidden at the side of the shop. At first Sin thought it was off limits to the public, but Boyd walked in without pause. A short hallway opened up before them and led to another display room. Several racks of clothing and shelves of shoes filled it. Boyd stood to the side, gesturing to the racks that held men's clothing.

"These are the new arrivals. It's best to check here before the good items disappear too quickly on the main floor. The shoes are especially good to peruse here first."

"Come here a lot? You don't seem very hard up for cash."

Boyd's gaze fixed on a rack of clothing, but his lips thinned again. "My mother's wealthy but, until this position, I wasn't necessarily. I've never had to worry about having a home but as for money for food or supplies, it varied. I became accustomed to minimal spending when possible. And my..." He crossed his arms over his stomach. "I knew others who didn't have much money so we came here to get clothing. I bought my trench coat and boots here, so they do have some quality items."

With a slow nod, Sin tried to make a valiant effort at seeking clothes, but the other customers continuously distracted him. He wondered if any of these civilians would recognize him from the incident all those years ago. Even if Vivienne had tried to cover it up, it was still possible that someone would remember the face of the man who had been dubbed by police as the Vickland Psycho.

Sin wished he'd worn something with a hood to hide beneath. It wouldn't solve the problem completely, but he wouldn't feel so exposed. The Agency would easily handle the situation if someone recognized him and alerted the authorities, but that would not erase the horror of running into a witness; someone who had seen him slaughter a score of civilians.

"Look, I just need a new t-shirt."

"How much clothing do you have?"

Sin mentally cataloged his belongings. It didn't take very long. A handful of t-shirts, a couple of pants and one pair of boots. He didn't own a proper coat of any kind that was suitable for cold weather. Not to mention everything he had was threadbare and worn.

"Enough."

"What constitutes 'enough' for you? I've hardly seen you in anything aside from that."

"I have... a few items."

"A few," Boyd repeated, looking at Sin askance. "What? A pair of pants and possibly two shirts?"

"I have two pair of pants, for your information."

"My mistake." Boyd's faint smile reappeared. "And exactly how long have you had this clothing?"

Feeling decidedly unimpressive as a result of the conversation, Sin turned away and shoved some clothes around unceremoniously. "Since I was young and impressionable."

"I'm going to assume that means at least a decade."

Sin scoffed. "What difference does it make? They're clean and covering the essential body parts, aren't they?"

Amusement lightened the cast of Boyd's eyes. "Yes, but you've nearly worn the clothing through. It seems like you may have worn the same thing almost every day for decades. We should remedy that today. If your summer clothing is this threadbare I don't have high hopes for your winter choices."

Sin figured he had a few weeks left of the faux-summer they received in the post-war world, and didn't feel too concerned.

"'I probably could have sent my service slave out to do all this."

"Who?"

With a dismissive shrug, Sin made a more conscious effort to look at the stuff on the rack. "Some damn fool service staff member who was assigned to deal with me. He hates me almost as much as I loathe the sight of him. He delivers my food and supplies. I think it's deliberate so they can prevent me having to go out at all."

There was a black bomber coat that would suit his purposes during the winter time. The inner lining was old, but better than nothing at all.

"With how infrequently you buy new clothing, would you really want someone like that making those decisions?"

"Considering how people cringe at the sight of me, it doesn't really matter what I wear or look like, but I suppose you have a point." Sin considered the coat and then at the other racks. Surviving for years on the bare minimum made it difficult to figure out what was supposed to be a necessity.

"Hmm." Boyd pushed a plain black long-sleeved thermal shirt back so he could see it fully. He held the bottom out, his eyelashes sheltering his eyes briefly as he studied it before he examined at Sin in assessment. Without saying anything, he held the shirt out to Sin.

"Are you going to dress me like you?"

"What? No. It's in good condition. You don't have to get it if you don't want; I just thought you may want to try it on."

Sin tossed the shirt over his shoulder. "I'm just messing with you, sweetheart. No need to get all explanatory."

"Why do you call me that?"

The smirk widened and Sin reached out, pinching one of Boyd's cheeks and turning his face from side-to-side. He started to say something smart but the feel of Boyd's skin startled him, and the sarcastic comment got lost somewhere. Sin dropped his hand. He'd begun to say "because you're so innocent and cute" but that seemed ill-advised when it struck him that Boyd actually was attractive.

"Because you're... young."

Boyd turned away, his hand absently brushing the spot where Sin had touched him. "Some of the trainees said the same thing."

"That you're young?" Sin stripped off his t-shirt and tossed it aside.

Boyd nodded. "They were surprised. I suppose it's because I went straight to a high rank without a pertinent background. Even so, you were recruited much younger than I was, so am I really such a precedent?"

Sin pulled the thermal shirt over his head and shrugged his shoulders to loosen it up. "It's because you're off the street and don't have any experience in anything. It makes it seem like it's nepotism. In reality, it's just because mother dearest knew two rejects of society might get along, I think."

"You may be giving her too much credit."

"Probably." Sin looked down at the shirt again before yanking it off. There were two other customers in the area and they stared as he switched back into his ragged t-shirt. Sin started to snap his teeth

SANTINO & AIS

at them like he would have done to someone on the compound, but thought better of it. "I really hate civilians."

"Most people use a dressing room," Boyd said mildly.

"I'm not shy." Adding the thermal shirt to the jacket, Sin headed back to the front of the store. As he walked, he thought he heard Boyd mumble, "I noticed."

They returned to the outer room and Boyd made a beeline for the denim section. Sin hung back, not wanting to become immersed in the crowd. There were dozens of people rifling through the stacks and making a mess of the neatly folded clothes. If he'd known the store was going to be so crowded, Sin would have refused to go. It wasn't as though he gave a damn about his clothes, anyway. He'd only come because he wanted to spend time with Boyd.

It was a weird realization; almost as weird as the realization that he found his partner attractive. Sin had never considered who was good looking and who was not before, but he'd never expected to spend time following some kid around Lexington either.

Frowning, Sin pulled a black hoodie off a rack and put it on, drawing the hood over his head. He tried to focus on the task at hand but found himself growing restless again. A pair of girls kept sneaking glances at him, and it was starting to get on his nerves.

Boyd reappeared at his side with several articles of clothing slung over his arm. He held up a pair of black and red sneakers. "Do you like these?"

"I have shoes."

"One pair, right?"

"Do I need more?"

"Yes. If those get worn out, what will you use to replace them?"

Sin supposed they'd be an improvement for working out. "Fine."

"I found some pants and a t-shirt. And I'm not positive you'll like this sweater but it seems warm."

"Looks good. Can we leave?"

"Does it bother you to be here?"

"I don't feel comfortable around... civilians. In Lexington."

"Well," Boyd began. He paused, looked around, and spoke again. "I don't think anyone is paying any attention to you at the moment. Maybe we could stay a little longer? If it isn't a problem."

It was true enough. The only people paying attention to him were those girls and when he made more of an effort to listen, he realized they were commenting on Boyd's and his looks. Apparently, he had an amazing body and Boyd had beautiful hair.

"Fine," he repeated. "By the way, those girls would like to know what conditioner you use."

Boyd shook his head, smiling again. "I'll never tell."

"Maybe you should. You may even get a date out of it."

With a quiet scoff, Boyd turned to the nearest rack. "I hardly think that will happen."

"So little faith in yourself?"

"No. I'm uninterested in them."

By now the girls were aware of the attention they were getting. To Sin's irritation, one of them smiled at him encouragingly. He glared and one of them, a petite redhead, instantly dropped her bold gaze.

In the next half hour, Boyd managed to collect a bunch of clothes Sin didn't look at, and the group of girls stood right behind them in line. They stared openly and murmured to each other, wondering if the two of them were gay. The question surprised Sin so much that he turned to level them with another deadly glare. The conversation came to an abrupt end.

Boyd did not appear to be paying attention, and Sin wondered whether he would have been offended by the comment. Sin supposed people were quick to assume that long-haired Boyd with his androgynous face and thin build was gay. Pair that with the two of them shopping together while Boyd nagged him about things he needed to keep warm and the assumption made sense. Other than that, Sin didn't know if Boyd was gay and had never considered his own orientation. The only people that had ever shown interest in him sexually were Lydia and Harry, and that was likely because both of them were insane. There had also been Thierry, but that had only been a weak attempt at manipulation.

Irritation turned to idle curiosity so Sin surveyed his partner. Boyd had good features and what would likely be a decent build if he ever gained weight. It was impossible to tell whether objectively noting that a person had good features implied actual attraction, though. When Sin examined several other people in the shop, he didn't find any of them particularly interesting. Maybe the Agency had burned the ability to find others attractive out of him.

SANTINO & AIS

It was bordering on pathetic that in twenty-eight years, Sin had never given it much thought. He bet that even Boyd had a better understanding of this type of thing, and he barely had an expression. It was bizarre to even consider Boyd having sex with someone.

The thought sparked interesting mental images in Sin's head, and he smirked.

Boyd was drawn out of his reverie. "What?"

"Nothing," Sin said, declining to explain.

ELEVEN

NEW YORK CITY was worse than Boyd had imagined.

Most people knew that the former metropolis had been decimated and subsequently abandoned during the war, but what stretched below their current safehouse was beyond even the devastation of the Wasteland. Smashed bridges rusted above rivers that shone gray, blue and chartreuse with pollution, thousands of decayed cars sat untouched on once-busy avenues, and the jagged remains of bombed high rises jutted up from the ground into a mustard-colored sky. It looked uninhabitable, and according to the government it was, but that did not stop people from attempting to take over the bits and pieces of land that still maintained resources.

Dì Zhì, a large faction made up of Chinese nationals, were one of the groups attempting to claim the remains of New York as their own. The organization rivaled Janus in strength and numbers, and the Agency wanted to know whether Dì Zhì was still operating solo or if they, like so many others, were being consumed by the Janus machine. With a lack of insight to the organization's global plans or a contact on the inside, Boyd and Sin had been sent to do reconnaissance and collect information.

They set up their base of operations in one of the upper floors of an abandoned apartment building in the area that had once been lower Manhattan. It had required them to climb several floors in the darkness, but the view from the floor-to-ceiling windows gave them a good vantage point of the area Dì Zhì had claimed from a group of local survivors turned scavengers.

"The exits are here." Boyd pointed to the array of images he'd laid across the floor. It had taken them a couple of days to identify the exact building Dì Zhì had commandeered, and another to sneak in and get an idea of the layout. "But the basement has stable electricity and is a more likely place to store electronic data." His finger moved to the screen of his tablet which displayed an old blueprint of the building.

"Although it would be best to enter the building via the nearest exit and go downstairs, that won't be possible. The basement is only accessible from a point inside the building with a high concentration of Dì Zhì operatives and security." Boyd glanced at Sin. "Realistically, there's no way to disguise ourselves in order to infiltrate so we'll have to enter undetected. Owen's source squats in a building nearby and gave him a guess as to when Dì Zhì seems the most active, which should give us an idea of the best time to enter."

Boyd showed Sin a simple simulation he'd generated of the mission using the blueprints for the layout. The simulation ran as he spoke, illustrating his plan in quick detail and showing the locations of the different areas.

"At 0800 hours they switch guards on the eastern entrance, and the same at 0810 on the northeastern. Since we don't know which way will be quicker and we don't want to garner attention, we should enter separately. You can take the eastern and I'll take northeastern. There are utility closets about fifty feet in on each of those corridors. That should provide an initial hiding place if necessary. The rotation will continue with a full sweep of the building until 0825 hours. These corridors seem to be the least convenient so they'll most likely receive less attention. If we hide there until the sweep is past, we will be able to proceed back through the areas that have already been checked."

The simulation continued to run while Boyd pointed at the screen to two different areas.

"Access to the basement is through here and here. I'll bring the decoder with me which should allow us to breach the security on the room which might hold their tech. It was the locked one in the basement. We'll have a ten minute window before the next group of guards moves through so we'll have to be quick. Egress will be back the way we came, behind the sweep. We'll split up at this intersection and leave through the doors we originally entered. Once outside, we'll have to avoid the exterior guards, so I suggest leaving through this alley to the north and going directly to the van. Provided there are no unforeseen difficulties, we should be done and leaving here by 0900 at the latest."

At some point, Sin had turned away from the simulation. He was lying across the floor on his stomach and peering out the windows through a pair of binoculars. "Sounds thrilling."

"We have to leave in a few hours so I'm going to get ready soon. I suggest you do the same."

"I'll be sure to do that."

Boyd frowned but chose to ignore the flippant response. He went over the mission again and returned to one of the apartment's bedrooms to get ready for the mission. He put on armor beneath his dark clothing and coat, and wore a black cap to bring less attention to his hair. Upon returning to the main room, Boyd saw that Sin was finally paying attention to the simulation. They left together without much discussion, stowed their equipment in the underground garage where they'd hidden the Agency van, and split up at the predetermined time.

He was able to slip in the building when the guards were distracted with a shift change. The rotations and guard sweeps came as expected and Boyd found the corridors of the planned route to be largely unoccupied. He only had to avoid hostiles once, and wondered whether Sin was finding it as easy as he was, or whether he'd run into any snags. It was entirely possible that without the information they'd been given ahead of time, the mission may have gone awry. Although Boyd wasn't running into any major problems, it was because he moved quickly, to pre-designated spots, on a precise time schedule. Without that, there were already over a dozen instances where he could have been caught.

By the time Boyd reached the basement he was surprised to see that Sin had already arrived since the senior agent had been scheduled to enter after a ten minute lag.

"That was fast," he observed as he removed his backpack. "How did you get here before me?"

"Took a different route."

Boyd looked up from his backpack. "What? Why would you do that? With the timing, that should have been the best route."

"My route was easier and faster."

A flash of irritation went through Boyd. After all that talk of being more involved as a partner, Sin still never really acted like one. He wouldn't get involved in the planning of missions, didn't pay attention during briefings, and didn't give any feedback even if he had a better idea. Instead, Sin just did what he wanted on his own terms. Boyd had spent hours plotting out their course, and Sin just strolled

SANTINO & AIS

in, one-upping him, and making him feel like a fool. Not to mention, if anything ever went wrong he would have no clue where Sin was because he was never where he was supposed to be. It was against everything Boyd had been taught at the Agency, and it frustrated him to no end.

"Yeah?" he asked, unable to keep the challenge from his tone. He yanked out the decoder and set it to work on the lock. "And exactly what route was it? Or did you just charge in without thinking as usual?"

Sin's expression went from bored to annoyed in a flash. "I can't figure out if it's funny or embarrassing that you actually think you have superior knowledge of how a mission is carried out."

"Well, there's a reason we're part of a unit. No one person knows best which is why we all work together, including using the intel we receive from the others. My plan was based on that intel. If you had a problem with it or saw a flaw, why the hell didn't you say so before we started?"

"Because you got it into your head that you're team leader and didn't bother to ask what I thought. I guess since I apparently charge in without thinking and don't know how to do a job I've been doing for over a decade, it wouldn't have occurred to you." After giving him a scathing look, Sin turned his attention to the stairwell and corridor.

"What, so now the great Sin Vega is too afraid to speak up to someone half his size?" Boyd scoffed. "Don't blame me for not saying anything when you had the chance. You never bothered saying anything even though you could have told me the plan was terrible after I pitched it to you. Nothing stopped you but your own apathy."

"You're an idiot. If this is how you're going to act when I don't follow your orders, I would have kept waiting in the van."

The decoder flashed to signify it was finished. Boyd pulled it off the lock and yanked open the door. "This has nothing to do with whose plan it is; it's about sticking to the plan itself. What's the point of being your partner when I never know what to expect from you? Or when you won't even tell me your opinion? I may as well go it alone like I used to."

"Well maybe next time you should ask why I went the way I did instead of acting like I'm a fucking moron who doesn't know how to do my job." Sin scowled at the corridor as if willing someone to arrive so he could kill them.

Boyd opened his mouth to angrily retort but thought better of it. Frustrated, he turned his back on Sin and stalked into the room. As expected, the combination of electricity and air conditioning made it an ideal place to store electronics. There were different gadgets, computers, and devices inside. Boyd leaned over the table at one of the laptops and booted it up, wondering whether it was more efficient to copy the data from multiple machines or just steal them. Ultimately, he thought stealing the laptop presented too great a risk of the information being lost or damaged since he did not have a secure place to store it. Only when he had begun copying data did Boyd look up to see Sin still glaring at him.

"Shouldn't you be watching the corridor and not looking at me?"

"I'm not looking at you."

Boyd raised an eyebrow but kept the retort to himself. He finished copying information from one machine and moved to another. The third, he saw, was actually a mini server which was easily slipped into his backpack. "You could at least look around."

"How would I know what to look for since I'm so fucking stupid?"

"I guess you wouldn't since you never pay attention, anyway."

"Yeah, what would I do without you here to guide me?"

Boyd's attention skidded up from the laptop, his teeth gritting. His anger was rising and it was becoming increasingly difficult to mask the emotion. "Why are you trying so hard to annoy me? Do you want to force an argument so you have an excuse to go back to the way it was before?"

"I don't need an excuse for anything. I can do whatever the hell I want."

"What is your problem?" Boyd nearly yelled. He managed to lower his voice just in time.

"You acting like I don't know what the fuck I'm doing is my problem! I should have known your nice routine was just an act."

"What the hell are you talking about now?" Boyd threw his hands into the air, aggravation making it impossible to stand still. "Stop making all these random assumptions!"

Sin turned, stalking back to the door. "Whatever."

With the tension nearly palpable, the downloading of the

information took forever. Even as Boyd kept his back turned to Sin, he couldn't help running through the mission in the back of his mind. When the download was complete, Boyd erased any indication that they had been there.

They barely looked at each other as they fled the building. The deserted streets flashed by them as they ran, navigating the city to reach the underground garage where they'd left the vehicle. Within minutes of exiting Dì Zhì's base, they were on their way out of the city. It required them to go further out of the way to get to a working tunnel to cross the river into New Jersey, but the only people who noticed them was a group of scavengers. They appeared more astounded by the sight of a working vehicle than anything else.

The drive into Pennsylvania was silent. Boyd was hyper aware of Sin's presence in the passenger's seat and refused to look at his partner, but the longer they went without speaking, the more the tension increased. By the time they were within the state, Sin was practically exuding anger.

When Boyd stopped for a red light, Sin opened the door and got out of the car.

"What the hell are you doing?" Boyd demanded, incredulous. "Get back in the car!"

"No. I want to walk." Sin shut the door although the window was still open. "Later."

"Sin, we're over thirty miles from Lexington!"

"I'll survive. Just go back. Tell them we're returning separately— they'll know I'm not far."

"Sin! What if something happens?" Boyd shouted out the window.

Sin didn't respond. He turned to leave the street and easily swung himself over the railing at the side of the road. His boots crunched over an old and long forgotten memorial cross that had been pegged into the earth there.

"Sin!" Boyd called again. He watched as his partner disappeared into a grove of trees nearby. With uncertainty and anger warring with him, Boyd was torn on whether to keep going or to pull over and follow. When it came down to it, he wouldn't be able to force Sin back into the van and it would likely cause another argument. Apparently he did whatever the hell he wanted whenever the hell he wanted it, on or off a mission.

"Goddamnit," Boyd hissed.

He put the van in drive and took off, trying to ignore the conflict that had arisen and focus on getting home. Unfortunately, it was impossible. The more space he put between them, the more frustrated he became. Twice, Boyd pulled over with the intention of turning back to find Sin. For all that he was angry with the man Boyd couldn't forget the image of Sin walking silently away. But ultimately, Boyd knew he would not be able to find Sin at this point. As reluctant as he was to do so, he set out again.

HOURS LATER, BOYD was pacing his living room.

Paranoia produced increasingly horrifying scenarios of Sin being captured, hurt, or so pissed off that he decided to do something rash just for the hell of it. After a short period of time it occurred to Boyd to check the live feed to Sin's apartment. When he pulled it up and found the place to be empty, the questions only grew. Guilt became a weight alongside worry, and it was all muddied by surprise that Boyd even cared in the first place. Not about Sin's safety, but about the cause of their initial argument.

What did it matter to him what Sin thought? Why should he care if Sin had been rude? Why did he give a damn if Sin thought his plans were stupid?

Yet it did matter. And Boyd did care. And he didn't understand why.

Time seem to stretch endlessly. Eventually, Boyd gave in and decided to check the live feed again. At that point, they had been separated for eight hours.

At first Boyd did not see any movement in Sin's apartment. He watched for several minutes and was about to close the feed when the apartment door opened and Sin strode in. Boyd felt such relief that at first he did not notice how angry Sin appeared. He stormed toward the bathroom, his lean body tense and movements rigid. His jeans were muddy and he was damp, likely from the rain that had started to fall in the past hour.

On the way to the bathroom, Sin stripped. The camera picked up flashes of smooth brown skin, scars, and a glimpse of his tattoo before Sin disappeared into the bathroom. When he did so, Boyd did not access that camera.

After ten minutes, Sin reappeared on the feed that showed the living room and kitchen. Even though his focus should have been elsewhere, Boyd found his gaze running down his partner's body instead of paying attention to his moody expression. Beads of water still clung to his sculpted chest, trailing along muscles that narrowed to hips that were in danger of being exposed by a towel that was knotted at his waist. The possibility seemed even more evident when Sin jerked the refrigerator door open and pulled out a carton of juice.

Sin tilted his head back and drank straight from the carton before shoving it back into the fridge in exchange for a candy bar. Even with candy in his hand, Sin was glowering at thin air. The scene was incongruous and yet so much like what Boyd had become accustomed to with Sin. He watched Sin finish eating in two bites before pacing the small area with increasing agitation.

And just like that, Boyd's guilt returned.

Did Sin really regret the moments when they'd made progress and gotten along? Did he really want things to return to the way they'd been in the beginning? The possibility stung.

Boyd could not deny that he'd come to appreciate having someone to talk to; someone whose fleeting expressions of interest or near-camaraderie felt like a victory over the suspicious glares from the past. He didn't want to lose all the progress they'd made simply because of one ill-timed argument.

A wave of uneasiness prompted Boyd to reach for his phone. He dialed Sin's number before turning to the computer again.

On the screen, Sin had paused to lean against the counter with his arms crossed over his chest. When the phone rang again, he shoved himself away from the counter and snatched his phone from where he'd tossed it in the other room.

"What?" he demanded without seeming to look at the screen.

"Hi." Boyd closed down the feed.

There was a brief silence and then a flat, "What do you want?"

"I wanted to make sure you'd made it back alright."

"I'm not entirely incompetent at traveling."

"I wasn't implying you were."

There was another pause before Sin said, "Well, as you can see I survived. Are we done?"

"No. Look—" Boyd sighed, bringing a hand to his forehead. "It wasn't my intention to insult you on the mission. I was frustrated."

This time the silence was longer. Eventually all Sin said was, "I see."

Boyd thought about turning on the live feed again so he could see Sin's expression, but he cast the thought aside. He paused, gathering his thoughts. For all that he spent his life inside his head, sometimes he found it difficult to explain to others what was going through his mind.

"It isn't that I don't value your opinion; I just didn't think you were interested in the planning. I thought it would be most efficient if I planned it based on research you likely didn't want to do, and I assumed if you had a better idea than what I presented then you would tell me. I'm just... I'm just doing what they taught me in my classes. That's how they said it works."

There was another long silence followed by a rustling sound. Eventually Sin said, "Why don't you come to the compound and we can discuss this in person."

Boyd raised his eyebrows. He'd half expected Sin to hang up on him. "Alright. Where would you like to meet?"

"Come to my apartment." The line went dead.

Boyd slid his phone in his pocket and, without giving it much debate, grabbed his keys and drove to the Agency. He had never been to Sin's apartment and did not know what to make of the situation, but at least it did not seem as though Sin wanted to give up on their partnership. When Boyd got to Sin's building, he saw that it was more heavily secured than others, so Boyd removed his identification to show it to the guards by the main entrance. Once they let him pass, Boyd took the stairs to Sin's floor and encountered yet another pair of guards. They looked at him, confused, and Boyd stared back. He had not expected this level of security for Sin, and at first did not know what to do.

"You can probably get in yourself," one of the men said. He gestured at the electronic lock on Sin's door. "Everyone else does."

Boyd nodded, hesitated, and then swiped his card more out of a desire to be away from the guards than anything else. He'd barely taken a step into the apartment before Sin appeared. He was shirtless but now wearing a pair of black sweatpants. Surprise flashed across his face before it morphed into a look of anger.

"Are you fucking kidding me?"

Boyd froze. "What?"

SANTINO & AIS

"Why do you have access to my door?"

"I don't know. Have you asked HR?"

"And so you take it upon yourself to just fucking barge in here?"

"You invited me over!" Boyd protested. "You were expecting me any time now. I didn't think it was such a problem."

"You didn't think walking into someone's home without alerting them to your presence is a problem? You people think you have so much power over me that you can do whatever the hell you want."

"Would you stop with these bullshit assumptions?" Boyd snapped. "You keep accusing me of all these thoughts I never have."

"Well, whatever fucking thoughts you have are obviously not making themselves seen in the way of your actions. You act like a self-righteous, condescending little bitch on the mission and now you walk into my apartment as if you have the right. It never crossed your mind that you're crossing a line? It never occurred to you that you're invading my privacy just like everyone else does every fucking day?"

By now, Sin's voice was steadily rising. He didn't seem to care about the guards, or the cameras if he knew about them, and the guards did not knock on the door to intervene in the argument. Perhaps they found it amusing since it had been their idea.

"Look," Boyd said evenly, trying to stay calm so one of them would be. "The guard told me to come in. I never would have even tried it but I didn't expect them to have so many people guarding you and didn't know what the protocol was. I won't ever use the card like that again."

Sin just shook his head and proceeded to stare at the wall.

"I don't have ill intent when it comes to anyone, Sin," Boyd said. "Least of all you. I have times when I get frustrated or do something without thinking, just like anyone. I'm sorry for my mistakes but none of the issues today have been purposeful on my part."

Sin didn't respond or react enough to show whether he was listening.

"I didn't want to argue," Boyd insisted. "I only came to apologize. Earlier, I was frustrated after having spent hours on something that was completely ignored. Maybe it seemed like I think I know more about missions than you but I don't. I'm used to getting above average grades in school, being ahead of my classmates. It's the only thing

I've ever been good at, so it's very... frustrating and demeaning to me to think I failed. And when I get frustrated I say things I don't mean, and sometimes you seem to assume the worst of me no matter what I do. And..."

Boyd hesitated. He knew this was all on camera but at the same time it was important to him that Sin heard what had been on his mind all day. "And I don't want that. I don't want you second-guessing me based on one or two events and ignoring everything else in between. I thought we were getting along better lately. I wanted it to stay that way."

Sin still didn't respond and Boyd sighed, dropping his hands at his sides. Weariness overwhelmed him. He didn't even know why he'd made the effort.

"Forget it."

Boyd turned to the door but before he could touch the handle, Sin grabbed his arm and yanked it back. Caught off guard, Boyd stumbled and tried to pull away but Sin did not budge. The resistance only made Boyd try harder even though it had zero effect.

"Just fucking wait," Sin said, refusing to release Boyd.

"Let go of me."

Sin was as strong and unmovable as a mountain. The reality of being unable to get away grew more pronounced, and a mote of alarm made Boyd's heartbeat skyrocket. Sin slammed Boyd back against the wall, pinning him and leaning in.

"I said wait."

The panic that had started to set in was sidelined when Boyd focused on Sin's eyes.

Boyd made a conscious effort to try to calm down but the remnants of panic made him hyper-aware of their proximity. The smell of Sin freshly showered; his damp hair against Boyd's face; and his mouth shockingly close. Sin's lips parted as if he was going to speak again, but he didn't. He just kept staring at Boyd, his fingers loosening although they did not fall away.

"Why?" Boyd's voice came out a little rough.

The response wasn't immediate. Although aggravation was evident in everything from Sin's posture to the grip of his hands, he remained pressed against Boyd. His gaze skimmed Boyd's face, analyzing every detail and lingering in some places longer than others

SANTINO & AIS

before his hands moved to brace against the wall on either side of Boyd's shoulders.

The reality of Sin's body so close to his own caused Boyd's thoughts to scatter. It was impossible not to think about the beads of water he'd seen trailing down Sin's bare torso, and impossible not to notice how gorgeous he was. Boyd's eyes drew to Sin's mouth, full and tempting, before he forced himself to look up again. Not that staring into those green eyes made things any easier.

"What do you want?" Boyd whispered.

"You—"

Sin aborted the sentence and sighed, the sound thick with frustration. It seemed like he wanted to say more but could not get the words out, so he wound up closing his eyes with his brows knitted together. In that instant, his head tilted forward until their faces brushed and their mouths were centimeters away. Boyd drew in a sharp intake of breath and Sin's eyes flew open. He took a quick step back as if realizing what he'd nearly done.

When frustration became confusion, Sin backed up further and burst out, "It's just that you're really fucking annoying."

The moment was broken. Boyd pushed away from the wall.

"*That's* what you wanted me to stay and hear?"

"Yes. Well, no. I don't fucking know. I just don't trust you. I don't trust anyone. And I don't want to."

"Well, I don't know what to say to that."

"Don't say anything," Sin snapped. "Just shut the hell up and let me try to talk. Look, I like getting along with you. But I keep expecting you to come out of nowhere and act like everyone else, so it makes me be a dick. And I don't know what to do about that because my paranoia isn't just going to disappear. Anytime anyone has pretended to be nice to me in the past, it's because they wanted something and as soon as they got it, I was a fucking animal again."

Boyd watched as Sin began to pace the room again, running his hands through his hair.

"I just don't trust people, okay?"

"Well, I don't entirely either," Boyd said simply. "But since we both like getting along with each other why don't we keep aiming for that?"

"I don't know how to get along with people." Sin seemed disgusted by the admittance. "I'm twenty-eight and you're the first person I ever had a normal conversation with. You can't expect much from me. And if you do, you will be sadly disappointed."

"I'm not particularly extroverted myself so I can't promise I'll do much better. But I'm willing to at least try for this partnership."

"Why?"

"Because it's a significant portion of my existence at this point and since I prefer to get along with you rather than not, I don't see why I shouldn't put in effort."

Sin did not look entirely convinced. "We'll see."

TWELVE

THEIR SIX-MONTH ANNIVERSARY as partners was marked by their most violent mission to date.

Boyd hit the floor and skidded before he could catch himself. When he looked back, he couldn't see anything around the crates. He ducked down, shielding his head as bullets shot crevices out of the wall above him. The sound of men shouting and screaming echoed in the warehouse. He couldn't make sense of anything except that within a matter of seconds, chaos had exploded around him.

A man careened past his view and hit the wall so hard Boyd heard a disturbing crack, and blood splattered around him in rivulets. Boyd jerked back and peered around the crates sheltering him. What he saw may as well have been a dream.

Sin was the eye of a storm. Both his guns were drawn, shooting in different directions. His bare arms gleamed with sweat and blood. His expression was set in that distant, grim look Boyd had seen on the videos. The face of death.

As Boyd watched, Sin killed five men in succession, blasting out the backs of their heads with perfect shots to the foreheads, or felling them where they stood by hits to the throat and chest. The ones who came close received violent kicks that sent them flying backward. Even as they fell, others came at Sin like cockroaches. He sheathed the guns so fast Boyd hardly noticed it happening, and soon the fight turned to bare hands. Throats were ripped out, shoulders dislocated and people thrown through the air as if they weighed no more than a paper doll. One hostile screamed as he was flung against another man behind him. The two fell in a tangle and were nearly trampled by another rush of hostiles swarming Sin.

Sin used one of his attackers as a human shield against a thrown knife, and even as the injured man looked down in shock, Sin snapped his neck with a motion that was effortless but caused immediate death. And within a heartbeat, Sin was already turning to take on more.

Boyd stayed hidden, knowing he was not skilled enough to throw himself into the fray but also found himself unable to stop watching the slaughter.

It ended with an aborted scream, the thump of a body falling, and then the sound of a single pair of boots walking across the floor.

As expected, Sin was the only one left standing. Blood streaked his face, splattered his clothes and dampened his hair. It was difficult to tell if any of it was his, but aside from a slightly halting gait when he strode to Boyd's side, Sin seemed fine.

"Set the charges anyway." Sin's face was devoid of emotion as he surveyed the room.

Boyd was certain that part of a scalp was caught on Sin's shoulder. Boyd averted his eyes and moved out from behind the crates.

It was like seeing a real life version of some of the video games he had once played.

There was no way to avoid the blood when Boyd dropped down to finish arranging the explosive, so his hands came away smeared red. He tried not to focus on that, or the bodies strewn about, but he could not stop his eyes from darting to each one. Limbs were skewed at odd angles and still faces stared in surprise. It was a caricature of life cut short. Multiple lives. And by a single man.

Once the explosives were set, Boyd approached Sin with the detonator in hand.

"I'm ready."

Sin turned to leave.

Boyd didn't detonate the explosives until they were nearly a block away. The explosion rocked the van and broke out windows on some of the neighboring buildings. Fire erupted, casting flickering shadows across the street as they drove away.

At their brief stop at the safehouse, Sin showered while Boyd packed and did a sweep of the room. They were gone within twenty minutes with Sin taking a short detour down an alley to throw his bloody clothing into a dumpster.

When Sin sat in the driver's seat, Boyd was relieved. Although his part in the mission had not been as physically taxing as Sin's, Boyd's mind was spinning and he felt exhausted.

A quick glimpse of Sin's face showed that he was half-hidden by the night due to the city lights flashing by them. It made the unreadable quality of his expression seem tenfold, and lent weight to the silence between them. Although Sin was clean, Boyd still couldn't look at him without remembering the blood coating his skin, or the flecks of brain and flesh spattered across his clothes like he was some *nouveau art* installation decorated by pieces of a corpse.

Boyd tried to focus on their surroundings and the drive, but continued to replay Sin dodging attacks with inhuman speed or swiping his arm out in a graceful arc that caused a fountain of blood to spray everywhere. Boyd thought about Sin running up the side of the wall like a wraith; gravity seeming to mean very little with his sights set on enemies, and the way he had flipped backwards with both guns blazing—multiple hostiles left dead before his feet even touched down.

Forty men against one. How were those odds possible in reality?

Boyd looked sidelong at his partner and caught Sin jerking his own eyes away. He didn't say anything but Boyd could see the tension in his shoulders.

Wondering if Sin was injured, Boyd tried to give him a subtle once-over but it was too difficult to see in the dark. He didn't think Sin had received anything more than superficial wounds, so it was possible he was just stressed by the direction the mission had gone.

After all, the original plan had been simple. Set explosives and take out a terrorist node. The intel claimed there would be fifteen people max but they had found closer to forty. An attempt to keep the operation covert had failed when one of the hostiles stumbled upon Boyd setting his final explosive. He'd barely glanced up to see a gun in his face before Sin had thrown him to safety and killed the gunman. And, in the process, started the violence.

It seemed like a lot of trouble just to keep him unharmed, and Boyd was still unused to the idea of Sin actually protecting him. Especially when that protection ended in a massacre.

The silent car ride allowed Boyd to analyze the situation to the point where everything seemed abstract and more confusing than it had been before. Forcing himself to stop, Boyd reemerged from his daze only to realize that Sin was looking at him again. And again, Sin averted his eyes as soon as Boyd noticed.

Sin was worrying his lip between his teeth, fingers white-knuckled on the wheel, and shoulders hunched forward. Everything about his posture and expression was so high-strung that Boyd felt compelled to break the silence.

"Are you alright?"

"My injuries aren't severe."

"You're very quiet."

"I don't have much to say."

"Usually you have something to say by now."

Sin grunted. It was clear that even if his injuries weren't severe, they were still causing him some degree of discomfort. He'd stopped hiding his wounds so completely only recently, but it was still surprising to see.

After nearly a full minute had passed, Sin said, "You weren't exactly looking very chatty yourself."

Boyd supposed it was true enough. "I was thinking."

"About what a freak I am?"

"No." Boyd frowned. "I won't deny that the mission underscored how dangerous you can be but you've also saved me twice. I don't entirely know what to make of you, but I can say for certain that I don't see you as the out-of-control, psychopathic monster others seem to, or that you may believe I do."

Sin did not answer but Boyd caught a glimmer of surprise in his face when they drove through the path of a street light.

"What?" Boyd asked.

"I just... didn't expect you to say that."

"Did you think I would hate you now?"

"No. But I thought you'd be afraid of me now. It would make sense."

"Would it have bothered you if it had?"

At that, Sin made a face. "Why do you always need so many details?"

"Why are you always so reluctant to answer when I ask?"

Sin released a long-suffering sigh. "Because you ask questions that are uninteresting to me."

"The answers would be interesting to me." Boyd looked out the window, noting that they were moving out of the city and onto the highway. "Should everything be solely according to what you want?"

"Yes."

Boyd snorted, but there was a faint curve of his lips. "If you say so."

Sin smirked and some of the rigidness left his shoulders. Even though he clearly did not want to admit it, Sin looked relieved to find that Boyd still did not fear him.

The fact that Sin cared at all was mystifying when so few people in Boyd's life gave much weight to his opinions, but he understood how it felt to be alienated from everyone else and not want to lose a single existing connection. Even so, the contradictions Sin represented—the way he was violent and harsh with others but quiet and uncertain around Boyd—made him feel almost... special. Like his existence actually mattered.

He almost scoffed aloud at that embarrassing thought, and was glad when the shrill scream of fire trucks in the distance interrupted his ruminating.

Sin's eyes flicked to the rear view mirror before turning on the radio. He found a local station and within the next twenty minutes, there was a special report of a large explosion on the outskirts of town. There was no indication that the authorities had more information so Sin switched the channel. Obnoxious pop music filled the car and, with a grimace, he shut the radio off.

Boyd wondered what music Sin liked but did not bother to ask. He attempted to once again lose himself in the relative peace of the drive, but the scenery was not very engaging.

Trees were dark lines in the night, their colorful leaves hidden in shadow, and broken up by signs proclaiming the distance to the next cities. Billboards that hadn't seen maintenance in years left strange messages in their wake; shredded advertisements only partially illuminated with half the words and faces missing. Boyd wondered how many of those places were still in existence and how many had become just one more ghost haunting peoples' memories.

With the darkness seeping in from outside and the rocking of the van, Boyd was lulled into a doze. It felt like his eyes had barely closed when he was awoken by a change in his surroundings. He sat up and squinted at the lights around him, unable to stop a jaw-cracking yawn. They had pulled in at a 24-hour rest stop.

"I want to eat before we get back." Sin pointed to the diner across the parking lot.

Boyd nodded, unsurprised. Since Sin could get anything he wanted when they were off compound, he usually liked to stop for food. They filled the van with gas and headed over to the diner, crossing the distance as Sin adjusted his jacket and pulled his hood up over his head. It was an action that Boyd had begun to notice more often, as if Sin was perpetually trying to hide when out in public. He usually failed. No matter how hard he tried, Sin stood out.

The diner was not very different than the other diners they'd visited in the past. No one paid attention to them when they arrived, which was one of the good things about rest stops. They offered anonymity since most people were just passing through.

The hostess, a girl with black curls and a bored look on her face, perked up when they approached. She took in Sin, who stared back grimly from beneath his hood, before turning to Boyd. She grinned and stared him down.

"Hi, I'm Danielle. Welcome to Sam's Shake Shack."

Boyd nodded politely in return. He hoped they ended up in a booth away from others so they didn't have to overhear any pointless conversations.

Danielle started to lead them to a booth at the front but Sin ordered in a flat voice, "The one at the back."

She shrugged. "Sure."

The booth he'd indicated was set apart from the rest of the crowd. Danielle placed menus in front of each of them.

"The special shake tonight is strawberry shortcake if you're interested. It's pretty awesome if you like that kind of thing." When neither of them replied aside from Boyd nodding, she sighed. "Your waiter will be right here."

Sin opened his menu and didn't bother to say anything in return.

"Thank you, Danielle," Boyd said.

Danielle gave Boyd a bright smile and returned to her station at the door.

"How cute," Sin commented from behind his menu.

"Hmm?" Boyd perused the menu for something that would fit his Agency-ordered diet. He was set to train with David again tomorrow and he was going to have to account for every calorie he'd consumed.

"I forget that you're blond."

"Is it possible for you to make it through a conversation without insulting someone in some manner?"

"Most likely not." Sin snapped his menu shut and put it on the table, leaning back against the booth. His eyes were barely visible from beneath his hood.

"Well, if you want to say something, just say it. I don't like it when people play games."

"I guess I won't take out my set of checkers then," was the disinterested reply. Sin looked around the diner, checking out the other patrons.

Boyd shook his head and skimmed the menu. He didn't feel like getting into a roundabout conversation.

The waiter came over and put glasses of water in front of each of them. He was tall, gangly, and had shoulder-length brown hair.

"Hey guys, I'm Steve and I'll be your waiter tonight," he said dully. He looked stoned. "The specials today are the golden-crusted chicken pot pie with buttermilk biscuits, the tricolor pasta tossed with lemon chicken, and the strawberry shortcake shake."

"I'll have the grilled chicken three-egg omelet." Boyd handed Steve the menu.

"Potatoes or hash browns with that?"

"Potatoes, please."

Steve nodded, not writing anything down. "White or wheat toast?"

"Wheat."

"'Kay." Steve turned to Sin expectantly.

There was a pause where Sin stared at Steve and then asked, "What's a pot pie?"

There was another pause as Steve tucked some hair behind his ear and looked skeptical. Then he shrugged. "Uh. It's like, chicken, potatoes, peas and carrots and gravy baked into this crust stuff like a pie. It's pretty good. The biscuits are awesome, too. Buttery and stuff."

Sin considered this. "I want that. And a black and white shake."

"Cool. Drinks?"

"Just water for me," Boyd put in.

"Same."

Steve nodded. "'Kay. Let me know if you change your mind."

When the waiter left, Boyd returned to his observation of the other customers. Some men who were clearly truckers were at the counter and a number of customers were dotted throughout the room.

One woman was leaning against the table looking thoroughly despondent as she let her half-finished shake slowly melt in front of her. She kept dipping in the long spoon, pulling up bits of the half-melted ice cream, and letting it fall back into the glass. One of the truckers was watching her in between bites of his meal.

"I wonder what these people would say if they knew what I'd just done," Sin commented.

"I don't know." Boyd took in the mannerisms and expressions he could see. Everyone appeared, for the most part, very ordinary. "I imagine most of them wouldn't be able to conceive of it, let alone know how to react."

Sin contemplated the other customers again. "I think they'd be disgusted that we're capable of sitting down to have a nice meal afterward."

"Probably."

Boyd wondered why the idea of food didn't disturb him, but knew he couldn't change what had happened any more than he could change the functions of his body. There had been a time in his life when the blood and death would have been too much for him to handle, but those days were long past, and the Agency had helped to deaden the sentiments even further.

"Some of them probably wouldn't care, though." Boyd gestured at the woman. "She seems too depressed to notice much of anything around her. I wonder what her story is."

Sin finally pushed the hood away from his face. "Whatever her problem, big boy in the red jacket seems to want to solve it for her."

"He certainly does," Boyd mused. "I don't think he has a chance, though."

Steve came back with Sin's shake and placed it in front of him. It was impressively large.

"Anything else yet, guys?" When they both declined, Steve left again.

Sin stirred his straw in the shake and eyeballed it. He leaned forward and took a long sip, and then nodded as if in approval.

"I'm surprised you didn't get one of the other shakes," Boyd said. "Some of them sounded as though they may be sweeter than that."

"They also sounded like they'd make me vomit." Sin sat back and stirred the spoon, mixing in the whipped cream. "However, I may still get dessert."

"You have the strongest sweet tooth of anyone I've ever met. Only you would even consider dessert after a large shake like that."

Sin drank some more. "Sugar deprivation as a child."

"You're going to make yourself diabetic."

That was met with a scoff. "Like I'll live long enough to suffer the effects."

Boyd shrugged. "If anyone would in this line of business, it'll be you. Your skills are uncanny. I doubt you have to worry about much on missions for the foreseeable future."

"Aw shucks sweetheart, you're going to make me blush," Sin said around his straw.

"Oh, is that all it takes?" Boyd drawled. "I was under the impression your sensibilities were far less delicate. Sometimes you seem shameless."

Sin stopped drinking his shake. "Why?"

Boyd couldn't help a small smile. "I was teasing you. Nothing ever seems to get to you so if all it took to make you blush was a veiled compliment, I would be surprised."

"Oh." There was a pause. "It's somewhat sad that saying I'm less likely to die is a compliment."

"It is."

The waiter came by again, this time with a tray filled with plates of steaming food. He asked them again if they needed anything else and when Boyd shook his head, he left.

Boyd started with the omelet. Since it was the protein, it was the most important thing to eat. The food wasn't bad. He was hungry enough that anything warm and filling was welcome. Sin was devouring his pot pie at a rapid pace and using his large, fluffy biscuits to sop up gravy.

They ate in silence until Sin commented, "The hostess is noticing you again."

Boyd sighed under his breath. He did not follow Sin's gaze. "I wish she wouldn't."

"Why? She's pretty enough."

"Because I'm not interested. And even if I were, it's not as though it would matter. We'll be leaving soon and I won't be by here again."

"If she's leering at some man in a truck stop, I highly doubt she has a long term involvement in mind."

Boyd refused to look up from his food. "It doesn't change anything for me."

"Why?"

Boyd opened his mouth to say something dismissive but he stopped when he saw Sin had actually paused in eating. It was rare for Sin to show genuine curiosity in him and even rarer for him to ask personal questions.

Ironically, he'd assumed that Sin had made the same assumption so many others had, and he was reluctant to change that when they'd finally started to get along. He did not relish the idea of facing judgment from Sin the way he had from so many other people, his mother included. But it was likely better to get it over with now.

"Because I'm gay."

Sin pointed his fork at Boyd. "So if it was an attractive man would you go off with him?"

"I said I was gay, not that I have sex with everyone I see who's passably attractive. I'm not particularly interested in flings with anyone, whether or not they're male."

"Oh."

Sin speared another mound of his pot pie and chewed it slowly, staring at Boyd without much of an expression on his face.

Boyd hesitated, fork in hand. "Is this going to cause a problem for us as partners?"

This earned him one of Sin's half-skeptical, half-annoyed faces— the ones that implied he thought Boyd was ridiculous. "It doesn't matter to me one way or the other. I was just wondering if you'd ever actually been with a man."

"Ah." Boyd supposed it didn't matter if he answered that, especially since he often asked questions of Sin. "Yes, I have."

"Oh." One of Sin's dark eyebrows rose higher than the other. "Weird."

"Why is that weird?"

"Because most of the time you have zero personality. I can't imagine you being intimate with another human being."

"I hate to disappoint you, then."

Sin just shrugged, turning his attention to his food and occasionally the people around him.

As Boyd ate, he found his attention continuously returning to his partner. Although they'd eaten at diners before, for some reason it struck him today how strangely normal this all was. And how he actually kind of liked it. He enjoyed the chance to have a conversation with Sin, even if it was on topics he hadn't ever planned to come up between them.

Of course, the topic just made Boyd wonder about Sin's preferences and sexual experience. The man was undeniably attractive, and part of Boyd wished he hadn't been assigned a partner who looked like he could pass as a model on a worldwide circuit. His body alone was enough for Boyd to find his attention straying before he thought to control it, but the combination of Sin's face and the raw power he possessed only made it that much better.

Boyd could still recall Sin's hands that night in the apartment, and the way Sin had held him still without causing pain even though he was capable of so much destruction with the same strong hands.

Neither of them had ever brought that night up again, but Boyd couldn't deny the confusion that had come from that hard body pressed against him. Sometimes, when his thoughts wandered during quiet moments, Boyd remembered Sin's breath curling against his lips and those eyes, those damn unforgettable eyes, so close to his own.

Boyd skewered a potato and chewed on it in contemplation.

Although Sin was often glowering at others or being sarcastic, the more Boyd learned about his partner, the more he felt like he was getting reeled in. Boyd did not know what made Sin more attractive, that glare that fended others off and lent mystery to him, or the intriguingly normal and, at times, uncertain way Sin could be at quiet times like this.

Again, Boyd wondered what Sin's past was like with others. Did the fact that he'd pressed Boyd against the wall mean he was attracted to men, or had it all been a misunderstanding? How many people, if any, had braved that glower for intimacy? Although most agents were afraid of him, had that always been the case? He hadn't hesitated to ask Boyd about sleeping with the hostess, as if it would be perfectly normal to go to the bathroom for a quickie between a meal and dessert. Was that Sin's norm? One night stands with whoever was interested?

"What about you?" Boyd realized after the words left his mouth that he'd let the silence stretch a bit too long, lending the question a sudden air.

"What about me, what?"

"Your interests or relationships."

Sin stirred his straw around in the milkshake, regarding Boyd. It was impossible to tell what he was thinking, but at least he didn't brush off the question the way he would have in the past.

"There's not much to talk about in that regard."

"Who are you interested in, then? Men? Women?"

"I've grown to despise both."

Sin must have had some unfortunate ends to relationships in the past to have gotten to that opinion. It lent more questions, including whether that meant Sin was bisexual, but Boyd didn't voice them. He didn't think Sin would answer and even if he would, he didn't know what he would do with the information anyway.

They didn't say much through the rest of the meal. Boyd could feel the weight of Sin's gaze on him more than once, which wasn't unusual. Sin had a tendency to watch him on and off since they'd met. In the beginning, he had clearly been waiting for Boyd to slip up. Then it had seemed liked he was trying to figure out Boyd's motivations. Later, Sin just studied him, as if perplexed to find that someone like Boyd existed, or perhaps trying to determine what made Boyd tick.

Whatever the case, it was distracting and Boyd did his best to ignore it.

When they left, Danielle was sitting on a bar stool in a quiet conversation with one of the waitresses. After he and Sin passed he overheard her musing, "He's probably gay, anyway."

Boyd shoulders tightened. He barely resisted the urge to look back in exasperation or speed his steps. Sin waited until they were out in the dark parking lot to comment.

"What's your problem?"

"Danielle. I'm tired of people making such automatic assumptions that I'm gay just because of how I look. It's a stereotype."

"Hmm." Sin grasped Boyd's chin, moving closer as if to examine his face. His fingertips slid along Boyd's skin, brushing his neck before falling away. The feel of that gentle touch was so unexpected that Boyd almost stumbled. He barely heard Sin's comment.

"Maybe it's the hair."

Boyd's lips parted but he didn't know what to say. His skin tingled maddeningly where Sin's fingers had brushed it, and he resisted the urge to slide his own hand over the area. It was the second time Sin had touched him without warning, and again Boyd felt a thrill go through him and knot up his stomach.

"Could be," he said softly.

Sin didn't answer and soon they were back on the road to Lexington.

There was no way Boyd was going to be able to sleep when he was so acutely aware of Sin's proximity. A shiver shot up his spine at the idea of Sin reaching out to him again.

Part of him wanted those long fingers to slide back and tangle in his hair. That same part of Boyd couldn't help wondering what it would have been like had their lips touched that night in Sin's apartment. How would Sin taste? How firmly would he have held Boyd if they'd kissed? How would it have felt to be wrapped in those powerful arms, held tight against that powerful body?

Boyd was disturbed by his own train of thought but still found himself staring at Sin openly. He knew his partner was aware of it, but Sin didn't seem at all uncomfortable with the attention. His demeanor didn't shift at all until they drew closer to the Agency and, at that point, Sin's eyes became hooded and his body was once again rigid with the slightest trace of anxiety.

"Why don't you ever just run away?" Boyd's question, once again, seemed too abrupt in the quiet.

"Where would I go?"

"I don't know. Anywhere but the Agency. You could flee to another country where they don't have a strong reach."

"I wouldn't be any use on the outside. Someone who can slaughter a warehouse full of hostiles and still maintain an appetite isn't exactly inclined to the domestic life."

"Maybe, but have you tried? There are many types of jobs out there even in civilian life. Is the idea of a domestic life all that's stopping you?"

"No. It just wouldn't work."

"Why not, though? Are you worried about them noticing too soon if you left on a mission? Because if so I could cover for you."

The comment caused Sin to look away from the road. "Why would you ever do that?"

"Why wouldn't I? I'm your partner, so your well-being is important to me. I've seen the way you're treated at the Agency so if you wanted to leave, I wouldn't blame you. I could easily tell them I lost you on a mission."

"Did it occur to you, in this fantastic plan, that they would terminate you for losing me?"

Boyd waved his hand in a dismissive gesture. "It wouldn't matter. I'll die soon anyway. It may as well have some meaning by helping you. It would probably be the most useful thing I could do with my life."

Sin scowled.

"What?"

"I just think you're brain dead sometimes. You're almost like what happens when a completely thoughtless person meets a borderline one." A pause. "Besides, it would never work. This collar cannot be removed without surgery and it has a tracking chip inside."

"What if you found a black market surgeon who could remove the collar?"

Sin sighed. He never seemed to have much interest in the conversation if it was focused on him, especially if it was sympathetic in any way. "They'd have tracked me down by the time I was ready for the procedure to be performed. The Agency has connections internationally. We also have a European division. And in addition to that, the procedure is complicated. The collar is situated in a way which makes it possible to sever my jugular during removal. I don't know any random black market surgeons who I'd trust to not accidentally cut my throat."

"That does make it problematic. I see your dilemma."

Once again Sin just shook his head.

"Well," Boyd said eventually. "If the situation ever changes, my offer stands."

Sin didn't bother to reply.

When they got to the Agency and parked in the garage, Boyd hesitated when he got out of the van. He found himself strangely unwilling to leave Sin. It felt a bit awkward, as if he was acting like they were two people on a date trying to decide whether or not they should kiss at the front door.

"I suppose I'd better write the report..."

"I'll go too."

"You will?" Boyd asked in surprise.

"If it's some private thing you like to do, then I won't."

Boyd laughed. Trust Sin to make writing a report sound like he was going off to masturbate. "I do prefer the old library but I assure you, I'm not doing anything that can't handle a witness or two."

Sin's eyes caught on Boyd and held. "Let's go then."

On the way to the library, they encountered only one agent who ended up in the elevator with them. She appeared alarmed by Sin's presence and shifted as far from him as she could. Sin didn't seem to notice or care. Maybe he was used to it. He said nothing and followed Boyd to the technology station in the library.

Once they got there, Boyd typed the report while Sin watched.

At first Boyd tried to ignore it, but Sin's presence was very distracting. Boyd thought maybe Sin was making sure he wasn't being disingenuous and writing horrible things about the scene at the warehouse, but Sin didn't comment on the report at all. After several minutes, Boyd realized that Sin was staring at him. Only him. Not the computer at all.

The first time their eyes met, Boyd's fingers stilled on the keyboard and his stomach fluttered again. He wondered what Sin was thinking. What he wanted. How it could possibly be worth Sin's time to have followed him up here only to stare at him while he worked. Whatever the reason, Boyd found that he did not mind the attention.

After some time, Boyd sent the report and closed out of all the programs.

"Did you make it good?"

"Did I ever," Boyd said with a smile. "Stories will be told for years to come about this one."

"It's always good to have something to add to my résumé."

This time, Boyd outright laughed and did not miss the way Sin's lips curved up in return.

"Don't forget; you can put me down as a reference as well."

Sin snorted and pulled his hood up again. "I suppose I should go back to my apartment before they sent out a battalion."

"I should probably go home, too." Boyd couldn't muster much conviction. He paused and added, "We could walk out together..."

It sounded so stupid that he wished he could take it back. But if Sin found the comment odd, he didn't let on. He didn't even make a joke about it or twist the words like he normally would.

"Okay."

Boyd couldn't get the stupid comparison about dates out of his mind, which was ludicrous considering the circumstances. Sin was one of the only people he'd spent any amount of time with in a long time, but Boyd had spent time with Ryan as well. And as far as date analogies went, going to someone's apartment to eat dinner and watch shows fit much better than finishing a report about mass killings.

So why couldn't he ignore the flush of pleasure he felt at being able to extend his time around Sin a scant few minutes? Why couldn't he ignore the fact that Sin was so attractive? And, most of all, why couldn't he ignore that Sin had appeared equally reluctant to part as well?

They left the Tower and again stepped out into the clear night, Boyd tipping his face up toward the sky. Although autumn was cooler than it had been in his childhood, he couldn't deny that there was something soothing about the crisp air and colorful leaves that accompanied October. As they stood beneath one of the street lamps, Boyd's attention was drawn to the space around them.

The buildings of the compound were like statues in the night, but he could see spots of color scattered across them where lights glowed through curtains and windows. There were probably other agents returning home from missions right now, and still others getting ready to depart. In the quiet of the night that thought made him feel, just for the moment, like he was part of a greater whole. It was reassuring after having felt isolated for years.

They walked for a while but paused at the point where their paths would diverge.

"I'm parked over there."

Sin nodded and again made sure his hood was pulled down low. "See you around."

Boyd nodded and the two of them parted. He glanced back once on his way to his car. Sin was walking toward his building, his black clothing making him a tall, dark figure that slid in and out of the shadows like an apparition.

THIRTEEN

EUGENE YARDLEY WAS different in both attitude and appearance than any of the other insurgents Boyd had dealt with thus far in his career at the Agency. Up until now most of their assignments had dealt with recon, intelligence gathering, negotiating with informants, or small-scale attacks on disorderly factions that were being scouted by Janus. Eugene was a different case entirely, and Sin wondered how his partner planned to handle him.

The man was a former Janus operative who looked as if he should be watching a tennis match at a country club rather than standing in a back alley in a shady part of Seattle. His dark eyes were alert behind thin-framed glasses, and he did not seem intimidated by them at all. Eugene appeared nonchalant but the way his bodyguards surrounded him showed that he was not taking any chances.

Apparently, Janus was as fond of deserters as the Agency was. Defection led to death.

Sin wasn't involved with the actual negotiations and he wanted it over and done with. Their position in the alley was not ideal for an altercation. The street was narrow and surrounded by buildings with gaping windows, all of which gave a sniper a perfect line of sight. There was no place for cover other than a dumpster, and Sin had the suspicion that Eugene's bodyguards were more serious than common street thugs. If the kid could afford cashmere sweaters and diamond-encrusted watches in the post-war economy, he could afford professional killers. Fortunately, they didn't appear to be dabbling in gene-splicing or bionic modification.

"I'd ask how you boys found me but I'll assume you weren't the clever ones doing the finding."

"We have our sources," Boyd said.

"I doubt you have anything. You two are just little messengers for whichever government agency is currently trying to nail Janus." Eugene smirked. "Which is it this time?"

"We represent an independent group that is unrelated to the government." Boyd's expression remained impassive, the lie rolling off his tongue with ease. "I imagine you already heard of us from your time in Janus. We are often referred to simply as the Agency."

A dark smile stole across Eugene's face. "Right."

"We have some things we'd like to discuss but perhaps there's a better setting than this?"

"The setting suits me fine. I didn't know you Agency boys were so high maintenance." Eugene looked up at Sin and did not seem surprised when Sin's flinty expression didn't change.

"The ambiance doesn't concern us." Echoing the words, Boyd leaned against the wall nearest him, the dirty bricks catching on his jacket. "I simply thought you may be hesitant to discuss potential business in the open where anyone could overhear, especially given Janus' distaste for former members."

"I'm not fond of repeating myself."

As always, Boyd was unperturbed. "I'm sure your time is valuable, I will make this short. Our organization is interested in purchasing information from you. As you've recently been running into some financial difficulties and the information we seek is likely no longer of use to you, we feel it could be mutually beneficial for all."

Eugene rocked on the balls of his feet. It seemed more like he was considering negotiating the price on a new car rather than whether or not he would sell information on an organization that the United States considered domestic terrorists.

"While I'm sure it must be difficult for people such as yourself—meaning opinion-less lackeys who are sent on errands and kill quests without much say in what's happening or understanding of why it is—I'm... not. Is there a particular reason why the Agency thinks I'd start helping them now?"

"You're liable to be targeted by Janus as a traitor which no doubt would result in your torture and death." Boyd's shoulders lifted in a minute shrug before he moved on with the bluff. "Information from our sources implies Janus may be closing in on your location. We have the ability to aid in your disappearing from the grid should you choose to work with us. Depending on the information you provide, we could offer even better services such as a new identify and safe location."

This time Eugene aimed his cocky smile at his guards. "Am I hearing a broken record? I asked why I would help the Agency. I only left

SANTINO & AIS

because I didn't like what they were doing down south, not because I'm suddenly going to switch sides. If you think my loyalty to their cause has weakened, think again. You are nothing more than filth that blindly serves a government which sees itself as sovereign of the world. Eventually Janus or someone like them will crush you all and the citizens of the world will take back power."

Boyd glanced at Sin.

So much for plan A. If Eugene wasn't going to be of use, his continued existence was unnecessary. Marshal Connors wasn't taking any chances with Eugene leaking information to Janus that the Agency had sources close enough to feed them information on their defectors.

Negotiation was out. Neutralizing was in.

Sin moved. Within two blinks, one bodyguard lay on the ground with a bullet in his head while the other was flung across the alley to crash into a brick wall. The scene exploded into motion as the remaining guards rushed Sin. As Sin had suspected, these guys were well trained.

Sin traded attacks with one of the more skilled of the bodyguards and, in his peripheral vision, saw Eugene fleeing the alley. Baring his teeth in annoyance, Sin evaded a jab at his throat, twisted out of the way of a knee to his side, and barely dodged a bullet careening past his head. He flipped backwards and allowed his booted foot to crush the other man's throat in the process.

"Get cover!" he shouted at Boyd.

Sin dodged another bullet and sprinted down the alley after Eugene. The ground was damp from recent rain and Sin could hear the men behind him splashing through the puddles with heavy steps. The sound of the guards chasing him lessened as his legs pumped faster, distance growing between them and him. Eugene was moving like a man possessed, managing to somehow keep a block between them as he shot alarmed glances over his shoulder. His calm demeanor had vanished, leaving a pale young man who was terrified and likely knew without doubt that he was within seconds of the end of his life.

Ready to be finished with the mission, Sin moved faster. There were no civilians in the area, but if Eugene got any further, they'd hit the main street. Abandoning his plan to do it soundlessly, Sin opted instead for speed. He raised his gun and shot Eugene twice in quick succession in the back of the head. The ex-Janus operative dropped to the ground. Blood pooled into the gutter, mixing with rainwater.

Within the space of one second and the next, Sin had turned on his heel and run back the way he'd come. Somehow, he'd failed to realize that the sound of pursuit had died away.

A strange feeling churned Sin's gut in knots and skipped a beat in his heart. Distantly, Sin recognized it as fear.

Cursing himself, Sin raced back to the original location of the meeting. It had been further than he'd thought—several blocks, and two avenues. The seconds it took to make his way back stretched unbearably as Sin realized that he'd fucked up by letting Boyd out of his sight.

The sinking feeling was justified when Sin skidded back into the alley. Boyd was sprawled on his side with the remaining bodyguard standing over him. Sin raised his weapon and unloaded into the man, barely pausing before he ran to Boyd and pushed the corpse aside.

"Boyd!"

Boyd's jacket was ripped and damp with blood, as was his hair. A quick assessment of their surroundings told the story easily. After dispatching one of the hostiles, Boyd had fallen and slammed against the edge of the dumpster, likely hitting his head. The injury beneath his clothing was a mystery in the shadows of the alley, but it felt like a flesh wound.

"Boyd, get up," Sin snapped.

Boyd's eyebrows drew down and his face contorted with pain.

"We need to get out of here," Sin said, looking around again. In the distance, he could hear the faint sound of a siren.

After a second, Boyd groaned and made an effort to rise. When he was slouched, his hand went to his head where the blood matted his hair, standing out against the pale blond.

"Ow," he groaned.

"What the fuck happened?" Sin demanded.

"I don't know..." It was unclear whether Boyd didn't know the answer to Sin's question or if he was still trying to understand the situation.

"Forget it."

Sin stood up, grinding his teeth with irritation as he gingerly pulled his partner to his feet. He slid an arm around Boyd's waist and crushed him against his side, more carrying than supporting. Boyd stumbled alongside him, fingers clutching at Sin's clothing. It would have been easier to toss Boyd over his shoulder and run, but Sin was loath to draw attention to them so soon. He took as many turns as possible to put distance between them and the alley.

It wasn't long before the sirens grew louder and Sin had to give up on being discreet. When Boyd barely reacted, Sin cursed again and picked Boyd up fully. He could feel the warmth of blood against his own shirt when Boyd's jacket pressed against it. The fear grew stronger, stabbing at Sin and heightening his adrenaline.

The labyrinth of streets took ages to navigate. Sin moved without thinking, mind calling upon the map he'd studied before the meeting with Eugene, and calculating the distance to their motel. Only once did he have to duck into the doorway of a closed shop to escape notice. A group of drunken young people were stumbling by and Sin slid sideways, blocking Boyd's bloodied face and hair from view. It likely looked like they were doing something unsavory but, at the moment, he didn't give a shit. Taking the opportunity to examine Boyd further, Sin ignored the catcall that they drew from a passerby.

"Are you more alert?" Sin canted forward to hiss into Boyd's ear and reached up to seek the wound with his fingers. There was definitely a gash. It was bleeding a lot, but it was slowly clotting.

Boyd nodded, his movements slow and cautious. Pain was a faint undercurrent to his words. "I think so."

"Can you run? The motel is another twenty minutes away."

Again, Boyd nodded despite his pinched expression. "I can, but my chest—there's a wound. I'll slow you down."

"I can carry you," Sin added quickly. "You're bleeding a lot. It may be better."

Relief was unmistakable in the slump of Boyd's shoulders. "Okay."

As soon as the noises of the group disappeared down the block, Sin picked Boyd up and began running through the darkness again. He could feel Boyd's face pressed against his chest and his arms tight around his neck, and beneath the layers of their clothing, Sin could feel the beating of Boyd's heart.

Everything went by in a blur as Sin ran to their motel. It was in as equally shady an area as where they had met Eugene, but several portions of the city hadn't regained their stature after the economic collapse. The end result was boarded up businesses that had never acquired new owners, copious amounts of beggars, streetwalkers and drug dealers in equal numbers.

Their motel was one of the few in the area that afforded separate units in a ranch style that didn't require going near the management office. Sin moved silently through the shadows, melting into them and then separating himself once he reached the unit they'd requested. It was the one farthest from the parking lot and closest to the tree line of the surrounding area.

Sin set Boyd down when they were in the surveillance camera's range. He supported Boyd as if helping a drunken friend and Boyd played along, although Sin suspected that the stumbling wasn't entirely staged. When their door shut, Boyd doubled over by a garbage can.

"Goddamnit." Sin locked the door while Boyd got sick, securing the room and pulling the curtains shut.

When it was over, Boyd slumped against the wall with a gasp. Sin was already by his side, kneeling on the floor and undoing the buttons on Boyd's jacket. He pushed it aside and saw that the long-sleeved shirt Boyd wore beneath was cut open in an arc, the wound bleeding steadily. Not hesitating or waiting to ask Boyd's opinion on the matter, Sin picked him up again and crossed the room. Getting the motel room bloody would only draw attention to who had been occupying it once they were gone. Especially with the news of murders nearby. The last thing they needed on top of a trip to medical was having to explain the PR nightmare to Vivienne if Seattle cops started investigating.

"Do you know what I'm doing?" Sin demanded as they entered the bathroom.

Boyd inclined his head. His breath came out in a pained hiss and he muttered something incoherent. The only word Sin made out was "mess."

Glad that they wouldn't have to argue about this at least, Sin ripped the shower curtain aside and set Boyd down on the tiled floor inside. Both of them were covered in blood by this point so Sin switched the shower on—allowing the water to spray close to where they were crouched. It hit Boyd's face and hair indirectly, and Boyd's eyes shot open.

The water rinsed the blood off Boyd along with the filth that had collected in his hair from the alley. It wasn't the most convenient option but it was the one that allowed for as little movement of Boyd's head as possible after he'd been jolted around in their egress.

"I need to wash out these wounds without making this whole room look like a crime scene."

Sin knelt in the shower floor next to Boyd. The water was hitting Sin's side and soaking through his shirt but it didn't matter. He'd have to change anyway unless they made the trip across the country in bloody clothing.

At least it seemed to be making Boyd more alert. He reached up to pat at his shirt which was becoming damp from the water. Then, he pointed at his shoes.

"What about…" Without waiting for a response, Boyd leaned forward. His fingers were clumsy as he started to untie the laces of his boots.

"Forget that," Sin snapped, pushing his partner back against the shower wall. He immediately cursed himself for not being gentler. "Just be still."

Sin stood up and backed out of the shower, kicking off his own boots only because they would track blood across the carpet. The med kit wasn't out like it should have been in case of an emergency, but they hadn't anticipated injuries for such a small-scale mission. Swearing and ignoring the building tension in his body, Sin forced himself to focus solely on the matter at hand. His own issues could wait.

Unzipping the duffel bag with more force than necessary, Sin dug out the med kit and belatedly took off his gun. It was soaked from the water. In his haste, he'd forgotten to remove it before jumping in the damn shower. Stupid. When had he become so completely unprofessional over a couple of fucking flesh wounds?

Grinding his teeth in agitation, Sin turned away from his weapon. It would have been smarter to take it apart and let it dry out but that was less important now. If anyone came bursting in for whatever reason, the mood he was in would guarantee a throat ripped out, anyway. Guns weren't something he relied on.

He stripped his shirt off upon reentering the bathroom and crouched in front of Boyd. His partner was awake and pressing a hand to his head. He had managed to kick off his boots. They lay haphazardly on the bathroom floor.

Pushing Boyd's hand away, Sin examined the head wound again and saw that it was not very deep. He checked for signs of swelling or any sunken areas but found none. Ignoring the relief that met with this discovery, Sin tilted Boyd's chin up. Their gazes locked and Boyd's golden eyes finally appeared to have focused.

"Are you good?"

"The water helps."

Sin's fingers splayed across Boyd's face, pushing wet hair to the side. He let his hand stay there, pressed against Boyd's cheek, but then he shook his head and let it fall away before reaching for the antibiotic ointment.

"How the hell did those two idiots jump you?"

Boyd tried to sit up straighter, his damp shirt squeaking against the tiled wall of the shower. "I took care of one and two came back at me. One cut me and then I got him. The other was too close and disarmed me. Then I fell."

Sin applied the ointment to the wound, his voice coming out gruff. "That's the last time we split up. Got it? I run, you fucking run."

"Okay," Boyd said, subdued.

While tending to the deepest part of the gash Sin tried to be gentle, but Boyd winced and jerked away. He reached up to grasp Sin's wrist, not applying pressure or pushing Sin away, but merely pressing his fingers against Sin's skin. Sin stilled and looked down, meeting Boyd's eyes.

Boyd only looked up at Sin and nodded a single time. Droplets of water ran down the planes of his face, hugging the contours of his lips and chin. In that instant, an image flitted across Sin's mind... Him pressing Boyd against the wall as the younger man panted furiously, and the barest graze of their mouths.

Sin inhaled deeply, his body warming. The feel of water sluicing down his arm snapped Sin out of the daze, and he jerked his attention away. He shut off the water. A few drops fell from the shower head while water tinged pink with blood flowed toward the drain.

Clearing his throat, Sin backed off and grabbed a thick wad of gauze. "Hold this against the wound."

Boyd's fingers brushed against Sin's as he obediently took the gauze.

Clenching his jaw, Sin tried to ignore the deranged reaction his body was having to Boyd. Instead, he reached out to cut the already-destroyed shirt down the middle. Before he could do it, Boyd shot his hands out and threw himself backward. His knees snapped up, keeping Sin away.

"No—" The word wrenched out of Boyd. "Don't."

Sin leaned back in surprise, seeing raw terror in Boyd's face. He looked one heartbeat away from tearing away from Sin and fleeing the room.

Baffled, Sin could only stare. He had no idea what could have caused such an extreme reaction, especially in someone so unemotional as Boyd, and he felt a brief flash of impatience. He didn't know how deep the laceration was or how much blood Boyd had lost. They didn't have time for this shit; not when they were expected at the airport within the next several hours.

But the fear in Boyd's eyes stopped him.

"What if I just rip the part where the wound is?"

Even this suggestion scared Boyd. He remained coiled against the wall like a feral animal. The seconds dragged with Boyd panting harshly, not moving from his position as if he was petrified. It was then that Sin remembered that first day in the car when they'd driven along Dauphin street. The wild look, the labored breathing—the signs of post-traumatic stress written all over Boyd's face.

"Fuck." Sin's breath hissed out in a slow exhale. His impatience skyrocketed, but he beat it back and tried to figure out what to do. It was only after Boyd began to tremble that Sin reached up to touch the side of Boyd's neck. "Boyd, I'm not going to hurt you. I just want to stitch up your wound."

Boyd grabbed Sin's wrist but didn't shove his hand away.

"Just that area and nothing else," Sin said, keeping his voice low. He fanned out his fingers to cup Boyd's face again. This time, he moved it up in a slow caress. When Boyd's eyes closed and he leaned into the touch, Sin nearly lost his focus. He swallowed hard. "Just let me fix you."

Precious minutes dragged with Sin becoming lost in the feel of soft skin, and Boyd's fear visibly receding as he clutched Sin's wrist. By the time Boyd was back to himself, Sin felt like he was the one on the verge of losing control. There was too much closeness, too much tenderness, just too much…

"Are you okay?" he grit out, voice rough.

Boyd nodded but said nothing.

"Let's go in the other room. You need to get your head elevated."

The next several minutes were spent moving to the main room while trying not to make a mess, and propping Boyd's head up with pillows as he stretched out on one of the full sized beds. Sin sat next to him, using his knife to cut Boyd's already destroyed shirt at an angle that only exposed the very top of his torso and his left shoulder. The gash was deeper than Sin had thought.

"I'm going to stitch this up."

"Alright." Boyd gripped the covers and his chest rose and fell more quickly than normal.

Time stretched with nothing to fill it but the ticking of a clock, the hum of the room's heater, and Sin methodically sewing the wound with the precision of a surgeon. He'd done it often enough to himself to complete the task easily on someone else. But even as his hands moved confidently, closing the gash once he'd cleaned it thoroughly, his mind was churning.

This was all wrong. The entire partnership had evolved in a way that he had never imagined was possible. From the start, nothing had gone as he'd expected. He'd never expected to be intrigued by Boyd, or to find anything in common with him. He'd never expected to feel reluctance about allowing the younger man to die. He'd definitely never expected to eventually start enjoying Boyd's company, and especially had not expected this god awful attraction.

As soon as he'd noticed Boyd's features that day in the thrift shop, the entire thing had taken off at a speed Sin hadn't anticipated. He hadn't been able to stop noticing things about Boyd from that point on, which had manifested into a confusing desire to do… something, that night in his apartment.

After finding out that Boyd was gay and had been sexually active in the past, the situation had gotten worse. Trying to picture somber, expressionless Boyd without any of his inhibitions had somehow morphed into picturing him losing those inhibitions with Sin. The worst part was that the musings had not been purposeful—they'd randomly accosted Sin and then refused to leave.

180   SANTINO & AIS

Scowling, Sin prodded Boyd. "Don't fall asleep yet."

One of Boyd's eyelids rose. "You have a needle in me. I'm not going to sleep."

"It doesn't hurt that bad."

Boyd scrunched his face up and dropped his head back against the pillows. "It doesn't feel good."

The nagging feeling that had been plaguing Sin since he'd gone back to the alley to find Boyd on the ground returned.

"Sorry."

Boyd peeked down. "It's okay. There's no painless way to stitch a wound like this."

"That's not what I was talking about."

There was a brief pause. "Then what?"

Sin made a face. "What do you think? If I'd been on top of things, this wouldn't have happened."

Boyd's eyes opened wider. "It isn't your fault. If you hadn't gotten Eugene, we both would have been in trouble. The rest of this..." He gestured to his wounds and let his hand fall to the bed again. "It just happens sometimes."

Unconvinced, Sin finished stitching the wound, cleaned it, and applied a bandage. But even though his wounds were now attended to, Boyd still looked like a mess. They had several hours before they had to meet the Agency transport team so Sin reached for the pack with the intention of giving Boyd a fresh pair of clothing.

"If your head is feeling better, you should change. We have seven hours before the transport team will expect us."

That being said, Sin turned to walk back to the bathroom.

"Sin," Boyd called out.

Sin paused and looked over his shoulder.

One of Boyd's hands was holding together his ruined shirt. "Thank you."

Sin refused to maintain eye contact, shrugged, and retreated to the bathroom to clean up. He stayed in there probably longer than was necessary, detailing the shower and the tiled floors to get rid of all traces of blood. Afterward, he showered with scalding water. An intense need to separate himself from Boyd coexisted with a desire to make sure Boyd was okay. But Sin's automatic desire to tend to Boyd was starting to disturb him.

Why the fuck did he even care? It wasn't like Boyd didn't have medical training. He knew how to take care of himself, and if he didn't, he would die sooner than later. It was a fact of life. A basic tenet of their jobs. Yet here Sin was, babying the kid, and running through the streets in some mad rush to get him to safety.

And that wasn't even mentioning the actual panic that he'd felt at seeing Boyd sprawled on the filthy ground, covered in blood.

Sin turned off the water and stepped out of the shower. For what felt like the first time in a long time, he stared at himself in the mirror. It was usually something he avoided; he didn't like being reminded that he had grown up to be nearly identical to his now deceased father. Even so, Sin looked at his reflection and tried to figure out what the hell was different. Where had he gone so fucking wrong? When had he become just another weak person?

He would have thought that years of conditioning himself to not care about other people would have held out longer. Years of being alienated and turned into something barely human should have made him not as likely to get sucked in. But all it had taken was Boyd's determination, curious questions and cautious smile, and things had slipped out of Sin's control.

He was pathetic.

THE DEBRIEFING WAS scheduled for a full day after they returned to Lexington, and Sin's only motivation for attending was not hearing Carhart's complaining. He spent the duration of the meeting staring at his panel, zoning out, and avoiding Boyd's searching stare. The kid's eyes were like magnets, but Sin leaned his cheek against his hand and gazed out the window.

"Are you with us?" Carhart demanded at one point.

"Sure."

"Don't let me interrupt your nap," was the sarcastic reply.

"I wouldn't."

And the debriefing dragged on.

By the end, Sin was ready to return to the safety of his empty apartment where he could drown out his extraneous preoccupation with recent developments in peace. He was determined to somehow mentally retrain himself and get his brain back to the way it had been, before Boyd had come along and complicated everything by acting like Sin was a real person.

But that, too, was ruined when Boyd stopped him after everyone else filed out of the conference room.

"What?"

"Thanks for waiting." Boyd glanced at the door. After a hesitation, he turned to his messenger bag. "I wanted to give you something."

"Why?" Sin regarded the bag with confusion. "For what?"

Boyd removed a rectangular object that was wrapped in several layers of white tissue paper. He held it out to Sin.

Confused, Sin took the package. It was heavier than he'd expected. "Why are you giving me anything? What is it?"

"Open it and see."

Feeling utterly lost, Sin ripped the paper down the middle. It was a book—an archaic-looking hardcover book with a reddish-gold cover. The spine was elaborate despite the fact that most of the cover was faded with age. He could just make out the words 'Paradise Lost' on the spine.

"You're giving this to me? Why?"

"I've had it for years but after I saw your tattoo, I started wondering whether you would appreciate it more." Boyd reached out, his fingers brushing the cover. "It's a second edition. I wanted a first but they're too expensive. I was lucky enough to find this at an antique store I frequent." Boyd dropped his hands and then winced as if the movement caused him pain. "I wanted to give it to you as a thank you."

Sin had no idea what to say. A voice in the back of his head ordered him to give it back, but Sin's fingers only dug harder into the cover.

"Why do you keep thanking me?"

"Because you're nice to me. And you listened when I—" Boyd gestured to his shirt, looking uncomfortable. "You could have ignored me and you didn't. And I... I appreciate that."

"Oh." Sin stared at the book. "I see."

If Boyd was underwhelmed by Sin's response, he didn't show it or look surprised. He simply closed his bag and put it over his good shoulder. "Well, I'm going to leave. I have some errands to run today. I'll see you later."

Sin struggled with what to say, tried to force himself to utter a thank you, but the words locked up in his throat. Feeling like an idiot, he started to at least say goodbye when his phone rang. Caught off guard, the moment passed and Sin wound up not saying a thing as Boyd left.

Irritated, Sin took the call without even looking at the screen.

"What?" he growled.

"Problem, Vega?"

Sin glanced down at the book. He had a sudden desire to cover it up again, as if Marshal Connors could see it through the phone.

"No. What do you want?"

"You, in my office, in twenty minutes," was the chilly reply. "You're being sent out within the hour."

The call ended.

Sin left the conference room and headed to his building to drop off the book. It, and whatever he wanted to say to Boyd, would have to wait until his mission was over.

Feeling inexplicably gloomy, Sin wondered who he would be assassinating now.

FOURTEEN

It WAS THE end of November and Sin was mortified that someone had placed Thanksgiving decorations around the compound. He wondered if this was some pathetic attempt to make the Agency seem less like a life-sucking void and more like a normal job.

If so, they had failed miserably. Paper cutouts of fat turkeys did not a welcoming environment make.

He stood in front his apartment and stared at the thing that was stuck to his door. It was a cardboard decoration that looked like a horn with fruit stuffed inside. Sin searched his vocabulary for a word that would describe such an odd creation.

"Cornucopia," he pronounced slowly, and pulled it off the door. The guards on either side of it had all but ignored him until that point, but Officer Daniels actually snorted out a laugh.

All employees are formally invited to a Thanksgiving feast this Thursday, 11/21/19, at 1700 hours in the main cafeteria.

Sin shredded the invitation into small pieces. He did not know what had possessed someone to stick this to his door, of all doors, but he found it offensive. He wasn't even really American. Not technically anyway, he didn't think. Perhaps that was something to look into.

He tossed the paper on the floor and swiped his card to enter his apartment. Daniels laughed again as the door slammed shut. At least someone was amused.

After Sin's solo assassination assignment there had been a lull in Janus activity. In the past month, he had participated in a grand total of three missions and none of them had been very exciting. He spent most of his time exercising, reading or roaming the compound. In the past Sin had barely left his building, but lately he found that he had become bolder and less concerned with dealing with the other agents. Sin suspected it was because he was spending more time with Boyd.

A few months ago, Sin would sit in the dark for hours. He'd stared out the window or at the wall until his mind was blank. There had been nothing to do, nothing to think about regarding the future, and no reason to put much effort into anything aside from keeping his body fit. Sin's sole purpose had been for killing and avoiding the box. He hadn't cared or felt interest in much other than that. He'd had no desire to be around or to speak to anyone else. For the most part, that hadn't changed.

Except, of course, when it came to Boyd. His obsession with his partner had not diminished at all in the past month. If anything, it had grown.

He found himself thinking about Boyd at odd times, often wondering what Boyd was doing when they were not together. He wondered what Boyd did in his spare time, what he read, and whether Boyd spent time with other people outside the Agency.

Most of all, Sin wondered if Boyd thought about him in return.

But the wondering wasn't the extent of it.

There were times when Sin's eyes would linger on Boyd longer than was necessary. When he would fixate on Boyd's eyes or especially his mouth. Later, Sin would sit alone and think about how odd it was to desire someone after so many years of not even knowing what that would feel like. There were other times when he would think about the mission in Seattle and the feel of Boyd's bare skin beneath his hands.

And here he fucking went again.

He'd begun reminding himself daily that he was a killer. He'd been trained to be one since he was eight years old, and that was the only thing he was good at. He could barely have a conversation, what made him think he could do... anything else? Especially the things that played out in his mind late at night when there was nothing else to distract him, and he wound up biting his lip and touching himself, cameras be fucking damned.

It was almost a relief that Boyd had been sent on a solo mission with that idiot from 53. Apparently, Andrews would only agree to the meeting if Sin was not there. He wanted nothing to do with "that animal." The words didn't bother Sin, but the idea of Boyd going off on his own did. It was the first time Boyd had a solo mission of any kind with no backup in the vicinity. What would happen if Andrews turned on them and decided to take Boyd hostage or kill him to get out of the deal?

Sin hadn't voiced the concerns but Ryan had done it for him. He'd complained loudly that Sin should accompany Boyd even if he didn't

SANTINO & AIS

actually go to the meeting. Carhart had said there was no point and, by now, Boyd should be able to hold his own.

It was true, but the entire thing still made Sin, and apparently Ryan, uneasy. The thought reminded Sin of something else, something that he'd completely forgotten after finding out that Boyd was going alone. Before the briefing had started, Ryan had asked Boyd if Wednesday was his birthday.

The concept of a birthday was alien to Sin. He couldn't remember celebrating his own and didn't even know the exact date. He suspected that it was sometime in April, and he knew that he'd been born in 1991, but that was the extent of his knowledge. Despite that, Sin knew that other people, for some reason, considered them to be joyous occasions that called for celebrations. He wondered if Boyd was one of those people. Sin doubted it but still had trouble dismissing the date from his mind.

The manuscript of Paradise Lost drew his attention, currently resting on the small coffee table. It occurred to Sin that he could get a gift for Boyd, but the idea was pretty absurd. It also contradicted directly with the goal of getting over his Boyd fixation.

Sin made a dinner for himself out of prepackaged chocolate chip cookies and instant oatmeal. He stared at the sink and chewed mechanically, ruminating.

Even if he were to buy Boyd a gift of some sort, Sin had no idea what he would get. He knew next to nothing about Boyd except that he read a lot, wore black, had turned into a bit of a control freak over missions, and had some kind of past trauma. It was a problem, not just because of the gift, but because Boyd knew a lot more about Sin. It was also stupid considering Sin had briefly had access to Boyd's entire file. In the past seven months it had been locked again, but Sin knew someone who could still get to it.

Sin tossed the empty packages into the garbage and strode out of his apartment. This time, one of the guards spoke.

"Where you headed?" Daniels asked.

"What do you care?"

"I don't really, I'm just bored." He eyed Sin's attire skeptically. "The temperature is in single digits tonight, guy."

"Your point?"

Daniels held up his hands in exasperation. "Forget I said anything."

Sin gave him a look that said he planned to do just that. The guards in his building were no longer particularly hostile. Now they seemed almost curious about him and the lack of bloodthirsty rampages they'd heard so much about. Even so, Sin had no desire to be remotely friendly. They could die for all he cared.

Outside, a bitter wind stung Sin's face and pierced through his clothing, but he showed no outward signs of discomfort while striding to residential building C. The guards of that complex gave him more of a hard time but they had no real reason to deny him access to the building, and had no choice but to let him pass. Sin ignored the elevator and took the stairs two at a time.

After reaching the appropriate apartment, Sin took the liberty of ripping down another stupid cornucopia invitation before knocking. Someone from within the apartment shouted, "Coming!" There were clattering noises and the door swung open.

Sin was surprised that an agent, even a non-combative one, would be so careless as to open their door without so much as pausing to look through the peephole. But maybe it was better that way. Sin didn't enjoy the idea of standing in the hallway while trying to explain why he was there or dealing with anyone's overactive paranoia.

Ryan stood in his doorway in an over-sized red t-shirt and baggy boxers. His hair was sticking out in every direction and he had a can of soda in one hand.

"Hsin!"

Sin raised an eyebrow at the usage of his real name.

Ryan reddened. "Er—Sin."

He raised the other eyebrow.

"Hsin?" Ryan asked in confusion.

Sin gave him a flat look and strode into the apartment, not waiting for a formal invitation. "Give me your key card."

"Um? What?" Ryan blinked at him and closed the door. He darted to the desk to hurriedly closed his laptop.

"Your key card. Give it to me."

"That's not really... like, allowed." Ryan scratched the back of his head. "What do you even want it for?"

Sin held out his hand.

"Well, when are you going to give it back?" Ryan asked uncertainly, eyebrows drawing together.

SANTINO & AIS

It was very fortunate that Ryan would never be questioned by an enemy if this was the extent of his resistance.

"Shortly. I need access to personnel files. The entire ones, not the superficial version. I don't have the access code for that."

Ryan opened his mouth to question him further but the expression on Sin's face shut it instantly. "Uh... well, I guess. My access code is, um..." Ryan looked embarrassed. "0666." He handed the card to Sin. "But first, can I—"

Sin left before the younger man could finish. He took the stairs once again and determined that this building was designed identically to every other residential building, which meant there was most likely a technology center and lounge area on the third floor. Sin was pleased to realize that he was correct, and even more pleased to see that it was empty. He took a seat at the back of the room and swiped Ryan's card, waiting for the screen to load.

It welcomed Ryan Freedman and asked for the access code. Sin punched it in and stared at the screen before figuring out how to get to the area of the database that he wanted. His own card was limited to unlocking specific public areas of the compound unless they temporarily increased his access. Even then, it was limited to accessing mission files that he was involved in.

Ryan, on the other hand, apparently had free run of the entire database.

Sin typed in Boyd's name and found the file easily. There were multiple sub-folders within it and Sin took his time, going through all of them. He went through file after file, viewing images of certificates from academic awards and contests that Boyd had received throughout the years. Sin noted that Boyd had graduated high school early, skipping to college courses at the age of 15. Sin had never been to school himself but he figured that was impressive.

He skimmed the information about Vivienne but took his time reading about Cedrick Alan Beaulieu, a journalist and aspiring author who had perished during the bombings in New York City while covering a story.

There was an entire folder dedicated to Boyd's father, and Sin read every document. He was curious about the type of person who would marry and have a child with Vivienne. The woman seemed even less capable of intimacy than Sin was himself.

Cedrick had done well for himself in his short life. He'd gotten a position at a good newspaper at a young age and had gone on to dedicate his career to exposing political intrigue. Apparently some of his first stories had blown the top off a lot of scandals. There was a video attached to one of the files. Sin almost bypassed it before going back to watch.

It was a recording of Cedrick interviewing for a job. He appeared to be in his twenties at the time of the video, and was vying for an internship at a newspaper called The Sun. Cedrick was stockier and had darker hair and eyes than his son, but some of their features were the same. During the interview, it became evident that Cedrick was passionate about equality, justice, and the truth. He was the antithesis of Vivienne. Sin had no idea how two such different people had managed to procreate.

Then again, Sin had no idea how normal families functioned or how people formed relationships. The extent of his knowledge in that area stemmed from watching his mother interact with johns, and his father fucking every attractive human that passed him. Neither of his parents had been very interested in family life before they'd died.

Sin went back to his research and found a sub-folder labeled Louis "Lou" Krauszer. At first Sin thought it was an anomaly but after flipping through some of the files, Sin realized Lou was a childhood friend of Boyd's. His parents had been liberal politicians before the war and had both perished during the bombings of Lexington.

There were several police reports and mug shots of the teen. After his parents' deaths, Lou had gotten into petty crime. There were surveillance stills that depicted him and Boyd walking together, his arm thrown around Boyd's shoulders more often than not. Although younger Boyd had already adopted his usual style of all black attire and a generally serious expression, he had been more animated in the past.

Sin stared at this Lou person with a slight frown. The kid had a slender body, an unruly mass of curly blond hair and gray-blue eyes that perpetually twinkled with mischief. The dates on the images were as recent as four years ago, which meant that Boyd was most likely still acquainted with the boy. The idea made Sin frown further. He wondered why Boyd had never mentioned a childhood friend hanging around. What did this person think about Boyd joining the Agency? Did he even know?

That brought to mind another question that Sin had wondered about recently: what cover story did Boyd use on the outside world, anyway? Every agent with civilian ties had one.

Sin idly flipped through files as he tried to find recent data on the mop-headed teen. His search came up short and Sin scowled at the computer before returning to the main file. This time, he read it more carefully.

```
Louis "Lou" Krauszer
Occupation: None
Status: Deceased
Birth: 3/14/2000
Death: 5/23/2016
```

It was an abrupt end to a teen who had at least appeared to be relatively healthy. Although, it was possible that he'd suffered from the lung disease which had taken the lives of a lot of young people after the war. Curious, Sin kept looking to determine what had actually happened.

Again, Sin came up with nothing. Frustrated, he swore and flipped back to the main folder. He went through every file and finally found one that labeled "police-hospital reports, surveillance."

Several files populated the screen. Sin opened each one, pouring over them and found that Boyd had been involved in a mugging where he'd been injured and Lou had been slain. Further reading described an inept and somewhat crooked police department who did very little to catch the gang that was involved.

A follow-up report noted that Boyd's wound had not been critical. However, he had returned to the hospital a few days later and stayed awhile. Inexplicably, the file noted a third trip to the Emergency Room not long after his release. There was nothing in the file to explain the two subsequent visits, and Sin assumed it had something to do with the initial wounds. Possibly an infection or improper care. Sin doubted Vivienne had been attentive to her son.

Sin rapped his knuckles against the table, biting his lower lip and staring at the directory. There had to be more information somewhere. Refusing to give up, he explored further before stumbling upon yet another video file. It was also inside the surveillance folder and was labeled "First Bank-052316."

The video started with a view of a deserted street, still wet from a recent rain. The video was unstable and moved at a dizzying pace.

"—getting this, Seth?"

"Yeah."

The way the view shifted and then steadied led Sin to believe Seth, whoever he was, was recording on a mobile device. Seth sounded prepubescent but the first speaker's voice indicated he was older.

"Can't believe those fucking faggots," the older male muttered. The video swung to the side and a tall teen with black hair appeared in part of the shot. Behind the guy and further down the street, Sin was surprised to see Boyd and Lou barely visible at the edge of an alley. They were kissing. Lou was pressing Boyd against the wall and Boyd's hands rested on Lou's back.

They were next to the First Bank location on Dauphin Street.

The street sign brought Sin back to his first mission with Boyd and the way he'd reacted upon seeing the now-defunct bank. The pieces came together in Sin's mind, and his mouth tightened as the scene played out.

The dark-haired teen was now smiling at the camera with eyes that were shark-like. Empty. "Let's do this shit."

"Jared," Seth started to say. "Are you—"

"Come on," another voice boomed. "Ken, you in?"

"Fuck yeah."

"Where's Vince?"

"Getting the bat. Come on. I want to see if Jared actually does it."

Two teenage boys strolled into view; one Asian, the other white. Not long afterward, an olive-skinned teen appeared, flipping a bat with one hand. All of them, Jared included, wore a green bandanna.

"Tommy—" Seth said, but he was cut off by the Asian kid turning a glare on him.

"Shut the fuck up and get a good vid, Seth. If you fuck this up, I'll beat the shit out of you when we get home."

Seth's sigh was audible. The video shook when he trotted behind his friends. They got to the alley just in time for the video to catch Boyd and Lou separating and starting to leave.

Sin watched as Boyd's head snapped up. He took a step back,

reaching for Lou's arm. Before they could fully react, Jared grabbed Boyd and threw him out of the alley hard enough that he fell to his knees.

Lou charged up to Jared, face reddened. "What the fuck are you doing? Give it up—"

Vince came up behind Lou with the bat. A cracking sound came across the speakers as he slammed it into Lou's shoulder. Lou cried out, stumbling against the side of the building.

"Give up?" Jared demanded with a harsh bark of laughter. "Why would I do that? You wanted to start shit and now I'm going to finish it."

Lou was holding his arm but he looked over to where Boyd had gotten to his feet. "It was just a fistfight! Jesus Christ, accept that you lost and move on. It's not that big of a deal."

"Yeah, it was just a fight and this is just a fucking beat down." Jared jerked his chin at Boyd. "Grab the fag."

Chaos erupted on screen. The view skewed again but a litany of curses and shouts filled the speakers. When the camera finally righted itself, Ken was holding Lou on his knees, and Jared was smirking down at him while two of the teens restrained Boyd.

"Stay away from him!" Lou tried to surge to his feet but was kicked back.

"Stay away from him? You think you can call the shots, rich boy?" Jared's face transformed in a heartbeat; one moment mocking and calm, the next manic and twisted. He was now holding the bat. "Your parents ain't around no more, bitch. I'll do what I want to that fuck-ing faggot."

Jared cocked the bat back and slammed it into Boyd's side. Boyd cried out, falling to the filthy concrete before Vince yanked him up-right again. Lou screamed at him to stop, but Jared just smashed his heel to Boyd's groin and he collapsed to the ground again.

"Oh, sorry. Did he need that? Who the fuck knows with you fags. I'd think he'd be the bitch but maybe it's you, Louis. Maybe I'm ruining your Monday night."

Jared backhanded Boyd and blood spattered the sidewalk. As Sin watched, Boyd's eyes blazed through a fall of hair, his swollen and split lip was garish in contrast to his pale face.

"You motherfucking piece of shit, don't you *fucking* touch him again!" Lou shouted, his voice high and panicked. "Please, leave him alone!"

"Shut the fuck up, bitch. It ain't time to beg yet." Jared glanced at his friends. "Hold that little cocksucker. Make him watch."

For a moment, the camera zoomed in too much and blurred. Sin's fingers curled into a tight fist. He could still hear the screaming. Boyd crying and the hard sounds of fists hitting skin. The splatter of blood. The dull thump of a skull bouncing off concrete. Even without the video, Sin could visualize it. But then the video focused again.

Seth had zoomed out enough to catch a clear view of everyone on the scene. The thugs holding Boyd and the way Jared was still looming over Lou. It focused completely just as Jared kicked Lou in the face, causing globs of blood to fly everywhere.

Over Boyd's screams, Sin was barely aware of someone noting that Jared had broken some of Lou's teeth. Someone else said that it would make it easier for Lou to give head. Sin didn't look to see who had spoken. All he could see was Boyd.

"Please don't hurt him. Please! He won't bother you anymore, we promise." When Jared reared back with the bat, Boyd wailed, "I'll do anything! I'll give you money! Just—Please!"

Jared laughed. "Yeah, I bet you can, princess. I seen you up in Cedar Hills. But I'll take what I want from you later."

Again, the screen tilted wildly and blurred. When it re-focused, Boyd's shirt was ripped at the collar and he was down on the ground. In the seconds without video, Boyd had curled into a ball as Jared's friends kicked and hit him. They forced Boyd onto his stomach despite his desperate attempts to fight back. One sat on his back while the other held down his legs. Vince yanked Boyd's head back by a handful of hair, his chin scraping against the street.

"Please," Boyd choked out. "Please leave us alone..."

No one listened. When their tormentor abandoned the bat for a knife, Boyd began to scream. The sound made Sin recoil slightly, his stomach churning when Boyd's voice cracked. Sin knew Boyd was still pleading but the words were clogged with sobs. All Sin could make out was a keening "No!", just before Jared slammed the knife into Lou's stomach.

The camera zoomed in.

Jared smiled as he leaned close. "Now you'll keep your mouth shut, won't you?"

When he yanked the knife out, Lou fell forward on his knees.

"Boyd," Lou moaned. "Run!"

"No! Lou!"

"Oh, shut the fuck up," Jared snarled. He jerked his fist back and followed the first stab up with a slash across Lou's throat. Blood sprayed everywhere as Boyd howled. He bucked and struggled, trying to escape the two thugs that pinned him to the ground.

"Leave him alone! Please!"

Lou reached up to clutch the meat hanging from his throat. Blood spurted between his fingers like a fountain, gore staining his face, his hair, the white t-shirt he wore. Nothing remained of the boy he had been only moments ago. The boy who had kissed Boyd against the side of a building in the middle of the day.

When Lou tried to speak blood spilled from his mouth. He made a gurgling sound.

The camera began to shake.

"I said," Jared whispered. "Shut. The. Fuck. Up."

The third time Jared struck he punched the knife into Lou's heart. Lou dropped to the ground and convulsed, turning his head as if trying to see Boyd. Before he could complete the gesture, his body went perfectly still in death. Blood leaked away from him, staining a nearby puddle.

Jared leaned over and yanked Lou's wallet from his back pocket. He pocketed the ID and threw the wallet to the ground as Boyd's desperate screams continued.

"No, no, Lou! Help! *Help us!* Lou, you can't, oh God, *please—* I'll kill you, I'll *fucking kill you—*"

Boyd's face was spattered with Lou's blood, his eyes darting like a cornered animal. He had managed to escape the two boys holding him to fling himself towards Lou, but they dragged him back, laughing. Jared turned away from Lou's corpse and flashed his cold smile at Boyd.

"Hold him up."

They yanked him to his feet, and Boyd lurched at Jared. His weeping became guttural, his face twisted with hatred that only intensified when he was prevented from reaching his lover's murderer.

"You think you can do something?" Jared taunted. "You're nothing, bitch. Even less without Lou here to protect you. You couldn't even stop me from gutting that piece of shit."

Boyd froze. He stood there, thin and pale compared to the teenagers around him, and the fight drained from his body. He went slack in the hands still holding him tight.

"That's right," Jared whispered. "I want you to remember this forever. Remember how you let your little boyfriend die while you watched because you're too fucking pathetic to stop it. It'll always be that way. You're nothing and you never will be."

Jared moved closer and jerked Boyd's head up. Boyd stared back dully, expression deadened like it had been the first time Sin saw him through a two-way mirror at the Agency.

"Little piece of advice?" The knife glinted in Jared's hand, still slick with Lou's blood. He slammed it into Boyd's lower stomach. "Next time, pick a boyfriend who can actually back up the shit he talks." The knife plunged in again, ripped out, and Seth's voice hissed out from behind the camera.

"Someone's coming!"

The camera swung wildly, and caught an upside down glimpse of Boyd collapsing next to Lou's body before the video ended.

Sin sat and stared for a long moment before he replayed the video. This time he tried to watch with clinical detachment. He picked apart Lou's fighting technique with disgust at the boy's inability to defend himself and his lover. The sloppy way the gang leader gutted him was not much better, and Sin absently went through several methods of killing that would have been quicker and more efficient.

Sin had been a professional assassin by the time he was their age. As far as he was concerned, there was no excuse for the lack of skill.

Even so, he couldn't remain detached. The slow simmer of anger had boiled up until Sin's fingers were flexing with the need to hit something or someone.

It made no sense. There was no reason to be upset. Boyd had survived the attack. If Lou had lived, it was unlikely Boyd would have ended up at the Agency. It was better for Sin that the boy had died, but that didn't appease the building storm of his rage. All he could see was Boyd screaming, begging, and Jared laughing in his face. And Sin could identify exactly why it made him want to unleash his wrath.

It was the same reason why it pissed him off when anyone on the compound looked at Boyd the wrong way or made one of their stupid comments.

Sin shifted gears and turned his attention to the computer again. He tried to find out what had become of the attackers but was met with the same irritating conclusion that he'd expected. Lack of evidence, the police file had said, no suspects, unsolved.

Jared had gotten away with it.

Sin began opening programs and clicking things automatically. He printed out five pages and erased all traces of his history on the computer. Sin left the lounge with an expression that was a lot deadlier than it had been when he'd gone in. He took the stairs to Ryan's apartment again and he pounded his fist on the door loud enough to echo through the hall.

Ryan opened the door and took an automatic step back at the waves of anger radiating off Sin. "Did something happen?"

Sin pushed his way into the apartment. "Look these men up for me."

"What?" Ryan squinted at him before taking the printed images that Sin held in one white-knuckled hand. "Who are these guys? Is this all you have?"

"Their names are Jared, Tommy, Vince, Ken and Seth."

"What—"

"Just do it."

Ryan nodded hastily and shoved the mass of papers and magazines off his desk before taking his seat at the computer. He laid each photograph out in the newly cleared space and chewed his lip. "Are these surveillance stills?" He pushed his glasses up his nose, professional attitude taking over. "I need more to work with than this."

"They are near First Bank on Dauphin. That one's named Jared." Sin pointed at the picture. "He's the one I want."

"Okay..." Ryan dragged his eyes away from Sin and turned on a lamp with an extremely bright bulb. "First Bank on Dauphin Street in Vickland, huh? Used to be a nice area, wealthy folks, but it was prime spot for gang activity and looting after the bombings because it was really close to one of the blast sites."

Sin crossed his arms and said nothing.

"And it looks like they're in the same gang... with a green bandanna." Ryan's fingers clattered on the keys, lips pursing while he worked. It was another few moments before he sat up straight with an exclamation. "The Outlaws! They're in the news so much you'd think I would have remembered what color they wore."

"What's his name?"

"Wait," Ryan said, swept up in his research. "Okay, Outlaws formed before the wars... major beef with the South Side Boys, got worse over the years—" He muttered as he read out loud and skimmed the information.

"Jared Strickland suspected in multiple murders and rapes around Vickland but never pinned with any of them. He's a real shitbag. Has a terrible record dating back to 2010 when he was only fifteen. Seems to get off on slashing civilians and has a history of rape. It doesn't make sense that he's never been inside a jail for longer than a few months at a time. He has to be protected by someone in the police department or higher. There's even speculation about it in the Journalist Guild, although it doesn't seem like they ever found concrete proof."

Ryan motioned Sin over. Sin hesitated before moving to stand behind Ryan. He leaned over his shoulder, looking at the computer screen impassively. Jared's face stared back at him in a mug shot that dated back several years.

"Is, uh, this your guy?"

"Yes. That's my guy."

Ryan nodded. "A lot of his cronies are in jail or dead already but somehow this guy has survived. His crimes have piled up over the years but nothing has happened really. Sometimes there has even been evidence that was either ignored or miraculously went missing. He definitely has to be related to someone or else he has some kind of dirt on a big shot in the city."

The comment deepened Sin's frown. He fought the urge to ask what kinds of crimes had piled up over the past decade. Had it been the serial rapes in Vickland and Crandall Park that the crooked detectives had tried to pin on Sin? The murders were mostly gang-related although the cops had tried to imply Sin was behind it after going on some kind of rampage.

He didn't know if any of this was true but at the moment it seemed possible. Jared had obviously been an active psychopath for the last nine or ten years so the timing was correct. How ironic if it turned out the police had attempted to pin Sin with Jared's crimes, possibly even Lou's murder.

"There's a tape of one of his crimes in the Agency database," Sin said. "How could the police not use it against him?"

Ryan shook his head, seeming just as dismayed by the obvious obstruction. "My guess is that the Agency was keeping an eye on Jared since he was obviously a high-profile criminal."

"Maybe they wanted to recruit him."

Ryan snorted. "I wouldn't be surprised. I know they've hired lots of criminals and killers before. I guess sociopaths fit their assassin profile. In the end, they don't actually keep people like Strickland, though. It seems like he gets too much of a thrill out of doing this stuff."

"Where is the original copy of the video?" Sin asked.

"I'm thinking after the Agency copied it, the original somehow disappeared like all of the other stuff that tended to go miraculously missing with this guy." Ryan scanned whatever he was reading. "Oh wow, apparently he killed some rich politician's son a few years ago too."

Sin tensed at the words. So far he hadn't explicitly told Ryan that he was looking into the death of Boyd's friend and he didn't plan to. If Ryan saw it himself, it would be out of his hands. Fortunately, whatever Ryan was reading didn't seem to mention Boyd's name.

"That was pretty high profile for a while so there's some stuff on it here. Apparently he murdered this kid in broad daylight and then bragged about it to people afterward, showing the victim's identification as proof."

The venom that had been swirling in Sin's system began to burn. Jared must have thought he was untouchable.

"Where is he now?"

"According to what we have in the database about him, he's still a lieutenant in the Outlaws but really heavy into drugs. He's in a methadone program but still does heroin at the same time. And—Oh! He currently resides at 289 Hammond Place in the Industrial district. It seems that he's just squatting there but it's on his residency placard for some re—"

Sin was gone before the sentence could be completed.

ASIDE FROM THE Barrows, the Industrial District was one of the worst places to be in the city after dark. Even though the police enforced a midnight curfew it was still a haven of crime. Robberies were a frequent occurrence as were random acts of violence. The area was controlled by the South Side Boys so Sin had no idea why Strickland was living there. Perhaps it was close enough to the Theater District for him to feel safe.

289 Hammond Place was one of the abandoned tenements in one grid of the district. It was dilapidated and against building code, but no one was supposed to live there so nobody cared. Jared lived on the top floor. It appeared to be half hideout, half drug den; paraphernalia was scattered everywhere in the loft-like space that stank of sickness.

When Sin first spotted Jared, he observed from the shadows.

Time had not been kind to Lou's killer. Years of fighting, drugs and alcohol had aged him. Jared was emaciated and weak but still had the hard face and cold eyes of a killer; a clear product of the war and the streets that had likely welcomed him after.

Jared was sitting on a filthy mattress that sagged on the floor while peering out the window. His hands were trembling and he was covered in a sheen of sweat. He didn't seem to sense that someone else had entered the room until Sin moved away from the darkened corner.

Jared's head snapped up. "It's about time," he growled. "I feel like fucking shit waiting for you. I can't even get up."

Sin approached without speaking.

"Archie, what the hell are you doing?"

Sin stepped into a beam of slanted moonlight and Jared recoiled. He threw himself back against the wall, tremors increasing as he groped around in the sheets as if looking for a weapon. His fingers shook so much he could barely perform the search.

"Who the hell are you?"

Jared managed to get to his feet, but his breath was coming in uneven gasps. There was no smugness in his face, no attitude and mocking smirk. Jared seemed to sense that he was in the presence of another killer.

A better killer.

"I'm warning you, man, you're fucking with the wrong person."

Sin stopped in front of Jared and took him in slowly, deliberately. Jaundiced, diseased, underweight, and helpless. There was no match.

SANTINO & AIS

No challenge. But when Sin looked into Jared's eyes, it did not process that this would be cold-blooded murder. Sin only knew that Jared had to die.

"Dude—what do you want?" Jared held up his hands. "Money? Drugs? Fuck, man, just tell me what you want!"

Sin smiled. "I want you to remember this forever."

Jared's screams echoed through the Industrial District for over an hour. No one came to his aid.

BOYD'S HOUSE WAS dark when he entered after returning from the mission. His mind was already gearing towards the report he would have to type up in the morning, and the information he had received from Andrews. He was so distracted when he walked into the kitchen that he did not notice the figure sitting at the table until he flipped on the light.

His heart leapt to his throat and he dropped back into a crouch. Adrenaline raging, it took Boyd a second to realize that it was Sin. He froze.

Boyd had never told his partner where he lived and yet there Sin was, sitting at the kitchen table with his head bowed.

"Sin. What—How did you get in here?"

When Sin looked up, Boyd saw that his partner was spattered in blood. Remnants were barely visible on his hands, face, and neck; as if he'd tried to quickly scrub himself clean but hadn't been able to do a thorough job.

"I picked the lock."

"What? Why—?" The scene almost felt surreal but it was eclipsed by confusion and growing concern. "Did something happen? Are you alright?"

"I'm fine." Sin stood and moved further away from Boyd. He raked both hands through his hair, the movements unsteady. "Fine."

"Sin, what's going on?"

Sin's face was an empty canvas, but his eyes were intense, burning, and distant. It was an expression that was eerily similar to the one Sin took on in the midst of a fight. When he shut everything else out and became a tool of destruction.

Boyd hesitated. Was this the precursor to one of Sin's episodes or was he coming down from one? Whose blood had he so hastily tried to wash off? A civilian? An agent?

"Sin..." Boyd took a step forward even though his instincts screamed for him to run away. Being around Sin while he was in this state set off alarms of imminent danger in Boyd's body. If Sin was having an episode, he would hurt Boyd without even realizing it was him.

"Sin?" he asked uncertainly.

Sin reached out in a sudden motion that caused Boyd to flinch. Before he could stop himself, he took a step back.

This time, it was Sin who froze in place. He dropped his head again.

"I tried to...I mean, I found something of yours."

"What?"

There was brief, strained silence before Sin put something on the table and slid it toward Boyd. It was a driver's license.

Boyd started to grab it but stopped just short of touching the card when he realized it was also covered in blood. He took a closer look and the world around Boyd ground to a halt. His surroundings faded away until all he saw was Lou's cocky smile.

Hand wrenching away, Boyd stumbled back. Horror twisted his throat and the dread in his stomach spread like wildfire with nausea as thick as smoke—

That day slammed back into his mind with sharp, frightening clarity. The memories he'd spent years trying to suppress—

Lou's face, twisted in agony—that helpless, terrible certainty that moved between them when they realized it had all gone so horribly out of control and there was no stopping it—there was no changing the way that fight was going and Lou was going to die—

Bile was at the back of his throat and Boyd's arms jerked against his stomach.

He was going to throw up.

Boyd barely made it to the toilet before he threw up. The sound and smell only fed into the sensory nightmare. Boyd remembered snapping forward and vomiting next to Lou's body. The smell and taste of Lou's blood on his lips. The meaty sound of Lou turning into a broken corpse on the street. Eyes that had once been mischievous turning dull, lifeless, and staring at him from above a ravaged throat.

Pleading. Accusing. Denying. Dead.

It all kept coming back to that picture, the grin Lou had on that ID, in life, just minutes before everything had changed. Before Boyd, too, had died.

Turning away from the cold porcelain of the toilet, Boyd pressed against the side of the wall. He curled in on himself, burying his face in his knees, and tried to feel nothing. His chest heaved and no matter how hard he gripped himself, he still felt like he was falling apart. After spending years trying to deny and repress what had happened, the entire memory from start to finish was now ripped out and flayed.

Boyd dug into his hair with quaking fingers and tried hard not to cry, not to vomit again, but he didn't make it long.

He didn't even hear when Sin left.

FIFTEEN

NIGHTMARES PLAGUED BOYD the weeks following his birthday. He came to fear sleep, and alternated between overloaded emotions and feeling at a complete loss. He avoided his bedroom, the kitchen, and soon the entire first floor. He felt trapped in his house, but was even more afraid of leaving it to deal with the world beyond.

Memories were stark and cutting. He felt them like a second skin: throat raw from screaming, the impotence and horror of being held down, unable to protect Lou or even himself. He remembered dark shadows, bound wrists, his voice breaking, and terror that had eclipsed all else; even the person he had been before it all.

It felt like Lou's murder had happened yesterday. Like the years of systematically isolating every emotion as a weakness and destroying it had never happened. Every carefully crafted layer of avoidance, apathy, and denial, was ripped away and left a raw wound.

It took days for Boyd to be able to function at all, and even then he didn't know what to do. Disconnected thoughts cluttered his mind, all running in opposite directions: the blood meant Sin had killed Jared and brought the ID back as proof. The blood on Lou's face was all Boyd could see. He hadn't had enough time to recover.

He thought he wanted to see Sin but the second he laid eyes on him on compound, his heart constricted and his throat closed. He was afraid. Afraid Sin would ask questions he couldn't bear to answer, or that he would ask some himself about what had happened with Jared. Questions that would only rip that hole even deeper.

He couldn't meet Sin's eyes after that, and left the meeting early so they wouldn't be left alone.

He hadn't had enough time to recover. He needed more time.

He pushed everything away and avoided it, the only way he knew how to cope.

Two weeks after Sin had appeared in his kitchen, Boyd was called in for a briefing. When Boyd got to the conference room, Sin and Carhart were already there.

Sin was slumped in his seat, hood pulled over his head and nearly touching the ridge of his nose. He did not look up or speak. Anxiety flooded Boyd so he sat next to Ryan. When Owen and Jeffrey arrived, the red-haired R&D agent gave Boyd a sleepily disgruntled look for stealing his usual spot. He made a production out of sitting in Boyd's chair, and balefully eyeing him over a steaming cup of coffee.

"I won't bother to ask how everyone is doing," Carhart said, taking in Boyd's somber face and Sin's refusal to make eye contact with anyone. "I'm sure everyone's tired of doing nothing for so long, but the good news is that we finally arranged a meeting with Thierry."

When neither of his field agents commented, the general frowned. "Is there something I need to know?"

Boyd shook his head. Sin did not bother to reply.

"It's probably the weather," Ryan said after an awkward beat of silence.

Carhart rolled his eyes. "The meeting will be in France and is expected to last two days. That is all he claimed he can spare, and that's your window for getting the intel. Arrangements have already been made and you will be staying at Thierry's hotel in Paris. You leave tonight."

"He has a hotel?" Ryan asked. "I didn't know he was *that* loaded."

"Yes. But I don't really wish to discuss the man's money." Carhart looked from Boyd to Sin and back again. "I cannot stress enough the importance of this mission. He's willing to give us data on Janus' inner core, with a very high probability that it is legitimate. Before now, their inner core has been almost mythical because it's been completely out of our reach. This has the potential to change everything."

Carhart tapped a finger to the panel embedded in the table. An image of a young, dark-haired man hovered above the table. He was very handsome with a clever smile.

"Thierry is very fickle. His cooperation depends on his mood so you need to keep him happy. I don't care what you have to do as long as you stay on his good side. He's loyal to no one in particular and will go with whoever best suits his needs and whims."

"It should be noted," Jeffrey added, "that the area the hotel is set in is very high class. If you stand out too much," he raised an eyebrow at Sin, "then you may irritate Thierry. He does not want it known that he associates with questionable people."

Owen nodded, leaning against one hand. "You'll be going penguin-style."

"Sin?" It seemed as though Sin hadn't even heard him so Carhart slammed his hand against the table. "Wake up."

Sin peered at Carhart moodily. "What?"

"You need to do something about that hair. Report to Cynthia in Unit 16 immediately after this meeting."

Sin did nothing to conceal his contempt. "Whatever."

"It sucks for you guys, though," Owen said to Sin and Boyd as if he had not heard Carhart and Sin's exchange. "He gave you no time. Gave me no time, either. I had to get you plane tickets for tonight already, and I bet you a week's vacation that tomorrow he'll be expecting you to be bright-eyed and chipper, and…" Owen trailed off in confusion. He looked at Ryan, as if asking silently what he had been talking about. "And all awake. And chipper."

"He will," Carhart agreed. "He demanded that the meeting be tomorrow and no later or the whole deal was off. I don't enjoy playing his games but the current state of affairs leaves me very little choice. He is very particular about what he wa—"

"What I don't understand," Sin interrupted, "is why my presence is needed at all. My job is to kill. There will be no killing. I serve no purpose."

"Oh, I'm sure you can find the odd innocent bystander to rip into," Jeffrey drawled.

Sin stared at him and said nothing.

Carhart did not seem amused. His mouth tightened. "You're going because it's your job. You and Boyd are a team. Your job is to back him up when things get out of hand. This isn't a Warren Andrews mission where we know exactly how to handle him. Thierry is a wild card. We can't trust him. For all we know this could be a trap."

Sin glanced at Boyd. "He can handle it. Just put me back in my fucking box and stop making me go on these bullshit assignments."

Carhart sat up straight. His nostrils flared. "Jeff, give Boyd the overview. Sin. See me outside. Now." He stood up and strode outside. Sin rose from his seat and loped out of the room without a backwards glance.

"What the hell is wrong with you two?" Jeffrey asked Boyd. He slid two tablets across the table.

"Nothing." Boyd grabbed one of the tablets and turned it on, flicking through the documents on the touch screen. There was the mission outline, background information on Thierry, the information to download their tickets and more.

Shrugging, Jeffrey didn't press for more. "If you lose the password, you will be out of luck. The information is heavily encrypted."

"Okay."

"I'm sure you can read and you have an eight hour flight so I don't really see the need to tell you detail by detail right now."

"I understand."

Jeffrey gave up with an irritated sigh.

Ryan leaned closer to Boyd, speaking low enough to be unheard by Owen and Jeffrey. "What happened? You were both doing so well."

Boyd just shook his head, not wanting to go into the details. Although he'd spent some time around Ryan on and off over the last few months, Boyd hadn't told anyone about Lou. He couldn't come up with adequate words for Sin, let alone Ryan.

"I know it's none of my business but ever since that night Sin came to my apartment—"

The door slammed open with a crack, cutting Ryan off. Carhart reappeared, a black look on his normally affable face.

"Boyd. Get in my office."

Boyd felt his stomach drop. Any questions that had started to form in his mind as to why in the world Sin had been at Ryan's apartment fled when he saw Carhart's face.

"Yes, sir."

The general left as quickly as he had come, not giving an explanation for his actions. Boyd looked down at his tablet, reluctant to follow although he knew he could not ignore such a summons. After checking the rest of the information and ensuring he could access it on both tablets, Boyd left the conference room to head upstairs. When he reached the reception area outside Carhart's office, Amy advised Boyd to walk right in. He did so with some hesitation, pulling the door shut behind him.

Carhart was standing by the window, staring down at the skyline of Lexington. His shoulders were tense, posture ramrod straight.

"I don't suppose anyone ever told you how I met Sin's father?"

The question seemed like a non-sequitur but Boyd replied, "No, sir."

"After the war began, the military was a mess. Our Commander in Chief was dead, the Vice President was dead, the Secretary of

Defense... dead. The Pentagon was in shambles." Carhart pointed down through the window and Boyd moved closer, seeing that the general was indicating the remains of the gutted military base near the Wasteland. "My family died there. A wife and child. The war took everything from me, but when the Agency recruited me, I felt like I had a purpose again. And I moved up quickly because of my experience as a Marine. When the Agency bumped me up to rank 9, I met Sin's father."

Boyd was surprised to hear so much about Carhart's life, but he was more distracted by the hint of a smile in Carhart's voice at the mention of Sin's father. When Carhart turned to Boyd again, it had faded to a subtle quirk.

"He was such a cocky fuck. I disliked him at first, especially because everyone else loved him. I was quiet and he was outgoing, I was a loner and he was so damn charismatic. He baited me and we'd argue. But we worked together for a while and he saved my life more than once. It made me feel worthless at first. I was the one with the military background, the apt pupil, and he was some smartass street kid from the *favelas* and slums, self-trained and brash, learned everything he knew from street fighting... yet he was better than me."

Boyd thought Sin and his father sounded quite opposite, other than the brash part, but he said nothing.

"There was a time when things were especially bad. The government was still picking up the pieces and everyone was an enemy. Emilio was sent on long solo missions, assassination missions, he'd disappear for months on undercover stints. Our main form of communication was email for two years."

Carhart's expression was faraway. "When his assignment began to wind down and he was finally supposed to come home, something changed. I knew something was different when the tone of his mission reports changed and the e-mails stopped, but I never suspected why." Carhart glanced up at Boyd. "Do you know what changed?"

"Sin helped him?" Boyd ventured.

"You could say that."

Carhart walked around his desk and leaned against the front of it. "We expected Emilio for the debriefing but instead we got his son. In walked little Vega with his father's laptop, fourteen years old, skinny as a reed and with his father's intense green eyes. We still don't have

SANTINO & AIS

complete intel on the events that occurred during that time but as far as we gathered, r concealed his son's existence for six years as he trained him and took him on assassination missions. I think he'd been planning to get the Agency to recruit the boy but it didn't happen exactly as he had planned. We're not sure how Emilio died. We never saw a body, never got a straight answer, but it seems that he'd been dead a year before the debriefing and Sin had completed the assignments on his own."

The information stunned Boyd. "Why did he come in? Couldn't he have ignored the summons?"

Carhart spread his hands and his eyes cast down, troubled by what he was saying. "I don't know. I don't even know why he completed the missions after Emilio died. A normal child would have run away, I imagine. Unfortunately, Sin was never truly a child. Emilio was my friend but when Sin arrived here, he was half the age of any other agent and ten times as skilled a killer. What Emilio did to get him to that point, I can only wonder about."

Looking down at the tablets in his hands, Boyd nodded for lack of anything better to do.

"I always knew it was a bad idea to assign him missions but no one listened to me at that time," Carhart said. "They couldn't pass up so good a killer, especially one they thought they could mold from childhood. They didn't care about his age. Or the fact that there was something... wrong with him."

"Wrong?"

"Yes. Sin was always different. He knew nothing else but violence so he could react in no other way than with violence. He was like a dog that had been trained only to fight. He had no bark. It was all bite."

When Carhart continued, the traces of guilt, of shame, in his voice grew so obvious that Boyd reacted to the general's pain. He crossed his arms over his stomach and listened to each word that was so packed so full of self-loathing.

"The people here didn't help. They knew he was mentally unstable but still they used him and while they used him, they ridiculed him. They labeled him as a freak because he was so young and such an adept killer; they sent him to murder but flinched at him because he did it so well and without any emotion. He got older, colder, more violent. They treated him like a wild animal that could never be tamed, even if they could force him to do what they wanted at times. Eventually, the Agency began to worry. He was too skilled an assassin to give up but he was wild and out of control. They devised ways to control him without having to get rid of him."

Outside, the wind gusted loud enough to whistle beyond the glass that ran along one length of the wall. It drew Boyd's attention outside, and he kept it there even as Carhart continued.

"I promised myself I would protect Sin, but I couldn't do it. I didn't know how. He was so damaged. Delicate and hard at the same time, and there is no room for someone like that in this world. So, I didn't know how to fix all of the wrongs that had been done, and I continued in the same vein as the Agency by coming up with things like... the collar. I only did it to convince Connors to give him another chance because I can't stand to see Sin in that box where his claustrophobia pushes him further into insanity. So I gave him the collar, I pushed for us to try giving him a partner again, and even then I didn't think it would work. I didn't think you would last as his partner, but for a while it seemed..."

Carhart trailed off, his handsome face creased with weariness. "For a while I saw a side of him that I'd never seen before. But now it's gone. He told me that if I didn't put him back in the box, he would make me sorry. That he would force me to do it. I need to know why."

Boyd felt caught by Carhart's stare; by the history he laid out.

"We—" Boyd halted. What could he possibly say? "Something happened and it created some distance between us. He may be upset about that."

"And what is this something that occurred?"

"Just a miscommunication," Boyd said in a quiet voice.

Carhart did not look convinced, but he inclined his head. "Whatever it is, it needs to be sorted out. I don't think Sin was serious but if he starts to regress, things will go very poorly for him. He becomes volatile, impulsive, and that is almost always when he starts to lash out. And now I'm going to get to the real reason I called you in here. What happened to your remote? I know the chip has either malfunctioned or been destroyed."

Boyd had completely forgotten about the remote. That night in the cabin seemed to have happened years ago instead of months.

"It... I think it broke."

SANTINO & AIS

"It broke," Carhart repeated. "I didn't mention the remote before because Sin had showed considerable improvement in his behavior. But now that he has gone right back to where he'd been before, I feel it is imperative that you have it. And don't misunderstand—I do not want you to hurt Sin. I do not want you to ever use that thing unless there is no other choice."

Boyd nodded, but knew he never would. He had managed to stop Sin before without the collar and would try again. He would never shock Sin like an animal. Even so, he picked up the remote.

And just like that, Carhart shelved the emotions that had shown so clearly and was all business again. "Sin is with Cynthia getting ready. I suggest you do the same. Your flight is in a few hours."

Boyd turned to go but Carhart spoke before he got to the door.

"Sin is not the only one you should be worried about on this assignment. Thierry is a good source of information but he has a knack for putting us through hell in order to get it. Regardless of that, we must have it. The information he's hinting at could turn this entire war with Janus, Boyd. It could change everything. And I need you to do whatever it takes to get it."

The words added weight to already burdened shoulders. Questions ran through Boyd's mind; *what if I can't handle it right now? What if I screw up?* His hand went to his wrist before he could stop himself, feeling haunted by the past as he remembered his mother's warning of what would come of failing.

Boyd swallowed but inclined his head. "I won't fail."

And he wouldn't. He would do whatever it took.

THE AGENCY STAFF in Unit 16 gave Boyd a haircut and a selection of suits worth thousands of dollars. He changed into a charcoal-colored suit and a button down shirt, looking more sophisticated than he ever had in his life. Cynthia fussed at and complimented him before teasing that Boyd would be shocked when he saw Sin. Boyd had mostly ignored the comments, uncomfortable with the attention and physical touching, but forty minutes later, he realized she was right.

For the first time since they'd met, Sin was clean-shaven and his unruly hair was cut shorter even though he'd already run his hands through it. He was wearing a black suit with a tight gray t-shirt that showcased his sculpted torso beneath an open jacket. Even after the past two weeks of awkward silence, Boyd could only stare. Sin had always possessed a wild beauty, but now it was polished and unbelievably sexy. As they stood there, yards apart, Boyd noticed other people craning their heads toward Sin as they walked by.

Sin sneered and the spell was broken.

Boyd picked up his bag and crossed the lobby of the Tower. When Sin noticed him it was with a glance that was so passing it felt like a dismissal, and Boyd felt a pang of disappointment. The desire to fix things crashed down on him but collided with the wall that kept all of the horrifying memories away.

It could not happen now. He would fix things later. Breaking down in the middle of a mission that would require a heavy amount of social interaction would not help either of them. And being punished for a mission failure would only break him completely.

"You look good," Boyd said when they were side by side.

"I look like an idiot."

Boyd shook his head but fell silent.

Their transport turned out to be a semi-private jet. Boyd didn't know if Owen had arranged it, or if it was at Thierry's behest, but it was a direct flight to Paris that would arrive in eight hours. Not daring to sleep, Boyd spent the time going over the mission and, when that was finished, brushing up on his French.

Sin sat apart from Boyd during the flight and they only spoke when necessary. Boyd tried to focus on anything but his partner and the reasons for their distance, but even with the mission and practicing his second language to distract him, it wasn't possible. Boyd kept his attention on the window, on the fluffy clouds that looked so pure way up in the sky, but it proved to be a mistake when he dozed into sleep.

The nightmare assaulted him instantly and Boyd ripped himself out of it with the taste of blood in his mouth. His eyes flew to Sin but he was asleep. The relief was staggering.

Irrational fear clawed at Boyd's heart. With demons chasing him and the afterimage of Lou's body burned into his cornea, everything and everyone felt like a threat. Everyone seemed ready to hurt him. Including Sin. *Look,* that fear told him, *he already did in the cabin. Remember how strong he is. How he can overpower you any time he wants. It's only because he chooses not to that he doesn't. But what if he ever changes his mind?*

SANTINO & AIS

Boyd went into the bathroom, braced his hands on the counter, and took deep breaths to calm the pounding of his heart.

If he'd only been more successful in shutting himself down, if he'd only been strong enough to become irrevocably dead inside, then the ID wouldn't have bothered him. He wouldn't be having these nightmares. He wouldn't be afraid of the memories. He wouldn't make connections with what Sin could do to him rather than focusing on what he hadn't. He wouldn't be doubting himself on this mission. He would be fine. Everything would be fine, the way it had been before.

He was weak but he could be strong. Strong people did anything it took to do what needed to be done. He could do that, too. He could be someone else, someone better, for this mission.

Boyd splashed water on his face and scrutinized himself in the mirror. Outwardly, he was presentable and in control. That was all that mattered for now.

THEIR HOTEL SUITE had two separate bedrooms. Everything about it was decadent and luxurious, with rich décor and a wall of windows overlooking one of the few views in Paris with little lingering damage.

They both hovered in the main room, not speaking, before Boyd ended up choosing the far bedroom. He barely had time to fully gather himself before they were leaving to meet Thierry.

The dining hall was more opulent than the suites. Chandeliers hung from the ceiling with dangling crystals that made the light sparkle. Couples in elegant clothing dotted the space, with the occasional group of three or four, and Boyd paused just inside the room to scan their faces. When he didn't spot Thierry, Boyd turned to Sin to ask when a man came up behind them.

Thierry was even more attractive in person. He was just under six feet tall and had a sleek muscular build, his dark hair carelessly styled. He approached them with a smile, white teeth flashing as his eyes slid from Boyd to Sin and back.

"Hello, hello," Thierry said with genuine-sounding enthusiasm. "We meet again, Monsieur Vega. But who is this young man accompanying you?"

Sin did not smile. "You thought it was just me?"

"Yes, even despite our previous misunderstanding. But that is in the past, let us not be rude." Thierry turned to Boyd. "I am Thierry Beauvais. I welcome you to my home."

"Thank you, Monsieur Beauvais," Boyd replied with a smile. Wanting to give the best impression possible, he switched to French. *"Enchanté de faire votre connaissance, je me présente, Boyd Beaulieu. Merci beaucoup pour votre invitation."*

Sin's gaze shifted to Boyd but he didn't speak. Thierry, however, was delighted and his face lit up. He slid his arm through Boyd's, guiding him over to one of the tables so their backs were to Sin.

"Your French is excellent—almost native sounding," Thierry said in French. *"How did you learn? School, perhaps?"*

"I did take some classes but I learned from my mother."

They approached a table that was tucked into an alcove in the corner. Thierry settled on the same side as Boyd while Sin, who had lagged behind them, sat on the other side.

"Is she French, your mother?"

"Yes. She grew up here."

"Excellent." Thierry's smile turned a touch indulgent. He turned his attention to Sin and the two surveyed each other coolly. During the interim, a waiter glided over with three glasses and a bottle of wine.

"I find it quite amazing that your organization continues to find such beautiful specimens of masculinity to recruit." Thierry poured the red liquid into their glasses. "How very odd that I feel quite plain as I sit next to the two of you." Thierry paused with the neck of the bottle tilted towards Sin's glass. "For you?"

"No."

Seeming unsurprised, Thierry set the bottle down and returned to Boyd. *"Do you not find it interesting that the Agency only wants beautiful people?"*

"Perhaps they only send the attractive ones to you to make you believe we're all beautiful," Boyd replied, trying to subtly steer it back to English.

"Or perhaps they know beautiful young men are my weakness," Thierry replied in French. He picked up his glass and took a sip, looking at Sin over the glass. "Is that not correct, Sin?"

"I have no idea what the fuck you're talking about."

A smirk found its way onto Thierry's lips. He sat back and crossed one knee over the other. "Did you tell our young friend about our previous meeting, Sinful?"

"Why don't you do the honors?" was the flat response.

"Heh." Thierry turned his body to Boyd again. *"I am not sure how long you have known Sinful, but those outstanding features mask quite a terrible temper. He was quite cruel to me on our last meeting."*

Boyd glanced at Sin. He considered switching back to English again but was hesitant to do so. Carhart's words were a dark current in his mind and, with Sin looking uninterested in being involved, it seemed like it might annoy Thierry.

"I could see the two of you being at cross-purpose," was all Boyd said.

The sound of Sin's fingers tapping against the table made an audible, staccato sound.

"I was surprised that they were to send him again, although I have been told that he is considered the best in many capacities. A sad testament of our times when a powerful organization such as yours must be in such desperation to rely on one such as him, who seems incapable of understanding the importance of society—" Thierry pushed hair off Boyd's forehead. *"—and human interaction."*

Boyd started in surprise but recovered. *"Well,"* he said with a small smile, *"we all have our talents."*

"And what are some of yours?"

"Negotiation, I suppose. And strategies. I enjoy planning."

"Mmm. Interesting. You make quite the spy, I must say. Just like in the old movies—the beautiful, talented agent who is known more for intelligence than brawn. I am intrigued as to how you became what you are. You seem quite young for this profession."

Boyd thought Thierry was laying it on thick. It felt strange to have someone seem so interested in him, but he nodded and kept his expression amiable. *"I am, to an extent. I was recruited as a possible partner for Sin. My age is a bit atypical for my position."*

Thierry made a sound at the back of his throat and took in Sin's obvious irritation.

"A pity you were only recognized to be his partner. I can imagine you are capable of much more. Your looks, manner, your ease in talking to people—I have met many people in my time and it is not simply with kindness do I say that."

Right, Boyd thought. You probably say that to everyone.

"*Thank you,*" he said aloud.

The combination of Thierry's flattery and Sin's glare persuaded Boyd to try English again. "And thank you again for inviting us to visit your hotel. I've never seen anything like it."

"Thank you. It took a long time to restore it to what it was pre-war. I seek to give people a place they can enjoy, a place they can find luxurious."

"Paris is lucky to have a business owner such as yourself who is able to restore the glamour of the city. It would be a shame if there were another incident and this was all lost once again."

"We will see where the world takes us next." Thierry took in the other patrons, nodding once at a woman across the room, before gliding his attention back to them. "Would you like to dine or are drinks fine for now?"

Boyd glanced at Sin, who gave him no indication of what he wanted. "Perhaps we could discuss business over drinks."

"Mmm." Thierry raised his glass but did not drink. "*I think I would rather hear more about you tonight.*"

"What more is there to hear?"

Thierry reached out and squeezed Boyd's hand. It was almost as though they were the only two people at the table.

"*I am sure there is much more to you than your partnership with this one.*"

Boyd contemplated his glass, forcing a smile that he hoped appeared shy. In truth, he was taken aback. It had been years since someone had shown him this much attention and since someone had looked at him with such obvious desire. Thierry was setting a tone that would be hard to undo if it went further, but Boyd could tell just by the few minutes they'd been in each other's presence that distracting Thierry would be trickier than expected.

For now, he'd have to play along.

SIXTEEN

THEIR FIRST EVENING with Thierry had lingered well into the night and lasted for two bottles of wine. The discussion had centered on Boyd, France, and anything else that came to Thierry's head. The rapport was easy to build and for the most part, pleasant. To Boyd's chagrin, they'd never gotten around to discussing business.

Boyd had fallen asleep more relaxed than he'd been in weeks but it had been swept away by another nightmare. He woke feeling restless and unsettled, but dressed for a day of sightseeing. Another of Thierry's plans.

When it was time to leave, Boyd waited in the outer room for several minutes before knocking on Sin's door. It opened to reveal Sin shirtless and wearing a pair of jeans. His hair was uncombed and he hadn't bothered to shave.

"We're supposed to be downstairs in half an hour," Boyd said. "I'm done in the bathroom if you want."

"I don't see the point in going."

Boyd frowned. His immediate reaction was to argue but, in truth, it probably did not matter.

"If you don't want to come, I can go alone. It may work better that way, anyway."

"I'm sure it will."

"I just meant that it was likely Thierry would end up speaking French again and you would be bored."

Sin crossed his arms. "Yes, I am sure it will be very likely since you made sure that it would end up that way."

Boyd huffed out an impatient breath. "I just wanted to build rapport and I thought introducing myself in French would be best. I didn't know he was going to bring everything back to French for the rest of the night."

Sin took a step back into his room. "Why wouldn't he? You basically invited that cozy little situation."

Boyd was starting to grow aggravated with the conversation. "What does it matter either way? We need him on our side and this seems to be working. It'll get us what we need."

"Fine," Sin said. "Go get what you need. What the fuck do I know, anyway?"

Boyd threw his hands in the air. "Jesus Christ, how should I know? I never do anything right, according to you. You used to leave the negotiation to me, at least, but apparently now even having it work isn't good enough for you. Do you want to come with so you can point out all the things I'm doing wrong along the way?"

"No, go ahead. Keep fawning all over him and be fucking naive, and I'll stay here so you don't have to say a goddamn word to me just like you want."

Boyd jerked back as if he'd been hit. He opened his mouth, didn't know what to say, and felt anger grow in place of anything else. He jerked his coat off the chair, threw it on, and jammed his fists into his pockets. "I'm going."

Sin kicked his door shut, and that only made Boyd's anger rise. He stormed out of the room, slamming the door harder than necessary and jogging to the stairwell.

He was furious by the time he'd made it to the base of the stairs. Why the hell couldn't Sin just give him some space? What the fuck had he expected when he'd thrown Lou's ID down out of nowhere? That Boyd would fawn all over him the way he thought Boyd was fawning over Thierry? They were completely different situations. One required time to deal with the unexpected fallout, and the other was just business.

He had to pause when he reached the lobby, his head tipped down and hair hiding any fluctuations of expression he hadn't yet controlled. He drew in a deep breath and let it out slowly, trying to calm down. He wished, not for the first time, that Sin couldn't get under his skin like no one else ever had. He had to be approachable when he met with Thierry. He had to do this right. After another measured breath and a conscious loosening of his shoulders, his frustration slid beneath the wall he'd constructed inside.

Later. He could deal with Sin later. When he had the words to explain, Sin would understand. For now, the mission was all that mattered.

When Boyd left the hotel, a sleek black town car pulled up to the curb. Boyd got into the backseat next to Thierry.

"Thank you."

"And where is your partner?" Thierry asked with raised eyebrows.

"He will be unable to make it today. I hope my presence alone is acceptable?"

Thierry's eyes slid to the window where the hotel loomed beyond. "Did you tell him to stay behind, or did he decide to?"

"A little of both, I suppose."

"I see." Thierry waved his hand at the driver. *"Va."*

Boyd wondered if Thierry was unhappy about the turn of events.

"I could call him and ask him to join us if you'd like."

The car moved down the street and Thierry shook his head.

"That will not be necessary. Perhaps it is just as well. He was quite jealous."

"Jealous?" *More like pissed off,* Boyd thought. "What makes you think that?"

Thierry gave Boyd a sidelong glance. "Surely you must have noticed. He could not take his eyes away from you."

"I confess I was paying more attention to you than my partner."

It was true enough. By the time Thierry had started flirting openly Boyd had been so distracted that he hadn't thought to consider his partner's reaction.

Thierry's lips curved up. "Is that so?"

"It is."

"Hmm." Thierry extended a finger and slid it along Boyd's cheek. His fingertip ghosted down and over Boyd's mouth before moving away. "I was not surprised that he is jealous. I already find myself possessive of you. I envied Sin for being able to walk with you to the room last night while I was forced to return alone."

"Again, you flatter me."

"To flatter is to be false." Thierry put his hand atop Boyd's, squeezing. "It is rare for someone in your line of work to treat me as a man instead of an asset. That you are charming is a magnificent bonus."

Boyd smiled but couldn't help wondering how much of Thierry's words were genuine. After years of being despised for one reason or another, whether it was his personality, his connections or sexual orientation, it was hard to believe someone as successful and attractive as Thierry could truly desire him. Even the people closest to Boyd judged his every move and constantly found him lacking. Gentle caresses and words of adoration were foreign to him, but Boyd could not ignore that the deepest part of him craved it. Acknowledging even that much felt like a betrayal to the effort he had made for years to forbid those needs to enter his thoughts.

"Where are we going today?"

"Anywhere you want."

Before he shut himself away from the rest of the world, Boyd had read books about France and identified places he had wanted to see, but those occasions were like a distant dream that he could no longer remember. The obvious attractions such as museums would take the majority of the day, and Boyd's interest in shopping was nonexistent. It was tempting to suggest getting lunch and discussing Janus but after Thierry's comment about being seen as an asset, refusing the generosity of his time and attention would be counterproductive.

All Boyd could think to say was that he was fascinated by architecture and the history of the city. Thierry was delighted, and his driver took them on a meandering tour of Paris for the better part of the morning.

It went by in a blur of elegant streets, gardens, opulent architecture and gleaming gold, as well as monuments that had managed to survive three world wars. Those, however, were the exceptions. The French had gotten about as far as the Americans with complete reconstruction. As Boyd looked down wealthy streets and saw the destruction in the distance, he was reminded of the Financial District in Lexington.

They stopped for a late lunch at a cafe on Rue Cler and Boyd could not help looking out the window to take in more of the city. The streets in Paris were so different than Lexington. Back home there was a clear distinction between pedestrian and vehicular areas. Here, at least by the cafe, everything blended together on the same grade, with streets that were aesthetically pleasing to the eye even as fast-driving motorists whizzed by.

"You spoke of your mother yesterday." Thierry's comment dragged Boyd's attention away from their surroundings. He realized that Thierry had been watching, his face cast in muted rays of sunlight. "Did she not tell you anything of her home country?"

Boyd shook his head. "Nearly everything I know about France I learned in a book. I have some memories of her talking about Paris when I was young, but it's so vague I'm not even certain it really happened."

"From the little I have heard of your relationship with your mother, it reminds me greatly of the distance that existed between my father and myself."

The information caught Boyd's attention. Thierry's file had mentioned a falling out before his father's death but there had been no details. An annotation had claimed Thierry was notoriously secretive about his father, but that was at odds with the sight of him looking pensively into a glass of wine and discussing it with Boyd.

"Did something specific happen to cause distance?"

"He never liked my way."

"What way is that?"

At that, Thierry released a rich chuckle that eased away any traces of melancholy. "Expulsions from boarding school for inspiring rebellions, leading adults to believe anything I wanted, and, of course, seducing my male tutors."

"Tutors, plural?" Boyd asked, amused. "How many of them did you seduce?"

Thierry leaned forward conspiratorially. "Enough of them to ensure he hired women in the future. Although I suppose the elderly gentleman did not fall for my charms."

Boyd couldn't help a quiet laugh. If nothing else came out of this afternoon, at least he could marvel at a stranger who had managed to draw him out of a depression that had seemed so unrelenting mere days ago.

"You are a dangerous man, Thierry."

"Of that, you can be sure." Thierry stroked the side of Boyd's hand with his finger, the movement slow and deliberate. "My father did not appreciate the embarrassment that I brought to his name. Even before he knew I was gay, he held some distaste for my temperament as a child. It is unfortunate that my mother died when I was quite young. I fear I never knew the love of a parent properly. Perhaps this is why I have always sought it in other places."

Looking down at their hands, Boyd wondered how their lives could sound so similar despite circumstances that put them worlds apart. Was it an act? Practiced lines? It was impossible to tell just how much was real in terms of behavior, but the words could not be born of deception. The similarities were too stark and Thierry knew nothing of Boyd's life. He did not know that Boyd's mother had also held him in distaste seemingly from birth. That his father had died, leaving Boyd in the hands of a parent who was cold and detached. Or that being gay had only added to Vivienne's disdain.

Having a man like Thierry admit to sharing a similar upbringing caused something to crack within Boyd. A tiny part of the wall that locked his old self away and left only a skeleton of the boy he had once been. Someone unwanted and worthless.

The feel of Thierry's fingertips ghosting along his skin did not produce the electrifying tingle Boyd felt any time Sin touched him, but he could not deny that he felt a measure of comfort. So he did not push Thierry away. How could he when so many things Thierry said resonated so strongly within him? What Thierry said about looking for love elsewhere rang in Boyd's ears.

The temptation to turn his palm to Thierry's and reciprocate the touch was strong, but Boyd resisted. Instead, he began to speak.

"My mother… She was the same. She's never approved of me. I used to try so hard to be worthy of her praise but I have almost no recollection of it ever happening." Boyd tried to smile as if it meant nothing, but he knew it must look strained and bitter. "Of course, when it became apparent that I was gay, it didn't help my standing with her."

"We are much alike, you and I," Thierry observed. "Perhaps that is why I feel drawn to you."

"Perhaps."

Boyd fell silent. For all that Sin had criticized his approach it seemed that Boyd had succeeded in gaining Thierry's trust. Even so, time was running out and Boyd was reminded of that as the sky darkened outside the cafe.

He let out a quiet breath. "Thierry, I don't mean to be rude but we have to return to America tomorrow and I'm growing worried about having to go back empty-handed. I'd really like the chance to discuss work with you. Could we do that?"

Thierry patted Boyd's hand and sat up straight. "Yes, but not now. I would like to invite you to my home this evening."

Every time Boyd took a small step, he was expected to follow with a leap or bound. Holding hands was one thing but being alone in the man's house had implications Boyd was not sure he was ready to handle. He started to say no but the reality of the mission, of the Agency and his mother, forced Boyd to incline his head.

"Of course. What time would you like me over?"

"I have some things to attend to after lunch." Thierry made eye contact with a waitress. "I will drop you off at the hotel and return this evening. Please do explain to your partner where you will be so he does not think I have abducted you and rip apart my hotel."

"I will."

When Boyd returned to the hotel, he found Sin sitting on the edge of the couch with a tablet clenched in his hand. His dark brows were drawn together, expression severe.

Boyd shut the door. "Did something happen?"

Sin shook his head, tight-lipped. "I have a mission when we return."

"Just you?"

"Yes. Rank 10 mission." Sin turned off the tablet and dropped it on the table with a clatter.

Sin had never told him what rank 10 missions entailed but Boyd assumed it wasn't anything pleasant, especially considering the expression on Sin's face. Boyd sat on the edge of the armchair and sighed, covering his face with his hand. He briefly considered putting off this conversation but ultimately decided it was better to get it over with right away.

"I wanted to let you know you'll have the room to yourself for a while tonight."

"Why is that?"

"I'll be at Thierry's."

When Boyd uncovered his face, he saw that Sin was on his feet and staring with raised brows and slightly parted lips.

"Why the hell would you do that?"

"He wouldn't talk business today but he said he would if I came over. We only have until tomorrow to get what we need, so..."

Boyd thought that would be the end of it but then Sin lifted his hand and rubbed his forehead.

"You shouldn't go."

"If I don't, how are we going to get what we need?" Boyd demanded. "We're running out of time. I'll just go over, get the information, and come back. I'm only telling you so you don't wonder where I am."

"And you think it's going to be as simple as that?"

"No, but what does it matter? He said he'd talk to me if I came over so that's what I'll do. After today, I feel like I have an idea of how he works. I'll use that to figure out how to get what we need so I can stop worrying about it."

"If you have an idea of how he works, then you're aware that there's a good chance he'll want you to fuck him for it."

"Obviously that's a possibility. I'm not going over planning on that. I just want him to talk. But you heard General Carhart—the information is important. We can't go back without it."

The explanation did not appease Sin. If anything, his face became a mask of judgment. "So you'd actually do it then?"

"I don't know," Boyd said. "My plan is to get him to talk without going any further. But we're quickly running out of time and if nothing works and it's a question between that or going home with nothing—"

Boyd looked down, one thumb worrying at the wrist of his other hand. He'd promised himself he would be strong this time; he would do whatever it took to please his mother and even Carhart. No matter what, this mission couldn't fail. Her words, cool and unmoved, replayed in his mind. *We have facilities that would be ideal to give you an opportunity to recover from your lapse. Time need not be a factor. Is that what you wish?*

"I don't know," he said with more force. "I guess I have to plan for the possibility of that happening, too."

The shock on Sin's face made Boyd want to take the words back.

"Did it ever occur to you to say fuck the mission?" Sin asked, his voice scraping out low. "Or do you actually want to bend over for that manipulative piece of trash?"

"Fuck the mission and then what? Go back to the Agency and tell them sorry, I didn't try hard enough? They wouldn't let that pass. And—" Boyd's jaw tightened in resolve. "If a mission fails, it's not going to be because of me."

"If you don't listen to me, for the first fucking time, you're going to regret it."

Sin turned away. Everything made it so clear that he was furious, but Boyd did not understand why. Of all people, he thought Sin would understand why he felt like he had no choice.

"If you have a magical answer to getting the information from Thierry tonight short of working this angle, then tell me. I'd love to hear it. But if you're just going to tell me I'm doing the wrong thing and offer no other solution aside from failing the mission then I don't know what to tell you. I can't do that. I'm bringing the information back with us no matter what."

"You can't do that?" Sin spun around, his voice rising until it boomed in the otherwise silent room. "Mommy isn't going to terminate you, you fucking moron. What are you scared of, a trip to the Fourth? Man up—who cares? Have some dignity instead of being so quick to stoop to the lowest level just to please the fucking Agency."

"Man up? Do you even—" Boyd cut himself off. "You know what? Just don't. Don't try to pretend you know me. Or her. You have no idea what she will and will not do to me."

"And you obviously don't know shit about me if you think I haven't been tortured in every possible way at the Agency, and I still wouldn't ever become their little prostitute," Sin growled. "But go ahead, have fun."

"Yeah, well, sorry I'm not impervious to life like you."

Sin only shook his head, the lines of his face etched in contempt.

Anger and indignation warred until the tension in Boyd made him feel locked in place.

"I can't talk to you right now."

"That's fine," Sin said. "Because I'm fucking done with you. This is the second time I tried to help you, and the second time I completely regret the effort."

Boyd felt something unpleasant welling within him at the words, but instead of focusing on it, he stalked into his room and slammed the door. But even being alone didn't help; the atmosphere felt oppressed, giving him no way out. He dropped onto the bed and leaned forward, his fingers digging into his hair. Sin's words echoed in his head, jumbled by Carhart's and his mother's until he didn't know what to think. What to feel.

What was he supposed to do? He didn't want to have sex with Thierry but he couldn't go back to the Agency with nothing. He couldn't disappoint his mother. The consequences of failing...

His chest tightened at the thought; at the memory of pain lancing up his arms; his own screams echoing around him and the darkness closing in on every side. Terror eclipsing all else to the point that he didn't even know what was a dream from that time and what was a horrible mockery of reality. The memories of Lou's murder that wouldn't leave him and the knowledge every time he'd slept and woken that he was alone, completely alone without any recourse and no one would care and no one would help him—

Boyd let out a harsh breath. No, he couldn't do it. He couldn't. He didn't care what he had to do to avoid his mother's form of punishment.

Why didn't Sin understand? He had his own demons, his own fears that he would do anything to escape. Why didn't he get that rebellion was pointless for Boyd? The only worth he had was determined by his viability as an agent—someone who could find the means to an end that might satisfy his mother and the few people he had come to respect.

Even so, Sin's words haunted him. The first time Sin had tried to help could only mean Jared, but did he really regret it? Did he regret everything he'd done for Boyd?

I'm fucking done with you. I completely regret the effort.

The words cut deep even though Boyd knew he should have never expected anything more. Eventually, people always regretted expending effort on him. He had tried to explain this to Sin from the start. Had tried to explain to Sin that he was replaceable, forgettable, and so very often a disappointment.

But maybe if Boyd could only succeed in this, everything would be okay. He and Thierry would be in different countries tomorrow and likely never see each other again. The mission would succeed, and neither he nor Sin would be punished for failure. Maybe then, Sin would understand. Maybe then, his mother would see that he had tried. There would be no harm done and eventually, this could be forgotten.

Boyd told himself that but he couldn't forget the look of disgust on Sin's face.

SANTINO & AIS

SEVENTEEN

THE DRIVER BROUGHT them to Avenue du Maréchal Maunoury in the 16e arrondissement. The building they pulled up to was beautiful from the front; brick with white trim and looking more like an old mansion rather than luxury apartments. Thierry lived on the highest floor and it was as sophisticated as Boyd had expected. Though less ostentatious than the hotel, there were hardwood floors with tall ceilings, cream walls, and dark trim. Floor-to-ceiling windows lined one wall, overlooking Bois de Boulogne Park and what little could be seen of the River Seine.

"Welcome," Thierry's voice called from somewhere inside. He appeared moments later with bare feet and tousled hair. "I thank you for coming."

"Thank you the invitation." Boyd walked further into the room. "You have a very nice apartment. Even at night, the view is amazing."

"I take pleasure in surrounding myself in amazing things." Thierry kissed Boyd's cheek and put an arm around him. "And you, my dear, are frozen. Would you like some wine to warm up?"

"A little."

Thierry pulled glasses out of a cabinet and took them to a table where a bottle of wine waited. "Make yourself comfortable."

"Thank you."

A sleek white couch curved around the table, the fabric softer than Boyd had expected. He ran his fingers over the cushion, eyes drawn to the flames licking from the fireplace. When Thierry sat next to him and pressed a glass into his hand, Boyd forced himself to relax. Everything felt warm and inviting. The impression was furthered by the taste of wine filling his mouth, the smell overcoming his senses.

"I was pleased when you told me earlier you were interested in discussing our mutual acquaintances. Janus has been a growing concern for us and we're very grateful for any help you would be willing to give. After all, you're something of an expert on the topic."

"Perhaps. It was not always this way, though. At one time I was just a novice, barely understanding my place in it all."

Boyd nodded, pouncing on the opening. "As I understand it, you got into the business when you were eighteen?"

"Seventeen, actually. I was aware of my father's dealings with Janus since I was quite young. When he died, I simply took up the mantle."

"What was it like?"

A wry smile formed on Thierry's mouth. He tilted his head as if trying to figure how to describe the memories of his early life, before he had been at the heart of a geopolitical storm.

"To say they did not know what to expect from me would be accurate. To them, I was a spoiled boy trying to involve myself in affairs that were better left out of my reach. They did not respect me, even when I began to work for them."

"What did you do?"

"I refused to give up." Thierry's tone was light but there was an intensity in his face. Boyd wondered if Thierry was like him; if his memories sprang forth with a jarring vividness that could transport him to another time. "Their world, my father's world, it was something that intrigued me. For so long I felt as though I was without purpose and this thing, this strange thing that I do, it gives me purpose. After quite some time, they finally began to admire my tenacity."

Boyd nodded, looking away. He wondered if he would ever get to the point where he felt a purpose for anything instead of simply going through the motions of his life. He doubted it. His sense of purpose and any goals had been taken the night Lou was killed.

"Did you feel that way right away?" Boyd glanced at Thierry. "Having a purpose?"

Thierry set his wine glass down and rested his arm on the back of the sofa. "No, at first it was a game. Perhaps like chess. Or perhaps a spectator sporting event that I had helped to fund so that the teams could keep playing. It kept me busy, but I did not expect to become so immersed and to eventually care."

"What drew you away from working solely with Janus like your father had?"

One of Thierry's hands began sifting through Boyd's hair as he pondered the question. "I did not like the idea of putting all of my eggs in one basket."

"It must have been a trying time, when you were learning the ways

228   SANTINO & AIS

and who to trust. Did anyone take you under their wing and help you out?"

"Not at all," Thierry said. "It was only me and my ambitions. But what of you?"

Boyd was disappointed but not entirely surprised by the subject change. "Not at first. Things are changing over time, though."

"Sin did not guide you? Is he not an agent of some high degree?"

"He is but he wasn't interested in being my partner. In the beginning I think he was simply amusing himself by seeing how long it would take for me to fail."

"How unfortunate." Thierry's hands became bold, moving to stroke the side of Boyd's face. "It would have been quite terrible if I would have never been able to meet you."

"I doubt it would have mattered. You wouldn't have known what you were missing, right?"

"Perhaps that would have been the worst part."

Boyd avoided answering by taking another sip of his wine.

The night went by with languid indifference to the urgency of the mission. Conversation flowed as steadily as the wine, but failed to return to Janus or any of Thierry's other connections. It was not unlike the day before with Thierry managing to sidetrack Boyd in a dozen subtle ways.

An hour passed, then another, and the effects of the alcohol became obvious. Boyd's body felt warm and his blood buzzed through him. His head was starting to feel clouded, and once or twice he found himself saying a little more than he'd intended. Giving a few more details than he normally would. But he still tried to press Thierry for the information.

He asked about Thierry's life, how he knew about his father's involvement in Janus, whether anyone had ever visited his house. Boyd tried many angles but never broached the topic and before long, found Thierry refilling his glass.

When they had gone through nearly two bottles, Thierry drinking most of it, his flirtation became more pronounced. With the pleasant burn of alcohol in Boyd's system, the muted warmth of the fireplace, and the heat of Thierry's skin brushing against his, Boyd barely considered turning away the Frenchman's advances. Thierry was kind, handsome, and time was running out. Maybe if he gave in, Thierry would relent. Maybe that was what he had been waiting for all along.

The next time Thierry caressed him, Boyd allowed himself to lean into the touch. When Thierry leaned closer, Boyd didn't pull away.

Their lips met, gentle at first. Thierry's mouth was soft and the feel of his kiss was unfamiliar. That sentiment was echoed in the slide of a hand along Boyd's leg, and Thierry's other hand moving into the hair at the nape of Boyd's neck. The oddity of the situation was overcome by the power of a sensual touch after so long. The body Boyd had forsaken awoke at Thierry's hands, aided by the heat and wine.

Boyd's breath caught when Thierry's lips trailed down to his neck, but it still lacked the electric tingle that sucked away his thoughts like when Sin brushed his bare skin with calloused fingertips. There was no explosion of fire in his belly, no frantic gallop of his heart at just the slightest touch, but under the expert maneuvering of Thierry's hands, Boyd's desire stirred. Their lips touched again and the kiss was deeper this time. For the first time in years, Boyd felt the moist slide of a tongue against his lips and allowed himself to be pushed back onto the sofa.

Before he knew it, Boyd was letting out breathless sounds and arching against Thierry in a slow grind. His body was an instrument that Thierry played to perfection; causing him to rise to a crescendo and stopping just before the climax. Whispers of French sifted through the roar in Boyd's head but the feel of a hand touching his shirt nearly snapped Boyd out of the daze.

"Not the shirt," he whispered. "Or underneath."

If Thierry thought the condition was odd, he didn't let it show. They kissed again, and this time, those clever hands went for Boyd's belt. Every motion was orchestrated to perfection; Thierry obviously took great enjoyment in seducing his partners. He ran his mouth over the parts of Boyd he had been allowed to undress, touching and caressing, sucking and pressing light kisses until Boyd was trembling with the need to get off.

"Look at you," Thierry murmured, eyes feasting on Boyd. "If I could capture this moment…"

Boyd turned his face away.

Thierry worshiped every piece of Boyd as if he were a priceless piece of art to be handled with care, taking time to touch every inch of skin before he was covering his erection with a condom and pushing into Boyd. Thierry moved with slow thrusts that stoked a fire burning deep within Boyd and made him crave more.

He hadn't been touched like this in so long that, yet again, the memories came back. Blue eyes hovering over his and soft lips he'd kissed innumerable times smiling down. Their fingers intertwined as they tried to stay silent in Boyd's bedroom, even though Boyd never managed. Inevitably, his voice was always freed from him when he moaned his best friend and lover's name like a prayer.

But those memories were muted with the alcohol and heat, and Boyd grew confused by thoughts of other touches against his skin.

Rougher, tighter, and more electric touches.

Memories of Sin pushing him against the door and his hard body still damp from a recent shower, Sin crouched before him in the shower and the intense way their eyes had locked, every time Sin had laid hands on him casually but firmly because of the undercurrent of power in his body...

A thought came unbidden to Boyd's mind: if it felt this good with touches that didn't ignite his skin, what would it be like with Sin?

Boyd moved against Thierry faster, wanting more, wanting something he would never have, and bit down on his lip when he finally wrapped his hands around his cock and brought himself to orgasm. It was only when Boyd clenched around Thierry's cock did he move faster, throbbing inside Boyd and pushing into his core. When Thierry came, it was with a low moan.

At first, they didn't speak. Thierry rolled onto his side, dark hair tousled and forehead damp with sweat, and brushed a kiss to Boyd's cheek. It should have felt good, but with the passion beginning to cool, Boyd crawled out of the haze of desire. The circumstances one-by-one fell back into place until the reality of what had happened was undeniable. And then, Sin's words returned.

I still wouldn't ever become their little prostitute.

Boyd tried not to flinch.

The wine still muddied his thoughts, the post-orgasmic bliss slowing his movements, but none of that was enough to make him forget the situation. He was on a mission. Thierry was his mission. Whatever it was Thierry had wanted from him, even if it was just to have sex, Boyd's ultimate goal was the information. At that, Boyd felt something close to shame. He did not deserve Thierry's kindness.

Sighing, Boyd sat up. When he glanced down at Thierry, he did not miss the small flash of disappointment.

"Thierry," Boyd said. "About the information—"

A phone rang and Thierry rolled onto his side, reaching for his pants. He answered the phone in French and stood, walking to the other side of the room. His voice dropped too low to decipher and, after gesturing at Boyd, Thierry stepped out of the room. When he didn't immediately reappear, Boyd got dressed. By the time Thierry returned, Boyd was putting on his shoes.

"Unfortunately I must go, dear one. My assistant is arranging a flight as we speak."

Boyd abandoned his laces and surged to his feet. "But we haven't had the chance to talk."

Thierry tied the sash to a robe that hung on his muscular frame and flashed Boyd a smile. "Do not fret. I have the information on a flash drive. I will send it with you when my driver takes you back to the hotel."

"Oh." Boyd tried to find the words for this situation and could only muster a quiet thank you.

"I hope that you will want to see me again someday." Thierry finished tying the robe. "Perhaps this was not just for work?"

Boyd found himself nodding, not wanting Thierry to know that this had only been for the job. For the Agency and Janus. "I enjoyed my time with you," he admitted. "I enjoyed spending time with someone who understands."

"I am glad to hear it."

DURING THE RIDE back to the hotel, Boyd worried about the flash drive Thierry had given him. He'd claimed it contained the information the Agency wanted, but there had been no way to verify at the man's apartment. Relief and anxiety whirled round and round, making it impossible to do anything but focus on the tiny object burning a hole in Boyd's pocket. He barely looked out the window during the drive. He was still lightheaded from the alcohol, still on edge from the reality of his actions, and nearly threw himself out of the car when they arrived at the hotel. A frantic need to check the data overcame

Boyd. It was so manic that when he burst into the suite, he did not realize something was off until an object nearly slammed into his face.

Boyd dodged out of the way, jerking his head to the side as something crashed against the wall. It took a second for him to realize that the destroyed object was the remote to Sin's collar.

"What the hell?" Boyd demanded, peering through the darkness at his partner.

"What the hell, yourself." Sin's voice was frozen and the look on his face caused Boyd to take a step back. Everything from Sin's expression to the tension in his body was humming with hostility.

Taking a deep breath, Boyd tried to collect his thoughts. "Sin, I know what you're thinking but I wasn't—"

"Don't give me your fucking—" Sin crossed the room so fast that Boyd threw up his hands defensively. "—bullshit!"

Sin shoved Boyd against the wall and leaned forward until they were nose to nose. Red flags went off and Boyd's mind skipped back to the night in the cabin; the sight of glittering eyes without a trace of recognition. But Sin did not look on the edge of madness now. He just looked angry.

"You like fucking with me, don't you?" Sin demanded.

"I'm not fucking with you! Won't you just let me explain?"

Sin slammed Boyd back again, causing his head to snap against the wall. A spike of pain shot down Boyd's neck but before he could even think how to maneuver away, his wrists were being wrenched up and pinned above his head. Boyd found himself crushed to the wall with Sin's body, every part of them aligned and their faces close enough to touch. His breath caught.

"What are you going to say?" Sin's mouth pressed against Boyd's ear, his voice low and thick. "You weren't going to use it? Then why was it in your pocket? Why did you bring it? Everything you say is bullshit, and a lie, you just screw with my mind and I'm stupid enough to—to just let you—"

A growl of frustration vibrated in Boyd's eardrum.

Boyd had a hard time concentrating on Sin's words. His thoughts kept zeroing in on the feel of his wrists crushed in Sin's grip, and the immovable press of Sin's body against his own. The vulnerability of the position made it difficult to understand anything but the rising fear at being unable to move.

"Let me go," he whispered.

"No." Sin's grip only tightened. A sigh guttered out of him, warm against Boyd's neck. "I want to hurt you so bad right now."

Boyd grit his teeth and pressed his head back, his heart a painful tattoo in his chest as he tried to think of something that would take him away from the clawing sense of helplessness.

"What do you want from me?"

"I want you to go away." Sin's voice was dropping lower, so low Boyd would not have been able to hear if they'd been further apart. "You fucked my head up, you did this to me, and I want to hate you so bad."

Uncertainty nipped at the opaque fear that had begun to shroud Boyd's mind. "What the hell did I *do?*"

"You made me think that—" Sin pulled back, their faces practically pressed together. "I just wanted to—" Sin's throat clicked when he swallowed. "He was a helpless, emaciated, drug addict. And I ripped him apart because of what he did to you, and you—you acted like I was a freak. And I know I'm not—I'm not normal, but seeing you sit there with *him,* making nice and letting him touch you, and then you let him take you home to fuck you."

"Goddamnit Sin, it's not the same thing!" Boyd could feel his breath quickening, the words twisting together as he tried to explain. "Thierry was for work. Everything with you is different! Just—Just let me go. I can't talk when you're holding me down. But I don't think you're a—"

"It doesn't matter. I just want you gone."

Sin released Boyd's hands but Boyd hardly got the chance to feel relief before Sin was touching him again. He looked torn between pulling away and yanking Boyd back, wanting to leave but not wanting to let go. His hands were shaking when they pressed against Boyd's neck, and then slid up to cup the sides of his face. Sin's fingers dug in hard and their foreheads touched, faces once again so close that the air was shared between their mouths. Sin's breath came in ragged pulls.

"I wish I could hate you, Boyd."

Boyd reached up to curl his hands around Sin's wrists. He didn't know what he planned to do but when he felt Sin's heartbeat pulsing against his fingers, it sidetracked all thoughts. He smoothed his thumb across Sin's skin, feeling the rise and fall of his tendons and veins. Sin shuddered and tilted his head forward again, making it impossible for Boyd to function when they were so close. With his hands free, Sin was no longer a terrifying force with unknown intentions. The swelling terror dissipated and was replaced by confusion and a need to... to do something. Boyd had no idea what.

Sin's eyes were too close, too phenomenally green and burning into Boyd from beneath thick lashes. It was hard to form thoughts, hard to explain all of the complexities of the situation, and when Boyd's lips parted, any words he'd planned to say failed when their lips brushed. Sin stilled against him.

This time, Boyd shuddered. His fingers twitched against Sin's wrist and his head tilted slightly. Just enough to feel that maddening touch against his lips again.

"What—" His voice sounded too husky the first time so Boyd stopped and started again. "What do you want me to do?"

Every word caused their lips to brush together more, and Sin unconsciously leaned into it.

"Nothing."

The word brought their mouths together again, this time with more pressure. Sin leaned in, his fingers digging in harder and his body pressing in closer. Even with the violence still emanating from him, Sin seemed incapable of creating space between them.

Boyd shakily exhaled. "Then—"

Sin's mouth crushed against his.

The kiss took away any control Boyd had. A ragged groan wrenched from the depths of his throat. Before realizing he'd parted his lips, their tongues were slicking together in a way that made Boyd's knees weaken. Suddenly, Sin's taste was all around him; intoxicating and making him crave more. Every time he'd been attracted to Sin and had ignored it, every time he'd wondered what Sin would feel like pressed against him, came back to Boyd in an overwhelming wave of desire.

Boyd wanted—*needed*—more. He had to taste every centimeter of Sin and feel every millimeter of his body. He had to swallow every muffled moan and dig his fingers into those hard, muscular arms. His desperation matched Sin's, and Boyd groaned when Sin tangled fingers in his hair and ripped his head back while continuing to explore his mouth. The hunger in it, the hot frantic pace, sent sparks of fire shooting through Boyd until he was breathless. They panted against each other's mouths, teeth clicking together when the kiss turned sloppy and wet. A low swear escaped Sin's mouth when one, or both of them, began grinding against the other almost unconsciously.

Sin yanked Boyd forward like a rag doll, and before Boyd's spinning mind could even comprehend the fast motions, he was on the floor with Sin on top of him. There were no gentle touches and sweet caresses; only raw animal need and the forceful grip of hands that could rip a man apart with no other weapons.

Boyd threw his head back and gasped, arching up to grind against Sin with intent. His hands scrambled across Sin's back, fingers gripping and digging in; seeking a place to hold while fighting the urge to run them all over Sin's body. He was so powerful, so dangerous, and completely amazing as they humped against each other with a filthy rhythm that made Boyd want to beg for more. More touching, more pressure, more Sin...

They didn't stop kissing. Sin didn't seem like he could stop. It was all nipping and sucking and jaws working hectically. Boyd had never experienced anything like it.

When Sin's lips left Boyd's, the loss was nearly devastating until Boyd felt Sin's hot breath traveling down his neck. Moist heat was accompanied by the wet swath of Sin licking him, followed almost immediately by the scrape of teeth and a bite.

"Oh God!" Boyd's body jackknifed. *"Sin."*

Their bodies locked together, but Boyd needed more. Suddenly, the layer of clothing between them was too much. He sucked Sin's tongue back into his mouth and found himself lost in an ocean of sensation that caused him to reach down to rip Sin's jeans open with clumsy hands.

Nothing else mattered anymore. No thought or doubt about the mission was strong enough to override the lust that made Boyd want to feel their naked cocks sliding together.

Distantly, he knew it was wrong. He'd just been with Thierry. Sin was angry. They were both losing control and maybe it was a mistake... But the sound of Sin's deep voice groaning undid Boyd completely. He ripped Sin's jeans down past his ass, arching his back and lifting his hips so Sin could return the favor, and then fucked up against Sin shamelessly.

"Oh fuck," Sin hissed against Boyd's mouth.

Boyd found himself nodding without knowing why, moaning in encouragement and grinding their dicks together. The friction was good but not enough. He needed to touch Sin, to feel that naked cock in his hand, to taste it... Boyd reached down, stroking Sin's dick and pressing his thumb to the sticky slit.

"Fuck!" Sin's breath sobbed out against the side of Boyd's face, his entire body trembling. He trailed messy kisses down the side of Boyd's face before latching onto his throat again. He sucked hard, teeth digging in, and was making Boyd lose his mind.

All thoughts of Thierry, of the previous two hours, were gone. Boyd could think only of Sin's taste and touch and the need to be filled with his thick cock. Having his legs shoved back or being flipped over while Sin drove into him hard. The image was so vivid, so fucking hot, that Boyd's breath hitched and came out in a wet moan, his fingers pumping at their dicks until they were slick with pre-come. Sin moaned against his neck and the sound only made Boyd's lust grow more intense, the need to be fucked by Sin almost escaping his mouth... But then something went wrong.

A hand sliding under Boyd's shirt, inching up and too close... Too close.

Tension arced through Boyd like ice, cooling the heat that had just been burning so brightly. "W-wait!"

Boyd grabbed Sin's wrist but Sin slammed Boyd's arm down impatiently, pinning it to the floor while their bodies stayed crushed together. And just like that, the yawning darkness of fear took over.

"Sin, don't!"

His shirt was lifting, cool air hitting the skin of Boyd's abdomen, and he couldn't move, couldn't stop those questing fingers. He was trapped beneath a stronger body, being held down, they were holding him down—

Boyd panicked.

"No!"

The word wrenched out of him, terrified, and he began to struggle. He didn't feel it when Sin's grip changed or when the weight of his body started to pull away. Boyd was blind to everything around him. All he knew was that he was trapped, someone was exposing his chest, his stomach, everything was wrong. Boyd barely registered that he'd started to scream.

"No, no, don't touch me!"

The next thing he knew he was sitting up, his knees clenched to his chest with shaking fingers, hair awry. Boyd's heart pounded against his ribs in a painful rhythm that was too fast to sustain.

Sin only stared in confusion. His lips were swollen from the savage kisses, his hair unruly and clothes half undone. Slowly, the confusion in his face was replaced by something else, something that made his eyes drop while he fixed his clothes. Without a word, Sin stood and walked into his room.

Boyd stayed crouched on the floor, still shaking. He couldn't comprehend what had just happened; the vestiges of panic were still shifting their way around his pounding heart and in the scattered thoughts of his mind. When he was finally able to come to grips with the situation, he hissed out a harsh breath against his knees, and after several minutes, Boyd got to his feet. He glanced at Sin's door but did not approach it and instead retreated to his room.

He told himself to sleep and deal with this all tomorrow, but his mind was on overdrive despite the pressure of exhaustion on his body. Boyd lay there for what felt like hours, his teeth gritting as he tried to gather some semblance of control.

When morning came, Boyd moved on autopilot to gather his clothing and gear, patting the pocket of his pants to reassure himself that the flash drive was still inside. By the time he had cleaned up and changed his clothes, Sin was already in the outer room with his bag packed by the door.

The cold silence filling the room was suffocating.

At first, Boyd continued to pack without speaking. But when twenty minutes passed without words and everything was ready, he took a step closer to his partner.

"Sin, I..." Boyd started, his voice seeming abrupt in the quiet.

Sin's eyes lifted from his steady contemplation of the wall, but he said nothing to coax Boyd to continue. The indifferent set of his features made Boyd's throat close. The words that had been difficult to say before now felt impossible under the weight of the previous night. Even without that, what could he say? *I didn't mean to hurt* you? I need some time alone to think? I never meant for any of this to happen?

None of that would mean anything.

"I—was never going to use that." Boyd gestured at the remote.

"Okay."

Boyd swallowed. "And, last night, I—" Sin's went back to staring into space but Boyd pushed on. "I panicked."

Sin resumed staring at the wall.

"Sin, please—"

"It doesn't matter," Sin said. There was no inflection in his voice. "I'm not usually in the habit of wanting to finish someone else's leftovers."

Boyd recoiled. He struggled before trying, "So—if it hadn't been for Thierry last night..."

"I don't want to talk about it anymore. It's bad enough that it happened at all."

Sin stood and walked to the door. Boyd trailed after him, wanting to know what he meant, whether Sin regretted it because of how it had ended up or whether he'd wished it had never happened, just like he'd regretted ever helping Boyd. But his expression was so stormy that Boyd let it drop.

When they left for the airport, they spent the next ten hours without exchanging a single word.

THE LAST THING Boyd wanted was to attend the debriefing, especially when he'd already written the report on the plane, but he trudged to the conference room upon their return to Lexington with Sin a silent shadow behind him. When they entered, Ryan grinned.

"Hey Boyd."

"Hi."

"I'm busy right after this," Ryan said, when the door opened and Carhart came in. "But can I call you later? I wanted to see if we could set up a training thing like we talked about before."

"Of course," Boyd said with a nod. He had nearly forgotten about Ryan's desire to learn the foundations of self-defense, but he couldn't focus on that now.

"I was think—"

"First of all, good job, Boyd," Carhart said as he sat down. He made eye contact with Jeffrey before continuing. "Not only did Thierry come through for us for the first time, but you managed to develop a romantic relationship with him that may be helpful to us in the future."

Jeffrey's fingers paused on his tablet and he peeked up at Boyd from beneath his eyebrows. He somehow managed to look disparaging and smug at once without saying a single word. Meanwhile, Ryan looked at Boyd in surprise which was mirrored by Owen.

Boyd kept his expression impassive but felt a spike of irritation. He hadn't planned to tell everyone about the details of France and he certainly did not plan to use the same tactic with Thierry in the future. Wanting to change the subject, he removed the flash drive from his pocket. It had been encrypted, preventing Boyd from looking at the contents on his own so he had no idea why Carhart was positive that it held anything valuable.

"Do you want this now or later?"

"Jeffrey will take it. He's been decoding the information since early yesterday, but it's always good to have a hard copy."

Boyd gripped the drive. "Yesterday?"

"Yes, Thierry emailed the information early yesterday morning. We haven't gotten far yet, but judging from the level of encryption—well, Jeffrey can explain it."

Boyd stared at the general, his mouth going dry. Jeffrey had begun to speak, but Boyd couldn't hear the words. He was too busy calculating the time difference, figuring out that Thierry had sent the information after lunch but before Boyd had gone to the apartment. The anger he felt only intensified when he realized that Sin was looking at him for the first time all day. Boyd ignored it, staring at the table.

He'd been played. Somehow he knew it unequivocally. Why else would Thierry refrain from telling him about the information? That he'd already sent it? Why else would he string Boyd along as he drank glass after glass of wine? Had that been to make him more compliant? Had any of it been real? The things in common, the words of comfort, the compliments...

Had it been anything more than a carefully crafted game?

All that second-guessing, and the hesitation, and the arguments with Sin, and the possible degradation of their partnership—for nothing. For a man who'd manipulated everything just so he could fuck an agent. And the whole time Boyd had known Thierry was known to be manipulative, he'd known he could be a seducer, but he'd told himself that he'd had no choice.

He should have known better than to believe someone who was kind to him, who acted like there was something worthwhile in him. He should have known it was a trick.

"There are essentially two files I'll need to decrypt; what looks like a public-key cryptosystem and a one-time pad. The public-key will take a bit but I should be able to crack it. But the OTP will be a hassle. If—"

Owen perked up. "OTP? Who with who?"

Jeffrey stopped in the middle of whatever he'd been about to say. "What in god's name are you rambling about now?"

"Your—" Owen waved a hand in front of him. "I mean. *You're* the dude going on about OTPs."

"One-Time Pad, not whatever ungodly nerdy thing *you* thought of," Jeffrey scoffed. He turned to Carhart before the conversation could degenerate further. *"As I was saying.* If they did that right, it's unbreakable."

Carhart looked prepared to fly to France and throttle Thierry. "So then it's pointless?"

"Not necessarily." Jeffrey straightened his back. "Thierry plays games but I doubt even he would have given us information we could not decipher. I have some ideas for dealing with this, including checking into some extra files on here that may be nothing. If I were a betting man, I'd say I'm going to have to decipher both main files and somehow combine the information between the two before I can fully understand what exactly is on here. But this is the level of encryption I would expect from Janus, so it lends credence to the idea that it may be legitimate. I just won't know until I'm done."

Carhart absorbed the information. "How long are we looking at?"

Jeffrey flicked a screen on his tablet. "Hard to say, sir. It could be weeks; it could be months. If I didn't have access to the sort of equipment I do here at the Agency, it could have potentially been years. A lot of it depends on how difficult or random the algorithms are. The one thing I know for sure is the OTP will take a while. I'll have to rely on Thierry to have given us a clue for that or we will get nowhere with it. But I'm confident I can figure something out."

"Leave it to that bastard to give us information that may be out of date by the time it's decrypted," Carhart said, disgust heavy in his voice. "I guess we will just have to take it on faith that he didn't screw us."

Jeffrey smirked at Boyd. "Oh, I think some of it could be taken for fact."

Boyd didn't say anything. He shut down for the rest of the debriefing, blocking everyone out. When Carhart dismissed them, Boyd did not move until the rest of the unit trickled out one-by-one. He sat still and waited for Sin to leave. When the senior agent didn't move, Boyd got to his feet and started to hurry away.

"I hope you realize how badly you fucked yourself."

Boyd was half tempted to keep walking but Sin's words made him pause. "What do you mean?"

Sin pushed back his chair and stood, hands sliding into the pockets of his hoodie. "I mean you should have listened to me."

"Look, if you just wanted to keep me behind to say 'I told you so', I don't see the point. You said I would regret it. Knowing now how everything turned out, I do." Boyd spread his hands. "Happy?"

"No." Sin released a low sound. "It's strange how I thought I had you figured out."

"What the hell are you talking about?" Boyd snapped. "Weren't you the one trying to get me to go off with some random girl in the diner? Why was one time of casual sex so acceptable to you there but suddenly so terrible when I made a mistake thinking I had to do it with Thierry?"

"Because doing something for yourself and doing something for the Agency are entirely different things, you idiot. You pretty much submitted a résumé to become a valentine, and you're attempting to compare that to sleeping with a waitress?"

"Valentine?" Boyd echoed in confusion. "What are you talking about?"

"Are you kidding?" Sin jerked his hands out of his pockets and gestured sharply, seeming almost speechless before he found the words he wanted to convey. "You are the fucking worst. You were so willing to do anything for the cause, but you don't even know basic things about the cause you're rushing off to do anything for." He looked so disbelieving that Boyd was not surprised when it defaulted to anger.

"A valentine is a usually young, attractive field agent who is sent on missions that require things of a sexual nature. And you put your name in the fucking hat."

"What?" Boyd burst out. "But no one ever said anything about that. I don't want to have my name in for that kind of assignment!"

"Too late, idiot. You basically asked for the title. Why the hell do you think I kept telling you not to do it? Because I was so desperate to ensure that you stay chaste?"

"But—" Boyd gestured wildly, his eyes flicking around the room to search for an answer. "How was I supposed to know when no one told me, not even you? You just acted like I was an idiot the way you do for any other mission plan. I thought you were just pissed because it was Thierry. Why didn't you explain?"

Judging from the look on Sin's face, he thought Boyd was a hopeless idiot.

"I didn't know you were completely ignorant. Don't blame me because you were so quick to fuck for information. I tried to warn you, and you didn't want to hear what I had to say. You dismissed my advice like you always do."

Boyd started to pace the room. "Well, how do I tell them not to mark me that way? I only meant it to be a one-time thing, and even then it was because of the circumstances."

Sin grabbed his arm, appearing to lose all patience. "Don't you get it? Are you fucking oblivious? It's not up to you! Now that you put the idea in the air, they'll take it and run."

"But there has to be something I can do," Boyd nearly shouted back. He jerked his arm away. "I don't know, a—a review board, or—what if I talked to General Carhart? What if he put in a word for me? I'd be terrible at that kind of assignment. They wouldn't even want me for it. There has to be some sort of oversight that I can contact or lobby... Even if it's the Marshal."

By this time, Sin was just shaking his head and rubbing a hand across his face. "They own you, Boyd. Don't you get that? They *own you*. They don't have to ask for permission. The only thing you had going for you was that you were just a glorified babysitter for me. Now you let them know that you can be used for something else."

Boyd searched for something in his partner's words or face to take away from the finality of his words, but there was nothing. His breath quickened at the reality of the situation. The idea of what he could be asked—told—to do, and the knowledge that he had gotten himself into this predicament all on his own, was overwhelming. He pressed the heels of his hands against his face. What could they make him do? What he would do if someone tried to pull off his shirt and he panicked? What would his mother do to him if he failed a mission because of that? If she punished him it would only make the fear worse and the cycle would continue and—

He felt his eyes pricking. He let out a rough breath.

"Fuck."

"Exactly," Sin said.

EIGHTEEN

For the past several days, Sin had seen no reason to leave his apartment. He'd ignored the knock on the door when someone had come seeking his supply card and he'd ignored the phone when, oddly enough, Ryan had called. He hadn't even bothered to leave in order to go to the gym. Being around people on the compound was an unnecessary risk when he already felt like breaking someone's face just to watch them bleed.

He'd thought the anger and humiliation would dissipate over time, but it didn't. Sin felt the same hostility toward Boyd and the same scathing hatred about himself. The whole valentine situation didn't help matters. In fact, it only made things worse. It was now painfully obvious that Boyd knew nothing about the Agency, and even then he refused to listen to Sin's advice. In that regard, absence was definitely not making the heart grow fonder, and Sin was pretty firm on the idea that Boyd was semi-retarded.

Except he wasn't. He was just a dumb fucking kid.

If it were anyone else, Sin would think that Boyd deserved everything that would inevitably come to him with his newfound status. He'd been too self-assured and cocky to heed warnings, and too stubborn to even question his own decisions, or wonder why Sin had been so adamant. But it wasn't anyone else. It was Boyd.

During Sin's self-inflicted isolation, that thought returned multiple times a day. He tried to squelch it and tell himself that Boyd would just have to learn from his mistakes. That it was for the better. Maybe he'd finally understand what he was involved with. But none of that made Sin feel any better. Instead, he realized that if he hadn't been acting so emotional and jealous, he would have thought to explain and none of this would have happened.

After years of being ostracized by humanity, Sin allowed some stupid little civilian boy's rejection to hurt his feelings. Up until now, he hadn't even thought such a scenario was possible. But then again, until recently he had never expected that he would go out and try to avenge anyone's pain either.

And what a brilliant plan that had been. His attempt to do right by Boyd had completely backfired. And it just kept backfiring.

The worst part of it all was that Sin now knew he was as pathetic and needy as everyone else. Despite the years of isolation, despite his father's training, despite hating most people in general—he'd still wanted Boyd. As a friend at first, and then as something more complicated. A complication which had led to him visualizing stabbing Thierry in the throat while he'd been forced to sit for hours and watch Boyd flirt with the fucking moron. The jealousy had morphed into complete fury at the thought of that pathetic little man getting to touch Boyd when Sin couldn't even talk to him anymore.

And then, of course, the remote.

Disgusted with himself, Sin paced his apartment. He tried to stop thinking but it was impossible. No matter how hard he worked out, how determinedly he tried to force himself to sleep, the thoughts returned. The fear in Boyd's face, the silence, the mental images of Thierry touching Boyd, fucking Boyd, then... the hotel. Boyd's mouth, his hands, their bodies pressed together so perfectly, and then again— rejection. Fear. Horror on Boyd's face.

It shouldn't have hurt so bad, but it did. Even now, days later, Sin's stomach went hollow at the thought.

Fuck, Sin wanted to hate him.

When his phone rang, Sin nearly chucked it at the wall. Instead, he glanced at the screen and answered.

"What?"

"Get to my office within the hour," Connors' deep voice came across the phone gruffly.

"With bells on."

A mission would be a great distraction. He was actually looking forward to being gone.

Sin was out of the apartment within minutes, ignoring the guards as he passed, and the bite of the wind outside. He didn't look at anyone even when he felt their stares on him, and kept his head down and hood up. When Sin got to the Tower, he took the stairs to Connors office on the top floor. Swiping his card in the stairwell door, Sin stepped inside the administrative level which housed both Connors' and Vivienne's offices.

"What are you doing up here?"

Sin stared down at Ann, uninterested in the oncoming altercation. "Your father has summoned me. He can't live without my presence for long, you know."

Ann's face tightened, her lip curling. Her loathing of him pretty much topped anyone else's in the Agency but at least she had a good reason.

"I can't believe they allow you on this floor. It's amazing how high your clearance continues to be despite your crimes."

"Yeah, well," he said, summoning a smirk just to push things, just to make her angrier even though Sin knew he deserved her hate. "Apparently your father didn't think what I did was such a big crime, did he?"

The smack echoed throughout the empty lobby and he didn't even blink. He barely felt it. The smirk never left his face.

"Fuck you." She turned and stormed in the direction of Vivienne's office.

"Not without dinner first," he called after her. Despite the words, he had an almost immediate flash of a memory; milky white skin tattooed by a web of scars. No matter how unaffected he tried to act about it, Lydia would always haunt him.

Sin continued toward Connors' office. He glanced at Samuel, Connors' assistant, but walked past, ignoring the way the man watched him.

Most agents spent the majority of their careers without ever meeting Marshal Jacob Connors even though their every action was dictated by his commands. Connors ran the Agency but very little was known about his history or how he'd gotten involved with it.

Sin knocked on the door and looked up at the camera with a kissy face as he waited for Connors to admit him into the room. There was a buzz, the light next to the doorknob turned green, and he entered.

It was probably the largest office on compound and was far more luxurious than Carhart's. Despite that, there were no personal effects to be found in the room, no hints about his life before the bombings and the war, not even a photograph of his wife or daughters. It was Spartan and cold, just like Connors' personality.

"I just saw your lovely daughter." Sin sat in the chair across from Connors. "She's as hostile as ever, Jacob. You must be proud."

"She's as hostile as she needs to be. She's as wary as she needs to be. This explains why she is still here and why her twin is an invalid." Connors' steel-gray eyes glared at Sin from under bushy silver eyebrows.

"You're a cruel man, Jacob. Poor Lydia."

"Poor Lydia was an idiot and I do not wish to discuss her further, especially not with the creature that is responsible for her condition."

"She's responsible for her own condition. She's the one who deemed it necessary to drug me and then get the brilliant idea to sexually accost me."

"Precisely. And that is why I do not further wish to discuss her."

Connors once again focused on his writing. Sin slumped in the chair and noted that the office was far warmer than his quarters ever were. Maybe they turned the heat down in his apartment on purpose. Some kind of weird, passive-aggressive torture. Unfortunately for them, his father had trained him to fight during a mission in Siberia during the winter. It would take more than a non-working thermometer to get to him.

After some time, Connors finished whatever he'd been working on and pushed a tablet across the table. Sin noticed that Connors watched him as though waiting for a reaction.

Sin turned on the tablet, stared at the image, and snorted. "Wow."

"Question?"

"Isn't this the guy who rebuilds poor neighborhoods and donates all of his money to charities?"

"Yes."

Sin nearly laughed. "Wow."

"It should be noted," Connors said icily, "that he also donates a considerable sum of his money to Janus, which in turn leads to them purchasing arms."

"Feeling the need to justify yourself, Jacob?"

"Why would I feel the need to justify myself to something like you?"

Sin shrugged and continued to read the assignment. When he finished, he really did laugh. "So this guy is so squeaky clean that you have to manufacture dirt on him? I don't appreciate having credit for my assassinations given to random, inept hit men."

"Do you understand the assignment?" Connors asked in a clipped tone.

"Yes. Although, you realize that it won't be complete for a few weeks. Not more than a month though."

"That's fine. Just get it done and don't fuck up." The warning tone in Connors' voice made it clear what would happen if he did.

"I'll try not to, darling, I really will." Sin stood up and slid the tablet into his pocket. "I'll need supplies and money."

"Fill out a supply card and see Charles. You're given clearance for whatever you need for this assignment."

Sin turned to leave but just as he began to open the door, Connors spoke again

"Are you fucking Vivienne's boy?"

Sin froze. "Why would you ask me that?"

"It's a yes or no question, Agent Vega."

"No. I'm not."

Connors snorted softly. "Didn't think so. The moment I actually believed you were sexually functional, I'd have you neutered. Dismissed."

Sin grit his teeth, hand tightening around the doorknob. It was hard not to turn around and give Connors what he deserved, but Sin forced himself to keep going. He didn't know why Connors asked him that and right now he didn't care. He was just thankful for an excuse to be off compound for a few weeks.

THE ASSIGNMENT INVOLVED a string of hits in different cities all over the world. After a couple of weeks, Sin grew weary of playing tag with his targets.

The purpose of this all was a man named Anderson McCall, a wealthy American who'd been in the clergy before the war and had dedicated his life to helping needy people afterward. He was well known nationally as a figure of hope and generosity, and had been loved by the public. The only problem was that he was a big supporter of Janus and their efforts to overthrow the US government. He would not have been considered more than a mild annoyance if it hadn't been for the fact that 40% of Janus' arms had been purchased with money that he'd donated to them.

A straightforward assassination would turn the man into a martyr so the Agency was using a different tactic this time. For months, they'd worked to create ties between McCall and several investors of questionable moral fiber. A direct connection between McCall and several men involved in drug trafficking and child prostitution rings had been established, and already his name was becoming tarnished. In two weeks it would come out that he'd been systematically having these questionable business partners murdered in an effort to clear his name and ensure their silence. When it was done, the story would go that McCall would kill himself after being overcome with guilt.

Of course, Sin was the one killing McCall's partners but no one would know that, and the man's memory would be blackened forever. It was a dirty job and Sin wasn't happy about being forced to do it, but he had to give a nod of credit towards the Agency. They covered every base. They'd managed to access bank accounts, phone records, create ties between McCall and known hit men... it was disturbing how thorough they were. But it was still dirty work.

His father had taught him how to do his job, kill the mark, and not question things even when they were obviously questionable. But missions like this got under Sin's skin. He didn't mind straightforward assassinations of political figures and terrorist leaders when he knew next to nothing about them. He didn't mind taking out hostiles and destroying their bases.

He did, however, mind playing games and planting evidence, knowing details about a man's life and destroying every part of it. It was usually enough that he was ending it.

Sin's irritation was ratcheted by the fact that, even when wandering a market in Morocco with his face wrapped by a shemagh while following a target, he couldn't stop thinking about Boyd. He was sure that his partner would have a more clever way of tracking these guys down and planting evidence that didn't involve following them for hours.

The annoyance tripled when Sin developed the habit of obsessively analyzing every word that had been exchanged between them on the mission in France. It replayed in his mind whenever he had downtime during the weeks away from Lexington, and almost always degraded into him being frustrated and aching when thoughts inevitably turned to that night in the hotel. He'd regretted it at first and blamed Boyd for leading him on, but when Sin thought back to the wet slide of their tongues and Boyd's hand gripping his dick... Sin knew the only regret he had was that he would never be able to touch or taste Boyd again.

One thing Sin had learned from this entire situation was that he wasn't cut out for any of it. He didn't know how to be someone's friend. That had been made apparent by the brilliant idea of murdering someone as a present. And Sin definitely didn't know how to approach someone as a lover without somehow scaring the hell out of them. The entire situation had confirmed something Sin had known since childhood; something he never should have forgotten or tried to move beyond.

He was a killer and nothing more. It was what he was good at, his only real skill.

Everyone had a role to play in life, and that was his.

It had been obvious from the start, and it was why his father had decided to train him. He'd known that Sin wasn't normal. His psychotic episodes and the events that had happened in Hong Kong had proved that. Even at the age of eight, Sin had been capable of violence and had possessed such an intense distrust of people that he'd been able to justify it.

For years he'd been alone, he'd trusted no one and he'd liked it that way. He'd lived his life with a single purpose, although at times that purpose had grown fuzzy in his mind. There had been times when he'd asked himself why he did the things he did, why he went back to the Agency, why he worked for people who thought of him as no more than a tool. There had been times in his teenage years when he'd debated leaving, thinking there had to be something more. But the ideas had always faltered and disappeared when he'd realized that there was nothing else for him.

Sin didn't know how to interact with people and even if he learned to pretend, he had never wanted to. The reality of not being able to function in society had always sent him back to being unquestioning and doing what he was told to do, just because he couldn't figure out what he'd rather do instead. When the confusion and doubt had lasted too long, Sin had reminded himself of his training. His father. But even then, there were lapses.

The first real lapse in his training had been over the girl; the young girl being raped by a group of men. Flashbacks had hit him, then darkness, then the feeling of watching himself from afar. The men died, then the girl ran from him, scared of his violence and his ability to murder, then the scavengers... the scavengers who'd allowed a girl to be raped but who came running to kill her rescuer just so they could loot his body afterward. It'd ended with more bloodshed than he'd intended to cause.

Sin had been thankful for the years he'd spent on the Fourth after that. He'd spent the time attempting to destroy the part of him that had such a soft spot for the helpless.

Then Boyd had come along. He wasn't helpless, but somehow he stirred those same feelings in Sin. Suddenly, there was a person in his life who didn't treat him like a monster. Someone who acted like a friend; the first friend he'd ever had.

Sin didn't know why the urge to protect the closeness with Boyd had morphed into something sexual, but he wanted the feelings to be gone and it was obvious that it was going to take more than a couple of weeks of isolation to achieve that.

It was February 9 by the time Sin was entirely through his list. Everything was going smoothly. The evidence was already pointing toward McCall. All of the murders had been completed execution style and linked to the Russian assassin Alexander Trusov, a former lieutenant in Russia's Federal Security Services before the collapse of the Kremlin during the war. Trusov was missing and presumed dead, but several phone calls made to his cell phone had been traced back to McCall's office in Louisiana before his disappearance.

During this time the accusations were widely reported, and McCall had become reclusive and hid in his New Orleans home. He'd discontinued all projects due to the worsening media storm, and interviews with family members described a depressed man who appeared to have lost all hope.

The rage that had begun to build during the course of the mission was beginning to boil over.

This wasn't the first time he'd found himself taking a side during a mission. He'd realized that he actually had morals on another mission as well. The Agency had ordered him to assassinate the Prime Minister of Italy in front of her three kids because she didn't agree with their solution regarding Italian rebel groups. Sin had nearly bailed on the mission, and had put off the assassination for days. By the time Sin got to New Orleans, he had gone too far to consider backing out now. He'd helped the Agency destroy McCall's life. He may as well put the poor bastard out of his misery.

It was devastatingly easy to break into McCall's house. The entire place had some Greek revival feel to it and could have been quite beautiful, but the inside it was anything but decadent. Most of the furniture was old and there was little ornamentation. The walls were covered with framed awards for his deeds and pictures of children who benefited from McCall's various urban youth projects.

The nagging feeling in Sin's gut became more insistent when he crept up the long, winding staircase to his target.

"I don't know, Nicole. I just—I just don't want to talk right now. No, I'm fine. I'll be fine. I don't know. I just need to be alone."

Sin followed the voice to the master bedroom and noticed that the door was wide open. He could see McCall's thin form facing away from him inside.

"It doesn't matter anymore. It's all over. Everything I've done—and now my own family doubts me? I'll call you later. I have some work to do, some arrangements to make."

There was a pause and Sin slipped into the room, closing the door softly behind him.

"I'll call you back later. It doesn't matter, Nicole. Goodbye."

McCall let the phone drop to the floor at his feet. He continued to stand facing the window.

"Are you here to kill me, then?"

Sin raised an eyebrow and leaned against the door. "I'm here to make you commit suicide, actually."

McCall turned around, surprisingly fearless. He looked older than he had in his picture, appearing to be in his sixties rather than fifties. It was as if he'd aged ten years in the past three months. His gray hair was uncombed, milky blue eyes red-rimmed and surrounded by dark circles.

"So you mean to say," McCall said. "That you're here to kill me."

Sin shrugged. "Semantics."

McCall moved to his desk, reaching for a bottle of gin and a tumbler. His entire demeanor reflected weariness and resignation.

"Would you like a drink? Or are we to get down to this right away?"

"I don't drink but you're welcome to. It actually suits my purposes if you do."

"Oh? You're going to poison me?" McCall sounded almost amused. "How absurd."

Sin shrugged. "Hey, it wasn't my idea. I just do what I'm told."

"Ah." The older man nodded and poured his drink. "So you're not acting of your own accord?"

Sin crossed the room to stand next to McCall's desk. "Does it matter? It doesn't change anything."

"Ah, well, I'd just hoped that the reason for this smear campaign would be explained to me before my death." McCall picked up his drink although he let it hover next to his mouth for a moment without taking a sip. "Oh yes, of course." He set the cup down on the table again and pushed it across the table at Sin.

"You're making my job very easy," Sin said as he pulled the vial out of his pocket and poured the clear liquid into the glass. "Drink."

"And what if I said no?" McCall queried as he sat at his desk. "How would you force me to drink it? I'm not going to resist, trust me at this point I'm far from caring, but I'm curious what your plan was."

"I'd tell you that I'll kill your sister if you make this any more difficult than it has to be."

"I see." McCall was silent at first but ultimately grabbed the tumbler and downed the entire contents in a single gulp. "How long do I have?"

"An hour."

"Ah." He nodded again and fiddled with the empty glass. "What precisely was it?"

"An overdose of the painkillers you take for arthritis."

"I see. Well, sit down, young man. No need to stand there hovering over me."

Sin didn't know what to make of the man, but this was not how he had anticipated this mission going. It was just making things worse. He sat in the chair opposite McCall's desk and for a while, they just stared at each other. The only sound in the room was the ticking of the antique grandfather clock in the corner. It annoyed Sin. The whole situation was too dramatic. It would have been better to poison the man discreetly and never have to be in his presence at all.

"What's the matter?"

"What?"

McCall spread his hands. "You looked angry just now."

"Could be."

"Maybe because you've killed an innocent man?"

"Could be."

"Maybe you feel guilty because of it."

Sin sighed. "Maybe. But it changes nothing."

McCall leaned back in his chair, causing it to squeak. "You aren't how I imagined my assassin to be. You're too beautiful and tragic."

"Are you kidding me?"

The older man smiled. "Well, there is no denying that you're a striking young man. But there's something dark about you. You remind me of a boy I once knew, a survivor of the war."

"So he went around poisoning people?"

"No." McCall gave Sin a patient look. "But like you, he didn't have much say in his life and did terrible things to survive."

"You're making a lot of assumptions, old man."

"Am I? You admitted to feeling guilty."

Sin tilted his head back against the chair. "You do realize that I just poisoned you. That I'm not lying. That you will be dying very shortly."

"Yes."

"So what's the point in trying to butter me up?"

"I'm not. At this point, I have nothing left to live for." The bitterness on McCall's face aged him a few more years, lines appearing in his forehead and around his mouth. "My family has betrayed me, they don't trust me and they won't even believe me over the media. My sister-in-law has taken measures to prevent me from visiting my nephew. After all the good I've tried to do for children..." He poured another drink with a trembling hand. "If suicide wasn't a sin, I'd probably have done it already."

Sin did not look away from the ceiling. "Sorry."

The word came out cold, but Sin meant it. He *was* sorry.

Even so, his face remained perfectly blank despite the turmoil that roiled inside of him. Right then he wanted nothing more than to be the cold-blooded killer that everyone said he was. The monster who could kill anyone. Sin didn't want to care about this man's life. He didn't want to care about this man's death. Sin didn't want to care about anything at all.

He was suddenly reminded of the night he'd killed Jared Strickland, how ripping the man apart had haunted him even though the death had been deserved. It was so strange how some things affected Sin while others barely niggled at his conscience at all.

"Well, I'm sure you don't want to hear about my troubles," McCall said. "I just wish you would tell me why. Why this has been done to me. Am I that much of a threat? Is it—" He hesitated even now. "Is it because I've shown support for anti-American factions?"

"I'd say donating millions of dollars towards Janus is a tad more than 'showing support.'"

"So that's what it boils down to." A quiet laugh. "The American government never ceases to amaze me."

"Well, technically you are a traitor to the nation that's allowed you to prosper and become a millionaire. You are aware that Janus purchases weapons to kill Americans with the money you donate to them? That they perform terrorist acts and have killed children in the process?"

When the words met dead air, Sin's skin crawled. He sounded just like Connors.

McCall got to his feet and moved to the other side of the desk. He showed no fear when standing next to Sin, and did not hesitate to look into Sin's face. He didn't blink, didn't speak, his countenance did not shift from the bleak lines of resignation. But still, it felt like an indictment.

Sin did not move or break eye contact with his victim, even when his body tensed, automatically defensive and poised to fight. But from McCall, there was nothing to fear. Instinctively, Sin knew that. There were no hidden weapons or secret alarms—no panic room. Just his target and him, and the evidence of the passage of time in McCall's watery eyes.

"Have you ever killed an innocent man before?"

Sin thought about the last time he'd felt like this on a mission. The scene played out in his mind like a shimmering apparition. The screams of his target's children when her head had exploded into a mass of blood and gore. But then, Sin had been able to walk away. He hadn't been chained there, waiting to see the fallout like he was chained to this room as he waited for verification that McCall had died.

"Maybe not a man."

"So, you've killed women?"

256   SANTINO & AIS

"Yes."

"Children?"

A muscle in Sin's jaw ticked. "No."

McCall nodded. He traced Sin's face with eyes that were becoming heavy-lidded. He leaned back against the desk. "Do you have parents?"

"Why are you asking me these stupid fucking questions?" Sin got to his feet and stalked to the window, feeling the phantom weight of a stare burning into his back. It was a bad move and he was being sloppy. He should have forced McCall to stay in his chair, to stop speaking, and just watched him die without ever exchanging a word.

"Does it bother you?"

Outside, the sun was trying to burst through a spread of wispy clouds. Rays broke through and gleamed down to the sprawling trees and trolley line still festooned with ancient beads wrapped around it hundreds of times.

"Does it bother you to talk to a man whose life you've ruined?"

"Yes," Sin snapped. "And I didn't ruin your life. My employers did. I'm just a tool."

"A talented tool. I doubt just anyone could pull off what you've done."

Sin inhaled through his nose and closed his eyes, blocking out the conflicting view of aged beauty outside and the nightmare of his existence in this room. A cagey feeling was encouraging him to leave, but the mission had been clear that he was to see this through to the end. If he left and McCall contacted someone for help, if the concentrated amount of poison was found in his system, everything would be called into question. The mission would fail.

"How old are you?"

"It doesn't matter."

"Do you have children?"

Sin shook his head, appalled at the idea of creating something like him. Fucked in the head chemically, violence and murder in his blood.

"Do you have parents?"

"No."

"Did you ever know your parents?"

"Yes," Sin growled. "Stop asking me questions."

"Am I upsetting you?"

"Yes!" Sin spun around to face McCall and for the first time, the man took a step back. "Just die silently."

McCall went back to his seat, unsteady hand grasping for another drink. "Are you entitled to murder peacefully?"

There was nothing to say to that.

"Do you believe in God?"

A huff of laughter welled in Sin's throat, incredulous and half-mad. He was really on the goddamn edge. "There is no God, old man."

"Is that what your parents taught you?"

"My mother was a mentally deranged prostitute. My father trained me to kill. Christian mythology didn't come up." When McCall's brow puckered, the lines around his mouth deepening with a frown, Sin released his hair. "Don't you look at me like that. I don't need your pity. I don't need your fucking Christian forgiveness, either. I'm a monster and a killer and that's what I'll always be." The words came out in a rush but Sin was starting to lose focus. Something scraped at the back of his mind. A memory trying to wiggle its way to the surface. "The worst thing to happen to me was being born, not anything after. My birth was nothing but—"

The memory erupted to the surface. A faint haunting voice and the tat-tat-tat of gunfire echoing in his ears. The sounds were accompanied by an image. Parts of Sin's recurring nightmare, but this time vivid instead of the fragmented illusions of a dream. Blood streaked on grass and long, tattooed fingers clawing at dark earth.

"Your birth was an act of God and inevitably, that is what my death is."

Sin looked at McCall blindly, breath coming faster. "What?"

"I said your birth was an act of God. Everyone is put on this Earth for a reason. Everyone has a purpose." He regarded Sin. "I don't think this is your purpose, but maybe it's mine."

"What the hell are you talking about?"

McCall blinked and set his glass down. Movements slowing, chemicals working through his blood stream; Sin could practically smell the approaching death.

"Maybe you need to feel this guilt."

"Guilt won't change anything."

"What about love?"

"That word means nothing to me."

"Nothing at all?" McCall was starting to look pale, his posture

SANTINO & AIS

sinking and words loose. "You've never cared for anyone? Never wanted to be kind to someone for no other reason than... than their happiness?"

The one person he'd been trying so hard to push out of his mind came to the forefront at McCall's words.

"If that's the truth than I'm sorry for you. Living life with nothing but your orders and your self-hatred will never allow the opportunity for change."

Now instead of seeing a fragmented death scene, Sin saw Boyd's smile and the way it lit up his face. Instead of seeing bloody fingers curling and green eyes staring at an unseen attacker, Sin saw Boyd's slim fingers clutching the remote right before he threw it at Sin in desperation. Instead of a field of grass and streaks of blood shining under the moon, he saw Boyd illuminated only by the dashboard in the passenger seat, looking over with a softened expression. He heard Boyd's quiet laugh, remembered looking at each other as he'd knelt before Boyd and tended to his wound, the way Boyd had trusted him to protect him when they were surrounded by enemies, and Boyd looking at him so hesitantly in the hotel in France.

But that was over now. All of it. And it was his own fault. Because he didn't know how to act like a real person. Because he was psychotic. A freak.

The slow burn of shame crept over Sin, eating away at the last shreds of self-control. Sin bolted from the room without waiting to confirm that the light had gone out of McCall's eyes.

NINETEEN

ON FEBRUARY 11, Carhart called Sin and informed him that he was to meet Boyd at a motel in Toronto.

There was a small group there being run by an alleged core member of Janus named Alexis Denis. She was gaining support and expanding membership for a new cell in Canada. Unlike the other members of Janus, Alexis did not have the privilege of being anonymous. She had a history that was documented here and there, and was known to be an intellectual and a former advocate for peace. Sin and Boyd were to negotiate with the woman, try to turn her to their side or, if that was not possible, bring her back alive for interrogation.

It was right on the tail end of his McCall mission and Sin's mood had not improved. It had actually gotten worse as he watched the fallout unravel on the news, as McCall was demonized even further by the media after his supposed suicide.

It was one of those times where Sin could identify that he was on the edge and needed to be left alone. He was too angry and fraying at the ends after weeks of consistent murder.

Having a mission with Boyd was a terrible idea, and Sin knew it from the start. They hadn't seen each other in over a month and everything in Sin's head was so conflicted, so twisted and confused, that all he could think to do was keep Boyd the fuck away. But the mission was unavoidable.

Sin arrived at the motel later than expected. He found Boyd crouched over a table, a tablet in front of him while he made notes on a pad at his side. When Boyd glanced up Sin saw dark circles smudged beneath his eyes, but there was a moment when Boyd's face lightened. He stood up straight, lips parting to speak, but when Sin kept his own face a blank mask, Boyd's gaze dropped back to the floor.

"Hello," Boyd said.

Sin dropped his bag on the floor. "What are we doing?"

"Search and retrieve," Boyd replied. "I did some recon yesterday. The location is monitored by a variety of security devices—motion and noise sensors as well as cameras aside from men who are assigned to patrol. More of it can be explained on site, but the structure is an old tourist attraction. There are four buildings, one story each, and I'm not positive but I think I have an idea of which one she may be in." Boyd reached into a bag next to him and slid a box across the table to Sin. "I picked up GPS wristwatches in Artillery to aid us."

"And what's that supposed to do?"

"We can track each other." Boyd pulled off the wristwatch he was already wearing and demonstrated to Sin as he explained. "She's likely to be in the northern or western building. If we split up, whoever finds her first can alert the other. If you press the button, the other person has a limited ability to track you through GPS. If you hit the button three times, the screen will be masked and appear like a regular watch. I thought this would be the easiest way to stay in contact while remaining radio silent. They seem to be monitoring radio waves and I don't know what channels we otherwise would be able to use without being overheard."

"Why don't we just plan to meet at whatever point at a certain time and bypass all of this?" Sin began to check his weapons, weariness making his movements sharp as a dull throb began in his temples.

"We could, but this would be more effective. Their security cycle is very quick, leaving us a small window. In the past, we've run into issues when we didn't know what the other person was doing and this can solve that. There's also an emergency signal built in. I've scouted a location for when we have her detained, but if anything goes wrong we can activate the emergency alert to call for backup."

Sin ripped off the hoodie he'd worn on the plane from Louisiana and swapped it for a black long-sleeved shirt. A glance in the mirror showed that he looked like shit; bloodshot eyes, unshaven for days, hair a total fucking mess. His body felt like it had been filled with lead, and he wished he'd been able to sleep on the way over.

"Let's just go in together. It would be faster than splitting up and we can communicate. Even with the emergency signal, there's no way for me to actually talk to you and relay information unless you want me to text you every time something crops up."

"I thought of that, but as I said, their cycle is very quick." Boyd's tone, while remaining neutral, was growing tight. "The buildings are large and don't appear to have many easily accessible hiding places within so if we're together it drastically increases the chance we'll raise an alarm and have to abort the mission. You're faster on your own anyway, and I might be able to blend in easier individually. And as for texting, I was thinking we would only alert the other in the event of needing backup or having found Alexis."

Sin knelt down to lace his boots tighter. "It just seems like over-complicating the whole matter. Besides, you said you pinpointed her possible location."

Boyd shoved the tablet away. "I said it was possible, not that I knew for sure. I have it narrowed down to two of the buildings with the likelihood higher in one. I spent two days trying to think of the best way to deal with this situation based on the compound layout, technology, guards and number of hostiles, and you haven't looked at a single blueprint yet. Can you just not challenge my every idea for once?"

"Why don't you listen for once?" Sin snapped, standing. "But I forgot, you don't have to. You know it all. And that's worked out so well for you lately, hasn't it?"

Boyd's back stiffened. His voice dropped several degrees when he spoke. "When you show up and tell me I'm wrong after I've spent a couple of days studying the situation and layout, it makes me a little less likely to scrap everything to accommodate your delicate sensibilities."

"What the fuck were you rambling on about, if that wasn't telling me the situation and layout?" All shreds of patience were blown. "I think I got the picture. You want to run around with no form of communication just because you're afraid you might get seen rather than go in together and simplify the matter. And for someone who doesn't even have basic knowledge about the organization you work for, it's pretty hilarious that you have balls to be on a high horse talking down to me about how to run a mission."

Boyd slammed his hands on the table. "You know what, Sin? I get it. I'm a terrible fucking agent, everyone's a better agent than me, everyone knows better and I should just fucking disappear. My plans never work and I shouldn't base anything on the successful missions I've had in the past because clearly I don't know what I'm doing. I can't ever be right because you've been at this so much longer than me. Everyone has. Is that what you want to say to me?"

After everything that had happened in the past few weeks, Sin was unmoved by the outburst. "I said what I had to say. If you don't want to listen, fine. Be a dramatic little bitch about it. It wouldn't be the first time."

Boyd's breath was coming faster and his eyes were bright with anger. "Fuck you."

"No thanks, sweetheart. That brief moment of insanity has passed."

Boyd's mouth fell open but he didn't say anything. The sharp edge of regret made Sin turn away, not wanting to look at Boyd anymore.

They finished preparing and by the time they were en route to the location, Boyd had transformed. His face had hardened and all of his actions were too abrupt, too harsh, and too fast. When Sin tried to address him, Boyd did not respond. It was like he didn't even hear. He seemed to have transcended to some zone of reality where sound was muffled by the constant throb of rage. Sin knew the feeling, and also knew it was his fault that Boyd was there now.

When they got there, the car rocked when Boyd hit the brakes harder than necessary. He threw the car in park and unbuckled his seat belt in the same movement. Before Sin could ask what plan they were going with, Boyd was grabbing the duffel bag from the back seat and striding through the trees to the Janus cell's location. Sin took out one of his guns and followed, looking around. He didn't even care about the plan anymore. He was over the whole argument and just wanted to grab the woman and go somewhere to crash.

They didn't speak as they approached what had once been an expansive parking lot in front of the huddle of buildings. Sin paused at the perimeter, but Boyd kept going, his breath puffing out in a cloud.

"Boyd—"

Boyd dropped the bag and charged to the center where floodlights illuminated the lot. The whirring of cameras followed his movements, but Boyd walked straight into the open without bothering to protect himself at all. He kept his hand at his side, but in the failing light of the day the glint could be seen off his gun.

"Oh, what the *fuck*," Sin hissed. He closed the distance between them and grabbed Boyd's arm. "What the hell do you think you're doing?"

Again, it was like Boyd did not hear him.

A flurry of snow drifted from the sky, the wind blowing it in dizzying patterns as several people appeared from different buildings around the lot.

"Stop immediately or we'll shoot!" one of the men yelled. "Identify yourself."

"I'm here to negotiate," Boyd yelled before raising his gun and blowing the man's brains out.

Sin could only stare. Before he could comprehend that Boyd had just killed in cold blood, he was on autopilot. Five men were pointing guns at Boyd and that was all that really mattered now. It was too late for reason, especially with Boyd walking towards them with reckless abandon, either not caring or not noticing that he was three seconds away from being pumped full of bullets.

In the brief second it took for the men to wrench their stupefied gazes from their fallen comrade and point their guns at Boyd, Sin reacted. Twin Rugers appeared in his hands and he took out the men before they had a chance to fire a single shot.

Boyd had already approached one of the buildings and did not look back. He kicked the door open and entered, barely dodging a bullet that skimmed past his arm. It was probably only due to the initial confusion that more of the men were not pouring into the area with their guns out.

"Boyd, what the fuck are you doing?" Sin shouted, running after him.

He was only a couple of seconds behind but when Sin burst into the door, he was nearly hit by two bullets. Sin swore and threw himself to the side, trying to gain sense of the situation while evading fire. His speed typically made it easy, but trying to find Boyd when he was on some kind of fucking rampage was making it hard. Further down the hallway, Sin saw Boyd still walking with purpose. The hostiles must have seen Sin as the larger threat because as Boyd got further away, their fire focused on Sin.

They aimed their guns at him, yelling orders to each other and requesting backup. Sin scanned the area to take into account the position of hostiles before he dismissed the threat, ducked out of the way of the gunfire, and sprinted after Boyd again. He sheathed one gun and tried to grab Boyd but was unable to get a grip when a bullet hurtled toward his face. Sin dove out of the way as more hostiles appeared and, this time, Sin saw Boyd stumble as a bullet hit his armor.

The sight prompted Sin to slide fully into mission mode. He turned his back to the wall, eliminating one-third of the people in his perimeter with single shots to their heads. Alternating between taking out the people trying to kill Boyd and protecting himself from the fire behind them, Sin was caught at a standstill. It took only minutes to clear the main room so no one was swarming at their backs, but that was enough time for Boyd to get too far ahead for Sin to cover him. Reloading his guns with spare magazines, Sin ran after Boyd again. They were almost immediately caught by another rush of hostiles flooding into the next room.

He shot two men nearest Boyd in quick succession before hitting a third hostile between the eyes while dodging fire from the corridor. Dropping to the floor and rolling, Sin eliminated three hostiles approaching Boyd, and managed to avoid being shot from two different directions by scrambling into the shadows of a nearby doorway. Sin was barely out of breath but now that he was still, he could feel two other locations on his body that had been grazed by bullets.

There was a pause in gunfire while his opponents tried to trace where he had gone. During that time, Sin kept himself flat against the narrow alcove and tuned in to the sounds around him. He placed one man's hurried effort to reload at the top of the staircase, and another's nervous panting behind a desk in the room across the corridor.

He could hear the clicking of a magazine but before it could pop into place, Sin zeroed in on the man on the staircase like a crosshair. He stepped out of the alcove and gunshots echoed deafeningly in the hallway when he fired, and killed, the man. The other hostile popped up from behind the desk, with two more men down the hallway behind him. Sin spun away, hunching and darting forward, attempting to keep his body a small, fast-moving target. Bullets ricocheted around him but Sin sprinted out of range of fire in a deadly dance that depended on reflexes and luck.

When he caught up to Boyd again, it seemed that the younger agent was still uninjured due to the full body armor he'd worn under his clothes. Even so, it was only a matter of time before someone aimed for his head.

Alarms went off and lights flashed. Boyd aimed at a small box on the ceiling near a major junction of hallways and the alarm died with a lingering wail. He kept going.

"Boyd! You fucking idiot, *stop!*"

A bullet grazed Sin's cheek and he aimed without looking, only realizing afterward that the hostile he'd killed had been a teenage boy. Gore and blood spattered the walls, the ceiling, and covered the floor in pools that oozed larger by the second. Dead bodies were littered around like flies swatted from the air, and some of the recruits were now running away from the action. People were screaming, a few were crying, and the deafening echo of gunfire created a cacophony of sound. Bullet holes dotted the walls, scattering drywall, insulation and paint flecks around them in a flurry like the snowfall outside.

The barrage of bullets stopped. Echoes resounded around them of people crawling over their dead comrades and trying to drag the wounded to safety. It was unclear what caused the sudden ceasefire but Sin used the opportunity to catch up to Boyd. He grabbed Boyd's arm, yanking him backwards with a growl.

The sound of running footsteps echoed down the corridor and Sin raised his gun, preparing to fire. He'd almost pulled the trigger when he caught sight of brown hair and a female figure charging towards them, a pistol lowered and held at her side. Either Alexis Denis thought she was invincible, had some ridiculous notion about killing Sin, or actually had interest in negotiating. Whatever the case, she did not pose an immediate threat, and was probably the one that had called for the ceasefire.

"Some fucking negotiating, kid!" Alexis yelled as she approached.

Boyd's head turned. Before Sin could react, Boyd's hand jerked up and he shot her in the head.

Sin wrenched Boyd back and it took every fiber in his body not to hit the kid. Every ounce of self-control not to make this opera of failure even worse.

"You fucking moron!"

He dragged Boyd back the way they'd come, practically carrying him when the sound of galvanized hostiles echoed through the maze of corridors. The shouting increased in pitch, probably as they found their leader's body, and Sin could hear pounding footsteps behind them. He didn't stop to engage, and Boyd was finally allowing himself to be led. Cracks had appeared in his blank mask of rage, and now Boyd's face was white and pinched with shock. He stumbled, clinging to Sin, but still managed to have the wherewithal to detonate explosives he'd apparently set in the building while Sin had run around getting shot.

An enormous explosion rocked the compound, followed closely by four others at varying lengths away. The chase faltered, and although some hostiles still followed, their numbers were reduced by the dust and debris raining down from the ceiling. Somewhere deeper within the building, there was a metallic groan.

When Sin burst outside, they were met with thick black smoke, the burn of flames, and a sudden, even larger explosion nearly throwing them to the ground. Alexis' people were fleeing the buildings in ragged clusters, most injured or overcome with smoke, but some still in pursuit of the men who had destroyed their base, and likely, their entire cell.

"Stop them!" someone screamed through the night.

Sin released Boyd and spun around, feet sliding on the slick ground. He fired both guns and neutralized anyone who may have been a threat. When it was done, when the light layer of snow began to darken with blood, Sin slammed one gun back in his holster and grabbed Boyd again, not even waiting to see if he would follow on his own. The confusion caused by the blasts gave them the cover necessary to get out. The snow fell heavier as they fled through the forest.

By the time they reached the vehicle, Boyd woke from his trance. He reacted just enough to pull out the keys and unlock the doors, and had already turned on the engine when Sin got inside.

Boyd sped through the snow, his breath coming fast and hands trembling on the wheel. He said nothing. No explanation, no apology, and seemingly no awareness of the damage he'd just done.

Sin's adrenaline stuttered and slowly eased into anger. "If you want to kill yourself," he hissed. "Leave me the fuck out of it."

Hair hung around Boyd's face, masking his expression. "Understood."

DESPITE THE NIGHT passing in growing horror, the next morning Boyd still could not understand his own actions. The mission in Toronto felt like a nightmare he would wake from if he just waited long enough.

He'd nearly scalded himself while crouched in the shower with the water on full heat, but the blood would not wash away, even when the water went cold. He knew it stained him deeper than skin level.

Boyd had crawled out of the shower to lie on the couch, curled up with his head in his hands.

He'd killed in cold blood. He was a murderer.

Alexis. The guard at the entrance. The other members of her group who could have gone home safely if he hadn't forced Sin's hand and unleashed the tidal wave of violence that his partner was capable of. And Sin—he'd been injured multiple times. He could have been killed.

And it would have worked. If Alexis had been willing to negotiate even after they'd slaughtered so many of her people, she certainly would have been open to negotiation if they'd done the mission as planned. All those people would be alive and safe.

All those people.

Everything from the past month, from his whole life, was coming to a head. Boyd felt it in the weight of every thought. Felt it in the acrid black pall that suffocated his every breath and made his eyes burn from losing all moisture for tears.

He was at the end of everything; had been even before that mission. The one last fraying strand holding him together had broken at their argument in the motel. Such simple words, such a typical argument, but Sin's mocking tone had caused something in Boyd to snap after weeks of feeling as though he was coming apart at the seams. His head had been full of white noise that reached a crescendo on the drive to Alexis' base and, by the time they set foot in the forest, he'd fallen off the precipice and into a clean rage that had guided his every action.

Boyd barely remembered making the decision to shoot that first guard. While floating in a haze of anger, self-loathing and shame, the burning need to lash out at the world consumed him. Distantly, he wondered if that was what happened to Sin when he had an episode. Maybe Boyd was losing his mind, spiraling into psychosis, and fulfilling everyone's wishes and expectations in the process. From the abuse people had heaped on him in the weeks after the France mission, it seemed like that was their goal.

When the debriefing came around in the morning, Boyd thought about not going, but he knew he deserved any punishment he got. During the drive to the Agency, Boyd felt like he was heading to his own execution. When he parked and crossed the courtyard, he felt like everyone was watching and waiting to see him suffer and burn.

Boyd kept his expression impassive and head held high, refusing to give them additional ammunition.

The rest of the unit was already seated in the conference room when he arrived. Carhart's hands were folded in front of him, his gaze flinty. Everyone else was silent. They looked nervous. Except for Sin, who stared at the table with his hood pulled down low.

Once Boyd was seated, Carhart turned to Sin as though he had been waiting to unleash his fury. "What the hell did you do?"

"Killed a bunch of Canadians, obviously."

Carhart slammed his hand against the table. "What the fuck is wrong with you? Don't you have any goddamn self-control?"

"Is that a real question?"

"Sin, I swear to God—"

"And what's he supposed to do about it?"

"Sin, stop." Sin pinned Boyd with a lethal glare at his words, but Boyd turned to Carhart. "It was my fault."

All attention snapped over at Boyd's quiet admission. Ryan in particular appeared shocked.

Carhart's anger wobbled and his features creased in confusion. "Was negotiation out of the question?"

Boyd found himself unable to lie but equally unable to admit that he had not even tried.

"This mission was important," Carhart seethed. Each word came out in a tone laced with anger Boyd had never heard from the general before. "Death was to be the absolute last resort. This woman could have provided valuable information on Janus, information about its leader and the core members—people she knew personally! So this time you're going to give me more than some bullshit, half-assed answer. I want details, I want to know exactly what went down and why. I have to answer to Connors for this. It's not just your failure. It's also mine and everyone else in this room."

Boyd's heart slammed against his ribcage. Carhart was right. They could all be blamed because of him. He opened his mouth to confess but Sin cut in before he could.

"We were completely surrounded. He tried to gain access to her, but there were fifty to a hundred hostiles in that location. Did you people really think they were going to let us carry the woman out without a fight?"

Boyd's eyes flew to Sin.

"I'm not really surprised," Ryan spoke up. "They chose Alexis to represent their group in Canada because she was unrelenting and known to train her people to be the same. Even if she would have attempted to negotiate, her men would have never backed down without a fight."

Carhart continued to glare at Boyd, waiting for him to speak, and Boyd felt trapped by those accusing cerulean eyes. He quelled at the idea of evading the punishment he deserved, but if he didn't lie, then Ryan and Sin would be implicated. He didn't understand why they were covering for him, why they didn't just let him be sent to the incinerator. But he didn't want to be the reason they were hurt.

"It was a difficult mission," he said at last. "We were surrounded. Amid the chaos, the danger to our lives, and the fact that the plan fell through, I made a decision based on the circumstances, and shot her."

The frustration did not leave Carhart's face. He looked ready to storm out of the conference room but managed to turn to Ryan and Owen, asking sharp questions from between grit teeth. "What will become of the base in Canada? Do your sources think Janus will send another rep?"

Ryan chewed on his lower lip. "Honestly, all is quiet on this end. My contact has been distant and frankly, I'm not sure how long I'll be able to get information out of them. I have ears in Toronto as well, but they don't seem to know much more than what was reported on the news. I still can't really get over the fact that one of Alexis' rookies called the local cops..."

Owen shook his head and appeared more alert than usual. "I doubt anything'll come from that, though. There's enough controversy with the insurgents in the first place that even if they investigate, they have to be all political about what they say."

"Beyond that," Jeffrey spoke for the first time, "the accounts the rebels gave were scattered and incoherent. It sounds as though they were all so startled by the events that they did not properly see anything. There are five conflicting stories. They can't even seem to agree on whether a bomb exploded or an earthquake hit, though the earthquake theory is absurd given that it's Toronto." He glanced at Boyd. "Maybe they were just confused. Did they seem that way to you, Boyd?"

Boyd could not make sense of what was happening. Why were they

SANTINO & AIS

doing this? Why did they even care, especially Jeffrey? Why weren't they letting him take responsibility?

"Many of them did seem like new recruits," Boyd said in a low voice.

Jeffrey nodded. "Honestly, they're probably too scared to do much other than figure out if they want to regroup right now."

Carhart pushed his chair back, causing it to screech against the floor. "Connors is irate. If this explanation doesn't fly with him, expect some kind of repercussions." He did not bother to apologize to Sin for his earlier accusations. "If this goes wrong it will not only be bad because of the loss of Intel, but it will be a PR problem as well."

Boyd knew the moment PR was mentioned that he would be hearing from his mother.

"Anything else on the table?" the general asked.

"Yes. I have decrypted a little more of the flash drive. However," Jeffrey held up a hand as if to forestall any reaction, "it's not connected enough yet. So far I have a lot of information that isn't complete. Monterrey seems to be a large theme, and there is some information regarding security for some type of event. There's also a list of rebel groups from across the world, but none of it is completed enough to indicate what it's for. It doesn't have any addresses or names so it can't be a contact list. I'm still not positive it's all legit, but it seems more likely. I won't be able to confirm this until I've had a chance to tackle the second file."

Even at that news, the tension in Carhart's body did not ease. He got to his feet, looking away from his unit.

"Fine. That may help our cause, but don't expect this situation to be over quickly. I'll be in touch."

When Carhart left, Boyd was right behind him. He did not look at anyone, or give them the opportunity to speak to him, before he left.

TWENTY

EVERYTHING WAS A disaster.

Sin left the conference room soon after Boyd, walking quickly to his apartment with a strong desire to be left the hell alone. The entire mission had been an utter failure and now one or both of them would possibly be sent up to the Fourth or terminated as a result. His only hope was that Vivienne would intervene and Carhart would spin things the right way. Connors would never let them get away clean unless someone covered their asses.

He ignored all the guards after entering his building and slammed his apartment door shut. The action did nothing to alleviate his agitation, so Sin began to pace. He replayed the mission in his mind yet again, and came up with the same explanation. There was no doubt that the catalyst of Boyd's little freak show had been their rapidly deteriorating interaction. It seemed like no matter what happened, things just kept spiraling down further to make the situation between them worse. And now it had spilled over into a mission.

Sin was still stalking around when someone tapped on his door. Half hoping it was Boyd, he yanked it open and was confused to see Ryan.

"What the hell do you want?"

Ryan looked at the guards that stood on either side of the door, and shot Sin an impatient glare. "Can we talk? It's about, ah... a mutual friend. Y'know."

Sin stepped to the side, allowing Ryan access before slamming the door again.

"To what do I owe this pleasure, Freedman?"

Ryan took off his gloves and rubbed his hands together. He was visibly nervous and his eyes flitted around the apartment as if he couldn't or didn't want to look closely at Sin.

"I'm worried about Boyd. I wanted to know what really happened on that mission."

"Why? So you can go write out a full report?"

Color flooded Ryan's face. "You know, I'm Boyd's friend. I actually care about him, and worry about him, and want him to be okay. I'm

SANTINO & AIS

not going to go running to report back to anyone, for your damn information."

Sin gave the younger man an assessing look. Ryan was so easy to read that it was unlikely he'd be capable of any kind of subterfuge.

"What does this information mean to you?"

"I told you. I'm worried about him! He's had a really bad few weeks, especially the other day, and now he blew a mission this bad? I feel like—" Ryan faltered, twining his hands together. "I just get the feeling something bad is going to happen. Like he's going to go off the deep end."

Sin held up his hand to prevent Ryan from continuing. "Bad few weeks how? He didn't even have any missions while I was gone."

"He didn't," Ryan admitted. "But, like, whenever he did come to the compound... I dunno. People have been hard on him."

"People are always hard on him."

"Yeah, but it's worse now! Somehow the thing about him being a valentine got out. I have no idea how, and it pisses me off so much that maybe Jeff or Owen said something to someone outside the unit. I mean it's also possible that one of the staff noticed when his official status was changed and word got spread that way, but people definitely know."

When Sin just stood silently and waited for more information, Ryan threw his hands up.

"You know how most of these fieldies are! You know better than anyone! Do you remember what they used to do to you when you were a kid? How they'd back you into a corner and try to... do whatever? Well, what the hell do you think they've been doing to Boyd? Especially now that they have confirmation about him being gay. Last week they made a spectacle of him in the courtyard right in front of everyone, I heard. They jumped him and made a big show about how he couldn't take them on even though he's rank 9, and spit on him while he was down. A whole courtyard of people just watched and left him there on the ground bleeding. And you know Boyd, he just keeps everything inside. It's only a matter of time before he snaps!"

Boyd *had* snapped. Sin now had no doubt that their stupid argument set off something that had been building for days.

Sin wanted to demand the names of the people involved so he could go show them what a rank 10 could do. No matter what happened between Boyd and him, the part of Sin that risked taking bullets to keep Boyd out of harm's way wanted to crush the people who dared to hurt him.

"I don't know what to do about any of this," he said. "I completely fail at sympathy. My solution to this problem is gutting them all, and I've already tried the murder-to-avenge Boyd's honor thing, and it didn't pan out. He and I, we don't communicate very well. In fact, I'd say we rather fail spectacularly at it. It's better if I stay the hell out of his problems at all."

"No, no, *no!*" Ryan shouted. "Jesus, you both *do* fail at communication! I don't know how two such smart, talented people can be so damn stupid. Either you ignore each other or you insult each other! And I know you both care about each other! He was so torn up about all of that France stuff—"

Sin frowned, wary. "What exactly do you know about France—"

"—and he thought you hated his guts, but I can tell just by your attitude that you don't. The way you treat Boyd is like 500% better than the way you treated your previous partners and everyone damn else, but he doesn't want to see that, and you just want to be a dick and push him away!"

"Well, what the hell do you propose I do about it?" Sin retorted. "As you can see, we've managed to turn our little fight into a colossal fucking failure on every level of the failure scale."

"Just go talk to him, damn it!" Ryan gestured his arms and took up the pacing that Sin had abandoned moments ago. "Just... just tell him what you told me, if nothing else. Tell him you want to go and kill those fuckers because of how they treated him. That it makes you angry because you care. Because right now? Right now I bet he thinks he doesn't have anyone at all."

Sin pressed a hand to his face and thought about their tentative friendship, and how it had been disrupted before it had fully forged.

"Maybe he doesn't want me to talk to him."

"Of course he does."

"How would you know?"

"Because I know! Stop being so insecure and go find him before he gets himself into more trouble! *Please.*"

The unseeing mask Boyd had worn the night before came to Sin's mind. The way he had thrown himself into danger with no regard for his own safety.

"Fine. Where is he?"

Ryan nearly sagged with relief. "He has to write the report so I bet he's up in the libr—"

Sin was out the door before Ryan finished the word.

BOYD HAD JUST shut the door to his mother's office when he felt a stinging ache. He blinked, stunned more from the act than the strength, and brought a hand up to his face.

A touch, any touch, from Vivienne was so rare that it took Boyd a shocked second to realize that she had hit him.

"What is the matter with you?" Vivienne demanded, her voice low and furious in a way he didn't think he'd ever heard. "Have you no intelligence? Is there a shred within you worth saving? I am of half a mind to mark you for termination now and be finished with you."

Vivienne strode back to her desk, jerking the chair out with a clatter. She leveled a hard stare at him and Boyd followed the unspoken directive, moving to sit before her desk. He tightened his fingers around the arms and kept his back straight.

"Do you understand how difficult it is to be a woman and succeed in this type of environment? Years of accusations against my integrity simply due to succeeding in a male-dominated world and I was able to avoid it all. Yet you have managed to bring it all into question again through your inability to consider the situation."

Boyd started to speak but she stopped him with a raised hand. "Do not."

He closed his mouth.

"While I cannot blame you for your dedication, I am disgusted by your actions. Do you realize the stigma of the valentine status? Do you understand the consequences of your actions?"

"I didn't know," Boyd said. "If I had—"

"Ignorance is not an acceptable excuse," she interrupted. "The fact that you appear to have volunteered for the status puts you in a class of your own. If you had put more faith in your ability to negotiate through words rather than in bed, neither of us would be in this embarrassing predicament. Or perhaps you used Thierry's alleged recalcitrance as an excuse to engage in acts with the first known homosexual you encountered?"

"It wasn't like—"

"Because from my perspective," she continued over his protestations, "you wasted no time in establishing yourself as a promiscuous homosexual degenerate. With our blood relations, every one of your transgressions is reflected on me. A fact which I am steadily growing to detest."

"I was just trying to succeed in the mission." The words already seemed destined for failure as they left Boyd's mouth. "I didn't want to disappoint you."

"If that is the case, your ability to achieve the exact opposite of your goal is astounding." Vivienne sat back, her hands intertwining and pale eyes frozen. "As I understand it, Jeffrey Styles is in the process of continuing to decipher the information, yes?"

Boyd nodded, not daring to speak.

"Very well. That does imply that the information is legitimate. It is possible the debacle will end with a small measure of success. However, understand this much: you have officially been given the designation of a homosexual valentine operative."

Boyd's stomach sank at the words spoken aloud. But he knew; the whole compound knew.

"As you were capable of acquiring information that we assume to be useful, it implies that your skills in that department are adequate." The words came out tight with distaste. "However, now the onus is on you to hold up to that standard in future assignments. Should you refuse or fail, it will appear as though you believe yourself to be too good for dirty work, I will be held accountable, and it will only resurrect this situation. If you had been intelligent enough to avoid this issue in the first place, we would not be having this conversation. However, you have proven yourself to be incompetent, and now I must do damage control. Do you understand?"

Boyd nodded again. He didn't bother asking if there was a way to remove the designation. He knew the answer would be no. The sense of hopelessness that had been plaguing him intensified, a black hole threatening to swallow him. He almost wanted to tell her she didn't have to say anything further because he knew, had always known, how worthless he was. That she'd always been right about him.

"And should the topic arise, I expect that you will make it clear that it is your own degraded values that caused you to make that choice. I want nothing to do with your promiscuity in the rumors, do you understand me?" Vivienne's mouth flattened into a line. A beat of silence passed before she asked, "Are you having intercourse with that creature of a partner?"

"What?" Boyd could not keep his surprise from the surface. "No. Why would you—"

"I suggest you keep it that way. Your reputation is poor enough without adding that abomination to your record. Now. Onto your latest disaster. Do not attempt to lie so blatantly to me as you did to General Carhart. I am well aware that the fault is yours alone."

Boyd hesitated, unsure of what to say, and Vivienne's eyebrows rose. "Do not underestimate me. It is my job to be informed. I have an extensive network of contacts and access to countless media outlets. After reviewing the varied reports, I have been able to pinpoint the most likely chain of events, and I am still at a loss as to your motivation. What on Earth possessed you to believe you could enter the facility in such a manner? You had adequate time to formulate a plan."

Again, he hesitated. There was no way to explain. But even without his admission, a knowing look slid across his mother's face.

"Ah. I see."

"What?"

"You were feeling childish again, no doubt. Are you truly so pathetic that suicidal tendencies are your only means of coping with anything that does not go your way? If you are so intent on dying, be more efficient about it. Your behavior thus far is shameful."

Be more efficient about it...

Her words were a reflection of Sin's, and Boyd's wall of protection cracked. His scattered thoughts came together to form a single conclusion. The two people he felt most connected to, the two people he wanted to be close to, felt the same.

If you want to kill yourself, leave me out of it...

"I am finished with this conversation," she said. "I expect marked improvement from you in the future. The Agency does not have time to deal with incompetent children and neither do I. Be thankful that I care enough about my reputation to sometimes protect yours. Dismissed."

Boyd got to his feet. When his fingers curled around the doorknob, there was a moment when he wanted to ask her so many questions. Whether she'd ever loved him, whether he'd ever made her proud. But he couldn't voice the questions because Boyd knew what the answers would be.

And they were right. They were all right. It would be better if he was gone.

It was time to remove himself from the equation.

Boyd was already analyzing the best way to do so when he left Vivienne's office. He walked with a purpose for the first time in what felt like months.

In the past, Boyd hadn't planned well enough and it had cost him. But the Agency had taught him how to prepare better than high school ever had. He was a murderer now; it shouldn't be difficult to achieve his own death. He just had to plan for maximum lethality so no one could interfere, and ensure that no one would look for him until he was well beyond the point of revival. To achieve that, Boyd had to file the report, take full responsibility for everything without implicating the others, and avoid seeing anyone from the unit.

With that plan in mind, he strode to the library. As usual, it was deserted and Boyd sat at his usual table, running through wording and different explanations. It had to match what the others had already said, but still make it clear that it had all been his fault. He stared at the computer, fingers poised to type, and then felt the presence of another person in the deserted room.

After the events of the past few weeks, Boyd was not surprised to see Harry.

"Well, look who's here. The little bitch who doesn't know how to keep his mouth shut."

Boyd dismissed Harry and focused on the computer again.

Harry crossed the room. He planted one hand on the table and used the other to grab Boyd's hair, forcing him to look up.

"Thanks to you, my pay has been docked for months. The bitch in payroll just says to me it's my own problem for getting temporarily demoted."

Boyd jerked his head away. "Leave me alone. I'm doing something important."

"Doesn't look nearly as important as me losing my fucking pay because you shoved your nose into my business."

"Maybe you shouldn't have been a pervert."

Harry put his other hand on the table and leaned down with glinting, predatory eyes. "Do you ever think that maybe your partner wants it? Maybe that's why he shows off for me. He knows it turns me on when those cock-sucking lips start talking all of that trash."

The detachment Boyd felt gave way to anger. "He doesn't want anything to do with you, you piece of shit. You're pathetic and see only what you want in the world even when it's a complete lie. No one in their right mind would ever want to be near you."

"That's where you're wrong."

The chair was yanked out from under Boyd, throwing him off-balance and causing him to crack his chin on the edge of the table. Boyd tried to push himself up but Harry grabbed a handful of his hair and used it to slam his face into the table. Boyd grunted when Harry bent him over the desk and pinned his chest to the top. Harry was like a wall of muscle against his back.

"Sin doesn't want you," Boyd grit out. "He would kill you in a heartbeat if it wouldn't inconvenience him by being sent to the Fourth. You're a psychotic sex offender who's been stalking him and is deluded into seeing something that isn't there. I hope he castrates you and shoves your balls down your goddamn throat."

Harry shoved his hand down and between Boyd's thighs, squeezing his scrotum. "What's that you were saying about balls, bitch?"

Revulsion coiled in Boyd's stomach. "Get off me," he seethed.

"No. No, this is what I'm talking about." Harry massaged Boyd through his pants. "You get me all fired up and then pretend not to want to play ball." He squeezed harder, and ground his growing erection against Boyd's ass. "Maybe you're like Vega. Maybe you just want it rough."

The feel of Harry against him and the disgusting words sent a shot of adrenaline soaring through Boyd. He hooked a leg behind Harry's ankles, knocked him off balance, and managed to scramble away. Once they were away from the table, Boyd turned and swung his fist in an arc, slamming it into Harry's jaw. The guard barely reacted.

"If you ever hurt him again," Boyd panted. "I will kill you."

"Give me a break, bitch. You're nothing. My cock would split you in half if I fucked you."

Harry wet his lips when he came at Boyd again, evading every attack with surprising agility. When Boyd finally managed to cause Harry to stumble, he turned to run to the door but a hand gripped the back of his neck and yanked. Boyd twisted and started to slam his knee into Harry's groin, but Harry caught his thigh and threw him down onto the floor. Boyd grabbed the side of a low credenza to pull himself up, and sprawled backwards when a large fist careened into his face.

Briefly stunned, Boyd could barely react when Harry dragged him up by the neck.

"I saw you out in the courtyard the other day. Saw you on your fucking knees like a bitch while Moua spit in your face."

Harry tossed Boyd towards the credenza and the wide mirror that was bolted to the wall above it. A crack split down the middle when Boyd's forehead collided with the glass.

"I started expecting mommy to come to your rescue, but she didn't. No one gives a shit about a little faggot like you."

He dug his fingers into Boyd's hair and slammed his face into the mirror again. The spider web of cracks expanded, and Boyd blinked when blood flowed from an open cut and went down into his eyes. The steady flow of warm liquid made it difficult to see, but he reached an arm back to slam the heel of his hand into Harry's face. The guard grunted but didn't budge. He bumped his hips against Boyd's ass and dropped one hand to once again get a good grip between his legs.

"You want it, don't you?"

"Fuck you, you disgusting psycho," Boyd hissed when Harry's free hand shoved his face against the splintering glass again. "I'll kill you. I will *fucking kill you!*"

"Yeah, baby, keep talking." Harry ground his hips against Boyd again, breath coming hot and fast against the back of his neck. Boyd grunted, straining against Harry, and felt a fissure of panic when he heard his belt buckle clatter against the credenza.

"Get off me," he whispered. "The cameras—"

"Who do you think watches the cameras, slut? My people. And they know all about you, you faggot ass valentine." Harry undid Boyd's pants and rucked them down, his hands shaking and breath coming in loud gusts.

"You won't—" Boyd's words cut off when a shard of broken glass came close to his eye. He flinched away, a strangled keen escaping his mouth at the realization of how trapped he was. "You won't get away with this."

"Who's gonna stop me?" Harry guttered out. He'd undone his own pants and now Boyd could feel bare flesh against him; the unmistakable length of an erection pressing along his crack.

"Vega? Yeah, maybe. Maybe not. He didn't stop Moua in the courtyard. Didn't find him after, either. And I fucking *wanted* him to crack Moua's throat, slut. I waited for it, hoped for it, so I could have a reason to drag him back to the Fourth and have him all to myself again. He didn't then, but maybe someone actually fucking his bitch will make him angry enough to flip out."

Harry slammed Boyd's head down to the top of the credenza so hard that Boyd saw stars. His blood slicked against the wood, smearing against his face. His head was twisted at an angle with Harry's hand tangled in his hair. Boyd could barely see Harry's reflection in a skewed portion of the broken mirror. He was lost in some fantasy, eyes dilated, face flushed as he humped Boyd's ass. When Boyd tried to throw the guard off him, Harry wrenched Boyd's arm around and twisted it until agony exploded down Boyd's shoulder.

"Yeah," Harry hissed. "Keep fighting, bitch. But I know you fucking want it. You want dick so bad you even begged to have it on missions. I bet that's why Vega's not around, huh? He wants you for himself."

"No. He's—" Boyd's voice came out so low and strained that he broke off, breath burning to be released as his chest was crushed against the edge of the credenza. Even now, he wanted to tell Harry he was wrong. It wasn't like that. Please just leave Sin out of it...

"No?" Harry mocked. He twisted Boyd's arm harder, his hips moving faster. "I saw you two in his apartment that night pressed up against the wall. We all did. Maybe he got you first, but after I fill your ass, we can all have a turn."

Boyd heard Harry grunting, his breath picking up, and the unmistakable sound of him spitting into his hand. Boyd felt revulsion roil his stomach, the need to be sick warring with his need to escape, but resignation sank in heavier than the need to persevere. He was locked in place, exposed, and so helpless that Boyd felt this chain of events must have happened for a reason. Maybe this was his punishment. Maybe he didn't deserve to fight.

The horror he felt at Harry's weight on his back would mean nothing in a few hours. He was going to die today, anyway. All he had to do was deal with this now, and soon it would all be over.

Boyd repeated the words in his head like a mantra, but still recoiled when Harry's fingers shoved against his crack and slid down. He listened to the excited grunts and mutters coming from Harry's mouth, and braced himself for what was coming.

It was then that Boyd saw something reflected in the glass.

Hands appeared around Harry's head and in two clean movements, snapped his neck.

Boyd felt the weight disappear from his back, watched Harry drop to the floor, and found himself staring wide-eyed into Sin's reflection.

Inexplicably, Boyd started to shake. Despite his resolution, relief made him lightheaded. He fumbled with his clothes until they were back in place, and was almost afraid to turn around, but he did.

Harry lay dead at Sin's scuffed boots, but Sin didn't even glance down. His attention was only on Boyd. When Sin's lips parted and he drew an unsteady breath, Boyd's chest tightened. He pressed himself against the blood-smeared credenza and stared up into the raw expression on Sin's face. He almost looked...

The door slammed open and a high-pitched whine shot through the air. Sin fell to his knees and clutched at the collar as guards flooded the room.

"Sin!" Boyd shouted and surged forward, but a guard pushed him back. Someone else started trying to revive Harry.

"More," someone snarled, and Boyd knew they meant the voltage.

"No," he pleaded. "Stop!"

The whine sounded again. Sin didn't resist even when the waves of electricity slammed through him with more power.

"You fucking idiots, *stop!*" Boyd shouted. "He didn't—"

The words faded when Boyd ripped his gaze from the man with the remote and centered on Sin. Pain twisted Sin's face, his green eyes were narrowed and damp, but he still had not looked away from Boyd. And then he shook his head wordlessly, telling Boyd not to interfere.

It didn't matter. Boyd couldn't stop himself. He shoved the guards aside and started to lunge at the one holding the remote, but a single, strained syllable brought him to a halt.

"Boyd."

The hoarse whisper silenced Boyd more than an army of guards ever could, and he bit back an anguished growl. Sin was trembling now, sweat covering his skin. It must have taken all the breath he had to squeeze Boyd's name out of his lungs, but he had done it.

Boyd grit his teeth but made himself stay still even when Sin fell unconscious. With the threat neutralized, the guards began to shout questions at each other.

Someone yelled that Harry was dead, someone else was asking what happened, and one of the guards kicked Sin in the side. Boyd reacted like a wild animal, pitching himself forward with single-minded anger until someone caught his arm and restrained him. It was Luke Gerant.

The guards dragged Sin away and took Harry's body with them once they'd pulled up his pants. The library was still again, and Luke and Boyd were suddenly alone.

Boyd was left reeling. In the space of minutes, everything had changed.

"You're bleeding," Luke said. "You need to go to the medic."

"No." Boyd wiped his arm against the blood on his face. "I need to see Sin."

"You can later. Right now you need to see the medic."

"But Sin—"

"After a shock like that he will be unconscious for a while." Luke put a hand on Boyd's shoulder and squeezed. "You won't do him any good if you're injured and acting out of control. You need to get yourself together if you're going to help him."

"But it doesn't—"

"*Boyd.*"

Boyd sucked in a breath. He looked at the floor, at the broken glass and sprinkles of blood, and pictured Sin in the box. Drugged and helpless, and at the mercy of Harry's friends.

He had to stop it, but Luke was right. To help Sin, Boyd needed to be in control.

TWENTY-ONE

"SIN'S BEEN TAKEN to the Fourth," Boyd said as soon as he was in Carhart's office. "How do we get him out?"

Carhart watched Boyd from under his eyebrows, taking in the obvious signs of recent injury. "How did you manage to get into trouble in the two hours since we all parted?"

"That isn't important. The issue is Sin—"

Boyd broke off when the general remained sitting with no urgency in his frame. Carhart already knew, and he wanted Boyd's version of events. The pit in Boyd's stomach opened, aching like sickness at the prospect of having to explain to that man he had come to respect so much.

"Harry Truman." Boyd nearly spat the name out. "He's a guard with friends on the Fourth. He has—had an obsession with Sin. I saw him trying to assault Sin one day and reported him. Apparently he was told today he would be pay docked while suspended, so he was angry. He found me in the library while I was writing my mission report. He blamed me and..."

Boyd hazarded a peripheral glance at Carhart, wondering if that was enough, but the general's expression had not so much as shifted. Boyd swallowed and pressed on.

"We fought and he tried to... assault me but Sin snapped his neck. He was protecting me, his partner, like he's supposed to. And even without that, Harry has attacked him in the past. Sin shouldn't be on the Fourth. It's not his fault. If anything, it's my fault because he was defending me." When Carhart still didn't speak, Boyd kept going, trying to press upon the general why this was so unfair. "Sin had warned me to stay away from Harry. He told me not to file the report. He told me this would all happen, but I didn't listen. I didn't listen to him, and now he's locked in that box because of *me*."

The words turned ragged at the end and finally, weariness spread across Carhart's face and aged him before Boyd's eyes.

"Unfortunately, the decision is not up to me. And I don't think Connors will feel especially generous about helping Sin after what happened last night."

Boyd moved closer to the desk. "I should be the one held accountable, sir. It's my fault. Last night was my fault. I'll go on record saying it."

Carhart sighed. "And today?"

"What?"

"Connors doesn't think I'm rational when it comes to Sin. He thinks I'm not objective. And as of now, there is not yet an official report regarding the event until I get a copy of the video, but the unofficial story has already begun to spread."

Boyd's heart sank. Every word spoken in the past few weeks, the things Harry had uttered today, it came together and Boyd knew what people were saying. He asked anyway.

"What is the unofficial story?"

"McNichols is saying you've had a vendetta against Harry ever since witnessing a disagreement between him and Sin and that you created lies to go after him. He's telling everyone he's seen the video, and you deliberately provoked Harry so Sin would have an excuse to kill him."

Boyd knew how the people on the compound felt about him, and he knew Carhart was censoring the story. Somehow, he was sure McNichols had claimed Boyd had been ready to fuck Harry and then cried rape when Sin appeared.

"It's a lie."

"I know that. But others won't. Harry was well-liked among the guards. You know as well as I do that you and Sin are spectacularly hated. I need the video so I can expose the truth."

"So then how do we speed that process? Do we petition the Marshal?"

Carhart leaned forward and pressed his elbows against the desk. "Why are you so determined to help him? For the past few weeks I've been sure that your partnership was coming to an abrupt and unfortunate end. So, why now? What happened?"

Boyd didn't think even he fully knew the answer to that. Everything had been moving too quickly to have a chance to reevaluate the situation.

"He's my partner. I had his back before with Harry, and now he had mine. Whatever the fallout is from Harry's death, from that mission, from anything… I'm involved, and it isn't right if he alone has to pay the price. Especially since if one of us had to pay, it should be me. I just want to make it right."

Carhart studied him at length with one finger ticking against the desk. The minutes seemed to drag but Boyd knew it was only seconds. Even that was too long when Sin was locked in the box, unconscious, and at the mercy of Harry's friends.

"Stay here," Carhart said. "Don't talk to anyone, don't do anything. The less visible you are right now, the better this will end."

Boyd agreed, but he couldn't sit still. When Carhart left him in the office, Boyd alternated between pacing and staring down at Lexington's skyline. It couldn't have been more than midday but the sky was dark except for the occasional bolt of lightning sparking across the sky. When the rain started, Boyd listened to the constant patter against the window. He slid down to the floor with his bandaged head tilted against the glass and imagined the thin barrier vanishing, him tumbling forward and down to the courtyard so far below. The mental image was so real that Boyd jerked back, startled. For a second he had almost felt as if he were falling.

Pressing his palms to his eyes, Boyd tried to ease the anxiety that wanted to bubble over and take away his control. Only two hours ago, he had wanted nothing more than to fall into oblivion. Now, all he could think of was Sin quaking on the floor and silently begging him not to intervene. Then there was that look on Sin's face before the guards had come... For just a heartbeat, Sin's face had been so open that Boyd thought he had seen regret, guilt, and horror in those damp eyes and had heard it in Sin's shuddering breath. But had it really been there?

The door opened and Boyd leapt to his feet.

"What happened?"

"No go," Carhart said, his voice curt. "Connors already has the video and he claims that he will view it when he has the time. Sin is to stay where he is until Connors decides otherwise, or until an assignment comes up that is imperative enough for his release."

"But we have to get him out." Boyd scrubbed at his wrist. His fingernail scratched his skin through his shirt and he paced faster. "It isn't right."

"There's not much more I can do, Boyd. When it comes to Sin, this is how it goes. Why do you think Connors keeps him active even though the rest of the compound thinks he's a monster? The Marshal is well aware that every incident had a trigger. He just doesn't share the information with the compound because he likes to keep Sin isolated. Harry's death will only feed into that and mythologize Sin even more."

"But—But right now—"

Carhart looked like he was at the end of his rope. He shook his head, unable to appease Boyd anymore. "We have to wait or the situation could be exacerbated. If you make Connors angry, it will be worse."

"I don't give a shit about—"

Boyd stopped himself abruptly, in words and movement. He tried to control his breathing, tried to tell himself this wasn't helping his cause. It wasn't helping Sin. All that mattered was Sin. Boyd sucked in a breath, trying to reach through the anguish of the past twenty-four hours and find a measure of calm.

"I understand."

FOUR DAYS PASSED with Boyd pacing his home, waiting.

He hated it.

Every second he was there, Sin was suffering, and it was all his fault.

Boyd did not dare leave his house for fear of being unable to stop himself from storming the compound and demanding Sin's release.

The waiting was not easy, especially when Boyd was trapped in his house. Harry's attack and his own stifled desire for death were resurrecting things better left forgotten; the memories brought to the surface by his home. He stayed on the second floor where the phantoms of his past couldn't dig as deep. He avoided his bedroom, but still found himself worrying at his wrists and rubbing the skin raw beneath his shirt. Every time he realized what he'd been doing, Boyd felt a flood of shame and nausea.

In the beginning, he concentrated on breathing and avoiding the issue. Denial was the only thing that had ever protected him from harm.

By the second day, he had changed focus. The moment Sin had been taken for killing Harry, Boyd's personal mission had shifted. Instead of plotting suicide, he brainstormed ideas that would gain Sin earlier reprieve in the event that Connors left him on the Fourth for an extended period of time.

As each day dragged with Connors refusing to acknowledge the situation, it seemed likely that an extended incarceration was exactly what the Marshal had in mind.

On the third day, Boyd discussed the situation with Ryan over the phone and, upon hanging up, Boyd started to form a solid plan.

When he hadn't gotten word by the fourth day, Boyd decided he'd given Carhart enough time. He couldn't sit idly by forever. He had to gather the intel needed to determine the secondary course of action.

On day five, Boyd was ready. He drove to the compound and ignored the stares he received. Not all were hostile, but Boyd avoided eye contact with everyone just in case. Especially with the guards. He developed tunnel vision and walked in a direct path to the Tower, taking the stairs to the top floor. Surprisingly, his key card still allowed him access.

Samuel Goldberg was the name of Connors' assistant and he wore a polite smile that did nothing to mask his absolute disinterest. When Boyd approached his glass desk, it was not dissimilar to being in the presence of an android.

"Good afternoon, Mr. Beaulieu."

"I would like to request an appointment with Marshal Connors. Could you tell me when he is next available?"

"In reference to what?"

"The incarceration of Hsin Liu Vega earlier this week."

"Ah. Him." Samuel glanced down at the holographic interface of his computer. "An appointment you say?"

"Yes. When is he next available?"

"Let's see... August 15th, 2020. Does 0700 hours sound good to you?"

Boyd's lips pressed together. That was six months away.

"Marshal Connors must be incredibly busy for the next available booking to be so far out. Is he going on vacation?"

"I don't see how that could possibly be any of your business, Mr. Beaulieu. Marshal Connors is the head of this organization. It is foolish to expect him to cancel dire meetings to discuss the incarceration of a known troublemaker. If you would like to see him in August, now is the time. The spot will close soon."

"I would argue that the meeting I'm proposing is equally dire, considering the circumstances."

"Mr. Beaulieu." Samuel's smile was overtly condescending. "You have a very limited worldview if you think your partner's incarceration is on the same level as the inner workings of this Agency. The fact remains that there isn't an opening until August. Would you like to see for yourself?"

Samuel flicked the floating image so that it spun towards Boyd. Connors' schedule for the next several months was visible to Boyd. His eyes flew over it, trying to remember as much as he could. After a minute, Samuel swiped the calendar back to his side of the desk. "Now, if there's nothing else..."

"He can't afford even a few minutes between meetings? He's only moving from floor to floor, is he not?"

"As a matter of fact, no." Samuel's tone somehow managed to skate the line between derisive and polite. "You are a fool if you believe all of his business is carried on in this building. Tuesday he will leave the compound for Europe."

"Would a phone conversation work, then?"

Samuel's polite facade evaporated. "Unacceptable. Take the appointment in August or take none at all. Unless Marshal Connors specifically asks me to make such exceptions, it's impossible."

"I see." Boyd stepped away from the desk. "Put me in for August, then. Thank you."

Samuel hardly acknowledged him, but he did type something that ended with a rather forceful keystroke. Boyd waited to call Ryan's personal phone until he was driving away from the compound.

"Boyd," Ryan said the second he answered the call. "Any news?"

"Yes and no." Boyd rolled to a stop at a light. "I think I have a plan. But I might need your help."

"Of course!"

"And, do you know how to contact individual guards?"

"I can probably get into the directory. Who do you need?"

"Gerant. His name is Luke Gerant."

"WHAT THE HELL are you doing? You can't be up here."

Boyd slowed his stride down the hallway of the Fourth Floor Detainment Center. The woman blocking his path looked incredulous but not overtly hostile, which was better than he had expected from most of the guards working the Fourth. The temporary clearance increase Ryan had programmed into Boyd's card had worked magic, getting him through every automated checkpoint so far. Now it was time to see if the falsified documentation would pass.

"I was given temporary clearance."

Lifting a palm-sized tablet, Boyd swept his thumb across the screen and a mini hologram of a document appeared above it. The guard snatched the tablet and scrutinized the hologram. Through the faintly glowing blue lines, Boyd saw her name tag read 'Kendris.' Once she saw Marshal Connors' signature on the bottom, Kendris flipped the document in a circle and then zoomed in with a flick of her fingers. The official digital watermark shown faintly in the hologram.

After giving Boyd a suspicious look, she read each line. "What the hell is this?"

"If you read it, you'll see it gives me clearance—"

"To release Vega to his apartment, yeah, thanks, I went to kindergarten, too." Kendris held up the tablet. "I *mean,* this makes no sense. This isn't protocol. We get orders through chain of command, not through agents prancing around with special clearance straight from the Marshal."

Boyd shrugged. "I'm just following orders."

"And why are those orders coming to *you* instead of Lieutenant Taylor?"

"How should I know? Maybe agent protocol is different than guard protocol. And since Vega *is* an agent..."

Kendris glared at the hologram. "I'm going to call on this."

"Go ahead, but you'd have to check with General Carhart or Marshal Connors if you did. And the Marshal is out of the country for a few days on business and General Carhart is indisposed."

"Well, isn't *that* convenient."

"Not really, since it's making you be a huge pain in my ass." Boyd shifted his weight and glanced at the time glowing beneath the hologram. "Look, can we move this along already? I don't know about you guards and your *protocol,* but agents actually have work to do. We don't get paid to stand around all day, questioning every document that comes our way. Maybe if we'd wanted to be glorified secretaries we'd have stayed at your level instead."

Kendris' face darkened and she pointed at the bruises and scabs on Boyd's face. "I heard what that's from."

Boyd stiffened, forcing himself not to react to her words.

SANTINO & AIS

"I'm one of those who thought Truman went too far with Vega, and I'm hearing a lot of rumors about what went down that day. One of them says he tried the same with you. If that's the case, it wasn't right." She slammed the tablet against Boyd's chest, her hand visually cut in half by the hologram. "But right about now, I can see why he wanted to bash your face in first. You agents always think you're so much better than us, but I got news for you: we control the compound, not you. So you'd better treat us right. Now get the hell out of my sight."

Kendris buzzed the entrance behind her and stepped aside. Boyd shoved the door open without bothering to look at her again.

"Gladly."

He was stopped by three other guards on the way, but none of them scrutinized the paperwork as closely as Kendris had. It didn't take him long to reach his destination but by the time he approached Sin's cell, Boyd's heart had clawed its way to his throat.

Luke and another guard stood at the entrance, peering through the reinforced glass and quietly conversing. Boyd's stomach knotted at the expression on Luke's face, but he didn't ask what had happened or why Luke looked so concerned. For Luke's safety, no one could know they had been in contact.

"Guards," he said. "I have orders to release Agent Vega."

Luke recoiled, for all the world looking like yet another offended guard who was annoyed at Boyd's appearance on the floor.

"How is that possible? Typically we're sent direct orders about the release of one of our inmates."

The other guard looked from Luke to Boyd apprehensively. "Who's Agent Vega?"

Luke flashed the younger man, obviously a rookie, a mildly reproachful look.

"Vega is Sin's last name," Boyd said. "I realize it's unusual but I'm just following orders. Your colleagues have already examined it, but," Boyd held the tablet out, "feel free to examine my orders for the fifth time."

"I will."

Luke took the tablet and activated the hologram. He half-turned from the cell as if blocking the rookie from viewing the document, but Boyd knew Luke was ensuring his actions were in full view of the cameras. He spent almost five minutes with his staged examination and even took the time to compare the forgery to another. By the time the show was over, Boyd felt close to vomiting. He couldn't stop looking at the box.

It was more horrible than Boyd had ever imagined. A literal box and it was so *small...* When Sin had said he would do anything to avoid it, Boyd had not thought it would really be like this. The construction was unfit for even an animal.

"While this is unprecedented, the documents are in order." Luke spoke to the rookie again. "When a prisoner is released, unless Marshal Connors, General Carhart, or Lieutenant Taylor is here, the person would have a document such as this. When checking the document, make sure it has the Marshal's signature and watermark, otherwise it isn't authentic. In that case, backup should be called immediately and the person taken to Containment."

"I suppose this is as good a time as any to train," Boyd sniped. "Should I fetch you some tea and crumpets? Might as well relax while you're at it."

Luke handed the tablet back to Boyd. "You should watch your mouth."

Boyd slid the tablet into his bag and didn't rise to the bait. It would have been believable for them to go back and forth, but he couldn't stop looking through the glass wall of the cell. "Why do I hear nothing in there? Did you kill him while no one was looking or is he just too traumatized to think after what you people do to him?"

"That's actually what we were discussing before you arrived, Agent Beaulieu." Luke maintained eye contact with Boyd, somehow making it clear that he was not exaggerating about what he said next. "We are concerned that he may be dead by now."

"What?" Boyd's voice came out too loud. Panic made him lose the calm facade of his act. "Why?"

"He had a head injury and then he was sedated. It has been quiet since and we are not allowed to enter or unlock the box unless given direct orders, which we now have."

Luke moved to the door and hovered in front of the keypad, blocking it from view. There was an audible release of pressure when he gained access and the loud click of a bolt snapping back.

Beckoning Boyd to follow, Luke approached the metallic box that sat in the center of the cell. An IV tube disappeared into a small hole

SANTINO & AIS

in one of the walls, hooked to a bag mounted on the side where they could refill it without having to open the door.

Boyd's heart thumped harder when they got closer. He couldn't stop running his eyes all over the thing, unable to imagine that Sin was truly locked inside. He would not even be able to stand in there; he would barely be able to move. For someone so claustrophobic, it had to be unbearable.

"Open it." Boyd's voice came out in barely a whisper.

Luke hesitated, hands poised over the keypad. His apprehension was visible, and it seemed as though he wanted to tell Boyd to stand back just in case, but then Luke just punched in the code. There was another long beep, but this time Luke had to punch in another series of digits, this one longer than the first, before he was able to open the door.

"Shit," Luke hissed.

Boyd crowded in behind him, nearly shoving the guard out of the way to see his partner.

Sin was half-slumped against the wall. His hair was limp around his face but it did not cover the deep purple bruises spreading across the side of his head like spilled ink. His hands rested at his side, fingers curled and bloodied, fingernails raw and jagged. There were bloody hand prints all over, as if Sin had pounded on the walls for hours. Or days. His skin was ashen and, worst of all, he did not seem to be moving.

He looked dead.

"What the *fuck?*"

Boyd was at Sin's side in the space of a second, reaching for Sin's wrist to feel for a pulse. One was covered with a tamper resistant bracelet where the IV was fed, but it looked damaged.

He could not look away from Sin's slack face and fear made Boyd's hands tremble to the point that he couldn't feel Sin's heartbeat. It took him a second, but as Luke watched with growing horror, Boyd found Sin's pulse and exhaled. The relief was debilitating.

"He's alive. But I need to get him out of here immediately and get these drugs out of his system because what the *fuck—*"

What had started as calm and reasonable ended in a snarl. Boyd inhaled and attempted to get his panic back under control, but it was difficult with Sin looking closer to death than life.

"I'm already on it." Luke disabled the IV with yet another code that was punched into the bracelet. He pulled it off Sin and threw it on the floor, his face twisting in disgust now that he was hidden from the cameras. "Fucking ridiculous," he muttered

Luke moved forward awkwardly, the top of his head brushing the ceiling of the box as he walked around Boyd, avoiding Sin's bent legs, and the toilet which was smudged with blood.

There was only a small space that wasn't occupied and Luke knelt there, gripping Sin's chin in one hand and studying him.

"What are we doing?" he asked in a low voice.

It was bizarre seeing someone be able to so casually touch Sin.

"We're taking him to his apartment," Boyd said. "I can't carry him on my own. I need help, I don't care who."

Boyd knew he was going to have to gather the dregs of his impassive mask once they were within the camera's range, but he didn't know how. He couldn't look around the box without some evidence of blood showing the pain and panic Sin had to have been in.

Luke slid both of his arms under Sin's arms, grunting as he tried to hoist him up. He stumbled, almost falling under Sin's weight. Luke caught himself and managed to tilt awkwardly against the wall with Sin sagging against him.

"Damn," Luke muttered as he backed out of the box, half-carrying and half-dragging Sin with him. "He's a lot heavier than he looks."

Boyd moved in on the other side to take half of Sin's weight as soon as they had more room. With something to do with his hands, and the feel of Sin solid and mostly whole, Boyd managed to take on his role again.

"Will you be able to escort him to the apartment or do I need someone else? And regarding the drugs," he said, unable to keep the sharpness from his voice, "will there be any side effects now that they've been stopped?"

"James!" Luke called to the rookie as he shifted to get a better grip on Sin. "Radio Travis and tell him I need him to cover me while I give Agent Beaulieu an escort."

The rookie stared at the scene with confusion before grabbing his radio and fumbling with it, trying to find the right switches.

Luke glanced at Boyd over the top of Sin's bowed head. "It would be wise to take him to the Med Wing for further evaluation. He might have a severe concussion or worse, and he has been unconscious for quite some time. However, if the orders are to return him to his quarters I would advise that you request further instruction. I assume he is to be watched in some way to monitor his condition. While he has never shown side effects before, I'm not sure what will happen in this case. He has a strong tolerance to the drugs and they normally wear off quickly once they are no longer constantly added to his system, but given his head injury, I'm not sure what his response will be."

Boyd nodded but his mind was racing. He knew he should take Sin to the medical unit but could he afford to? What if Connors discovered his ploy? Boyd's entire plan rested on the fact that he could barricade the two of them in Sin's apartment before anyone realized what had happened. It was the only place on compound he could have a believable reason to bring Sin that he should also be able to defend until he knew Sin was okay. Now, more than ever, Boyd wished he could have brought Sin off compound without it raising alarms.

Boyd thought he could probably count on some leeway time before someone nosy enough thought to contact Samuel and for Samuel to get in touch with the Marshal, but it was still risky. Not as risky as leaving Sin untended, though.

"The medics," Boyd agreed. "But we can't drag him there the whole way. We need a gurney."

"I know where to find one."

The next thirty minutes passed in a blur despite a constant fear that they would be discovered before returning to Sin's apartment.

The medical staff was at least professional, a fact that surprised Boyd. At this point, he'd expected everyone on the compound to hate Sin.

One of the doctors swore at the sight of Sin's bruises and bloodied hands. He had treated Sin several times after being released from the Fourth, but never like this. He proclaimed that the guard on duty in Maximum Security had stalled before allowing one of the technicians to administer the sedative in Sin's IV. Although the drugs kept Sin in a stupor, both Luke and the doctor informed Boyd that it was better than the alternative, which is what had happened this time. The claustrophobia had likely induced complete terror, which had undoubtedly triggered a psychotic episode that had led to Sin trying to knock himself out.

They tested the amount of drugs in Sin's system and ran a CT scan, but when they said they wouldn't be able to immediately examine the results or test Sin's responses until he was awake, Boyd convinced them to let him bring Sin home.

Once they were in the open air of the courtyard, Boyd stole a glance at Luke. "Thank you for this. I know it puts you at risk."

"You're welcome."

Luke led Boyd on a roundabout route to Sin's building that ran along the perimeter of the compound and lent a shield in the form of trees. Even with documentation, any number of people could take the opportunity to sidetrack them with Sin slumped on a gurney between them.

"I don't agree with some of the things he has done," the guard continued. "And I don't think he's entirely sane, but in the real world he'd get psychiatric help and not this kind of abuse."

Boyd glanced down at Sin. His face was turned to the side, the sheet half-covering it. "I know he's done terrible things, but there's so much more to him than people know. He just needs someone to believe in him."

Luke nodded and just before they reached Sin's building, he said, "I think being around you helps him."

Boyd scoffed. "I don't help anything at all."

"You're not giving yourself enough credit. He's different now. You don't know because you didn't see what he was like before."

Boyd shook his head and didn't bother to answer. Together, they entered the building with little trouble. The guards greeted Luke with enthusiasm and barely looked at the documentation. One of them, Daniels, joked that he'd been bored guarding an empty apartment for the past week. Luke replied that they could switch jobs.

Their act was playing well all the way through, but Boyd was anxious for them all to be gone. Once they were inside Sin's apartment and had transferred him to the sofa, Boyd sagged in relief. After staring down at Sin for a moment, Boyd turned to Luke and affected the composed detachment again.

"I'm fine now, guard," he said imperiously. "You can return to your post."

Luke's mouth quirked up but he hid it and nodded. When he was just inside the door, he adopted a leering smirk. "Good luck with your... friend."

Boyd nearly released a half-hysterical laugh.

When Luke was gone, Boyd locked the door and set about removing the surveillance. It damaged the walls and took quite a bit of painful wrenching on his end, but he managed to rip most of the cameras down. The one in the bathroom mirror was most problematic as he had to figure out where it was located based on his memories of the live feed. He wound up prying the mirrored cabinet out of the wall just enough to find the camera tucked in a recess behind it. When it was done, Boyd was careful to put things back to rights in the bathroom. He did not want Sin to know where the camera had been.

Through the duration of the surveillance removal, Sin was still. But by the time Boyd finished, Sin's breathing had grown deeper and he stirred more often.

Boyd tried to find something to barricade the door but there was nothing in the apartment large enough except for the sofa. It was futile, anyway. They couldn't stay in here forever.

By the time the sun was setting, Boyd was sitting on the floor next to the couch with Sin's gun in reaching distance while he methodically dismantled the cameras. He tried to stay as quiet as he could and put the pieces in an empty supply box he'd found beneath the kitchen sink.

When the cameras were destroyed and the pieces tossed in the box, Boyd returned to his spot on the floor and waited. He watched the numbers change on the clock, saw when the gray sky pitched to a bleaker black, and listened for the door to slam open.

But nothing happened.

No one knocked and no one called.

Yet, it was impossible that nothing had been reported. He could only assume that Connors did not yet know what happened, or there was some other interference that was delaying the inevitable confrontation that would take place. When it happened, Boyd was prepared for whatever they decided to do to him. It didn't matter as long as they let Sin have some peace.

While Boyd waited, he watched Sin.

At some point he had rolled onto his side and curled up, one hand pillowing his cheek and dusky lashes brushing his face. His full lips were parted, his brow smooth, and he looked comfortable despite the bruises that covered him. The sight pulled Boyd out of his brooding contemplation of the door, and he could not stop himself from touching the bruises on Sin's forehead. Boyd tensed, half-expecting a hand to grip his wrist, but Sin did not stir.

Boyd felt as comforted by the ability to touch his partner as he was alarmed by the fact that he could.

During the night, Sin woke up twice but was so disoriented that all he could manage was slurred speech and mumbling. He stared at Boyd with glassy-eyed confusion and sometimes thought he was still on the Fourth. Once, he started to thrash back and forth, harsh whispers of breath escaping him and accompanying the occasional word in Mandarin.

Unable to stand back and watch, Boyd crouched by Sin's side and put a gentle hand on Sin's cheek, murmuring reassurances.

"It's okay, Sin; it's Boyd. You're out of the box. I'm here. You're safe. I won't let anyone hurt you..."

When the nightmare faded, Boyd threaded his fingers through Sin's hair to soothe him. He trailed his hand along Sin's temple, smoothed his hand over his forehead, and then found his fingers in Sin's hair again.

Boyd waited for those intense eyes to snap open and for a sarcastic voice to demand to know what he thought he was doing but, instead, Sin sometimes leaned into his touch. He was so out of it, so incredibly different than his usual self, that Boyd didn't know what to think. On the one hand, he felt special to be privy to such a moment, but on the other, Sin's vulnerability frightened him.

The idea of anyone taking advantage of Sin in this state made Boyd feel cold inside. The things Harry had said echoed in Boyd's ears, and he couldn't help wondering how far the guard had gone.

To distract himself, Boyd got up and filled a container with warm, soapy water. Sin was still dirty and bloody so Boyd spent the next hour sitting on the coffee table next to the couch, gently cleaning Sin's face, torso, arms and feet—the parts he could reach without disturbing Sin's pants.

Boyd left Sin's hands for last. He ran his fingertips along them to see what they felt like when they weren't gripping him painfully.

Boyd was lost in the feel of Sin's skin when a soft sound caused him to glance up.

A glimmer of green showed beneath Sin's lashes. "You're not real," he whispered.

"Yes I am."

Sin mumbled something inaudible but all Boyd could understand was a quiet "sorry."

"Why?" Boyd asked, voice low.

He didn't expect an answer and didn't get one. Sin fell asleep again. The night marched on.

Boyd was exhausted and his eyelids felt heavier by the hour, but he would not sleep until he was certain the drugs in Sin's system had worn off. Still, Boyd found himself in a constant doze. He was kneeling by the side of the couch with his head on a slow, sleepy collision with the edge, when he heard talking on the other side of the apartment door.

He scrambled to his feet just as Vivienne appeared in the doorway. She shut the door firmly behind her, contempt freezing her features in a mask. In that instant, Sin half-woke and tangled his fingers in Boyd's sleeve.

Surprised, Boyd saw cloudy eyes locked on him.

"Don't go," Sin murmured.

"I'm not going anywhere," Boyd said. "You can sleep."

Either comforted by the answer or too tired to care, Sin's fingers slid from Boyd's sleeve and he collapsed back onto the couch.

"What did you expect to gain from this?"

Boyd wrenched his eyes away from Sin to turn to his mother.

"Exactly what I got. Sin's freedom for now."

Vivienne's heels made a dull noise on the carpet when she walked further into the room. "Your wish was for temporary respite that would lead to worse consequences than if you had simply been patient?"

"Maybe that's all it will be in the end, but I couldn't stand by and do nothing."

"The charges against you are severe. Insubordination, forging official documentation, entry to the detainment center without permission, misappropriation of Agency assets, destroying Agency equipment..." She crossed her arms. "I could continue. Do you not understand the consequences of your actions? Forging the documentation alone could be grounds for termination."

"It doesn't matter."

"Because you wish to die?" she asked with repugnance.

"No." This time when Boyd answered her, there was strength in his voice. He didn't look down at the floor and wait for condemnation like he had on the morning of Harry's attack. "Because this is more important."

"You are a short-sighted fool."

"Maybe."

Vivienne stood in the moonlit room, shadows casting darkness across her pale face. She turned back to the door.

"You're leaving?"

"I am remedying the situation."

"How?"

She didn't respond and something icy cold wrapped itself around Boyd's spine, making him shudder. He was across the room and grabbing her wrist before she could open the door.

"How?" he demanded, louder this time.

Vivienne looked down at his clasped fingers. "You will unhand me at once."

"Not until you tell me what you're going to do."

She tried to yank away but could not escape Boyd's grip. "I will have your partner removed by force and deal with you later."

"No you won't."

The finality in Boyd's voice seemed to shock her. Her lashes lowered, and ice hardened her voice to an edge. "What did you say to me?"

Boyd faltered, but one glance at Sin reminded him of his purpose.

"I said I'm not letting you have him," Boyd said. "Not until he's better. He does everything Connors wants, and he was still ready to let Sin die at the hands of those guards on the Fourth. With the mood on the compound now, that could still happen. So I won't let anyone touch him and I won't leave his side until he can defend himself. I will fight to keep him safe with every ounce of strength I have left. After he's capable, I won't resist anything you do to me. I know this is all my fault so I will willingly accept my punishment. But until then, if you're getting reinforcements, tell them to expect a fight."

He released her wrist and her hand fell away from the door. He couldn't tell what she was thinking, but for the first time Boyd realized he didn't care. It should have scared him to outright defy her but he only felt resolve.

Vivienne regarded Sin.

"You intend to cause a massacre in order to preserve one man's safety for even a short few days?"

Boyd nodded.

"Why?"

"He's my partner."

"That answer is not acceptable. Answer me why you would go to such lengths for such a paltry goal."

"Because saving him from torture and possible death is the furthest thing from paltry to me." Boyd stood between her and Sin, blocking her view as if that could protect Sin. "I know you don't believe human connection is important. I know you've never cared for my taste in friends. I know this may be reckless and could end in even worse. But I don't care. He protected me when no one else cared what happened to me and I'm going to do the same for him no matter what it costs me. He's my partner and he's my friend and no matter how stupid this may seem to you from the outside, it won't change my mind."

Vivienne's lips tipped down on the very edges like the twitch of butterfly wings.

The silence stretched, taut and liable to cut.

Boyd knew how it would end, could almost see her calling the guards in to restrain him and drag Sin away, and knew he would not hesitate to raise his gun at anyone that dared put their hands on the man behind him.

But that didn't happen. Instead, she inclined her head.

"Very well. Agent Vega has already served most of his punishment and it would not do to have him incapacitated indefinitely. I will see to it that you both remain undisturbed for the minimal time required for him to recover. However," she added in a voice tinged with acid, "I can make no guarantees for you. I will speak with the Marshal, yet given your astounding disregard for protocol it should not come as a surprise to you should you meet with dire consequences."

Boyd stared at her, thunderstruck.

"Thank you," he managed to say.

Vivienne's jaw clenched in a way that made him wonder if she was annoyed by the words. She turned her back on him but paused before opening the door. "You have tried my patience far too often of late. I expect you to consider your actions more carefully in the future. And Boyd—" Her eyes glinted in the darkness when she half-turned again. "If you lay a hand on me again, I will not be this lenient. I am your superior. You will treat me as such."

"Of course, Mother."

Her glare was full of warning, and then she was gone. He heard her giving clipped orders to the guard as the door swung shut.

Boyd stood in the middle of the room, staring at the door in a mixture of disbelief and wonder, before returning to his position next to the sofa. Sin had not stirred. He was lying on his side with one hand dangling over the edge.

Releasing a quiet breath, Boyd pushed some of Sin's hair back from his forehead and let his hand rest there, feeling the heat of his skin.

"It'll be okay, Sin," he murmured. "I promise."

TWENTY-TWO

Faint light breaking through the clouds signaled morning. Boyd's eyes snapped open and panic lanced through him.

It took some time to remember that he hadn't fallen asleep, he'd allowed himself to sleep, and that everything was okay for now.

He was still on the floor with his knees crimped and upper body leaning against the end of the sofa. He could practically hear his body creak when he straightened.

Squinting in the gloom of the apartment, Boyd saw that Sin was still asleep. He watched the gentle rise and fall of Sin's chest and couldn't help noticing how Sin's eyebrows and fingers twitched, his expression shifting with his dreams. There was something vulnerable in the slight parting of Sin's lips, the fall of hair across his face, and the movement of his eyes behind his eyelids.

This time Boyd did not hesitate to run his fingers down the side of Sin's face, brushing along those high cheekbones and down through the scruff on his cheeks. Boyd's fingertips danced along Sin's jaw and paused at his chin. His thumb shifted, rising up to brush against the full moue of Sin's mouth. His lower lip caught against Boyd's thumb, showing a glimpse of white teeth.

Sin shifted, his eyebrows drawing down and fingers jerking. Boyd yanked his hand away, feeling guilty.

His touch must have drawn Sin out of sleep because all of a sudden Sin's eyes were open and squinting at Boyd in the mostly dark room. The sleepy, tousled confusion on his face made Boyd's regret at having woken him, dissipate. Having Sin look at him without any guardedness or suspicion felt like a once in a lifetime chance.

Boyd smiled. "Hey," he said, keeping his voice low.

Sin frowned, his gaze diverting between Boyd and the door before flitting around the room. He moved to sit up and Boyd almost reached out to stop him, but withdrew his hand just as fast.

"We're in your apartment," Boyd explained.

The drugs seemed to be working out of Sin's system because when he spoke, he no longer slurred.

"How did I get here?"

"I brought you here with Luke Gerant."

Sin's brow furrowed. "Gerant—what? Who released me?"

Boyd's hands hovered between them, not feeling confident that Sin was ready to be moving around just yet. "Are you certain you want to talk about this right now? You were injured and should probably try to rest."

"No. Tell me."

Boyd sighed. He sat back on the carpet. "I... might have forged official documentation ordering your release."

"Why would you do that?" Sin's deep voice was hoarse from disuse but still managed to sound incredulous.

Boyd was starting to feel nervous. Now that Sin was awake, he couldn't help worrying that maybe his help would be unwanted. Sin hadn't wanted Boyd to interfere in the library. What if he wouldn't have wanted interference later either?

Boyd picked at carpet fibers on the floor and couldn't meet Sin's eyes any longer.

"You shouldn't have been in there. I should have taken full responsibility in the debriefing, and they should have taken me right from there. And even the way it happened... You never wanted me to report Harry in the first place. So you shouldn't..." His fingers dug lines into the carpet. "It never should have fallen on you to pay the price in any of this."

"It doesn't matter now," Sin said. "It's already done."

Boyd shook his head. That didn't change the facts but it was pointless to argue. He would end up dead soon, anyway. If not by the Agency, then by his own hand.

Sin nudged Boyd's knee with his foot. Boyd looked up, startled by the touch.

"Stop spacing out. You still haven't explained anything."

"I—" Boyd crossed his legs in front of him, struggling to put the events into a coherent explanation. "I was told to leave you in there. I thought you wanted that so at first I tried to comply with the rules. But I couldn't let you stay there indefinitely like they planned. So I timed it when the Marshal was gone. Ryan helped me hack temporary clearance onto my card and forge a document for your release, and Luke helped me bring you here."

Sin massaged his temples, once again squinting at Boyd. "You're insane."

"Maybe. Are you sure you feel alright?"

"This has happened to me before. With the exception of a headache and feeling slow, I'm fine," was the dismissive response. "What the fuck happened with Truman?"

Boyd did not believe that Sin was fine. He'd seen the man hide bullet wounds and knew Sin was capable of repressing pain, but he let it slide while making a promise to himself to remain diligent.

"Nothing. Just—A stupid situation. I was alone and he was angry. He attacked me and then you came."

"Yes, but why did he attack you?" Sin demanded. "That stupid fuck must have had a death wish."

Boyd redirected his attention to the carpet again. He didn't mention Harry's actual wishes. "The harassment report I filed for you meant his pay was temporarily docked. He wanted me to pay for it. It's nothing important."

"What an idiot." Sin stood but seemed to be at a loss. "Why didn't you just leave me up there, Boyd? Do you realize how much trouble you can be in?"

"I know. But as I said, I had to do something. All I cared about was getting you free. Now that I've achieved my goal, I'm fine with taking responsibility for my actions."

"Great. So you're fine with being terminated?"

"If that's what happens, I still won't regret my actions." Boyd pushed himself to a stand. It felt like every single muscle in his body hated him for it. "But..."

Boyd hesitated. He'd thought he would be doing everyone a favor if he killed himself. If he said something now, it might mean Sin would stop him. But if Sin wanted to stop him, wouldn't that mean there was something in him worth saving? But why would that have changed now? The mission in Toronto had only been a week ago.

"But, what?" Sin snapped, as impatient as ever.

"I've been wondering something."

"What?"

Boyd's arms crossed his stomach.

"I know we both said a lot of things to each other. But I really thought you hated me. You said you regretted ever helping me before, and I feel like you have good reason to regret it again. So I don't really know where we stand anymore. If you want a different partner..." Boyd studied the pattern of light on the wall past Sin's shoulder. "I just need to know if I should arrange that."

This time, it was Sin who looked away. "I said that because I was so disgusted at everything that happened in France. I hated myself for being an idiot, but I never hated you."

"How were you an idiot?"

"Because I was—" Sin appeared to think better of what he'd been about to say. "Because I was angry. You wouldn't talk to me, and then there was Thierry who I just hated in general. I was angry because you walked into valentine status. I was angry about the remote. And then—Anyway, I'm sorry for the things I said to you. I just couldn't handle what was going on and I didn't know how. I just get angry. But I didn't mean it. Any of it."

"Even what you said on the Canada mission?" Boyd asked, searching the shadowed planes of Sin's face.

"Any of it," Sin repeated.

For the first time in months, it felt like the very air no longer pressed in around Boyd; like he wasn't being crushed by a growing weight that wouldn't lift.

"Okay." Boyd sucked in a breath and, nodding, said louder, "Okay."

It was easier to pay attention to the world outside the room, like the weak sun trying so hard to break through the clouds. The events unfolding in the apartment did not seem real, but Sin's words left little room for misunderstanding. A hand brushing his elbow caused Boyd to once again focus on Sin. It was the second time he had touched Boyd since waking up.

"I'm going to shower." Even battered and bruised, Sin still looked beautifully uncomfortable when he murmured, "Thank you. For everything."

Boyd smiled, small at first but it grew as Sin fidgeted with the pockets of his loose black pants.

"You're welcome."

Sin nodded and backed away, eyes not leaving Boyd until the door closed between them.

Three words had changed everything.

The need for a suicide plan faded with the knowledge that not every person who mattered to Boyd felt only loathing for him in return. He couldn't be that useless, that unwanted and reviled, if the one person he had hurt and caused injury to still wanted him around. He couldn't be that loathsome if Sin didn't hate him.

Maybe, for now, things could be okay.

But now, Boyd had no idea what to do. It had been much simpler when he only had one last evening to plan.

When the sound of rushing water emanated from the bathroom, Boyd realized he had been doing what Sin accused him of only moments ago—spacing out. Shaking himself, Boyd went to the kitchen. He needed something to do to prevent himself from falling into constant reveries.

He decided to make something for Sin to eat but all he saw in the fridge was raw fish and meat. Boyd stared at it, nonplussed, and then opened the freezer. Nothing. Not even a single microwave dinner.

What the hell was he supposed to do with this?

Boyd had no idea how to cook. He was almost resentful of Sin's kitchen for its complete lack of ready-made meals.

He searched the nearest cupboards but all he found was a jar of peanut butter and a loaf of bread missing a few slices. That was doable, at least. Boyd had placed them on the counter when he heard his phone jingle. At some point he'd missed a text from Ryan telling him that Carhart was looking for him and asking if everything was okay.

Boyd sent a quick reply to Ryan and tossed his phone on the kitchen table. In that brief time, Sin had finished what had to be the quickest shower in history. He was already walking out of the bathroom and adjusting the ties on a loose pair of sweatpants while Boyd opened the jar.

"I see you made a garbage heap of my cameras."

"I did."

"Good."

Sin entered the kitchen and leaned against the counter. His hair was damp and combed away from his face, the bruises more prominent than they had been before, but Sin was definitely more alert.

"You sure went out of your way to do everything possible to piss them off."

"It wasn't the reason I did it, but I do know my mother was angry. I imagine Connors will be even more so."

"Was your mother here?"

"Briefly."

"I thought I'd heard her voice..."

When Boyd finished making him the peanut butter sandwich and slid it across the counter, Sin ate it in a few large bites. After he was finished, he grabbed the container of peanut butter, scooping it out with his fingers and eating it plain.

"Why haven't they brought me back yet?"

"I don't know." Boyd's eyes caught on Sin's curved lips and the faint sheen of saliva on his fingers when they slid out of his mouth. Realizing what he was doing, Boyd opened another cabinet. He found a can of soup. "My mother planned to help. She said she would allow you to recover here. I imagine it has to be cleared through Connors, though."

"Why in hell would she do that? She doesn't particularly care for me, you know."

Sin sat on the counter and continued to spoon out peanut butter with his fingers. He swung his legs idly and his feet bumped into Boyd. Whether it was on purpose or accident Boyd didn't know, but it was so relaxed it made Sin seem nothing like the man who had so recently been delirious and on the verge of death.

Boyd set the can of soup on the counter, trying to ignore the light jostling of Sin's foot. It was impossible to keep from looking at the casual way Sin slipped his fingers in and out of his mouth. It made Boyd remember their tongues clashing in France; the way Sin tasted. With it came the unbidden question of how it would feel to have Sin's lips—

Boyd snatched the jar away from Sin.

"Stop. That's—unsanitary. Eat it with something that's not... your fingers."

"Tastes better this way." Sin licked his hand clean. The longing look he gave the jar made him seem completely unaware of what was going through Boyd's mind.

Good, Boyd thought at the same time as, *Bastard.*

Boyd concentrated on making the soup. That was perfectly appropriate, and not a strange thing to be thinking about when his partner was still recovering from serious health issues.

"So?"

For a moment, Boyd couldn't even remember what they had been talking about. He pushed the can into the opener installed in the wall, and watched it rotate.

"I don't know. I didn't expect her to agree, let alone help. She did say it would be inconvenient if you were incapacitated indefinitely. Maybe it's that. Or maybe she assumed it would be too irritating to deal with me after I told her I wouldn't let anyone take you until you could defend yourself."

Sin watched Boyd pour the soup into a bowl, gaze following his every movement.

"I'm confused," he said finally.

"About what?"

"Because I don't understand why you did all of this. I understand that you feel responsible for me being in the box because of Truman, but why are you still here?" Sin seemed to realize how his words sounded because he scowled and shook his head. "I didn't fucking mean it like that. I just mean, I don't downshift this fast. You had me on ignore for a while now. Why are you suddenly being so nice? Not just getting me off the Fourth, but everything. The cameras, taking care of me, standing up to your mother. Do you feel bad for almost getting my head blown on that mission or something?"

Boyd stopped with his hands braced on the edge of the counter. "I might have been upset at times, but my opinion of you never changed. With or without Harry, with or without the Canada mission, I would have done the same. I know what it feels like to be abandoned in terrible circumstances and I would never do that to you. You're my partner and that means something to me."

"I see..." He watched Boyd heat up the soup, still looking unsettled but not doing anything to move the conversation forward.

"Now that I think about it, why were you in the library, anyway?" Boyd asked.

"Ryan came to my apartment to inform me of some things that had occurred while I was on my solo. I wanted to speak to you about it."

"Oh." The word carried some weight. "Did we already discuss it?"

"Not really. I guess I just wanted to make sure that..." Sin tilted his head back against the cabinet and looked at the ceiling. "That you knew where I stood. That I don't despise you, and I just think you're really annoying most of the time."

Boyd's lips pulled to the side. "Thank you. I think."

Sin stopped staring at the ceiling and grabbed Boyd's shoulder, pulling him closer. Boyd didn't resist. He brought his hands up without thinking and nearly rested one on Sin's hip before he caught himself. Instead, Boyd placed his palms on the counter on either side of Sin's legs instead.

"I had more to say," Sin said, still looking frustrated. "But it doesn't come out right when I try. I always say the wrong things."

Boyd nodded but he was so caught by their proximity, by the green of Sin's eyes, that at first he struggled with his own words.

"It's alright," he said at last. "As long you don't hate me, it's enough."

"That is not enough," Sin growled. "Not by a goddamn long shot. You just have no idea, Boyd. No fucking clue."

"About what?"

"Everything. Why I acted the way I did...Why I was so pissed off. It will never make any sense to you because I don't know how to explain."

"So try," Boyd pressed. "Please."

"I don't know how."

Boyd started to encourage him again, but Sin was so agitated that he let it drop.

He started to back away but Sin lifted his hand with measured care and cupped his chin, tilting it up. Boyd took it as an invitation to attempt to read all of the unspoken words in his partner's face. Once, long ago, Boyd had been good at reading body language and the subtle nuances of a person's countenance. With Sin, it was nearly impossible. Until now.

Now, Sin didn't hide the flash of hesitancy before sliding his thumb over one of Boyd's fading bruises, and making Boyd's heart pound so much faster.

Calloused fingertips brushing his face shouldn't have had such a powerful effect on Boyd, but he could not contain a shaky sigh. He leaned into the touch, closed his eyes, and for one instant, forgot everything else.

No longer uncertain, Sin pulled him closer and then their chests pressed together. Boyd's face cradled in the crook of Sin's neck, and he swore Sin's lips ghosted over his hair.

It couldn't be real.

"It's better if I don't have to talk," Sin whispered very close to Boyd's ear.

Boyd nodded in understanding but wondered at the slight tremor in Sin's voice. He leaned back slightly so he could see his partner's face and did not miss the way Sin's eyes flicked down to his mouth.

The sound of someone clearing their throat made Boyd's heart leap for a different reason. He jerked away and spun around.

"I'm just making him soup—" he blurted out before even registering who had entered the apartment.

Sin glared at Carhart. "What do you want?"

Carhart stared at them from the doorway, face awash in skepticism. It seemed as though he couldn't understand what he'd walked in on.

Boyd inched away from Sin, locking away his initial flustered reaction. "Good morning, General Carhart."

Sin slid off the counter, bare feet slapping against the floor. He picked up the jar of peanut butter again, obviously unconcerned about Carhart's presence.

"Okay then." Carhart shook his head and blinked twice. "Now you—" He pointed at Boyd. "I'd like to know what the hell you thought you were doing. And I don't want to hear about how dire Sin's situation was and how you had to do everything in your power. You could have gotten yourself, and him, killed. The next goddamn time—"

"Don't start in on him."

Carhart's glare swung over to Sin. "What?"

Sin scooped peanut butter out of the jar again. "Just leave him alone. You can yell at me."

"When I find a good reason, I will."

"Can't wait, General Carhart."

Boyd put a hand on Sin's arm. "Stop."

Again, Carhart gaped at them incredulously. He glanced around the apartment as if waiting for the real Sin and Boyd to come out. When his gaze returned to Sin and saw him eating peanut butter off his fingers, Carhart snorted.

"Look, Boyd," he said in a more even tone. "If you were anyone else, you would be dead now. Don't let that make you cocky. If you pull a stunt like this again, the Marshal won't let you off the hook a second time. You made him look like an idiot, and you're lucky it was something that was easily covered up. The general population thinks Sin was officially released."

"The guards will know," Sin pointed out.

"And they'll know to keep their mouths shut," Carhart replied. "It isn't difficult to get rid of the lot of them and replace them with low-ranking and not progressing field agents. That's what most of them are, anyway. You're lucky that can't be said for the two of you. You're currently irreplaceable in your own rights. It would be a mistake to use that information and let it turn you into a liability instead of an asset."

"I understand, sir," Boyd said. "I'll be more mindful of my actions in the future."

"You had better." Carhart gave them a hard look. "Get your shit together."

When Carhart was gone, Boyd raised his eyebrows. "That went... well."

"Yeah, his bitching was down to a minimum."

Boyd nodded and finished preparing the soup. He put two bowls on the table with some of the bread.

"Sin. You're not angry with me for all this, are you? I know it's stupid to ask that so far after the fact, but if I *did* make it worse for you than if I'd left you alone..."

"No," Sin said. "No one's ever done anything like that for me before."

"Good." Boyd released a low breath. "If you'd been angry too, I would've felt like I'd done the wrong thing."

"You did the wrong thing to the Agency." Sin grabbed a paper towel and wiped his hands. "But you did something good for me. They wouldn't have let me out until there was a mission. I would have been there for weeks. Maybe months. So don't feel like... it was wrong. Okay?"

Boyd waited for a sign that there was something more to it. That after everything, it couldn't be as simple as this, but Sin noticed the hesitation and glared.

Flashing Sin a slight smile, Boyd finally said, "Okay." Needing something to distract him from the doubts, he indicated the table. "I don't think even I can ruin microwaved soup but I suppose we're about to find out."

Sin considered the soup with some suspicion. "What is it, anyway? They order all of this crap for me."

"Vegetable beef."

"Vegetables, huh?"

Sin regarded the table as if it was an IED, but eventually sat in the chair opposite Boyd. He stuck one of his fingers in the bowl, sucking off the broth. "Not bad."

"Have you never heard of spoons?"

"I told you it tastes—"

"Better that way. Yes. I heard you." Boyd pointed at the bowl. "Stop stalling."

"Are you trying to distract me?"

"From what?"

Boyd expected Sin to say more but, instead, he just shrugged and offered a half-smile.

Boyd wondered if Sin meant what had happened before Carhart's interruption; as if Boyd was trying to distract him from the way they had touched. The last thing Boyd wanted to do was forget the feel of Sin against him, but the tender embrace they'd shared only moments ago already seemed very far away.

TWENTY-THREE

THEIR DOWNTIME LASTED until the end of March.

When Sin received notice about a briefing, he was almost thankful. In the month-long lull he'd done little more than read, exercise, and think about Boyd. It didn't seem wise to go to the gym after the Harry incident and Sin primarily stayed in his apartment. Confinement had never bothered him, but this time the lack of cameras allowed his self-imposed isolation to be almost pleasant.

Even so, Sin was bored.

He had some trepidation about the walk to the Tower, but the claims Boyd had made in the past couple of weeks appeared to be mostly valid. The air was less rife with hostility, and Sin only garnered the usual side-looks and mutters of 'freak' or 'monster.'

After the investigation, Carhart had made it clear to guards and field agents alike that anyone conducting themselves like Harry Truman would be dealt with immediately in the future so that events did not escalate to the same degree.

The general also had his admin do a thorough review of the guards manning the cameras at times when Truman had exhibited similar behavior, and proceeded to crack down on Harry's clique so swiftly that they seemed to have disappeared from the compound overnight. And all of it had been approved by Connors.

Sin didn't know why the Marshal was attempting to act like anything less than a shark-eyed sociopath, but he supposed it had something to do with the massive amount of Janus data that Jeffrey had finally begun to decode.

At least people were now smart enough to leave Boyd alone.

Sin entered the conference room to see Carhart and Jeffrey looking way too chipper, Owen stirring heaps of sugar into a monstrous cup of coffee, and Ryan clacking away on his ancient keyboard. He grinned at Sin when he entered, but Sin regarded the R&D agent without comment. The kid was okay enough, but Sin was tired of hearing about Boyd going over to his apartment.

"Where's Boyd?" Ryan asked.

"How should I know?"

Ryan blinked, clearly taken aback. "Um. I don't know? Because you talk to him a lot?"

"Well, I thought you were his new best pal." Sin dropped down into his chair. "Seems like you talk to him more than me."

Ryan's face went from confused to amused, and he gave Sin a knowing smile. "Ah, I see."

"What is it that you see?"

"Jealous, are we?" Ryan asked, voice light, teasing, and a far cry from the awed tones he'd previously used when speaking to Sin.

Sin glared at Ryan before switching gears and leaning closer with a smirk. "Yes. Very. Didn't you know? I want you all for myself."

Ryan's smug expression vanished. "W-What—"

Before he could continue, the door opened and Boyd entered the room. He nodded at everyone in silent greeting before taking his place beside Sin.

Still flushed, Ryan offered Boyd a weak hello before sneaking another glance at Sin. Sin winked and Ryan scooted away, peering at his laptop.

Boyd glanced between the two of them.

"I hope you two had a good vacation," Carhart started. "Because it's officially come to an end with a big assignment."

"It's still a vacation if you ask me," Jeffrey said, snider than usual.

Sin crossed his arms on the table and put his head down. Big assignment meant long, tedious briefing.

"After months of working diligently on the files that Thierry provided, Jeffrey finally decoded it in its entirety."

Carhart accessed the embedded panel on his end of the table and a hologram appeared in the center of the table. It was an image of an expansive building large enough to take up several city blocks in what appeared to be a metropolitan area.

"Do you recognize this building, Sin?"

Sin reached out to flick his fingers through the hologram. "Should I?"

"I assume you've been to Monterrey considering it was where one of your father's residences was."

"I wasn't allowed to leave the house." Sin's tone brooked no room for further discussion on the topic. He had no desire to talk about his father, but Carhart never seemed to remember that. "Does this have relevance?"

Carhart sighed and gesturing to the hologram. "This is the Joel K. Solar Convention Center, also known as JKS, located in the heart of Monterrey, Mexico. Before the war, Monterrey was an important industrial hub in Mexico and one of the leading centers of business. It was one of the few cities in Mexico that sustained heavy damage during the war but years later, there was a large scale restoration operation. Now, the city is one of the few booming places of industry and commerce in this Hemisphere. The population consists of expats from around the globe. In this case, mostly wealthy artists or businessmen."

"And?" Sin asked without patience. "So there was a history lesson on the drive?"

Jeffrey glared at him. "Don't interrupt. He'll get to the point."

Carhart was unfazed. "The JKS is directed by a former American who has the privilege of being related to a core member of Janus. A man named Hale Clemons."

A hologram of a man appeared next to the JKS and slowly rotated. He was in his fifties and had dark hair shot through with silver but was otherwise unremarkable.

"So, you want us to blow it up?"

This time, Carhart glared at Sin. "No. The place sits on a lot that is 2 million square feet. There are hundreds of exhibition rooms, conference halls and auditoriums. On November 11 of this year, eight months from now, there will be a large event at the JKS called the Global Arts Exposition, an exhibition of works by several famous artists who specialize in works visualizing freedom, hope and the new world. It will be so large, and need so much security, that no other events will be held on the property during that period of time."

"Is the Exposition a cover for something else?" Boyd asked.

"Not exactly but, according to the data on the drive, on the same night there will be another event at JKS that is being undisclosed from everyone except Clemons. He's using the Exposition as an excuse to heighten security at the JKS and hold a conference that representatives from all of Janus' cells will attend. Including their core members." Carhart looked at his field agents again. "This is a chance of a lifetime.

We haven't been able to pinpoint the location for a single member of their leaders, let alone the whereabouts of all of them at once."

Carhart pointed at Sin. "So by now, I'm sure you have figured out the purpose of this assignment."

"Wide scale assassinations?" Sin asked in a bored tone.

"Precisely. Check your tablets."

Boyd dutifully pulled out his tablet, but Sin didn't bother. Instead, he observed the rotating miniature of the convention center.

"I sent you the mission specs. There, you will find the names of everyone who is supposed to be in attendance. The eight men at the top of that list are our key targets, and then that entire wing of the building is to be destroyed so the rest of the reps are eliminated. So yes, Sin, you get to blow something up." Carhart raised an eyebrow. "And you're going to love this part."

"That just means I'm going to hate it."

Jeffrey smiled. "In order to effectively accomplish this mission, you will both go deep undercover in Monterrey. And we all know how you love undercover assignments, Sin."

Boyd leaned back in his chair with a look of surprise. Sin stared at them, disbelieving.

"Three months prior to the event, the staff at the JKS will begin hiring and training new security for the Expo. Sin will be one of those new trainees. And if you would check your files, you'll see your cover."

Sin frowned and slipped his tablet from the pocket of his cargo pants, flicking at the touch screen until he could access the data Carhart had sent earlier. After opening the file, Sin debated throwing the tablet at Carhart's face. The guy in the picture was his height and weight and had a similar complexion, but that was where the similarities ended. He had light hazel eyes, hair that had been dyed black and red, and he sported a multitude of tattoos and piercings.

"No."

"Yes."

"You've got to be out of your fucking mind."

"Obviously." Carhart reached out to swipe the rotating image of the JKS away to replace it with a hologram of Sin's cover. "Jason Alvarez was an American living in Northern Mexico. He traveled between both countries frequently and worked as security for major corporations. About a year ago, he was detained during a skirmish between our agents and insurgents using one of the locations he guarded as a meeting space. After it was clear that he was not involved, he was offered a position here. He was on the compound for three months before dying in training. He had no friends and no living relatives so no one knows he is deceased. His background fits the qualifications for a position at the JKS completely."

"He looks like an idiot," Sin complained.

"That is unimportant. He is similar enough to you in height, complexion and eye color to be the perfect cover. You will arrive in Monterrey in the first week of April. You will rent an apartment and you will seek similar employment until JKS sends out the notification for their hiring fair. That gives you six months to lay down roots and connections in Monterrey that will prevent you from looking conspicuous to anybody connected with Janus."

"You want me to be around civilians? Are you insane?" Sin looked between the rest of the unit. Everyone but Carhart and Boyd seemed as skeptical as he was. "I don't know how to be around people. This is going to fail really badly and then you'll throw me on the Fourth."

"It's not going to fail if you try," Ryan offered.

Sin shot the R&D agent a lethal look.

"Besides, Jason was not the nicest of guys. He had a similar temperament to you."

Unconvinced, Sin shoved his finger in Boyd's face. "And what the hell is he going to do during this time?"

"Boyd will be learning the city, making connections, and doing recon. Today, Monterrey is not only a center of commerce and tourism, but it also has an extensive criminal network that may either help or hinder you. After the Expo, Monterrey will likely be in chaos and it will be nearly impossible to leave in the same manner in which you will enter the country next month. You will need to develop multiple egress plans, have a variety of pre-planned hideouts, and hopefully have the right connections to assist you if needed. That is Boyd's role."

"So he gets to wander around the city for six months. What a fucking hardship."

Boyd smirked.

"He will also have a cover." Carhart pointed at Boyd, who stopped grinning at Sin to glance down at his own tablet. "Kadin Reed was chosen by Warren Andrews to be the representative for Faction 53, or the True Democracy Movement as they so arrogantly call themselves. Reed has agreed to let Boyd impersonate him at the Janus Conference. In exchange, we provide Reed with a cushy vacation in Hawaii under heavy surveillance."

"Kadin?" Boyd asked, sounding bemused. "Strange..."

"When the time comes, Boyd will attend the conference. Reed is not expected to arrive in the city until three days prior to the conference so until then your main concern is learning the city. Reed is known to travel and take extensive vacations so it wouldn't be a problem even if Janus thought he was in Monterrey early."

"I can handle that."

Sin leaned in and peered at his partner's panel. Kadin Reed was apparently a redhead.

"If Kadin was recruited, has anyone from Janus personally met him?" Boyd asked. "I'll need to know his mannerisms if I'm expected to impersonate him."

"Nobody has met him. This will be the first time Janus has contact with anyone except for Andrews," Ryan replied.

Boyd nodded and set his tablet on the table. "How am I to maintain contact with Sin? Will we be communicating covertly?"

Jeffrey's smirk appeared again. Carhart just shook his head.

"Monterrey is a large city with a huge population. There's no reason for the two of you to remain that discreet. You two will share a residence until just prior to the conference when Reed is to arrive at his hotel."

Sin sat up straight. "What the hell?" he demanded just as Boyd said in surprise, "We're living together?"

"Yes. A reasonable amount of money will be deposited into an account in Jason Alvarez's name. It should take care of all necessary expenses but when the funds run out, there will not be more. Whatever money you earn while working your initial job, you should use wisely. We have already secured an apartment in Jason's name under the guise that he will soon be moving to Monterrey with a roommate. You will both receive new phones under your assumed names but, with the exception of timed check-ins, there will be no contact unless there is an emergency."

Sin was still hung up on the fact that he would be living with Boyd.

For months. He was unable to figure out if the concept startled or appealed to him.

"What about my collar? Are you planning to remove it?"

"The collar will be replaced with an internal chip that provides the same functions. Boyd will receive a tracker as well."

Sin rolled his eyes.

"A tracker?" Boyd asked.

"A form of GPS unit," Carhart replied. "Temporarily, for the mission. Both of you will need to see Cynthia."

"You do not seriously plan to deface me with these tattoos, do you?"

Carhart smirked. "Jason was also a notorious chain-smoker."

Sin's mouth pressed into a thin line.

"If there are no further questions, I suggest the two of you go over your information and head to Cynthia."

Boyd pushed his chair back but didn't stand. He was reading his tablet like a good little agent, not complaining or annoyed by the assignment in the least.

"Are there any similar surprises I should know about for Reed?" Boyd asked. "What will Sin and I have for reference regarding how to act like them?"

Ryan grinned. "Kadin is an artist so that should be somewhat cool since you like to draw. I could probably contact my source and see if we can arrange a meeting."

"And Sin can watch some footage from Jason's field agent training," Carhart said.

Boyd nodded and glanced at Sin. "When do we leave?"

"Next week. So get going."

Sin got to his feet and shoved the tablet back into his pocket. He strode to the door and only paused to glare at Boyd over his shoulder. "Are you coming?"

Boyd seemed startled, but grabbed his messenger bag. He followed after saying a quick goodbye to the rest of the unit.

"This is bullshit," Sin snapped as soon as they were in the hallway. "I hate this assignment."

"We haven't even started it yet."

"It's not going to work. They've lost their goddamn minds if they think I can pull this off."

"You'll be fine," Boyd assured him. A tiny grin tipped his wide mouth up as they walked down the corridor. "It will be good, actually. You'll have the chance to test your skills at blending in while I'm there to give you advice. Unless it's so terrible to have to spend most of a year in Mexico with me?"

"It's the most terrible idea I've ever heard of."

"Well then, we'll have to find you a replacement. What about that supply agent who showed up the other day?"

"He didn't have your dashing good looks or dexterity, and I don't think he'd make a very good redhead." Sin shoved his hands in his pockets. He was being petulant and he knew it, but didn't give a damn. "I'm going to look like an idiot."

They stopped to wait for the elevator and Boyd nudged him in the side.

"That is very unlikely. What sort of tattoos does he have? And did I see something about piercings?"

"Typical meaningless nonsense. Barbed wire, cross, et cetera." Sin had surprised himself years ago by getting the Paradise Lost tattoo while on an assignment, but at least it meant something to him. He wasn't fond of the idea of looking like a punk kid who just wanted to get some ink.

"He has a lip ring and some earrings. It's ridiculous. Cynthia will enjoy defacing me, though."

Sin wondered what his partner would look like with red hair. He couldn't picture it. They observed each other in the empty hallway, and Sin saw Boyd's golden eyes focus on his mouth.

"I don't know," Boyd murmured. "I don't think it will be so bad..."

The words, and the intense way Boyd stared at his mouth, made Sin's heart thrum. The elevator arrived and Sin stepped inside, feeling less overheated and nervous after Boyd's gaze moved away.

The receptionist at Unit 16, or the Civvie Squad, was way too amused with the list of body modifications she'd received for Sin. Boyd was sent away to dye his hair or whatever the hell else Kadin needed, and Sin marched to Cynthia's office like he was heading to a death camp. She did her usual teasing spiel, went on random tangents about the love affair she'd had with his father over a decade ago, and then called in her assistants to start the transformation.

He wanted to refuse the tattoos but knew it was ultimately too difficult to explain missing modifications if it ever came up. When the work began on his body, Sin tuned it out by reading the rest of the file.

Most of Jason's family perished during the war and his remaining relatives had died due to exposure to radiation. He'd spent his adolescence in juvenile hall, became involved with gang activity, and was eventually sent to some kind of reformative school or boot camp. After graduating, Jason began to take jobs in security. He had a reputation for being a bad ass and a smart ass but was known to be good at his job, and had been employed by large corporations and wealthy individuals needing a bodyguard.

As for as his brief stint at the Agency, Jason had started as a guard but had died during training to become a field agent. It wasn't a surprise. Many people didn't make it through. It was one of the reasons why Sin grew annoyed with Boyd's insistence that he wasn't impressive or deserving of his rank.

The process of becoming Jason took several hours. Although Sin did not have to undergo any procedures to change his eye color, his hair was dyed, cut shorter and choppier, and Cynthia's assistant began to organize an entire wardrobe for Jason Alvarez based on the specifications in the file.

Eventually, the body artist arrived. The guy's name was Manuel and Sin hated him instantly for no other reason than the fact that he would be the one to tattoo a fucking barbed wire on his arm. The piercings came first, and then Manuel made a weak attempt at chatting while he inked a cross on Sin's hip.

"You look familiar."

Sin said nothing and flicked his tongue at the hoop that now curved around his lower lip. It was surprisingly tender.

"Yeah, you know who you look like? That crazy guy who works here. The—"

Sin looked at Manuel. "The what?"

The guy went still. "Nothing."

Cynthia laughed, although Sin could barely see her over the racks of clothing that had been wheeled in.

"There's nothing to be afraid of, Manny. He's harmless unless you get on his bad side."

Manuel glanced up at Sin with some hesitation.

"Or," Cynthia drawled. Her head appeared over a rack of denim. "If you mess with that cute partner of his."

At that, Sin sneered. "Shut the fuck up."

She just leered at him and disappeared behind the veritable wall of clothing again.

When it was over, Boyd had already left Unit 16, and Sin learned Boyd was being sent on a trip to meet Kadin Reed the following day.

In the week that followed, a low-grade sense of anxiety started to develop that Sin could not shake.

He lay on the floor next to the windows every night, restless, and working on transitioning into a smoker. Sin had hated the taste at first, but had already stopped finding it unpleasant. The continuous inhaling and exhaling was soothing, and Sin wondered if it came so easily due to his father having smoked so much around him as a child. The first day they would met, his father had offered him a cigarette.

With nothing to do but wait until April, Sin looked out at the lights of the city, compared the taste of mild versus menthol, and worried about the mission.

Could he fake being a normal person for so long? Could he even pass an interview process that would allow him to attain employment? Would the recruiters at JKS give him some kind of psych evaluation and realize he was wired wrong? So much could go wrong that Sin was continuously frustrated that Carhart and Connors were forcing him into an unmitigated disaster.

And then of course there was Boyd.

Eight months of living in close quarters.

Sin had no idea how he would manage when he had enough trouble keeping his behavior in check the few times Boyd visited him at his own apartment.

Something had changed between them on that morning in the kitchen, but neither of them pointed it out, and neither of them acknowledged the subtle flirtation that was undeniably there. But at the Agency, they could separate when the tension between them grew too thick; when they stared at each other for a beat too long, or when Sin found himself absently touching Boyd's hair, or when Boyd ran a tentative finger along his broken knuckles.

Here, Sin could wait until Boyd was gone to lose himself in a fantasy about alternate endings to that night in France, or what could happen if he acted on his temptations, while biting his lip and releasing the sexual frustration that had built for the past two months.

But in a shared apartment for months? Sin had no doubts that it would only complicate an already convoluted situation.

Even so, a part of Sin, the part of him that stayed up at night and thought of nothing but Boyd, wondered what it would be like if for the first time... something went right.

END OF EVENFALL VOLUME I

Books by Santino & Ais

IN THE COMPANY OF SHADOWS

Book One:
EVENFALL VOLUME 1: DIRECTOR'S CUT
EVENFALL VOLUME 2: DIRECTOR'S CUT

Book Two: AFTERIMAGE

Book Three: INTERLUDES

Book Four: FADE

Post-Fade Anthology: 1/27

Available at www.inthecompanyofshadows.com

Spin-Off: AFTER MIDNIGHT

Available at Amazon | Smashwords | All Romance Ebooks

ABOUT THE AUTHORS

Ais and Santino met fourteen years ago, and have been writing together in some capacity for at least a decade. They met in anime yaoi fandom, and eventually branched off into developing original characters for RPGs before entering the realm of original fiction. They have been writing and planning In the Company of Shadows since 2005, and are dedicated to improving their largest-scale writing project to date.

Ais has future plans to return to writing fantasy and has been developing ideas for an LGBT police procedural at some point in the near future. Santino's future projects are in the contemporary romance and paranormal genres.

You can find the authors at:

Ais:
    Email: mikaaislin@gmail.com
    Blog: https://aisness.wordpress.com/
    Facebook: https://www.facebook.com/ais.icos
    Twitter: https://twitter.com/aisness
    Instagram: http://instagram.com/aisness

Santino:
    Email: santino.hassell@gmail.com
    Website: http://www.santinohassell.com/
    Facebook: https://www.facebook.com/santinohassellbooks
    Twitter: https://twitter.com/SantinoHassell
    Instagram: http://instagram.com/thatdudesonny

Made in the USA
San Bernardino, CA
09 May 2018